Eric Malpass ̖
bank after leaving school, but his firm ambition was to
become a novelist and he wrote in his spare time for many
years. His first book, *Morning's at Seven*, was published to
wide acclaim. With an intuitive eye for the quirkiness of
family life, his novels are full of wry comments and
perceptive observations. This exquisite sense of detail has led
to the filming of three of his books. His most engaging
character is Gaylord Pentecost – a charming seven-year-old
who observes the strange adult world with utter incredulity.

Eric Malpass also wrote biographical novels, carefully
researched and highly evocative of the period. Among these is
Of Human Frailty, the moving story of Thomas Cranmer.

With his amusing and lovingly drawn details of life in rural
England, Malpass' books typify a certain whimsical
Englishness – a fact which undoubtedly contributes to his
popularity in Europe. Married with a family, Eric Malpass
lived in Long Eaton, near Nottingham, until his death in 1996.

ERIC MALPASS

Sweet Will

HOUSE OF
STRATUS

This edition published in 2001 by House of Stratus, an imprint of Stratus Holdings plc, 24c Old Burlington Street, London, W1X 1RL, UK.

www.houseofstratus.com

Typeset, printed and bound by House of Stratus.

A catalogue record for this book is available from the British Library.

ISBN 0-7551-0197-9

To John and Nick

CONTENTS

DRAMATIS PERSONAE

Edward Alleyn: A notable actor.

Richard Burbage: Another notable actor.

A Dark Lady

Robert Devereux: 2nd Earl of Essex; remained the Queen's favourite until he tactlessly forced her into the position of having to cut his head off.

Robert Dudley: Earl of Leicester. Member of Her Majesty's Privy Council. Master of Kenilworth Castle. Queen's favourite.

Richard Field: A London publisher. Like Sir Hugh Clopton, who became Lord Mayor of London, he was a Stratford boy who made good but had his thunder stolen.

George Gascoigne: A writer.

Robert Greene, MA Oxon. MA Cantab.:   A writer with a penchant for titles. (*A Notable Discovery of Cozenage* and *Greene's Groatsworth of Wit Bought with a Million of Repentance* make titles like *Macbeth* and *King Lear* look bald and pedestrian.)

i

Anne Hathaway:	Pitchforked into history by her marriage to William Shakespeare. World famous as the owner of "Anne Hathaway's Cottage", a considerable farmhouse that never belonged to her.
Philip Henslowe:	A brothel-keeper. His many sidelines included pawnbroking, moneylending, and putting on the world première of William Shakespeare's first play.
Will Kempe:	A clown. Interrupted a successful career to dance a jig from London to Norwich, after which he seems never to have been the same again.
Lettice Knollys:	Married (1) The 1st Earl of Essex, and so became mother of the 2nd Earl of Essex, the Queen's favourite. (2) The Earl of Leicester, the Queen's former favourite. She was the aunt by marriage to Sir Philip Sidney. This almost vulgar involvement in ENG.HIST. was perhaps helped by the fact that she lived to be ninety five.
Augustine Phillips:	An actor. Believed his friend Shakespeare was inhibited from writing anything of value by the censorship of the Lord Chamberlain.
Hamnet Shakespeare:	William's son, who showed much promise and then died.
John Shakespeare, Gent:	A Glover. Bailiff (Mayor) of Stratford-upon-Avon 1568. Father of William.

DRAMATIS PERSONAE

Judith Shakespeare: William's younger daughter and Hamnet's twin, for whom at first the world was rather difficult.

Mary Shakespeare: Daughter of Robert Arden of Wilmcote (a Gentleman of Worship). Wife to John Shakespeare, Gent. Mother of William.

Susanna Shakespeare: William's eldest child, who arrived in the world too soon but became a beauty.

William Shakespeare: A Poet. Later Gent. Publ. *Venus and Adonis, The Rape of Lucrece,* 154 Sugar'd Sonnets. Also wrote a number of plays.

Elizabeth Tudor: Queen of England. A woman of genius whom it is perhaps more comfortable to read about than to have met.

Joan Woodward: Stepdaughter to Philip Henslowe.

Henry Wriothesley: 3rd Earl of Southampton. A spoilt youth.

Citizens of London, Citizens of Stratford-upon-Avon, Soldiers, Courtiers, Attendants, Friends and Relations.

AUTHOR'S NOTE

These are the generally accepted facts: William Shakespeare was the son of John and Mary Shakespeare. He *did* attend the Kenilworth Revels. He *did* marry Anne Hathaway when he was eighteen, and she was twenty-six and three months pregnant. He did go to London. He did write plays, and act, and become a sharer in the Globe. Robert Greene did attack him in a pamphlet. He was a friend of Southampton. There was a Dark Lady. Hamnet did die. A few days before the Essex Rebellion, the rebels did persuade the players to put on *Richard II* at the Globe (it seemed likely to me that before doing so they would have had to get the cautious Will out of the way, so I invented the visit to Essex House). The players were called to account. He did buy New Place and eventually retired there.

John Shakespeare, after a highly successful business and civic career, did fall from grace suddenly and inexplicably. Why? Sack and sugar is *my* suggestion.

I have had the temerity to take two liberties with Queen Elizabeth. (1) To suggest that when she made her famous Tilbury speech she already knew the Armada was in disarray. (2) To suggest that the unknown play she commanded for the eve of Essex's beheading was *Richard II*. But I consider that both actions were in character.

The cottage in Chapel Lane is not to be confused with the one prosperous Will bought in 1602, presumably for his gardener.

The only *major* incident in this book that is purely fictitious is the production of the play at Kenilworth, and the consequent flight to London.

E.M.

CHAPTER 1

WHEN THAT I WAS AND A LITTLE TINY BOY...

Outside was silver. Inside was gold.

Under the moon, the roofs of the little town were a cluster of diamonds. Avon was a silver eel, burrowing among the silver-pennied willows. The fields were cloth of silver in an April frost.

Inside, the candlelight splashed gold on dark panelling, on the portrait of an Arden forbear; and on the plump hands, the plump jowls, the shining Humpty Dumpty pate of John Shakespeare.

Alone, by the dying embers, John Shakespeare had drunk a modest pot of sack and sugar to celebrate his good fortune. A son! A son, after six years of marriage. A son, to carry on the business. Perhaps, after all, the name of Shakespeare would not be forgotten in Stratford fifty years hence. He was very moved. "William Shakespeare, Glover to the Nobility," he murmured. He could see it, hanging outside the door: a dark wooden shield with the words in gold. Very tasteful. Glinting in the sunlight, creaking cheerfully on winter nights in Henley Street. "Glover to the Nobility."

He rose. He would have liked another cup of sack and sugar. But no. His slowness and pomposity hid a strong ambition, and a strong will. He had a long way to go yet; sack and sugar would not help him on his way.

It was time for bed. He picked up the candle. The shadows lurched and plunged like a ship in high storm. He went upstairs, where Mary Shakespeare, born Arden, lay in the great bed, her son in her arms.

The day had been clear and bright, the sky turbulent with white summer clouds, clearing towards evening for the coming frost. There had been a good deal of hey nonny noing. And justifiably so. Behind lay salted beef, mire, bitter cold, almost unmitigated dark, and the scurvy. Ahead: warmth, brightness, lovemaking and haymaking, those twin bucolic pastimes; a little enjoyable plotting for the gentry; and a good couple of months before one need start worrying about the plague. April, a pretty time, when even an untimely frost dressed everything in tinsel.

Elizabeth Tudor, Great Harry's whey-faced daughter, was in the seat of power. And by God she was staying there. Whey-faced she might be. But when Elizabeth frowned, great men turned pale. Or so it was said, though Mary Shakespeare, who liked the idea of a woman on the throne, believing as she did that most women had more sense in their little fingers than most men in their great hulking bodies. Most men! But not her sweet Will, sweet milky Will, flesh of *her* flesh, drowsy-drunk with *her* body milk, staring now with dark, unfocused eyes at the bed hangings. Sweet yeoman Will; she saw him striding over his Warwickshire acres, driving a straight furrow across the very heart of England. The Arden blood was safe. Stout Arden feet would still be planted firm on the English earth, when she and John were dust. Yeoman Will! There was one calling, and one calling only, for her William. The land, the land of England, the land at England's heart.

The tiny fists were clenched. The eyes were clenched shut. Mary brushed her lips across the fuzz of black hair; it was an act of pride and possession and ineffable love. She, Mary Shakespeare, had produced this exquisite creature from her own yeoman body. In patience and travail created she him. Her bowels yearned with love of him. "Sweet Will," she murmured, brushing again the soft hair. "Sweet Will."

She was a composed serene woman. She loved her husband, even though she had all the effortless superiority of someone, with a Sheriff of the County among her ancestors, who has married into trade. John Shakespeare might be a successful businessman. He might be an Ale Taster and a Borough Chamberlain, respected by all. He might be shrewd and clever. But he could not claim a Gentleman of Worship for a father.

She could. And hugged the knowledge to her as even now she was hugging her milk-dribbling, darling yeoman-to-be.

The oaken staircase creaked. John was coming up.

She knew the ceremonial. He would pause on the landing to snuff a candle. Then the door latch would lift. The door would creak open. John would make his entrance. Without a word to her he would wash his face at the ewer. Then he would cross to the bed, gaze down at her unsmiling... "Well, wife?" he would say.

The steps paused on the landing. Then the door latch jerked upward. The door opened, John came in, sluiced water into the bowl and dabbed his cheeks, crossed to the bed, gazed down at her. "Well, wife?" he said. But tonight he *was* smiling.

"Well, husband?" She too was smiling. In the light from his candle her smile glowed with a proud, inward joy. She was exhausted, emptied, filled with a delicious languor; yet exultant, because after six years of waiting she given the world a man; a man to till the earth and tend the beasts and fight and be sad and revel in food and music and laughter, to fill some woman's loins with ecstasy, to fill a long life with doing and loving.

The father looked at the son.

The son, eyes clenched again, grimaced. The tiny limbs jerked as in pain, relaxed. John Shakespeare held a thick, spatulate thumb against the perfection of a hand. The wrinkled fingers closed about it, clung trustingly. John was deeply moved. Strange to think that one day these little hands would shear the glove leather in the shop downstairs. "Pretty wanton," he said fondly. "The shop shall be his." John's comfortable Midlands accent took on the mellifluous tones he had always adopted when speaking to her late father. "William Shakespeare, Glover to the Nobility."

"Yes, John." By heaven, she'd stop that. An Arden, in *trade*? But that could wait.

She watched her husband with her dark eyes, her lean, clever face. Her lower lip curled outwards, showing a keen intelligence at work. She patted the bed. "Sit down, John."

The bed creaked under his weight. It was a creaking world, she thought, suddenly amused. The stairs, the door, the bed, a passing cart; perhaps, she thought, even the great globe itself, spinning in its God-appointed task of creating day and night.

The great globe, sun, moon and stars, God, a new-born child, a new life stretching forward to take a million twists and turns before it found the grave, man and wife, joined in spirit and flesh, here were enough mysteries to fill a universe.

"Tell me about your day, husband," she said, playing with his fingers, smiling gravely at her thoughts.

"Business was good in the market. Everyone crowding round, friendly, cheerful, because I had a son." He began fumbling with his shoe-latches.

She was no longer smiling at her thoughts. She was smiling at him, her husband. She was happy in his happiness.

"One gave me a charm to keep the child safe from witches," he said. "Another a balm against the itch."

"The charm. Let me see it." An aunt of Mary's had gone into a decline at the age of thirty, the direct result of witchcraft. Mary feared witches almost more than she feared the plague.

It was a sprig of parsley, tied with a frog's entrails. Mary touched it with her lips, laid it on the child's breast. She found it a great comfort. She was a sensible woman, and never left things to chance if she could help it.

"All wished me well," John said, taking off his furred gown. He slipped into bed, sighed with content, blew out the candle. "They are good people, the people of Stratford. Rejoicing with them that rejoice. Mourning with them that mourn. Good people."

They were, too. A little band of townspeople, huddled together in the leafy plain, beset and harassed by witches and goblins and foul fiends, by the ghosts of murderers and of the foully murdered. To say nothing of pestilence, palsy, marauding robbers, and the cruel quirks of the nobility. To say nothing of the blanketing darkness of night, the stranglehold of winter; to say nothing of the healing work of the doctors, experimentally lopping off a limb here, hopefully applying a salve of bat's blood to an open wound there. Let one of these citizens put a foot wrong spiritually, and he risked the stake; politically, and he risked the wrath of princes; morally, and he risked being stretched out on a red hot griddle in Hell for ever and ever and ever and ever and ever.

They were on a tight rope, every man Jack of them. Yet they were happy. They quarrelled with relish. They did everything – danced round the Maypole, sang madrigals, made love, went to law, were melancholic, enjoyed the bear baiting and the players – all with relish. They lived their damned uncomfortable lives with cheerful, acrimonious gusto.

On eastern slopes, Cotswold shepherds blinked in the level rays. Stiff from their bracken beds, shivering in the fresh morning, bleary-eyed and unshaven, they nevertheless seized their pipes and did a little routine hey derry downing. They felt it was expected of them.

No one expected any hey derry downing from the swineherds. *They* lay in the muck, nuzzling up to their simple charges for companionship and warmth.

A light wind danced across England, sweeping away the trailing vapours of night like a pert maid dealing with cobwebs. Trees, fields, hedgerows, doubly new-born to a new spring and a new day, preened themselves. Smoke stood up, blue and clear, from cottage chimneys, before the breeze swept it off into the dance.

London, waking, seethed like a disturbed ant-hill. At the Tower the wind tossed indignant ravens about the sky, and breathed, tormentingly, spring into a hundred clammy cells. At Tyburn they were testing ropes, sharpening knives, heating cauldrons. They worked merrily. They were cheerful lads, and on a brisk, sparkling morning like this they felt glad to be alive. The crowds were forming already; decent, respectable wives and husbands, their hands resting fondly on their little one's shoulders; the children well scrubbed, each tiny fist clutching a laundered piece of linen. ("Dip your kerchief in the gentleman's blood, dear.")

At Kenilworth, Robert Dudley, Earl of Leicester, was going through the accounts. God, he hoped Elizabeth wouldn't take it into her head to visit her sweet Robin this year. He just couldn't afford it, damn it. It never seemed to occur to her for one moment that these things cost money.

And a few miles away, in Stratford, John and Mary Shakespeare woke to the thin crying of a child; and looked at each other in wonder, knowing that, after six years of waiting, their dreams had become reality.

May began wet that year. Then the sun came out, hot and lusty. Everything steamed, everything smelt: the growing things, sweet and heady; the river, dank and rotten; growth, ripeness, decay, all hung and clung on the still, hot, moist air.

Plague weather.

It came, of course. Despite the prayers to the Virgin and to the old, dark, half-forgotten gods of the Arden forest, it came. Despite the burning of camomile and the sprinkling of vinegar; despite, or some said because of, all the efforts of the medical profession, it came.

It came first to a dank hovel down by the river, carrying off the brat of a feckless good-for-nothing called Meg Bates. (The town never forgave Meg for starting up the whole dreadful business, and as soon as things settled down again she was arraigned for witchcraft and burnt alive, after which everyone felt a bit better.)

Plague! A word to strike at the heart, to banish happiness, to foreclose on the future; a word to drain all strength and purpose from the limbs.

The house in Henley Street became a fortress. Mary, that serene woman, held her William desperately to her bosom, and watched her imprisoned husband and her little girl for every change of colour and breathing. None came. Death dragged his obscene harrow across the town, and went his way.

The citizens were overjoyed at his going. They rang a merry peal, cheerfully burned poor Meg Bates, and began again the eager, urgent business of living. Mary opened the shutters, John re-opened his stall in the market, the little girl went out to play, and William went on with his life of feeding and sleeping as though nothing had happened. He had crossed his first hurdle.

And now he was beginning to see his world for the first time. The movement of trees, green fingers probing a blue sky; the swaying, encircling world he saw from his rocking cradle, a world of dark wainscoting and small windows, lit sometimes by golden candles that held his stare for long minutes.

But these things were almost as remote as the stars. His world was still, really, his mother's breast, his mother's arms, his mother's face, smiling in tenderness. His world was tenderness. His world was the firm flesh, the clear spirit, of an English gentlewoman.

The world grew wider. Sometimes he would be perched up on his father's market stall in High Cross, thronged by faces and bright ribbons and coloured awnings, by shouts and laughter and a chatter that flowed on forever like a brook; by the smell of horses and linen and leather, the warm, strong, friendly smell of people. Round the big fire at home, the shadows dancing. Above all, the country, with his sister. Green meadows, daisy chains, sunlight, the swirling Avon. Life – teeming, exultant, proliferating – was all about him.

By the time he was ten, he was in love with every one of its million facets, good, bad, beautiful, ugly. Above all, with beauty. Beauty was his mistress, and would be to the end.

But when he was eleven, he found another mistress – at Kenilworth. And fell in love all over again...

Robert Dudley, Earl of Leicester, walked with his new love in the gardens of Kenilworth.

He was a brave man. But he didn't relish telling his new love what he had to tell her.

He cleared his throat. "The Queen, my love, is coming to the castle."

"*That* bitch," said Lettice Knollys succinctly. She turned. "I will make her so jealous she will want to scratch out my eyes – *and* yours."

He said uncomfortably, "All that was long ago, my love. Nowadays Elizabeth and I are simply friends."

He hoped he was right. Otherwise, once Elizabeth arrived, there would be two bitches fighting over a bone; and *he* would be the bone. He even thought about the oubliette in the keep for Lettice. But no. He didn't want *her* ghost at large in the castle for the rest of his days.

Nor was this his only trouble. A visit from the Queen cost more than even an Elizabethan earl could well afford; with courtiers, court officials, servants, hangers-on, performing bears, horses, dogs and falcons; to say nothing of a deposit of filth to be cleared up and a new crop of bastards in the town.

There was no doubt about it. Leicester was going to have a difficult and expensive time.

Young William was aggrieved. He wanted to stay and play by the river.

John Shakespeare, on the other hand, was bursting with pride. An invitation to the princely revels at Kenilworth Castle! In the privacy of his chamber, John swept a low bow. "Your Majesty, may I present? My wife. My son Will. Yes, Majesty. A good lad, who will follow in his father's humble footsteps. A glover, Majesty; to, if I may say so, the nobility." Tenderly, reverently, he kissed the royal hand.

Mary Shakespeare wore her usual expression of cool amusement. She was bidden to Kenilworth Castle; not, God save the mark, as the daughter of Robert Arden, Gent. But as the wife of a Borough Chamberlain. Her seat would be among the more prosperous tradesmen. It would be further back, and harder, than the seat to which her birth entitled her. But no matter. It was the seat her husband's position had won for her, and she would take it with pride.

She had, years ago, met Robert Dudley. Mary, wife and mother, felt her blood quicken as she remembered the handsome, swaggering, confident creature that Elizabeth had created Earl of Leicester, had presented with a royal castle, had called her "Sweet Robin". She wondered whether they would meet again. "Mary Shakespeare, my lord. But I was Mary Arden, then. Yes, a good lad, my lord. William. His heart is set on the Warwickshire soil of his ancestors."

Yes, a good lad, Will. Amenable. He went to the Grammar School, and was polite and courteous to Simon Hunt, the Master, and soaked up Latin and logic and arithmetic like a sponge. He listened carefully while his father showed him the ins and outs of the business, and explained how he wanted Will to concentrate on the gloves and let the butchering side run down. He listened with equal care while his mother drew for him the cares and delights of his future life as a yeoman farmer. And if he sometimes felt a little confused, he never showed it. He cheerfully determined, he didn't quite know how, to satisfy both loved parents to the utmost of his ability. That was his nature.

Robert Dudley had been wrong, he thought glumly, about Elizabeth. And it was small comfort to remind himself that almost everyone was, almost always, wrong about Elizabeth. We shall meet as friends, he had hoped, as old, sad lovers, passion spent. Well, passion might be spent, but jealousy wasn't. In Elizabeth, jealousy survived love and passion and even hope.

Fortunately, he had arranged such fantastic revels for the occasion that even a jealous queen ought to be wooed out of her sulks. All he could do now was ensure that nothing went wrong. He did his best. Kenilworth Castle stopped dreaming among its sleepy meadows. It came to life; with trumpet and drum, with fireworks and fusilades of cannon, with awnings and bright pavilions, with gods and goddesses and nymphs and satyrs. The people came from all around, from Coventry and Warwick and Stratford and the small hamlet of Birmingham; on horse and on foot and by coach and by carrier's cart. Here was what they loved above all things: noise, jostling, crowds, stink – and a glimpse of those bright creatures, far nearer to the angels than to themselves – the Nobility. Nothing like the princely revels had ever been seen before. They were splendidly costly.

But they were not a success. Leicester was on tenterhooks. One smile at the Queen, and Lettice sulked for days. One glance at Lettice, and the Queen started throwing things. The nymphs and goddesses, with ten thousand lusty men-at-arms about the place, needed eyes in the backs of their heads. Some of them became quite neurotic. But not as neurotic as the Queen. A salvo of guns was fired every time she rose, went out, came in, drank wine, or went to bed. It upset the royal nerves. And when it wasn't cannon it was lutenists, or fireworks, or a Latin recitation, or the inevitable "Greensleeves", or a masque with herself as the Queen of Beauty and Honour. Or a banquet, with tumblers and clowns. Or, at night, the screams of nymphs and goddesses fleeing for their honour from clanking soldiers across the Castle lawns. She began to long for the peace of Whitehall or Nonsuch. Robin had overreached himself.

She supposed, she thought sadly, he'd always been a bit of a parvenu. She didn't mind ostentation: everyone was ostentatious nowadays; she was herself when it didn't cost too much. But to weary one's Monarch, in an attempt to take her mind off a doxy like Lettice Knollys: that was unforgivable.

It was scarcely light when the Shakespeares prepared to leave Stratford. And the July dawn was milky with mist. The stable lamp glowed in a golden haze, like an aureole about a sainted head, like a ring around the moon. Beards were festooned with diamonds, the rumps of the horses steamed.

Down by the river, he knew, the mists would linger till mid-morning. Then – a luminosity in the upper air, the mist tearing and shredding like old lace, to reveal the sun and the sparkling water and a world new-made. He felt the water, embracing naked limbs. He felt the summer sun, burning into cheek and forehead. He felt the grass, cool about bare feet. He thought of a whole, long summer's day of boyhood – idling, fooling, swimming, dreaming. "Mother, do I *have* to come?"

"Will, dear, of course you must come. The Queen will be there. And Kenilworth is a great house."

"Greater than Grandmother Arden's?"

"Far, far greater," she said, smiling.

William didn't believe it. You couldn't build a bigger house than Grandmother Arden's. Why, the great hall, he vowed, was as big as Stratford market place. But now his father was joining in. "What is wrong with the boy?" he asked tetchily.

"He wants to stay and go swimming," Mary said, amused – awaiting the storm.

"Swimming? *Swimming?* When he can see the gentry, and the new fashions, perhaps the Queen herself?" John was deeply shocked. Social climbing was the national pastime; more so, even, than bear-baiting or composing madrigals. Anyone who preferred swimming to hobnobbing with gentry was a fool. John hoped he hadn't got a fool for a son. Will was a good lad. But there *were* times when John couldn't help wondering... "No more of this nonsense," he said. He swung Will on to the cob's withers, and clambered up behind him. They were off.

John and his horse had much in common; both were short-legged, tubby and ponderous. Mary, on the other hand, rode a sleek, impatient, high-stepping creature; again, not unlike herself.

John sat his horse like a sack of oats. Mary rode proud, erect. Put her on a horse, and she was filled with an eager joy. It was as though she had been given wings. She wanted to gallop, to fly over fences, to shout exultantly.

Will never took his eyes off his mother. So slim, so erect, so – so feminine. He was already drawn to the attractions of femininity – the softness, the lightness, the darting wit. He adored his mother. She could be tiresome, of course. Today, for instance, making him come on this stupid outing; but she was a mother to be proud of. An Arden, the same name as the great forest that filled the heart of England. An Arden: she never forgot it. She never let her husband, or her children, forget it. William, at eleven, had already learnt the exact class distinctions that ruled his times.

They rode on, in misty silence. Only the clip-clop of hooves, the creak of leather. Will looked about him fearfully. Here, perched between the comfortable solidity of father and horse, a lamp glowing at the horse's neck, he was as safe as one could ever be. Nevertheless, trees loomed like giants out of the mist. They crouched low over the riders, reaching down with predatory claws. Thick pockets of fog lurked in their branches, swayed and moved like grey ghosts which, in fact, they probably were. He didn't actually *see* any hobgoblins. But they were all about, scurrying from the path before the horses' hooves, gibbering in the tree tops. He knew it. Or suppose a foul fiend suddenly appeared in the path, and the horses bolted, and he, Will, was thrown at the monster's feet! He drew closer to his father's warm body. Robin Dell's grandmother had once met a foul fiend face to face, on just such a misty morning as this, and had given Robin and his young friends a very detailed description of the occurrence. Will, remembering, felt the hairs curling at the base of his neck.

His father said, "Today, dear boy, can, if you so apply yourself, be a landmark in your education."

"Yes, father?" Surely that tree had edged a little nearer!

"I want you to observe how I comport myself with the gentry. Nothing familiar; a touch, even, of obsequiousness is never amiss."

A wood pigeon clattered from a high elm, sending Will's heart racing. "The gentry, in my opinion, appreciate a touch of the obsequious."

"Yes, father?"

"Train yourself also to observe their gloves. Many will be wearing the London fashions. Observe details. Such knowledge can be invaluable."

"Yes, father."

Mary, who had been riding ahead, fell back beside them. She waved a hand to take in, vaguely, the misty south. "Somewhere over there", she cried, "is Arden land."

Will peered. He couldn't see a thing. But it didn't look inviting. A foggy, dewy, haunted land. He saw himself trailing a lonely plough, hobgoblins flocking round like birds, nipping at his ears. He thought perhaps he'd rather be a glover.

John said, "A tradesman can learn much of value by observing the gentry. Let him gain a *little* of their polish, and they will be flattered and treat him respectfully. Too much, and they will kick him downstairs."

A quiet voice said, "Husband, what has Will to do with tradesmen?"

There was an edge to the voice that John did not like. He said, "He is the son of one. And I intend that he shall *be* one."

Will said, "Very well, father. I think I should make but a poor farmer."

Mary reined in her horse. She'd got a word or two to say to all this. But no. The time was not ripe. Angrily she cantered on ahead. Will, sensitive as always to mood and atmosphere, was anxious. Mother was displeased. With him? Apparently. He sighed. He peered through the murk to where the Arden acres lay. He supposed he *would* have to be a farmer after all. He couldn't disappoint Mother.

It was quite light now, though mist was still all about them. But no longer silent. There were voices, the sounds of hooves and turning wheels, faces appeared out of the mist and were swallowed up again, buildings loomed, vague and insubstantial. "The town of Kenilworth," Father announced knowledgeably.

They rode on, forded a little stream. And suddenly his mother cried, "Will! Look! Oh, look!"

He peered ahead. And gasped, in fear and wonder and delight.

Something was towering above him in the swirling mists, vast, ponderous, a pile of red sandstone whose tops were lost in the mist. Grim, forbidding, mysterious, for in this changing light it was impossible to define height or width or depth. Lights glowed yellow in traceried windows. It was more than a building, a habitation of man. It was royal England. It was more beautiful, and more terrible, and more cruel, than anything Will had either seen or imagined. He felt sick with excitement.

Somewhere a cornet sounded. The crowds in which they were now moving stilled; then scattered from the road. A troop of horsemen in the Earl's livery rode bravely by towards the Castle, followed by a straggle of riders, gentlemen and ladies, who stared disdainfully ahead as though the crowds scattered in the hedgerows were so many dandelions and dog daisies.

All except one: a woman enveloped from head to foot in a hooded riding-cloak. She, alone, looked at the people; with what they, the people, hoped was love. And a murmur ran through the crowd, like the susurrous of wind through reeds on the seashore: "The Queen, the Queen, the Queen, the Queen, the Queen."

Hats were doffed. The women curtseyed. The Queen stopped, and stared. William saw a pale, intense face, a wisp of red hair beneath the green cowl; and was lost, forever, in love and adoration. Immediately he began to devise situations in which he could die for her; for that, now, was the one thing he wanted. Elizabeth Tudor, with one glance, had conquered him as she had already conquered most of her subjects. He waved his hat with wild abandon round his head. "God save Your Majesty," he cried.

The Queen's love for her people was very real. They were all she had to love. But sometimes she loved them less than others; and a misty morning before breakfast, with Robin disappearing into the fog with Lettice, was one of those times. She stared angrily. "Ha!" she ejaculated, high and sharp. Then without a smile, without a word, she was gone – to breakfast. She clattered over the bridge; and the cannons roared in salute. As Lettice Knollys sweetly remarked: "*Dear Robin! I vow he shoots off ordnance every time that woman goes to the privy.*"

Will watched her go, and the mist close about her. She hadn't worn a crown; but she rode with majesty. Her face had been angry; yet, at the same time, filled with a terrible loneliness. Her "Ha!" had been sharp and irritated, like the cry of a magpie. It would ring forever in his ears. But now, suddenly, it was as though the sun had grown impatient of being hidden, and shrivelled up the remaining mist like paper tossed on to a fire. Will saw Kenilworth, in all its brave glory.

The windows flamed in the sunlight. Steel breastplates, halberds, pikes, flashed and glinted. The great mass of sandstone was gay with flags and bunting and pennants, with striped pavilions, with the silks of the ladies, the stiff brocades of the gentlemen. Mary Shakespeare looked, and smiled. My Lord of Leicester had always believed in doing a thing properly. Then she looked down at her son.

He was absolutely still, staring, his cheerful, sunburnt face lost in an ecstasy of wonder. He couldn't believe it. So much of life, already, he loved: the river, the meadows, the flowers, the rough bustle of Stratford High Cross; horses, and the gentle deer, and the poor hungry cur. But this was something new; a richness, a beauty, that was beyond anything he could have imagined.

Today's programme had, as usual, something for everyone: a recitation from Ovid; a madrigal competition; a Lyon, set upon by Dogges; fireworks; a poetry reading, a jig, a merry daunce; a wearisome masque about Juno which, although it was written by George Gascoigne, Leicester's resident author and a master of simple prose, was surprisingly turgid.

It was, in fact, dreadful. Hurriedly written, unrehearsed, and pretentious. Lettice, playing Juno, was too busy watching Leicester bowing low over the Queen to cover up for not having learnt her lines; to be fair, they hadn't been worth learning anyway. The Queen yawned ostentatiously every time Juno opened her mouth. And when the Queen yawned, everybody yawned.

All except Will Shakespeare, who did not yawn. Will was entranced. He had seen the players often when they visited Stratford, of course; but he had been too young for them to have made an immediate impression on him. Now, suddenly, it was as though all he had seen then, all he saw now, was of one piece: something he had always known suddenly took on a terrible beauty and significance. The gorgeous costumes, the words, the gestures! Grown men and women, playing at being gods and goddesses of ancient times! Will thought it was a wonderful idea. He hadn't fully realised the grown up world could *play*. The knowledge gave life yet one more gay and delightful facet. When *he* grew up *he* was going to play. But he would want something better than this to play in. All these words were being wasted. He yearned for action, conflict, not all this posturing and mouthing. He fell into a waking dream, filled with the clash of conflict and of arms, of love and hate. His mother, glancing at him, was startled. The child was staring, bright-eyed, rapt, at – nothing. For one dreadful moment she feared he had been orelooked by a passing witch. She seized his arm. "Will! What ails you?"

He looked at her, with those brown, gentle eyes. "Nothing, mother." He nodded towards the actors. "Mother, when I grow up, can I so play?"

She said, sadly, knowing her Will, "No. This is only for lords and ladies."

He was silent. The kings and queens, the princes and the prelates, were still fighting it out in his head. But it was not for him apparently. For him, the glover's shears, the lonely plough, he thought sadly.

After that vile masque, Robert Dudley needed to stretch his legs. He decided to show himself.

He liked to give pleasure, provided it cost him nothing; and he knew that, to the wives and daughters of small tradesmen and country squires, the most powerful man in England, in mustard-coloured doublet, white ruff, and green velvet breeches, must give a great deal of pleasure. Besides, he liked to make sure he wasn't missing anything. It was often surprising what the common sort could produce in the way of charm and beauty.

Take that one, for instance. A tall, slim creature, nicely mature, a woman of spirit by the look of her. Well, what with Lettice and the Queen he'd really had enough of women of spirit for one day. But he could never resist a beauty. He doffed his cap. Since the lady was in the tradesmen's area his bow was a nicely adjusted mixture of the elaborate and the perfunctory. "Mistress –?" he murmured enquiringly.

She curtseyed, gracefully. And smiled, evidently amused.

He was put out. Usually the poor geese were so overcome they nearly fell over their own feet. Amusement was the last thing they ever showed. Awe, gratification, wonder, yes. But amusement! She said, coolly, "Mary Shakespeare, my lord."

What a vile clatter of a name!

"But you knew me once as Mary Arden."

"Ah." That was better. Good family. Though he had the feeling that he wasn't making his usual impression on this woman. So he tried the old game of approaching the mother through the son. "And this is your only child?"

"No, my lord. The younger children are with their Grandmother Arden. And there were two little girls who died young."

He turned to Will. "And you are enjoying Kenilworth?"

"Oh yes, my lord. But – I thought the masque ill done."

"William!" cried Mary, no longer cool. Families had been dispossessed for less.

She saw with alarm that two deep lines had appeared between the Dudley brow. "Indeed, Master William? And what is wrong with the masque?"

"It should to the barber's, my lord."

"I see." He straightened up, unsmiling. "What do you plan for the boy, Mistress Shakespeare?"

"A good yeoman, like his Arden forbears." She decided to strike while the iron was hot and John was out of the way. "To work for your lordship would be an honour for the boy – and for us all."

One of the tradesmen's daughters was eyeing the Earl with considerable interest – a pretty, vacant piece who looked half bowled over already. He was, he decided, wasting his time on this Shakespeare woman and her percipient but precocious brat. He said hurriedly, "Let him be educated to puberty. Then bring him to my bailiff. We will find work for Master Shakespeare."

"Thank you. Your lordship is most gracious." She curtseyed deeply. But the most powerful man in England was already on his way to bring sweetness and light to another of the common sort.

"Will," she fussed, "you *must* be careful. Men get their ears cut off for saying that sort of thing."

"But it was true, mother."

"All the more reason. Oh, here's your father. John, such news! I have met the Earl. And Will made a great impression. The Earl wishes him to join his service."

"No!" John was visibly swelling. "Our son, in the Earl of Leicester's service! Why, it could mean going to court."

Mary was silent. Then John remembered. "But the business. I had set my heart –"

She slipped her arm into his. "I know, John. You'd set your heart. So. The Earl must be denied." She smiled at him brightly.

"Yes," he muttered. "The Earl must be denied." But he said it without conviction.

Chapter 2

The play's the thing...

There had been a marriage in the Warwickshire village of Shottery.

A poor affair. A snuffling, perfunctory service, and a thin wedding breakfast with little ale and no bawdry. But what could you expect, with the bride's father in a new grave and grief making the bride's stepmother even more stupid than usual, and those two puritans, Fulk Sandells and John Richardson, taking charge of the proceedings in the absence of their late friend Richard Hathaway, called by worms to a wedding breakfast in another place?

And now. The few guests had gone home, every man Jack walking unaided, a shameful thing at a wedding. The grey spring day was slipping into a quiet, sad evening. Away across the fields a dog barked with inane persistence, accentuating the country silence. A petal from the clouded may fell listlessly to the ground. The blackbirds sang: a song that overflows with joy, or grief, according to the heart of the hearer. That was all that was happening in Shottery, on this marriage day.

Inside the thatched, red-brick farmhouse, the bride, the groom, the bride's stepmother, and the bridesmaid sat on stools about the empty grate. They were silent. Bride and groom waited nervously, hopefully, shyly, for bed time. Mistress Hathaway sewed, for a housewife could never allow herself the luxury of doing nothing, even for a moment; even though her tears blinded her to her work.

The bridegroom rose. With gentle courtesy, he gave his hands to his bride. She rose, embraced her stepmother, then the bridesmaid. "Goodnight, sweet sister Anne," she said fondly; knowing, but unable to express, many things: that a tender, sweet relationship was ending tonight, or at the least changing; that her marriage somehow underlined the bitter truth that Anne, seven years her senior, could not hope for a husband; that she herself was now caught up inexorably in the terrible wheel of begetting and birth and dying. She went up the ladder, followed by her groom.

Anne felt a tear clinging to her cheek. She brushed it away. Another. She rose, went towards the door. "May I go out, mother?"

Mistress Hathaway looked at her sourly. "What? Are we gentry, now, to walk abroad in our finery, our silks and ribbons?"

"I – don't want to go upstairs to change – now."

"Very well. But watch yourself, mind. Not that any lad's going to give *you* a green gown, at your age, that's one comfort," she said cruelly.

Anne went outside, and down the path. Already the cottage-garden flowers, no longer tended by Richard, were growing wild and rank. She had loved her father. But today her thoughts were for herself. Begetting and birth, she now knew, would never touch her. Death alone would not scorn to take the dry and withered spinster in the end.

She passed through the wicket gate, and into the lane. The blackbirds still sang. The dog still barked, behind the wood.

And Anne looked at her life, coldly, and clearly. She wept in earnest.

Tied to an obscure Warwickshire village, half lost among its dripping trees. Tied to her bitter-tongued stepmother, and them both tied, now Richard was dead, to lifelong poverty, as to a stake. Tied, by her soft, pale looks, her slow, quiet ways, to endless maidenhood; without a man to bring her joy in the long, dark nights, to bring her children, and bread, and save her from a thousand terrors.

She followed the tree-hung lane. To her left, a path wandered away across downland pasture. Should she follow the lane, or the path? The path, striding boldly across the rough pasture, beckoned. The lane, plunging deeper into the evening gloom of trees, frightened her. She turned left, across the pasture.

Will Shakespeare jigged happily along the downland path.

At eighteen, he had turned out well. His mother was proud of him: an open country face under chestnut hair; a sturdy, if rather stocky, frame; and still the pleasant, amenable ways of the boy; eager (perhaps sometimes over-eager) to please everyone.

His heart quickened. A girl was coming towards him in this lonely place. A girl in a frock of softest blue.

She came nearer, and he saw that the frock was of silk, with pretty ribbons and laces. His heart beat even faster, thinking for a moment she was gentry.

But no! This girl walked shyly, hanging her head as deep as a pretty harebell. A gentlewoman would already have been staring at him arrogantly. This must be a country girl, yet decked in finery. He was intrigued.

So was she. Low though she hung her head, she was woman enough to know that a very personable young man was approaching; a young man as rich and warm in colouring as a horse chestnut new dug from its shell.

In Shottery? She knew all the oafs of Shottery. And anyway, this was no oaf. Despite the loneliness of the spot, she couldn't resist having a peep.

His doublet and breeches were of fustian, his hose of wool.

She was relieved; though also, perhaps, a little disappointed, so desperate was her mood, to see that he wasn't gentry. Had she met a gentleman in this solitary place, she wouldn't have got away without a tussle. Gentlemen were partial to country wenches. Country wenches were fair game, like deer, wild boar, or foxes.

For that moment, she lifted her head and looked at him. He saw eyes of the same soft blue as her dress. Eyes, surely, that had been weeping. And at this thought compassion welled in him, so that he put aside the discovery that this was no young girl, but a woman in her middle twenties already with the first glaze of spinsterhood upon her.

All his life he had been falling in love at first sight: with flowers, with music, with clouds and sunlight and laughter and friendship. Now, for the first time, he fell in love with a woman. Pale as the moon, gentle as thistledown, soft as the breast of the dove. "Who are you?" he asked quietly.

She told him. Her voice was low, and gentle, an excellent thing in a woman.

Anne Hathaway: a beautiful name, a sweet-sounding country name, a name to write lovingly in the margins of books, as he had so often written others: Eliz. Regina, Elizabeth Tudor, Wm Shagsper, Will Shaxspere, William Shakespeare.

His quiet voice gave her confidence. She saw him looking at her low-cut bodice and imagined, poor fool, that it was her unusual clothes that interested him. "I have been bridesmaid at my sister's wedding," she explained.

"Ah."

If his voice was gentle, his face was smiling and compassionate. She said, boldly, "You are not of Shottery, sir?"

"No, I am Will Shagsper, of Stratford."

Her reaction was disappointing. He said, importantly, "I serve my Lord, the Earl of Leicester."

That was better. The very name of the Earl could strike terror into country hearts. But he'd overdone it. She paled, and took a step backward. Another second, he thought, and she'd be running for her life. He said hurriedly, and with a smile of great charm, "I am only a ploughman to my Lord." She look relieved. But he couldn't leave it at that. "I am of Arden blood," he explained. "I but learn husbandry of the Earl, the better to farm my family lands."

Damn, but he'd frightened her a second time. He said, again with that melting charm, "It is darkling, Mistress Anne. And it is said that goblins are free to roam the moment the sun touches the rim of the earth. Will you let me see you to your home?"

Poor Anne! She stammered and blushed. Goblins and Ardens and noble lords were all too much for her; but the young man seemed kind. And he *was* quite right about the goblins. It was a well-known fact.

In the distance, a few lights glowed, dim and yellow. Shottery. They turned towards them. They walked in silence, Will tongue-tied for once.

They reached her cottage gate. She turned and faced him. She searched desperately for something to say. She, Anne Hathaway, was doing what she had never thought to do, what she had yearningly seen so many other girls do – standing at her gate in the gloaming with a lad. But if she couldn't speak soon, he would be gone, forever. "Thank you," she managed, "for your company, sir."

Again, that smile. It seemed to light up the dusk, to take away the chill of evening. Unconsciously her body swayed, ever so slightly, towards him. And in that moment she knew she was in love – a mere boy, five, six, seven years her junior. A stranger who took her hand in both of his as one holds a frightened bird and said, all compassion, "Mistress Anne, you have been weeping."

"Not any more," she said with a smile and a great sigh.

"Meet me again," he said.

Again she hung her head, the pretty, pretty harebell. "If – you – so – wish," she said.

He bowed, as graceful, she thought, as any court gallant, and was away; serious, dazed by the sudden surge of first love; elated; anxious, surely a woman like her could never love a stripling like him; rhyming Anne, Dian! A poet who, at eighteen, now loved a woman.

Mistress Hathaway looked at her stepdaughter sourly. "What is this, then, walking abroad when only witches are afoot? Seeking out the Hobgoblin Puck, are you, for I vow no true *man* will ever look at you?"

"Peace, woman," said Anne, scarcely listening. There was no doubt about it; the flushed, bemused, ecstatic Anne who had just entered the house was not the same person who, an hour before, had wandered so sadly out of it.

She struck her stepmother dumb, which was no mean feat.

Nobody (except the Queen, of course, and that exception made up for a lot) loved Robert Dudley, Earl of Leicester.

For one thing they all believed, rightly or wrongly, that he had gone to the trouble of murdering his wife Amye so that he might marry the Queen; thus, ironically, putting himself in a position where the Queen could never marry him. Being Elizabethans, they disliked him more for the certain failure than for the suspected murder.

It was very unfair. He deserved some credit. Like so many of his contemporaries, he combined a cold will, a ruthless ambition, a raging egoism, with a selfless desire to help his country to greatness.

He also took a sincere and constructive interest in the theatre. So that when he met his new servant Will, he did not forget the eleven-year-old boy who had also shown an interest in the theatre. "Ah! Master Shakeshaft, who thought my man Gascoigne's masque ill-writ."

Both the Earl's voice and features had a built-in sneer. Will swallowed and trembled. His fear fought his youthful swagger – and lost. He said, "Shagsper, my lord. Will Shagsper."

"The devil. I'll call you what I will." Cold eyes stared at Will keenly from beneath cleft brows. Will waited, sweating. The Earl was deciding something – a week in a dungeon, for insolence? A whipping? Will's mouth was dry.

At last the question came – itself like a whip lash. "Could you do better, youth?"

"I – I could try, my lord."

"So. Write me a piece that will last for half an hour on the stage. In *your* time, remember, not in mine."

To write! To hold a pen in his hands, to feel the clash and tumult of character in his brain, to set it down! The Earl said, "I will provide pens and paper and ink. See George Gascoigne for them." He turned away.

"But sir – my lord?" cried Will.

"What?" His lordship was furious. *He* terminated interviews.

"My – my lord. I can say nothing in half an hour. I need four, five hours."

"Well, you won't get them. If you *can* write, which I very much doubt, we shall know in the first five minutes."

He went his way fuming. Insolent pup! "Will Shagsper, my lord," correcting *him*, Leicester. "Will Shagsper, my lord." By God, he'd teach this cock to crow another tune.

But in fact where his beloved theatre was concerned, Robert took no chances. George Gascoigne *had* for once written vilely. The boy had been right. And the youth – for all the brashness, the infuriating self-confidence – had impressed him. There was, Robert felt, a depth, a power that excited him. He wasn't going to risk missing a useful scribbler.

He went to see George Gascoigne. "A youth – Shagsper, or some such outlandish name – give him pens, ink, paper, a room if he needs it. He is to produce a half-hour masterpiece."

"Really?" George Gascoigne looked amused, and contemptuous. *He* was the writer. He didn't want any young cubs snapping at his heels. "What do we know of him?"

"Nothing. Except that he thought your *Juno* vile."

"Well, well. What an introduction, my lord." Master Gascoigne smiled thinly.

"It *was* vile," said his lordship. He didn't need to worry about the feeling of others, unless they were his superiors, and there were precious few of those left in England.

Gascoigne was silent. He had long ago learnt the bitter taste of insults, and had found the way to deal with them. He swallowed them without a word. But not down into his belly. He held them, like gall, in his throat; and spat them out, venomously, at those who could not spit back.

The Earl said, "We will have the play in the Great Hall, with madrigals, and a jig or two. If it be good – well. If it be, *like yours,*" he underlined with relish, "*vile* – then we shall have much sport." He was silent. Gascoigne, watching him, saw his cold eyes glint with humour, like ponds in January sunshine. Gascoigne added to the merriment by twisting his thin lips into a smile. The two men, despite contempt on one side and hatred on the other, understood each other perfectly.

Will's mind was whirling and whirring, like some powerful, but yet unharnessed, machine. A play, characters, conflicts, words buzzing in the air like angry bees, gestures, swords, cannon – ! But none of this was any good without a plot. God in Heaven, he *hadn't* a plot. All this fever and ferment and action in his brain, and he had no peg to hang it on. Never would have.

Still in the throes of panic, he went to see George Gascoigne. "Sir, my lord said you would give me pens, paper."

Gascoigne lolled in his chair, gazing up insolently. Will, refusing to listen to the voice in his brain which cried insistently, "You can't write a play," said importantly, "I am to write a play for my lord."

"About what?" Gascoigne tossed some quills and paper across the desk. They fell on the floor. Will stooped and picked them up. "About anything, sir."

"Anything is nothing. As you will soon discover, Master Shakewell." He stared up under his brows, venomously. "So you thought my *Juno* vile?"

"The actors, sir, did you no credit."

"Ah! A smooth tongue. But you know that the lady who played Juno is now Countess of Leicester, Mistress of Kenilworth?"

"No. I – I didn't know." Will thought longingly of his quiet life in Stratford. He was already thinking that mixing with lords and ladies was much too nerve-racking for him. It

seemed that if you'd still got both ears and your tongue by
the end of a week, you'd have done well.

George Gascoigne gave a waspish little laugh. "I'm sure
she will be mightily interested in your judgment."

"Sir, it would be unkind to tell her," Will said urgently.

"Unkind, Master Wagspear? But surely, we who think well
enough of ourselves to pass judgment on a masque should
be prepared to stand by our judgment? Certainly I shall tell
her, young man."

As a glover, serving in his own shop, he would not have
been open to so many and great dangers. He thought of
himself ploughing a lonely, untroubled furrow under the
Wilmcote elms. Was it too late? He said, with more
assurance than he felt, "She will think nothing of it. A
humble, unlettered servitor of my lord's?"

Gascoigne swung his feet down from the desk. He rose.
He pushed his face close up to Will's. "Believe me, Master
Shaking-at the Knees," he said earnestly. "My lady will think
a great deal on it. My lady is not an easy woman. My lady
welcomes a critic like a bear the mastiff's bite." He sighed,
with satisfaction. "She will tear, little man. She will tear."

Will stared back, fearfully, into those hostile eyes. Then he
bowed, turned, and came away.

Back to Stratford, he thought, while he'd still literally got
a tongue in his head. Father, I have sinned, let me have the
business after all. Mother, give me that farm you promised.

Then he thought of the play. His chance! He'd write such
a play that my lady's anger would be forgotten. Such a play
that my lord would protect him henceforth like the apple of
an eye!

He remembered an old tale, that seemed to have
everything he wanted: kings, queens, a Prince of Denmark,
ghosts, murder and revenge, a love interest, a wild dramatic

setting. He didn't know how he was going to get it into half an hour, but he'd do it somehow. He hurried back to Shottery, running, panting, skipping down the leafy byways. The farther he came from Kenilworth the more he thought of his play, the less of the Countess. She couldn't bear him any ill will, once she had seen his play.

The evening sunshine was in his eyes, striking a forest of spears through the trees, turning the white road into a dazzling screen.

A shadow lay along the middle of the road, pointing at him, like a level lance threatening his very being. It struck Will, lost in his play, with sudden menace. Half-blinded, he peered ahead. A woman, straight, still, darkly silhouetted, to whose head both sun and golden hair added a perfect aureole! A woman, hands held slightly forward and outward, in a classic gesture of welcome, or love, or benediction.

He crossed himself. He wasn't, he flattered himself, religious. But there was no point in taking chances; and though he knew it was unlikely that he would come across the gentle Mother of God in an English country lane, he knew it wasn't impossible. Nothing, in these days of the world's youth, was impossible.

But it wasn't Mary, Mother of God. "Anne!" he whispered, all his love breathing in the soft syllable.

"Will!" she cried happily.

He took her hands; strong hands, for so gentle a creature, strong from the hard, unceasing toil of a country household. "I am to write a play for my Lord of Leicester," he said.

She smiled up at him; uncomprehending, but with open admiration. That was one of the things he liked about her. Some people, he felt, didn't really appreciate him; but Anne did. They'd met several times now; and on each occasion her admiration had warmed him like summer sunshine. She was, he thought, a girl of unusual perception.

But he loved her for more than that. He loved her for her sweetness, her gentleness, her quiet country beauty. She was one with sleepy, leafy Warwickshire, with the ambling tree-hung streams, the lanes that wandered all day and came to nowhere.

He slipped an arm about her friendly waist. They left the lane. They followed a path that ran beside a cornfield. The corn was tall, and green. The sun tangled with the willows. The western sky was an outrageous daub of ochre. Elms and sycamores enfolded them lovingly. He kissed her lips, for the first time; and she sighed and clung, and her shy lips again sought his. "Do you – love me?" she whispered. He nodded. The sun edged down, and dusk crept in under the trees, a breeze of evening troubled the willow leaves and ran like puppies among the corn. For Will, it was a brief hour he could have wished to last for ever: love in his heart, a girl in his arms, a play in his head; and the slow pavan of the coming night danced before his eyes.

He kissed again, fortifying himself against the long hours of absence. He tried to pull her down on to the grass. She broke away, angry and fearful. "Sir, would you give me a green gown? My mother would kill me." Her eyes were wide with anger. So. She was not the milk and water creature he had fallen in love with. She was a girl of spirit.

"A – a green gown?" he said, not understanding.

She took his hand, steering him back towards the lane. Gaily she swung his arm back and forth, eager to make up for her anger. "Oh, Will, do you really love me?"

"Of course," he said. For a poet, it was not the most poetic of utterances. But his mind was on other things. He had heard a new phrase. As always, he had to have it understood and docketed for future use. "A – a green gown?" he said again.

"Country matters," she said shortly. "Oh, when lovers lie in the meadows, and she comes home with grass stains on the back of her dress, they say, 'He hath given her a green gown.' 'Tis very foolishness." She was no longer holding his hand. She was irritated. They stopped outside her cottage. "Why are you angry?" he said.

She stood, feet primly together, staring down at her toes. Gently, with finger and thumb, he lifted her chin. Her face was sad. "Why are you angry?" he whispered, brushing her lips with his own.

"I don't know," she said miserably.

Nor did she. She only knew that she loved, and was loved, miraculously, when she was on the verge of spinsterhood; that she knew, already, with a woman's instinct, that this Will would always be a will-o'-the wisp to her, that he was too deep and wide for her ever to know more than a little part of him, that she must always be content with a little. Yet she knew that, for her, a little of Will Shagsper was better than the whole of anyone else. She also knew that love was more than tenderness. It was green gowns and strivings and moanings under the stars, and this she wanted and did not want, this she both feared and yearned for; this was a battle she could never win, because he whom she loved desired above all things the victory.

She managed a sad smile. She lifted her hand, and moulded the back of it, lightly, under his chin. "Will," she whispered. "Sweet Will. Sweet Will-o'-the-Wisp." As she went into the house she was not weeping, but a single tear hung on her cheek, and caught the candlelight, and fell to the stone floor.

Will was drunk with the beauty, the excitement, the multitudinous richness of life. He capered and ran. He laughed, wild maniacal laughter, he wept, he did not know why. Something was happening in the eastern sky. A lightness, a growing brightness. Some far, distant town was afire beyond the furthest horizon.

No. The moon edged out from behind a little hill, swung clear, sailed, bland and smiling, into the sky. What an entrance! "Bravo," cried Will. "Bravo, old moon!" He clapped and capered. The water meadows dreamed in the moonlight. The summer night was soft, heavy with the scent of may blossom. The stars were diamonds on a velvet tray. The young poet stared at the moon. The moon stared at the poet. It seemed that they had known each other a long time. Theirs was a love affair that went back through the slow ages of man. William inhaled deeply, as though to take into himself this rich and silver loveliness. "On such a night", he murmured, "on such a night as this –"

Someday, at more leisure, he would recollect this moment.

George Gascoigne handed back the manuscript without a word. Will, waiting for the cries of delight and wonder, was disappointed. "You – you like it, sir?" he faltered.

"Well – " Gascoigne was silent. "It's certainly a well-packed half-hour," he said at last.

No more than that? Will was affronted. He had written *Hamlet, Doe Not Tarrie* at white heat. It still rang in his head like the clash of swords. He *loved* those characters, heroes and villains alike. And now: a well-packed half-hour! But he was already learning. He asked, humbly, "Will my lord show the play, do you think?"

"Certainly he will." Gascoigne held out a hand for the manuscript. "There is one point here," he said, turning the pages, "where I think I could help you. It is where the King's brother kills the King to gain the crown."

The crux of the whole play! Gascoigne said, "It seems to me, as a play writer of no small experience, that the drama would be heightened if he were also to kill his own wife so that he could marry the Queen."

"But he hasn't got a wife."

"You could give him one," Gascoigne said sweetly.

Will went home, gave Claudius a wife, and had him push her over the battlements. Re-reading it, he had to admit that Gascoigne had been right. It was the most dramatic scene in the whole play.

And Gascoigne, still sitting in his little room in the tower, surrounded by quills and papers and books and the cluttered properties of the theatre, Gascoigne thought: Well, that should be one young playmaker less snapping at my heels. After *Hamlet, Doe Not Tarrie* has been produced at Kenilworth, the only course open for Master Shake-at-the-Knees will be to take to his heels.

Always assuming, of course, that he still had heels to take to.

She met her Will-o'-the-Wisp in the white cornfields under a white moon. She drew him to her, gently, softly, almost as a mother might hold a son. She smiled in wonder at the crisp hair, the eager eyes. Her body melted and swooned with love. Her body, that had been hardening itself for expected spinsterhood, softened and yearned. She touched his hair. "My beloved is mine, and I am his," she murmured, knowing sadly it was not true, her beloved would never be hers, always a part of him would dance away, out of her grasp. Or perhaps it would be true to say that a part of him, a major part perhaps, she would never see, perhaps no one would ever see; there were deep, secret places of the soul where no man, or woman either, might ever penetrate.

She ached to enfold him with her love. Not green-gown loving, she thought anxiously. But she would be kind, kind and tender as moonlight on gossamer. And then, perhaps – ? He had never mentioned marriage. But tonight, under this amiable moon, might he not do so, young though he was?

But all he wanted to talk about was his play. "Tomorrow night, Anne, in the Great Hall! With my lord and lady on the front row" – he swallowed anxiously at the sudden thought of my lady - "and the Ladies and Gentlemen, and my Lord's Officers, everyone watching. You – you will come, Anne?"

"Come? *Me?*" She was terrified. "*Me*, come to the Castle?" She had seen that sombre pile, arrogant behind its moat. The thought of being on the *inside* of that moat appalled her.

"Of course. You shall sit with the author."

"But – I have no clothes for such a grand place."

Yes, he supposed that was true. He hoped she would manage not to look too countrified. Still, he'd asked her now. And, anyway, he needed someone to impress. And, most compelling reason of all, of course, he loved her, didn't he?

"You will look more beautiful than the greatest lady," he assured her. It was a bit trite, but it suited Anne, poor simple Anne. She glowed with pleasure. And then they were silent, lost in the wonder of moonlight and the stirring, rustling, country night.

Lost, most of all lost, abandoned, drowned in the wonder and the tenderness of love. He, blinded by the white, burning brilliance of this moment to everything – to ambition, to future happiness, to poetry itself; she, accepting at last, with sad, overwhelming tenderness, the urgent desperate demands of love.

"If I have to sit through 'Greensleeves' once more I shall scream." That was Lady Lucy on the second row.

"God's blood! You can't scream here," said Sir Thomas in a desperate whisper. "Robert would have your tongue to feed his dogs." He looked nervously about him. True, the Earl and Countess had not yet taken their places. But every single member of that audience would have been eager to advance himself by carrying tales to my Lord of Leicester.

His wife dug her jewelled fingers into a pearl-studded box. She chose a comfit, set it between her pouting lips. "But, Tom, I know just what it's going to be. Madrigals, a lutenist hey nonny noing, and a jig or a tale of bawdry to finish with.'

Sir Thomas sighed. Like all the nobility present he had been given a parchment on which, writ fair, was listed the entertainment. Now he tried to read it.

Despite the torches round the walls, and the wax lights, and the candles, the Great Hall at Kenilworth was not well lit. And reading was not one of Sir Thomas' readier accomplishments. Nevertheless he persevered, running his finger along the lines, muttering the words aloud. And at last he got the gist. "You are wrong, my love," he said. "The last item is a play by, I believe, some Stratford youth." He peered again at his parchment. "The Prinz of Danemerk or, Hamlet, Doe Not Tarrie."

"I can scarce wait," said Lady Lucy, biting the comfit with strong, yellow teeth. But now, suddenly, the Great Hall, with its brooding stone, its hellish draughts, its menacing shadows, became taut and tense. They all sprang to their feet, and put on bright and anxious smiles. The high and mighty prince,

Robert Dudley, Earl of Leicester, and his Countess, he in cloth of silver, she in cloth of gold, both smiling graciously, entered and took their places in the middle of the front row. The entertainment began.

Lady Lucy, peering uncomfortably round the great, high chair that housed the Earl, could hardly see a thing. But she did see a fat youth with a lute walk on to the stage. The youth struck an all too familiar chord. "O, God," said Lady Lucy. "What did I tell you?"

On the back row, among the scullions and the yokels, sat William Shakespeare, in very heaven.

True, Anne was not with him. Too honest to plead a headache, yet fearing in her country way that if she once entered the Castle she would never leave it, she had hurt him by refusing to see his play. But now that he was here her absence did not unduly worry him. He could scarce sit still for excitement. He looked at this audience, so meticulously graded: Earls and their ladies at the front, then Knights, Esquires, Gentlemen, the Great Servants of the House, the lesser servants, the common sort. And one day he, Sir William Shakespeare, of Stratford-upon-Avon, would be up there near the front.

With Anne? He wasn't quite so sure. He loved her, for her sweet and tender womanliness, for her soft voice, her gentle smile, not least for her unconcealed love and worship of him. But could she, with her quiet but rustic charm, go where he was going?

For writing *Hamlet, Doe Not Tarrie* had opened William's eyes. He had discovered in himself powers he had never dreamed of. The power to distil his overflowing love of the world into poetry; to create his own kings and queens and nobles, and make them do his will. *He* was no ploughman, no glover. He was a poet. He surveyed, in imagination, his corpse-strewn final scene. When he compared that masterpiece with some of the Moralities he had seen at Coventry and Warwick, he was amazed at himself. If that didn't impress my lord, then his name wasn't Will Shagsper.

The rest of the entertainment was interminably dreary. Much as he loved music, he had to admit that "Greensleeves" was beginning to pall. The appetite for it, he thought, sickens after about the hundredth hearing, and so dies. He made a mental note.

A madrigal, sung by two Countesses, a pretty Esquire, and a Gentleman. A knock-about Morality, showing Lust overcome by Chastity and Purity, much to everyone's disappointment, Lust being far and away the most endearing character. Another madrigal. "And now," announced George Gascoigne, tongue in cheek, "a most melancholy tragedie, the Prinz of Danemerk, or Hamlet, Doe Not Tarrie, by" – he peered short-sightedly at his parchment – "by Wilton – Wilson – Shagskeeper, of Temple Grafton."

Why were they laughing? Why in God's name were they laughing? This was a tragedy, not a jig.

Will, scarlet, listened to the guffaws of the yokels, saw the sneers and smiles of the gentry. He wanted to jump on to his seat, to cry, "I am not what he says. I am Will Shakespeare, of Stratford, an Arden. And you will hear of me, by God!"

He didn't. Will knew his place. He might be a poet, and an Arden. But gentry were gentry, and if they thought fit to laugh, then none could stop them. Besides, one crossed the Earl at one's direst peril. And on the list of Will's many excellent qualities, courage came rather low down.

"The scene," announced Gascoigne, "is the Castle of Elsinore."

Claudius and Queen Gertrude entered. Obviously, they were deeply in love; but, as Gertrude pointed out, there were two obstacles to their marriage: her husband the King, and Claudius' wife Mildred.

Will, alert to the audience's every reaction, was surprised to hear a sharp intake of breath at this.

And now something even more strange, and slightly alarming, happened. My Lord of Leicester peered quellingly round his great chair, a furious look on his red face. But by this time King Hamlet had come on and settled down for an after-dinner nap in his orchard, much fussed over by his treacherous Queen Gertrude.

Claudius came and poured poison in his ear.

King Hamlet delivered a very long speech and then died.

Claudius and Gertrude carried him off. There was a perfunctory clapping. So far, Will had to admit, they were a poor audience.

"Scene 2. The Battlements," announced George Gascoigne, stifling a yawn. But the yawn was false. If George Gascoigne knew anything, the next scene was going to prove the most dramatic in all literature. He was also getting nervous, questioning his own wisdom. He had chosen for the play young actors who had never heard of Amye Robsart. But *he* knew the old story and he had read the play. He was beginning to wonder whether his prepared excuse, that young Shagsper had interpolated the scene later, would satisfy the Earl. When the Earl was in one of his cold rages, Gascoigne reminded himself uncomfortably, he was not easy to satisfy.

Claudius and his wife Mildred entered, lovingly. Mildred sighed with content. "This castle," she said, "hath a pleasant seat; the air nimbly and sweetly recommends itself unto our gentle senses." She went and leaned over the battlements, represented by the back of a large settle.

Claudius looked at her. He turned to the audience. He leered horribly. "Now might I do it pat," he stage whispered behind the back of his hand.

George Gascoigne had been *right*. In that whole audience, ranging from sophisticates to clowns, no one over forty was breathing. You could have heard a pin drop. Will was gratified in the extreme. But few, had Will realised it, were looking at the stage any more. All eyes were fixed on the back of my Lord of Leicester's great chair.

Those who had programmes, and could read, were busily scanning them. Who was the rash youth who had written this? If Claudius was going to do what they thought he was going to do, they could only assume this Will Shagsper was bent on self-destruction.

But now Mildred was holding up the action. "How fearful and dizzy 'tis to cast one's eyes so low," she piped, leaning out well over the settle. She shaded her eyes. "There's one that gathers samphire, dreadful trade!"

The audience was still holding its breath. Claudius began to steal up on her. There was no doubt now what he was going to do. Throw his wife downstairs, or anyway over the battlements, so that he could marry the Queen! And this, in the Great Hall of Kenilworth, with Leicester himself on the front row! Lords and Ladies, grooms and scullions, Chamberlains and Stewards hugged themselves with a monstrous, fearful delight. There was only one person in that entire throng who was not giving thanks his name was not Will Shagsper.

Claudius was now standing just behind Mildred. He turned to the audience. In another stage whisper he apostrophized himself:

"Now Claudius, let thy resolution shine
And Danemerk's Crown and Queen shall both be thine."

And deftly seizing Mildred by the ankles, he tipped her over the battlements.

"God's teeth!" whispered George Gascoigne, awestruck. He'd expected it to be good. But it couldn't have been better if he'd written it himself; which God forbid, he thought devoutly. This Shagsper must have a veritable genius – for self-annihilation!

The silence in the Great Hall was absolute – for perhaps ten seconds.

William felt slightly uneasy. He'd expected them to be moved – moved deeply. But not quite so soon in the play. If they were like this already, they'd be emotionally exhausted by the end of the half-hour. Why, young Hamlet hadn't even appeared yet.

But now something strange was happening. My Lord was rising slowly and painfully from his chair. And, as he rose, the silence was broken; the audience sighed like a wave receding over shingle. A hissing, angry sigh as each man and woman wondered what it were best to do. Heads were going to roll; and when heads rolled even mere spectators were in a dangerous position.

The Countess too had risen. Her hard features heavy with anxiety, she stared at Leicester. "How fares my lord?"

Leicester, face and body twisted with rage, staggered towards the door on his wife's arm. He peered desperately, as though half blind. "Give me some light," he was shouting. "Give me some light. Some light."

Servants were rushing up with torches. The audience were rising, jostling, staring. The Officers of the Household were hurrying to help their lord. All was pandemonium. Most people's idea was to get home as fast as possible and stay there till things blew over. The last thing anybody was thinking about now was *Hamlet, Doe Not Tarrie.*

Except William.

William was aggrieved. Just because my lord had been taken ill, was his play to be abandoned? Did none of these people care what happened to the royal house of Danemerk?

Apparently not. He sat on his now lonely bench, and watched them with distaste. They couldn't get away fast enough. Thronging and pushing round the doorways. You might have thought the place was on fire. They realised, what poor Will didn't: that from now on anyone who had even seen *Hamlet, Doe Not Tarrie* would be Leicester's enemy.

Someone was hurrying across the Hall towards him. George Gascoigne. "Vouchsafe me a word with you, Shagsper," he cried while still yards away.

Will's mouth was suddenly dry. "The Earl – ?"

"Is marvellous distempered." He seized Will by the arm. He stared at him in wonder and astonishment. "Why did you do it? Are you *mad?*"

"Do – do what?"

"Mock Leicester in front of his peers, his friends, his servants. My lord is not a forgiving man, Master Shagsper. For him who offends my lord, it were better that a millstone were hung – "

Will wished he hadn't risen. It would have been easier to stop his knees trembling. "But I haven't offended my lord," he cried piteously.

The devious Gascoigne looked at him in wonder. "Of course – at your age you won't remember. Leicester had his first wife pushed downstairs so that he could marry the Queen and wear the crown."

It took William some time to sort this out. And then the awfulness of what he had done flooded in on him. "He – *didn't?*"

"Well, he says he didn't. But everyone believes he did. Which really makes your position even more unpleasant," Gascoigne said with relish.

Will swallowed. "What is my lord saying?"

Gascoigne sat down on the bench. "Well, at the moment he's talking of cutting off your right hand. But – "

It felt as though all the blood drained out of Will's head. The Great Hall of Kenilworth shuddered, like a ship meeting head-on a mighty wave.

"But he is curiously devoted to the theatre." Gascoigne held a pomander to his nose delicately. "I do not myself believe – though there I may be wrong, of course – I do not believe he would cut off a writer's writing-hand."

"You – you don't?"

Gascoigne patted his brow with a handkerchief. "Warm for late summer, don't you think?"

"You – you don't think he'd do that?" Will repeated anxiously.

Gascoigne shook his head. "No. Not the Earl. I think, when his choler's abated somewhat – " He appeared to fall into a brown study.

"Yes?" croaked Will.

"I think he'll decide to be lenient and cut off your left hand instead."

Will felt the shock of the axe. It would be as though the earth on which he stood had crashed into a great sun on its journeyings. He saw the spurt and fountain of blood – *his* blood. He saw a hand – *his* hand – jerking and clawing in the dust. "If I were you," Gascoigne said smoothly, "I should join the throng in that doorway and disappear before his men-at-arms find you."

Will didn't think he could walk as far as the door. For him, the Great Hall was growing dark. His limbs felt like water. "I'll give you a hand," Gascoigne said kindly.

Unsteadily they went across the Hall. "Where shall I go?" Will asked helplessly.

Gascoigne shrugged. He didn't care, so long as it was well away from Kenilworth.

Despite his terror, Will remembered something. "But Master Gascoigne, *you* suggested I give Claudius a wife and let him kill her."

Gascoigne stopped short. "Now see here, Shakeshaft. Don't you try to blame me. I suggested no such thing."

"But – "

They were at the door. Gascoigne gave him a push. He went through. A stone staircase. Empty now. He staggered down it like a drunken man. At the bottom a man-at-arms regarded him without interest.

He was in a wide corridor. And now he was catching up with some of the audience. No one seemed to notice him. More men-at-arms. And now – a high archway, a guard room fairly seething with soldiery. He'd never get past here! But he did. A bridge; a moat, swan and lily dappled. With a hundred others he crossed the bridge. There was Castle Green, with its cluster of houses, its smoke rising in the still evening air. He was free! Still trembling uncontrollably, still a hunted creature, still with the most powerful man in England as his enemy. But free!

His instinct was to lie in a ditch until dark. Then get as far from the Castle as possible.

But suppose they brought out the dogs! Those mastiffs, kept for setting upon bears, or poachers, or fleeing criminals. His flesh prickled. Even as he stood, desperately undecided, he could hear their baying from the grim and forbidding Castle.

He was too terrified to reason. Clumsily, drunkenly, he began to run and flounder along a road that could lead to Shottery, or Stratford, or London.

Or all three.

"I'll see how *he* likes being flung from the battlements," snarled the Earl. Luckily for Will he had, though usually a man of swift action, taken a little while to recover from the shock.

"The dungeon under the privies. That's the place for him," screamed his amiable Countess.

"Bring him in," ordered the Earl.

There was an embarrassed silence. "He – appears to have left the Castle, my lord," said the Captain of the Guard.

"He – appears to have – *what*, Master Grenville?"

Grenville swallowed. "Left the Castle, my lord."

"God's teeth!" The Earl was putting on weight. His complexion had of late grown red and mottled, and in anger it became suffused like a bladder of blood. "Then you'd better *return* him to the Castle, Master Grenville."

"Yes, my lord."

"And I advise you to do it before nightfall. Because tomorrow someone is going to suffer. And I don't greatly care who."

Grenville saluted, and clanked off, with an hour of daylight left in which to search the woods and forests and spinneys and copses, the coppices, brakes, groves, thickets and boscage of woody Warwickshire.

Leicester stared unseeing at his back. Two black lines lay between his little, yellowing eyes. His small mouth was twisted – but in misery rather than in anger. God, would they never let him forget? Amye and dear Elizabeth! Both lost, in one desperate throw. What had the fool said? "Let thy resolution shine/ And Danemerk's Crown and Queen shall both be thine." He gave a sharp, bitter laugh, like the yelp of a hurt dog. His Countess looked at him sourly. There was no doubt about it. Robin was getting damnably middle-aged.

The heart of England slept, in the light of the moon.

Only the hunters, the hunted, the haunted, the lovers, the tormented, the dying did not sleep.

The fearful, button-eyed mouse, the stalking cat did not sleep.

Little furry things, bunched in the hedgerow, sensed a silent shadow cross the moon, their enemy the owl, and did not sleep.

In the dungeons at Kenilworth, the summer night was cold. The prisoners shivered, and groaned, and did not sleep.

Leicester did not sleep. Self-pity kept him awake. Why did Amye stick in everybody's craw? He'd disposed of plenty in his time, and no one thought twice about it. But they couldn't forgive him Amye. Why? Dammit, the woman had had a mortal illness anyway. A terrible one. In a way you could say that being pushed downstairs and having her neck broken had been a kindness. If she *had* been pushed. But could anyone see it? No. Not even Elizabeth. Not even after two juries had decided the whole thing was an accident.

People, thought Leicester, had nasty, suspicious minds. He didn't think he cared much for human nature.

George Gascoigne did not sleep. The Earl had been more marvellous distempered even than Gascoigne had feared, and said explicitly that if Gascoigne were still in the Castle after first light tomorrow he'd have his tongue slit.

George Gascoigne did *not* sleep. He was too busy packing his belongings.

Anne Hathaway did not sleep. She lay and heard the furtive night sounds of the countryside, and yearned for William. She prayed he would be safe. She had only the vaguest idea of what he had gone to Kenilworth for; but she felt that for ordinary people to enter the Castle was to put one's head in a trap. Ordinary people were safer away from the nobility. The nobility would have you hanged as soon as look at you. She pulled the blankets about her. If anything happened to her Will-o'-the-Wisp, she would not die, but for her the world would end. "My love," she whispered, holding out her arms to the empty air, enfolding to her breast – nothing.

But why was she so fearful? He would come with the morning, bright and cheerful as the robin. Fate would not be so cruel as to take her Will from her.

Somewhere, a horse whinnied. Near at hand a cow grazed. She heard the cropping of the grass, the stamp of a hoof. She heard the snorting breath of the creature. She heard an urgent, breathless whisper: "Anne! Anne! It's Will."

No, no. A goblin, mocking her. Her own longings, tormenting her brain to madness. She lay still, on her lonely pillow.

Master Grenville, Captain of the Guard, did not sleep. Nor his men. Nor his dogs. They searched the woods. They questioned wayfarers. They hammered on the doors of lonely cottages, frightening occupants out of their wits. The men searched grimly. The dogs bayed and howled. Nothing encourages one to search diligently for a man more than the fear that if you don't find him you'll take his place being flung from the battlements.

Mary Shakespeare did not sleep. Beside her, her husband snored and wallowed.

John Shakespeare had always contained within himself two warring elements: ambition, fortified by a keen business acumen; and a fondness for sack and sugar.

For many years, sack and sugar was kept firmly in its place. You needed a steady hand and head, and steady feet, to go where John was going. He climbed, steadily. And, as his business grew, so did his civic appointments.

But when he was made Bailiff of Stratford-upon-Avon, he had reached his pinnacle. There were no other worlds to conquer. He had worked hard, he had gladly let the gentry wipe their boots on him, and where was the satisfaction? He had a wife who, he wrongly believed, despised him. An eldest son who despised the business; a second son who was a fool. The rust of self-pity soon began to erode a sturdy personality. And with self-pity came the comfort of the bottle.

Mary kept him going for ten years. Recklessly she mortgaged her own lands. She encouraged him to buy the two adjacent properties in Henley Street, and so enlarge the business. She even, in a last effort to appeal to his social ambition, persuaded him to lay claims to a Grant of Arms.

To no avail. The business went to pieces. The Grant of Arms was forgotten. Honest, thrusting John Shakespeare, blandly proud of all the bourgeois strands that made up his life, had become a sot.

And already the creditors were hammering at the door.

No. Mary Shakespeare did not sleep. Lying there in the darkness she looked calmly at poverty; at a life to be painfully built up again from ruin. For she was an Arden. Whatever happened, she must keep things going. Her own appearance must always be maintained. The house must be kept neat, clean. The table must shine, even if it held little food. Whatever happened, the Arden/Shakespeares were going to keep up appearances.

She wished Will were here. Sweet Will. Why, one word from her and he'd take over the business. But no. She would not be saved by her son's efforts, but by her own.

It was lonely, despite the children in the other room, and this snoring hulk beside her. "Oh, Will," she murmured, seeing the friendly grin, the cheerful, boyish face that had been so much a part of the days of her happiness. "Oh, Will."

"Mother," cried a voice on the stairs. "Father."

She shivered. For a moment she had thought it was Will's voice. Strange. It must have been Gilbert, talking in his sleep. Though Gilbert's voice was rough, not light and musical like William's. She must, she decided bleakly, have been imagining things.

Will Shakespeare did not sleep.

The hostility of this moon-washed world terrified him.

Far away he heard baying. He left the road and plunged into the forest.

This was a world where man was no longer master; a world where man was the quarry. Even the moon had a cold, sinister air. Goblins, ghosts, foul fiends were behind evey tree and bush.

Briars clutched and clung. Low branches tore and scratched. Heavy bodies moved furtively in the undergrowth. Wild boars, wild cats? He staggered on, tripped by brambles, terrified of man-traps. He came into open country, waded across streams, floundered across marshes, gasping and retching for breath. He kept the Pole Star at his back, but went without much sense of direction.

He was fleeing from, not to. He ran with his left hand, his precious, threatened left hand, pressed tight into his breast.

After a time he could no longer hear the dogs. He slowed a little, and began to wonder where he was going.

Certainly not Stratford. The son of a one-time Bailiff! Why, he'd be picked up in five minutes.

London! The only place he could hope to find a moment's peace of mind was in the throng and turmoil of London.

He must be five miles from Kenilworth now. A little of his natural resilience returned. But not very much. He still kept fondling his left hand with his right, assuring himself that it was there. He still felt faint at the thought of the shock of the axe, he still wanted to vomit at the thought of the blood.

London. He was mired, torn, bleeding. He couldn't reach London like this.

He thought of his mother. He thought longingly of the comfortable house in Henley Street. He could hide there, his mother would hide him. That cupboard under the stairs. In there, knees to chin, arms clasping legs, he would be safe, invulnerable.

The Earl, they said, had a long memory for an insult. He had been known to wait ten, twenty years for a bloody revenge.

No. It must be London.

But first he would call at home. A blessed but frantic hour with his mother and father while he explained, washed, changed his clothes; borrowed some money. Then off while it was still dark.

He came back on to the road, his ears cocked for horsemen. But the country night was still. "On such a night as this…" He remembered, with intense pain, the happiness of that other moonlit evening. Would such happiness ever return? Not for him, he thought sadly. The carefree boy of those days was dead for ever. Now the sickness was in his very heart.

He was approaching the lane to Shottery. Anne! He had scarcely given her a thought. He had given no one a thought. The whole world, all feeling, all creation, had been centred in his left hand.

Sweet, tender Anne! Not even his terror would let him leave her without a word. Craven he might be, but he had a tremendous, innate decency. He began to run, wearily, desperately, along the narrow lane to Shottery.

There it was again, above the cropping of the foolish cattle. "Anne! It's Will."

Had he said the Archangel Gabriel, she could not have moved faster. She leapt out of bed. Pulled a blanket about herself, tiptoed downstairs, carefully drew the bolts, noiselessly opened the door, stood there modestly in her shift and blanket.

Her eyes were wide, dark in the moonlight, frightened. Something terrible had happened, she knew it.

Will took her hand, enfolding it tenderly. He was the last man not to know what this was going to mean to her. She looked at him fearfully, lips parted. "Will? What – ?"

"I cannot stay. I must be miles away before daylight." His voice was steady. His compassion for her had already driven out his fear.

She went on staring, too horrified for speech.

"I have offended the Earl. He would" – he could not bring himself to name the hideous thing the Earl would do. "He would – hurt me."

Hurt her Will-o'-the-Wisp? Her arms were about him. Now *her* fears were forgotten. They would have to kill her first. "I shall come with you."

He was appalled. It was going to take *him* all his efforts to get to London, without having a woman on his hads. He shook his head. He even managed a smile. "No, Anne. My only hope is to travel quickly, alone. I must to London."

London, Cathay, the Pole Star? All were equidistant when seen from Shottery.

He kissed her cold forehead. "Somehow I shall send a message, when I reach London," he said. "And as soon as the Earl's anger has abated – "

But he knew the Earl's anger would never abate.

She kissed his lips, his eyes, his hair, holding his head between her hands, staring at him so that the memory of his features must surely be forever in her mind's eye.

He broke away. "I must go. The Earl – "

She let him go, and it was as though a part of her flesh had been torn from her body. She watched him till the muddy figure became indistinguishable from the soft grey shadows of the moonlight.

Then, moving like an old woman, she went back up the stairs. She lay in her bed, while a square of moonlight crawled up the plaster wall, and the stars wheeled outside the tiny window, and what she had just learnt beat on her brain like hammerstrokes: Will was in danger from the terrible Earl of Leicester. Will was fleeing for his life. Even if he escaped, he would never dare to return to Warwickshire while the Earl lived. Her Will-o'-the-Wisp had danced away, out of her life. Unless she could follow him to London. But the thought was impossible. London was another world. Such as she could never reach it.

Will! Will! Warm as a chestnut, happy as a lark, torn from her arms for ever.

The long years of spinsterhood, bereft of him she loved so tenderly, moved before her eyes as slowly as the moonlight across the drab and dreary bedroom.

The chamber door was flung open.

John Shakespeare floundered up through layers of sleep and confusion. He peered at the young man holding a candle in the doorway. His yellow eyes focused unsteadily. His slobbering lips found few words, arranged them, enunciated them thickly. "It's Will. Wha's Will doing – here?"

But Mary was already out of the bed, holding her son at arm's length, surveying the torn clothes, the cut cheeks, the blood-flecked hands. "Will – what's happened?" And even as she spoke she was at the ewer, pouring water, then at the press, finding clothes.

"Wha's Will doing – here?" John repeated querulously.

Will spoke for the first time. "Father! What – ? Are you – is he ill, mother?"

"Nothing a dousing under the pump wouldn't cure," his mother said. "Now, Will. What's wrong?"

She was washing the blood from his hands. He said, "I have made an enemy of Leicester."

She felt herself turn pale. "Of Leicester? How?"

"Too long to tell, mother." He was changing his shirt, his breeches. "I must – "

"Wha's that?" demanded John, floundering in the great bed. "What's that about my lord?" He was sobering up quickly.

"Never mind, John," Mary said peremptorily. But her husband was out of bed, staggering to the ewer, pouring water over his head. "What's that about Leicester?"

"I have offended him, father."

John stood swaying by the chest that held the basin, staring foolishly, while Mary pulled on Will's hose, fastened his points. "Offended Leicester? But this means ruin for my business."

"'Tis already ruined," Mary said unsympathetically.

John put thick fingers in the basin, pressed the water into his hot eyes. "Offended Leicester?" he repeated stupidly. His knees trembled grotesquely. His fingers shook. His fool of a son had put him in mortal peril. The Earl was worse than Jehovah. Jehovah only visited the sins of the fathers on the children. Leicester was quite capable of visiting the sins of the children on the fathers. "How?" he said helplessly. "How?" He thought this was probably a very bad dream, but he couldn't be sure.

Mary said, "You must to London, Will. You will be safe there."

"I know, mother."

"Wait here. I'll get you food, something for your journey." She hurried to the door. "John," she called impatiently, "he will need money."

Money? John was affronted. "There's no money, Will, and that's flat. Now if you'd come into the business, like a good son, things might have been very different. But – "

Will looked at the maundering, helpless, frightened creature that had once been Bailiff of Stratford. And again his compassion welled. "That's all right, father." He put his hands on the heavy shoulders, kissed the hot cheeks.

John looked maudlin. "London? I must give you a few precepts, lad. Now, what was it my old father – ?"

"He doesn't want precepts, John. He wants money. Come, Will." Mary swept impatiently out of the room. Will followed her down into the kitchen.

She found bread, a piece of salted beef. She looked at him fearfully. "Will, how serious? I mean, I am an Arden. If I could intercede?"

He shook his head. "Too serious. I wrote a play. About a man who kills his wife so that he can marry the Queen. And it seems – "

"Will, you fool."

He flushed with shame, nodded.

For a second her outcurling lower lip showed amusement. Her son, so to bait the mighty Leicester! She embraced him, the fool, with pride. "And you still live?" she asked incredulously.

"My Lord vows he will – take off my left hand," he whispered, hanging his head at the obscenity.

"Oh God." She shuddered, clutching at his left hand desperately. "Will, you must go. Leicester will be revenged. Did your father give you money?"

"No. He – he really hasn't any, mother. I can – "

"Here." She went to a drawer, pulled out a purse, pushed it into his hand. "But – " he said.

"We shall live," she said drily. "And you must be able to travel fast. Nothing talks so fast as money. And Will, when you come to London, seek out Richard Field. He is a Stratford lad. He will help, if only for the friendship your father had to his father."

"Oh, Richard and I are friends. He is prentice to a printer. I will find him, mother."

She moved her face close to his, shut her eyes.

He looked at her; perhaps, he thought, for the last time. A clever face, still young, pale, the marks of worry and hardship beginning to show. Her black hair hung in a long coil about her cheek. Two women: Anne, fair, soft, gentle, pretty. His mother, dark, intelligent, high-born, beautiful.

Two women who loved him. He wondered irrelevantly, what they would think of each other if they ever met. Not that they were likely to now. Life in Warwickshire would go on undisturbed in future by Will Shagsper, poet. Already he had a sharp pang of homesickness. He couldn't imagine that London any more than Stratford was going to be seriously disturbed by Will Shagsper, poet.

Her eyes were still closed. He kissed her cheek. "Sweet Will," she murmured. She saw him to the door. Soon he was indistinguishable from the soft grey moon-shadows of Henley Street.

Privately, Mary thought the Reformation was a lot of nonsense. The Ardens were of the old religion. She went down on her knees, crossed herself, and asked the Virgin, a mother like herself, to watch over Will. She also had a word with St Christopher, then to be on the safe side read a Collect from Cranmer's Book of Common Prayer, and burned a sprig of rosemary as a general discouragement to evil spirits. Then, sadly, she went upstairs. She had other children. But Will was her favourite. Friendly, cheerful, loving Will. She'd had such high hopes of him. And now, already it seemed, he'd thrown his life away. He was virtually an exile from Warwickshire. And a country youth, even one with Arden blood, could never hope to make his mark in London.

Even if he ever reached there.

Leicester's breakfast of small beer, beef and bread was doing little to improve his spirits.

A late summer chill was rising from the mere. Despite the tapestries on the walls, despite his furred gown, he shivered. The stone chamber was cold. Living in a castle wasn't all pleasure, he thought. There must be many a humble swain eating his breakfast in a snug room, warmed by the love of wife and children. Whereas he – rich, powerful – ate alone in a cold chamber; his son, ailing, soon he feared to lie in an even colder chamber in Warwick church; his wife – Lettice, he thought savagely, would warm no one – his wife preferring to gnaw her breakfast chicken bone and slop her succory pottage in bed.

When he thought how he'd worked – for England, for Elizabeth, for himself – by God, he deserved something better than this cold loneliness.

Perhaps, he thought glumly, the Queen would let him go and quell the Irish. He could think of nothing else that would lift him out of his listlessness and melancholy.

There was the tramp of armed men. The door was flung open. Grenville, the Captain of the Guard, entered, with three soldiers. He saluted. "Sir! The man Shagsper."

The Earl looked at him sourly. "Well?" Damn Shagsper, he was thinking. The fool deserved death. Worse than death! He deserved tearing apart. But he could write. Get rid of his cockishness, discipline him, and he might well write plays that Leicester's Men could act before the Queen herself.

Grenville stepped forward. He laid a bloody bundle on the breakfast table. Carefully he pulled aside the wrappings. Leicester stared down at a severed left hand.

Fastidiously Leicester moved his plate to one side. Grenville was a man of little delicacy, and he had put the hand rather close to the Earl's beef. Leicester studied the hand. Then he looked up at Grenville. "Shagsper's?"

"Yes, my lord."

"Tell me."

"We caught up with him, my lord, the other side of Stratford. I knew your lordship's intentions. So, rather than bring the man back, I executed justice then and there."

"Or, to save yourself trouble, found some peasant to act as substitute," the Earl said nastily.

He was looking at Grenville very hard. When he was in this mistrustful mood he could be very difficult. Grenville was pained. He lifted up the hand, the better for Leicester to see. "My lord, this is no peasant's hand. See, it is young, and uncalloused. And my men here will all bear witness – this is Shagsper's hand."

"'Tis so, my lord," said one.

"As God is my judge," said another.

The third said nothing, but crossed his eyes and spat. My lord ignored them all. In fact, he dismissed them. And as he finished his breakfast he went on studying the hand. It might be Shagsper's. It might not. If it was, well, that should have taken some of the cockishness out of the fellow, and he would still have a hand to write with.

He would, he supposed, never know. And the awful, the frightening thing was, he didn't care. He was appalled. He had never known himself not to be vindictive before. It must be a sign of age. After all, he was fifty. He must expect some deterioration.

He didn't care. He would just wait. If he heard of this Shagsper being successful, he could always use him, one hand or two. No playwriter, however successful, was likely to refuse an offer from the Earl of Leicester. If, on the other hand, he recovered from this present malaise and decided to be revenged, he could always trace Shagsper and have him done away with. To the most powerful man in England, such a thing was child's play.

Grenville blew out his cheeks in relief. That had been easier than he expected, much, much easier. There was no doubt about it. The old man was losing his grip.

"Here." He tossed a coin to each of his loyal soldiers. "Thank you, lads." Everything, he thought, was very satisfactory. It was better that one unknown clerk should go through the rest of his life one-handed, than that a young Captain of the Guard should suddenly terminate a very promising career.

CHAPTER 3

IT SHALL TO THE BARBER'S...

"Now Godde Bee Prazed," wrote Philip Henslowe devoutly at the top of the page on which he was recording his brothel takings.

His piety did him credit. And his thankfulness was more than justified. The brothels were doing splendidly, better even than the bear-baiting, and that was saying something.

His trade in goat-skins, his dyeing, his pawnbroking and moneylending, all were flourishing. On Sunday, he thought, when he went to make his weekly communion, he would offer up a special prayer of thanksgiving. In fact, the simple, honest fellow was about to go down on his knees and give thanks there and then when he remembered his other venture: the Players.

He remained seated. There was no doubt about it. When it came to the Players, he had not received from the Almighty the co-operation he had come to expect.

Nevertheless, his faith stayed unshaken in the special relationship that existed between himself and the Creator – a faith that had begun on the day that God, in his infinite wisdom and mercy, had carried off his master Woodward specifically so that Philip could marry his wealthy widow.

Thoughtfully, he put down his quill. He sat, pulling his worn gown about his knees, for already an autumn dankness was rising from the Thames to his cramped, cluttered little office on the South Bank. He rubbed his soft, pendulous nose, a constant habit when thinking (and when was Philip Henslowe not thinking: planning, plotting, scheming, or musing upon the infinite mercy of the Most High?). He remembered many things. If God had done His bit, so, frankly, had Henslowe. No one could say he had frittered away his God-given money. He had put every penny of Woodward's savings into landed property near his house at Southwark, setting up his brothels adjoining the London residence of the Bishop of Winchester (a juxtaposition that gave him much pious satisfaction, and earned for his good, hardworking girls the pleasant name of Winchester's Geese); using a field here, a yard there, for bear-baiting; considerately storing the goat-skins down-wind from the Bishop.

Yes, Philip Henslowe had a very flourishing little empire on the South Bank. But his land had one considerable advantage that even he had not fully appreciated when he first acquired it: the jurisdiction of the Lord Mayor of London ended half-way across London Bridge.

This meant that the Players, hated and feared by the largely Puritan City Corporation, could perform without let or hindrance. And Philip had a grand design, a concept so bold that even he trembled at the thought: to build an actual theatre on his land, to be used solely for the production of plays.

It would be a sensation. No more courtyards and balconies of inns for the Players. No more being pushed around from pillar to post. No more floating audiences, floating off as soon as the cap went round. The audience would be firmly inside; and they wouldn't be inside unless they'd paid. And once inside they would be a sitting target for men selling beer and apples and quinces.

Of course, London already had two playhouses, the Theatre and the Curtain, but they were out near Finsbury. But a playhouse on his land, just across the river from the City, and yet beyond the reach of the City magistrates; and flanked by brothels and beer gardens – why, he was giving London its first cultural centre.

As he sat, his slitted eyes saw, as in a vision, the hordes pouring across the river: the City sparks, the prentices, the wits from the Inns of Court, the – dare he hope? – occasional noble in his private barge; each, according to his whim, about to spend a satisfying afternoon at the play, the bear-baiting, or with my Lord of Winchester's Geese; each with a tightly clutched sixpence which would, sooner or later, find its way into Henslowe's coffers.

But – and it was a big but – the Players must show a far better profit before he could risk his money on a playhouse for them.

It was not their fault, of course. They were good lads. They'd flog themselves to death day after day. The trouble was that no one had written a decent play since *Ferrex and Porrex*. Nothing you could get your teeth into, that is. Philip Henslowe reckoned that if God would send him one good play writer, just one, he could make the Players a better paying proposition that the harlots. "O God, send me a competent play writer," he muttered.

There was a knock at the door. William Shakespeare came in.

Philip Henslowe took in the fustian, the torn woollen stockings, the sunburnt but hungry cheeks. "If it's a loan," he began sourly, "I shall need security. A ring, perhaps – " His keen eyes searched. But these were not hands that would wear rings. "Times are hard," he explained.

A loan was what William needed more than anything. But it was not what he had come for. "No, sir. I am Will Shagsper, of Stratford-upon-Avon. I – "

Ah! A countryman. Philip began to understand. He even smiled. "I'm afraid you have chosen an ill time to sell goat-skins, sir. Prices are – Nevertheless, I will see what you have to offer." He was about to rise when his man, Moreton, came in, wringing his hands. "Sir, terrible news, terrible news. Burton is slain in a brawl."

Henslowe sank back in his chair. "Then God damn and blister his soul forever in Hell," he cried uncharitably.

His rage was very understandable. Burton was one of the less witty University wits who, for a few pounds, wrote bookish plays while at the same time despising those to whom they sold them, the Players who acted in them, the audiences who watched them, and themselves for soiling their fingers with such plebeian goings on. But the trouble with Burton was that he'd written four acts of a play, all duly learnt and rehearsed by Henslowe's Players, and already billed for production, and had now got himself slain before delivering Act V. Just what you might expect from one of those arrogant, supercilious, affected – "Go and search his rooms," commanded Henslowe.

"Sir, I already have. In vain. And his room mate, Johnson, swears the last Act is not yet writ."

Henslowe stared. "Nor ever will be, now." What a situation! This came of dealing with those posturing university fellows. Not an ounce of responsibility among the lot of them.

Still, business was business. This yokel was still waiting with his goat-skins. He rose. "You must forgive me, sir. I – "

Will was a little confused. All this talk of goat-skins! His friend Richard Field had mentioned that good Master Henslowe dealt in plays. And, indeed, there had just been mention of an Act V. He said, "Sir, I am Will Shagsper, of Stratford-upon-Avon. A writer of plays. And I wondered – "

What in God's name did they know about writing plays in Stratford-upon-Avon? Henslowe said roughly, "You mean you haven't any goat-skins?"

"No. I – "

"Then why did you say you had?" He gave a peremptory nod to Moreton, who seized Will by the arm and hustled him to the door.

Will was furious. He, an Arden, to be manhandled by a servant! He shook the fellow off. He put a thick manuscript on the table. "Master Henslowe, I beg of you to read my play."

Henslowe said, "No. You read *my* play. Take your time. Then tell me whether you could write a last act."

He gave Will the play, and a chair. "A STICKE TO BEAT A WIFE WITHAL," read William. 'A COMEDIE By HENRY BURTON."

He sat down. An hour later he put down the manuscript. "I could rewrite the whole play," he said. "To advantage."

"I don't want you to rewrite the whole play, damn you. Could you write a final act by this time tomorrow?"

"Of course," said William. "How much?"

"Five shillings," said Henslowe, who usually had to pay a pound an act.

"Oh, sir," cried William, eyes shining. "I will write you such a last act as was never before seen."

"Do that," said Henslowe. He was feeling rather pleased with himself. This yokel would produce something. The Players would lick it into shape. Thanks to Henry Burton's untimely end, Philip hadn't had to pay a penny for the first four acts. So he'd got a five-act play for five shillings.

Even considering the rates prevailing, he thought, he hadn't done badly.

At the door the fresh-faced lad turned. "Sir, you will read my play?"

"I *always* read plays," Henslowe said wearily. "One day, if I live long enough, I may even find one that's worth reading." There was no doubt about it. At the moment, Philip Henslowe's mood was verging on the cynical.

The following afternoon, William was back. "Sir, you have read my play?"

Henslowe held out his hand. "You have finished *my* play?"

Will gave it to him. "It would be a better last act if it were a better play. If I might suggest, sir – "

"You might not." He read what Will had written. He read perfunctorily. Damned plays. He sometimes wondered why he wasted time on them. The bears, they were the thing. Steady. Why, only this afternoon old Harry, one of the audience's favourites, had put up a wonderful performance, clawing the bowels out of one dog with a single swipe, blinding another. Expensive, of course. Dogs weren't cheap. But it paid. You could afford to be cheese-paring with the Players and Winchester's Geese. But really first-class bears and dogs were worth their weight in gold.

He put down the manuscript. "You – you like it?" asked Will

"It will serve, Master Shagsper."

Was *that* all! "And – you did read my play, sir? *Hamlet, Doe Not Tarrie?*" Will had been busy in Richard Field's lodgings, taking out the offending scene and stretching the rest to five acts.

"I have, God help me. The most preposterous plot I've ever read in my life. And that's saying something."

As panteth the hart after the waterbrooks, so did Will's soul yearn for praise, for the one word of praise he had never yet had – might never have. "You mean – it is bad?"

Philip Henslowe considered. The play *was* bad. A lot of pretentious nonsense. Worse. It was completely unactable. But Shagsper's last act of *A Sticke To Beat a Wife Withal* was at least a good deal better than Burton's first four acts, though he'd never have told Will that. And a hack who seemed quite happy to write for five shillings an act was certainly worth cultivating. Why, if Philip buttered him up enough he might even go away and forget to ask for the five shillings.

He looked at Master Shagsper thoughtfully. He noted with satisfaction the torn clothes, the hungry cheeks, the general air of desperation. Here, if he wasn't mistaken, was a lad who lacked two pennies to rub together. Philip liked people who lacked two pennies to rub together. It made them so much easier to handle. He said, "Master Shagsper. I will be frank with you. This play of yours has a certain merit. But – well, look at it. This fellow what's-his-name is told by his father's ghost to kill his uncle. And what happens? He spends five acts trying to make up his mind. It's too thin, boy."

Will's heart sank. "Yes," he muttered. "Put like that I can see – "

"Besides, it's too heavy. All they want nowadays is to laugh."

William was looking more and more glum. "I – I could put in a comic gravedigger," he suggested hopefully.

Philip Henslowe rose. "Look, lad. You don't want to flog yourself to death on this serious stuff. Something light, that's what they want. Now listen. You write me a comedy. About identical twins. One meets the other's wife and she thinks he's her husband. You know. They love that sort of thing. You could call it – *A Comedy of Errors*. Now there's a title for you."

"I see, sir." Will didn't want to write a comedy of errors. He wanted to write about the death of kings. Still, if it was comedy or nothing – He said, "I think, sir, if you are satisfied with my last act, you owe me five shillings."

Henslowe actually put an arm round his shoulders. "And while you're writing it, boy, you can lodge with the Players. Do a few small parts, sell quinces during the interval, hold customers' horses – Here, Moreton. Take this fellow to Alleyn the guider. Tell him to lodge him. And if you serve me well, Master Shagsper, I will make you a hired man." After all, he was thinking, if he did promote Will to hired man, it would only cost him six shillings a week. And even if this Shagsper couldn't act, Henslowe had a shrewd feeling he might prove a useful botcher up of other men's plays; and, as such, cheap at the price.

"Oh, thank you, Master Henslowe." The one thing of which Will had dreamed, ever since that far-off day at Kenilworth! "And my five shillings, sir?" he asked. And got it. He might be a dreamy poet. But no one owed Will Shakespeare money for very long.

Moreton, as they went down the steep stairs, said devoutly, "Master Shagsper, you have been talking with one of the greatest benefactors of the human race."

"You mean Master Henslowe?" said Will. He felt vaguely surprised.

"I do indeed mean Master Henslowe. Oh, what an empty desert London would be without the simple pleasures he provides: the Players, the obliging ladies, the bear-baiting."

Will thought the obliging ladies sounded interesting, and would have liked to ask more. But a natural delicacy restrained him. So he said politely, "Bear-baiting is popular in London?"

"Popular? My dear sir, it is enjoyed by everyone, from the Queen downwards."

"Except, perhaps, by the bear?" Will said tentatively.

Moreton shot him a sidelong, irritable glance. He hoped the master he revered wasn't wasting his money on a fool "The bear?" he said, puzzled. "What has the bear to do with it?"

Frankly, Will didn't quite know. It was something he must think about. Bear-baiting must be a good sport, having a healthy and enlivening effect on all who watched it. Everyone said so. Even the Queen, for was it not called the Royal Game?

And yet? And yet? He had watched the baiting, and howled and yelled with the rest. And, afterwards, when all was over, had tried to tell himself he had caught his blood frenzy from the mindless crowd, knowing it was partly but not wholly true. There were things inside him – He was ashamed to find in himself such dark and ancient stirrings; and then, ashamed of himself for feeling ashamed. Was it not unmanly? And yet? With his love of all created things, with his ability to get inside the skin of others, even of a Russian bear, he didn't know.

He and Moreton were picking their way through the filth of the lane. But Will was no longer there. He was a bear, torn and in pain, locked in his cage, who hears the men coming to lead him out for the afternoon performance. He also hears the baying mastiffs, half mad with hunger. Despite his small brain and feeble memory, every quivering nerve in his body tells him what is waiting outside. His little eyes watch the men, any of whom he could kill with one blow if only he were free. But he is not free, they have him by the chain, they are heaving, prodding, whipping him out. Terror-stricken, digging in his toes, he is dragged to the arena of blood and pain and hate where he went yesterday, and yesterday, and all his yesterdays, and will go, did he but know it, all his tomorrows; to bear, yet once again, what is too terrible to be borne...

No, thought Will. Such suffering could not be right, even to please a Queen. But now he forgot the bear, and all else. For Moreton said, "The Players are at rehearsal." He was about to meet the Players!

In Warwickshire, the leaves were falling; gently, like tears; or drifting, like poor ghosts; or driving, madly, like an army of tattered revolutionaries, to the barricades of death. The leaves fell, the leaves lay, trodden, sodden, forgotten, to receive the rains, the frost, the snow, the sheer misery of winter. All the leaves of leafy Warwickshire were falling; and winter lurked behind the majestic autumn days.

There was frost at morning, now. The flowers that Richard Hathaway had planted were tangled and wet. Soon the blue smoke of a bonfire would climb in the Warwickshire air, under the golden, gauzy clouds of autumn, and Richard Hathaway's flowers would have gone to join their planter. Anne's stepmother mourned for a husband lost, Anne's sister rejoiced in a husband held and possessed. Anne walked alone, forlorn and desolate, mourning a will-o'-the-wisp that had danced like a star and was gone.

Then one day she had a letter from him. He was lodging with his friend Dick Field, at the house of Vautrollier, a printer, to whom Dick was prenticed. And everything was wonderful – or would be, he added as an afterthought, if she were only with him. London was a beautiful, exciting place, and he had seen the Queen's Palace of Whitehall, and the great houses of the noble in the strand, their gardens and lawns running down to the river and to the boathouses where the nobles' gilded barges lay. (He did not say that his friend Richard had pointed out one of these as Leicester's House, a remark that might well have sent William scurrying, his heart pounding, back to the shelter of Stratford, had the house not been shuttered and empty.)

Yes. William, who had already fallen in love at first sight so many times, had done so once again – this time with London. He had come to her to hide, trembling, under her ample skirts. He had come as a child fleeing to its mother; and had found, instead, another mistress to be worshipped, and conquered. The palaces, the churches, the gardens and open spaces, above all the Thames, that silver, crystal stream, with its hundreds of swans and the ships of all the world, so different from lonely, self-absorbed Avon!

And now, amid the stink and turmoil and fret of London he had found very heaven. With Moreton, he had entered a big, ramshackle, dilapidated room on Bankside. There was a low stage. There was a clutter of helmets and cloaks and swords, of farthingales and doublets and ruffs; there were a dozen men and boys on the stage, shouting, posturing, and gesticulating. There was a girl, sitting on a bench, watching, chin on hand.

Will stood in the doorway, rapt, a smile of ineffable peace on his face. This, he knew, was where he belonged. This was reality. Everything else – Stratford, the house in Henley Street, Anne, love between man and woman, even the mighty Earl – everything else was shadow, or at best a preparation, a road to be travelled before the real journey began.

Will leaned against the doorpost, still with that rapt smile, and sighed with deep content. The moth had glimpsed the

star. Will Shagsper, poet, of Stratford-upon-Avon, had come
where he belonged.

But Moreton, more convinced than ever that his master was
wasting his money on a fool, seized his elbow and bustled
him up to the stage. "Ned," he called.

A young man, no older than Will himself, darkly
handsome, arrogantly gestured for silence. He strode to the
edge of the low stage. "Well?"

"A new man. Will Shagsper. Master says lodge him and
use him for what you will."

Ned Alleyn looked at Will keenly. "What can you do?" he
asked sharply.

"I can write plays."

"God's Death! Can you drive a nail, paint a board, grasp
a pike, dance a jig, stop a brawl, sing a catch, swing a sword,
make the groundlings roar and weep and tremble, all in an
afternoon?"

"All that," said Will sulkily. "*And* write plays."

There was a great shout of laughter. For a moment Alleyn
looked furious. Then he too laughed, though a little
grudgingly. He jumped down from the stage, threw an arm
round Will's shoulders. "You should be useful, friend."

The actors, still laughing, crowded round, welcoming,
asking his name, introducing themselves. Will kept telling
himself that these were *Players*. He felt like a religious who,
rising from his deathbed, finds himself being given a cordial
welcome by the Communion of Saints.

But now, suddenly, the young man Alleyn was serious
again. He clapped his hands. "Come on. Back to work, men."
And to Will, "For today, Master Shagsper, you can watch our
antics. Joan," he suddenly called.

Will had forgotten the girl, sitting so lonely on a bench. She rose obediently, and came and stood beside Alleyn. "Take Master Shagsper," he said, "and explain to him what we do."

Will looked at her. She was about twelve – and exquisite. A perfect, grave replica of a grown woman, from the veil hanging from her black hair to her bodice and skirt of crimson velvet. She curtseyed, very self-possessed, and led Will back to her bench.

He bowed, and sat down, feeling clumsy beside her miniature grace. She said, never taking her eyes from the Players, "See. Each has his own part written in his hand. And the guider guides them, from that Plot which is affixed to the wall."

William watched, fascinated. True, each man held a scrap of paper, from which he read his words. But it was Alleyn, referring occasionally to the instructions hanging on the wall, who signalled to them when to speak, who told them how to speak, who checked them, encouraged them, who dominated the entire stage.

Will had often seen men working together as a team: harvesters, builders, thatchers. But he had never seen a team working with this absorbed, yet light-hearted, friendliness. How he longed to join them, to be one of them, to add his bit to the dramatic whole they were working to achieve!

Still feeling clumsy and countrified beside this child of the city, he said, "Is not Master Alleyn young to be a guider?"

She turned and looked at him. Her eyes were dark, like her hair; her features fine-boned, set, with none of the vague outlines of childhood. "He is not yet twenty," she said. "And already my stepfather has made him guider."

"Your stepfather?"

"Master Henslowe. He married my mother when father died. I am Joan Woodward."

"I am Will Shagsper." He smiled, sensing a sadness in this possessed little creature.

She looked away, without returning his smile. "Is not Ned Alleyn handsome?"

"Yes," said Will. He was, too, with a fine, commanding presence, and a voice sweet and rich and noble. If Will longed to join this good fellowship, he longed even more to call Edward Alleyn friend. And then was ashamed of his dreams. How could friendship be between Alleyn, the appointed leader of the company, a man already of great distinction, and Will Shagsper from the country, not even yet a hired man?

But now, Alleyn was dismissing them. They broke up, laughing and chattering. Alleyn, taking the drop from the stage in his stride, came hurrying across the room, unsmiling, holding out his hands. "Now, Will, let me show you your lodgings. It is not the Palace of Nonsuch, but you will have company – the Players, a few roaches, the odd rat from the river. Master Henslowe lodges his mastiffs better than his Players." He appeared to look appalled. "Mistress Joan, forgive me. I had forgot – "

She looked up at him. "I heard nothing, Master Alleyn." Will had the feeling that she would forgive this handsome, gifted creature far more than that.

Alleyn swept her a low bow. "Thank you, Mistress Joan, for entertaining our guest."

She curtseyed demurely. But Will saw, to his surprise, that the grave eyes were now dancing with laughter, a smiling lip was caught in white teeth. She poised, as for flight. Alleyn crouched, as for chase. Then she was away, bubbling with laughter, giggling helplessly, Alleyn after her, over the bench, across the stage. The leading actor, the grave lady of fashion, had, for a few moments, both become their age. They chased and fled and romped. Then Joan disappeared through the door. Alleyn came back to Will, panting, laughing, shamefaced. "Forgive me. But the little maid is lonely, in a dull household. Were it not for the Players – " he shrugged. "Besides, both Henslowe and her mother worship her. It is good policy to make much of Mistress Joan." He gave Will a swift, charming smile. "So you write plays, Master Will. And" – he held out his hand – "by a strange coincidence you happen to have your latest play with you. Let me see it."

Will was astonished. "How do you know?"

"A writer of plays always happens to be carrying his latest play. It is a law of nature."

Will pulled *Hamlet, Doe Not Tarrie* out of his doublet. "Mater Henslowe says it is the most preposterous plot he has ever read," he said miserably.

"Master Henslowe has never praised anything in his life, except his friend God. But he *is* a shrewd judge, of course. May I read it?"

"Please," said William. "And I shall welcome criticism," he added earnestly.

"If you do, you'll be the first writer who ever did. Writers are like oysters bereft of their shells." He grinned, put the precious manuscript in his doublet. "Now, let me show you to your lodging."

All the leaves of leafy Warwickshire were falling. Anne Hathaway sat on a three-legged stool, salting beans for winter, thinking of Will, wanting Will, needing Will. She did not weep. For all her softness, there was a strength in her nature that seldom allowed her the comfort of tears.

The leaves fell. The cold crept back to the stone-flagged floors, the nights grew longer, with only a candle to hold foul fiends, the hobgoblins, the multitudinous terrors of darkness away. Winter had always been a time of misery. But the coming winter cast the darkest shadow of them all.

Life was very heaven. He had been made a hired man. Every day now he rehearsed, carrying a pike; or walking, hands clasped, in a monk's habit or waving a sword and crying "To the battlements" louder than all the rest.

What he particularly loved was working with this close friendly band of brothers, all striving together to produce something pleasing, dramatic, and profitable. Surrounded by friends: the actors and hired men; Ned Alleyn, friendly but patronising; still, what could you expect? Little Joan Woodward, one moment a grave lady, the next a laughing, teasing child.

He had been well received. Quickly they had responded to his friendly, generous nature. Will, they agreed among themselves, was the pleasantest fellow to have joined them for a long time. His warmth brought out an answering warmth in them. It was very heaven.

Except for one thing. Conscience.

About Dick Field, for one. Dick, compared with Will's new friends, was a bit too serious and steady. He was a good fellow, and but for him London might well have swallowed the new arrival like a bird swallowing an insect; yet Will hadn't seen Dick since he joined the Players. This was no way to treat an old friend, he told himself angrily. He must visit Dick, spend an evening with him. But he was so busy…

About Anne, for another. He had left Anne because he was in mortal danger. Now, here he was, not skulking in his refuge, as honour demanded, but enjoying life more than he could have thought possible. And with every prospect of continuing to do so, so long as the Earl stayed out of London.

He was filled with guilt – not only because he was enjoying himself, but because Anne, whom he so dearly loved, was already growing dim. Worse! His disloyalty was horrifying. He had seen ladies in London who made his senses reel. Elegant, exquisite creatures, laughing, mocking, in long-waisted, pointed bodices and Spanish farthingales, scented like a garden in spring-time – creatures who seemed to inhabit a different world from poor, homely Anne's.

Conscience nagged away. He had been disloyal to Richard in his actions, disloyal to Anne in his thoughts. And if there was one thing Will hated it was disloyalty. In fact, this was something that distressed him a little about his idol Alleyn. Alleyn, while treating Henslowe with respect and courtesy to his face, would be spitefully witty about him behind his back. Will didn't like it. But who was he, he asked himself with disgust, to criticise another's disloyalty. First let him put his own house in order. He would go and see Richard Field this very evening. And occupy his thoughts with Anne.

But as they broke up from rehearsal, Alleyn said, very seriously, "Will. A moment."

Will stopped. The others disappeared, chattering like sparrows. Alleyn sat down on the edge of the stage. Will did the same. Alleyn said in a flat voice: "I have read your *Hamlet, Doe Not Tarrie.*"

Will's mouth was suddenly dry. As the days had passed he had thought: Has he forgotten all about it? Or is it so bad that he is embarrassed to speak of it?

Yet he had not dared to ask. So far, he had had no praise from anyone for his work; and he shrank from any further rebuffs. But now, he was going to hear another opinion, whether he wanted to or not. He braced himself, as for a blow, and was silent.

Alleyn re-arranged himself on the low seat, sticking out a long leg. He said, slowly, "For once I am in agreement with Henslowe's artistic judgment. It is the most preposterous plot I've ever read."

Will felt as though Alleyn had reached forward and struck him in the stomach. He knew in his heart that the only reason for his existence was that he should be a writer. Nothing else mattered. The trivialities that other men spent their lives in – loving, marrying, begetting children – none of these really meant a thing to him. To write! To hold a pen, and with that pen to summon up all human feeling, all nature, the proud and bloody history of man, the majesty of princes. Here was richness beyond a Midas. And, he began to fear, denied to him!

But Edward Alleyn was speaking again, still slowly, choosing his words. "On the other hand – "

Will licked his lips. "Yes?" It was a croak.

"On the other hand, a man – a man like me – could use your language to make thunder, the sound of the trumpet, the dancing of a stream, the tolling of a bell." He stared over Will's head. "Shall I tell you something?"

Will nodded, too overcome for speech.

"Henslowe would like to build a permanent playhouse, here, on Bankside."

Damn Henslowe, thought Will. Here they'd been, starting to have a fascinating talk about William Shakespeare, but no sooner had Ned uttered the first words of praise that Will had ever heard than he switched to this fellow Henslowe. But now Allen was speaking again, still staring away over Will's head. "He would then have the only site in London with brothels, bear gardens and a theatre all cheek by jowl. He would attract all London."

Who cared? Like all writers, the only thing Will ever wanted to talk about was his own work.

"All he lacks – and he will not build until he gets this – is a writer who will pack the theatre week after week, month after month."

William was beginning to take an interest again. He stared at Alleyn's dark, arrogant face.

"I think," said Alleyn, "that you have some of the qualities of such a writer. But you will need moulding. God knows you need moulding. For instance, you're too heavy. This Hamlet thing; after all, I'm a tragedian, but even I – "

"Actually," said Will hurriedly, "I had been thinking of putting in a comic gravedigger."

"You need more than a comic gravedigger. Look, try something lighter. Try one of these things about identical twins, you know, one of them meets the other one's wife, and – "

"I'd thought of that," said Will. "I thought I might call it *A Comedy of Errors*."

"Yes. Good title that." He looked at Will, for the first time smiled. "If Henslowe does build this playhouse, he'll pay anything to keep me, and by God, I'll see he has to. And if you turn out as I think you might – "

He grasped the edge of the stage, fell silent.

"Yes?" breathed Will.

But Alleyn's mind was off on another tack. "It's such a vile name. Shagsper. How do you usually spell it?"

"Oh, as the mood takes me. My father sticks to S-H-A-K-E-S-PEARE."

"That's better. It means something. Quite a martial ring." He stood up. "As I was saying. *If* I can make of you what I think I can – Then a combination of Henslowe, Alleyn and Shakespeare will take London by storm." He strode off, making a magnificent exit, leaving William stunned and breathless on the edge of the stage.

William was so elated that, instead of trudging over London Bridge, he had himself rowed across the Thames.

He stood on the landing-stairs at Paris Garden, waiting for the ferry, his extravagant penny clutched in his hand. An autumn freshness blew from the river, but he did not feel it. The evening was cloudless, the sun not yet at his setting. Will stared. The river with its swans and boats and trade; London Bridge, with its noble houses, its bright tumble of water through the narrow arches, its gatehouse tower with the heads of traitors stuck on poles. London, its vanes flashing in the sunlight. London, squalid yet magnificent; ancient of cities, yet under this dancing Queen spreading its Renaissance wings like a butterfly struggling from the chrysalis.

But for the moment Will saw none of this. The heads on London Bridge held him with a horrid fascination. Treason! The Elizabethans could be very understanding of human frailty. Let a man murder his wife with a meat axe, and they would hang him, quietly, even apologetically. But let a man be suspected of even a thought of treason and he was hated and execrated by the entire population. Nothing was too bad for him – hacked apart, like the carcase of a beast, but while still living and feeling; then his sightless head skewered where it could overlook the Londoners disporting themselves on happy summer eves.

And not only he. His family, friends, servants – all were suspect. The life of pain that followed a vicious racking was about the best any of them could hope for. Justice was forgotten. The word "treason" was a match; and the fuse would run, slowly but inexorably, to flash point at Tyburn or Tower Hill.

Brightness was in the air, in the waters, it fell on the spires and towers of London, it gleamed in the eyes of girls, the windows of houses. But Will no loner saw it. Those damned heads were in the way.

What world of suffering, he wondered, lay behind each man's journey to this unenviable eminence? And then he looked round fearfully, knowing that one such thought, once suspected, could bring a head to the cold comfort of those spikes. He pulled himself together. What was the matter with him? First the bears, now the traitors? Surely he was unmanly, pitying creatures all his fellows regarded with either amusement or loathing. The bears were a national pastime. The heads on London Bridge were a national institution. Visiting foreigners were taken to see both, and never failed to be impressed.

He tried to shake off his sudden melancholy. Across a band of dancing water, all London was laid out before him, gleaming and sparkling in the evening light. The London, he thought, awe-struck, that he and Alleyn and Henslowe could take by storm. London! Why, he was scarcely known, except as his father's son, in little Stratford. Could mighty London, the Court, the Queen herself, ever come to know his name?

His eyes came back to the eyeless heads of traitors. He shivered. A clod, a yokel wasn't likely to finish up in that exalted position. There was a lot to be said for being almost indistinguishable from the earth. Rising with the sun, tending one's flock, drinking from the stream, and rest at sundown. A hovel at the end of a leafy lane, where nobles, loyal or traitorous, would not think to soil their boots. Where – a sudden terrifying thought – the high and mighty Prince,

Robert Dudley, Earl of Leicester, would not lift flared nostrils hearing the name of Shakespeare. Peaceful days, lived close to the sweet earth; and a quiet end...

God's teeth, no! Not for Master Shakespeare. Master Shakespeare had to write. And wherever his writing led – to a life of cheerful poverty with the Players, to greatness, to Court, where treason, so it was said, hung in the air like a pestilence – wherever it led, there he must follow.

He was aboard, now. The prow of the little boat lifted, set towards the far bank. William stood in the prow. He no longer looked at the decaying dead. His eyes were on London, on the living, teeming, pullulating London that he and Alleyn and Henslowe would one day conquer.

Richard Field was damnably homesick.

He lay on his truckle bed, and watched a square of sunlight climb the wall and lose itself as the sun touched the roof of Paul's.

Just now, he thought, the mist would be lying like folded linen in the Stratford meadows. The apples would hang like little suns in his father's orchard, the beech trees of Warwickshire would be aflame, there would be cheerful preparations for Mop Fair and Michaelmas and Hallow E'en. He felt an almost physical, almost unbearable ache. He hated London, he feared his master, he loved a girl who mocked him; he was in a bad way.

It hadn't been so bad when Will was here. Will was a good fellow, but mercurial, thought the solid Richard. Will would never submit to the discipline of apprenticeship, for instance. And where were you without it? Richard was a great believer in discipline. And thrift. And hard work. Richard was going to grow up into an admirable citizen with, he hoped, a business of his own, a pleasant house and garden, and a wife and children who would do him credit.

He'd got it all mapped out. And he knew, though it was hard to believe it this evening, that it was worth being homesick for.

He wished Will hadn't gone off like that. Or rather, he wished he'd done it a bit more – graciously. At least come back and thanked him. Not that Richard wanted thanks. He just didn't like to feel disappointed in anyone. And he didn't think Will had behaved *quite* as one might have hoped. But perhaps you couldn't be as delightful as Will and stick to all the rules of good behaviour. The rules of good behaviour were for dull, solid citizens like himself, he thought glumly.

It would have been helpful, too, if Will had left some kind of address. A letter had arrived for him the day after he left, brought by a lad from the Oxford carrier's cart; and this letter had worried the conscientious Richard to death. Anyone who went to the expense of sending a letter by carrier, with a penny for special delivery at the other end, must have something urgent and important to say. But Will was lost in the maggot heap of London. Richard was helpless.

Steps were coming up the stairs, brisk, cheerful steps. No one in Vautrollier's gloomy household moved like that. Will, he thought, leaping eagerly from his bed and running to the door. "Will," he cried, holding out both hands, his plump, bland face beaming; glad not so much to see Will as to find that his friend hadn't just disappeared gracelessly without a word.

They stood, smiling, clasping hands. Will said, "Dick, I'm sorry, what you must think of me, going off like that, and never a word, but oh, Dick, it's all so wonderful, Henslowe has made me a hired man, six shillings a week, *six shillings*, Dick, and Edward Alleyn, the actor, has read my play and thinks – But Dick, how are you? How is the printing? How is your young mistress?"

"Homesick, dull and quite impervious, in that order."

Damn, thought Will. Here he was, bursting with joy and energy and an overflowing love for all creation. And poor Richard was in the dumps. He felt ashamed of his own good fortune. He couldn't tell Dick what Alleyn had said when Dick was stuck with seven years of bondage. Being a prentice wouldn't suit me, he thought. Hedged about by government laws as to what you might and might not do with your leisure, what you might wear and not wear. Bound to a peevish master. Drab clothes, drab company, drab life. No. Give him the easy comradeship of those rogues and vagabonds the Players. He said, compassionate as ever, squeezing his friend's shoulder, "I have a few pence. Let's find a tavern, drink to your mistress' chilly glances."

Richard looked delighted. "Nothing I should like more." Then he remembered. "But first – I forgot – the most important – This came for you, days ago. But I had no address. I didn't know – " He gave Will the letter.

Will looked at it stupidly. A letter, for him? Why, he'd never had a letter in his life. Letters were about death, sickness, disaster. He looked again. *Master Will Shapere.* The spelling was so-so, but he supposed he couldn't complain about that.

He broke the seal that fastened the single sheet. He read.

It didn't take much reading. Anne Hathaway was handier with a needle or a kitchen knife than with a pen. But she could say what she had to say. "Sweet Will, I am with childe, and very lonelie. Anne."

He had been in the foothills, climbing vigorously, breath controlled, thighs powerful, feet sure, spirit exulting in the struggle. Whenever he lifted his eyes, the gleaming peaks were there; high, majestic, and, for him alone among the many, *attainable*. Now, with dreadful suddenness, he had plunged back down the slope. He sprawled, bruised and winded, in the mire of the valley.

Strangely, his first thoughts were of everlasting damnation. He had never given much thought to religion. There were too many delights in this world demanding his attention. But now he began to wish he'd thought more about it. To an Elizabethan, Hell was very much more real, and far nearer, than Ethiopia. (And peopled by creatures more familiar. Everyone knew what a devil looked like. Most people had met one, and those who hadn't always knew someone who had. But the dragons of Ethiopia were thirty yards long and their eyelids rattled like tinkling brass. Such creatures, unlike devils and foul fiends, were outside normal experience.)

Hell! Was there not a special Hell reserved for the ravishers of the young? Were there not special torments?

But he hadn't ravished her. They had come together, in love, on a summer's night, in a gossamer bed of moonbeams. They had striven, and sighed and moaned to become one flesh; but instead their love had become flesh, to grow monstrously in the womb, finally to burst forth and smother, a destroyer of hopes, plans, lives. He remembered a foetus he had once seen preserved in a bottle. He shuddered violently. This was the misshapen creature that would grow, and grow, until it overshadowed all his life, a shadow in which achievement and hope would wither and die. A moment ago his future had been the bustle and good fellowship of the playhouse; the stretching of mind and intellect; with, perhaps, fame and success at the end.

Now it was brats and poverty by the damp, dank Avon.

He thought of his mother. God, what a son he'd turned out to be, what a disappointment! Not content to have angered the most powerful and vindictive man in England; not content to have been exiled from his native shire before he was twenty; but, before all this, to have shamed her womanhood by shaming all womanhood with his lusts.

No. It wasn't like that. That was how the Church would see it; how his father would see it, how Dick here would see it; how, perhaps, his mother would see it. But it wasn't like that. Anne would not see it like that.

He thought of Anne. Poor Anne, who had wanted and not wanted, who had been afraid yet in the end courageous, who had loved, and lost her love, and been left to carry alone the fearful burden of love made flesh. Compassion welled in him, so that tears trembled on his eyelids. All this time, while he had been strutting about the stage, laughing, chattering, good fellow Will, beloved by all – she had been suffering, and because of him. Oh vile, vile, vile.

His face was as frozen as if he had walked five miles in a blizzard. His jaws were stiff, his tongue swollen. It was like a dead man speaking. "I must to Stratford."

Will's long descent into Hell, and the shedding of all his hopes, had taken perhaps fifty seconds. Richard Field had watched him, waiting for a sign, either to speak or to remain silent. His round, sleek face was surprisingly understanding. "Bad news, Will? Not your father?"

"No. A girl. I – its – unbelievable, Dick. A child, from that? Not even – abed?"

Richard said gently, "What will you do, Will?"

"God's blood, Dick! Marry her, as soon as possible."

Richard could never have found himself in this situation. Richard's head could never let go command, even in the extremities of desire or fear or anger.

Wed first, bed second,
Peace and joy can then be reckoned.
Wed second, bed first,
All thy life shall be accurst.

So Richard's mother had always taught; together with taking care of the pence, letting not the sun go down on thine anger. She was a great one for saws. She had taught Richard well. Not that Richard, with his careful ways, needed much teaching. Where Richard was concerned, everything was under control.

Despite his bland appearance, he did not admire himself for this. Rather he admired men like Will, who dared to act without calculation, who could snatch a joy while he, Richard, was weighing up the pros and cons (by which time, as he knew, the joy had fled).

So Richard Field understood something of the motives and consequences of, and the emotional reactions to, an act whose recklessness was utterly beyond him. He said, "Don't be too rash, Will. The fault was not yours alone, remember."

Will looked at him in disbelief. "How *dare* you?" he asked venomously.

"It takes two to make a quarrel – or a child." He was watching Will closely. "Oh, she will suffer – five, ten years maybe. After that, the waters will have subsided. Whereas, if you marry her you don't love, both your lives may pass in misery."

"I *do* love her, damn you."

"Or pity her. Besides, have you forgot – the Earl?"

He had. When a man's life is turned topsy-turvy, he cannot remember everything. Even a high and mighty Earl is apt to be forgotten. But he said, desperately seizing his friend's forearm, "Listen, Dick, I am going back to Warwickshire, to marry her."

"Why?"

"Honour. Love. Oh, pity, if you like. What's wrong with pity?"

"And how will you live?"

"I can plough. I know something of my father's trade."

Richard grinned. "I knew you wouldn't let me down, Will."

"Let *you* down? What have you got to do with it?"

"Nothing, I suppose. I just enjoy seeing my friends true to their own selves. It means they can't be *un*true to anyone else."

Will gave him a quick look. Dick had said something worth thinking about when – if – the world ever got on an even keel again. He said, "I wish you could come with me."

"God, so do I." Dick was no longer smiling. The sun was down behind Paul's now, his room was almost dark. But in Stratford, he knew, the sun would be a red ball caught in the willow branches, and the grass would be already cool in the long shadows of the poplars.

"Shottery? Where the devil's that?" cried Edward Alleyn.

"Warwickshire."

"You can't go and live in Warwickshire, a man like you. Why, you're just starting to be useful. And if I'm not mistaken, you're *going* to be *very useful,* " he added softly.

"I – I know. But my father – "

"Oh, don't be so down, man. He'll recover."

Will shook his head. "The doctor has given him a nostrum of ground pearls. And if that has not cured him – "

They were in Henslowe's stuffy office. And now Henslowe spoke for the first time. Impatiently. "'Tis not his father, Ned. 'Tis a wench, carrying his child." The carrier could usually be relied on to part with unconsidered trifles of information, and Henslowe found it paid always to know a bit more about his hired men than they wanted him to know. Not that his pious soul would ever think of blackmailing them. They were far too poor for it to be worthwhile. Nevertheless, it paid him in small ways.

Alleyn's great laugh rang out. He slapped William on the back. "Then what an excellent reason for staying in London, Will."

Henslowe crouched low over his desk, peering. "How do you know it is your brat, Master Shakespeare?"

Will said hotly, "Because she is virtuous, Master Henslowe."

"Virtuous? With a brat inside her, and no wedding ring?" The godfearing man was deeply saddened. What was happening to the old standards? Why, he had known the time when such a one would have been flung into the river, weights tied to her sinful legs. He shook his head sadly. The world was an evil place. Sometimes he almost felt he would be better out of it.

Alleyn was looking at Will incredulously. "Are you seriously suggesting going back to the country to – to marry her?"

Will swallowed. "Yes."

"You fool. You poor fool."

"You'll find it hard to keep a wife on a hired man's pay," said Henslowe.

"I should not bring her to London."

"Why not?"

He didn't know why not. But Anne, in London? Anne could not live in London, he knew it instinctively. Wild flowers sometimes took seed in City streets. But they withered, and died. That is what Anne would do.

Ned Alleyn said, "Look, Will. The theatre's in your blood. You'll never be happy away from it. Stay with us, boy. This girl and her brat will never find you here."

"Even if she did," said Henslowe, speaking almost to himself, "there's always the river. Or Winchester's Geese," he corrected, quite to himself. A live girl was always more profitable than a dead one, he reflected virtuously.

You'll never be happy away from it. It was true, damnably true. He looked round the little room. A clutter of beards, wigs, make-up, manuscripts, plots, individual parts; the trappings of that lovely, magical world to which he had come so recently; could he just put it all behind him, had he the strength, the courage, to drive this knife into his own heart?

"I have to go," he said.

"And fall for the oldest trick of Eve?" said Henslowe scornfully. "Right. Go back to your byres and middens. Marry her. And I warrant you'll find she isn't pregnant."

William had been too numb and bemused, too occupied with his problems, to take in very much of what was being said to him. But now he rose. His fresh, boyish face was flushed. He said, with all the pride, the absurd pomposity of youth, "Master Henslowe, Master Alleyn, I am a man of honour. And she who is to be the mother of my child is a virtuous woman. I shall go to her, and marry her. I can do no other though" – he glanced wistfully at the theatrical clutter – "though the heavens fall."

Henslowe shrugged. "Marry her or not, you will not save her from the flames of Hell. Or," he added sweetly, "yourself."

Will shivered. But now Alleyn too had risen. He put a hand on Will's shoulder. "I think you're a fool, Will," he said.

"You're like a fox that leaves his snug lair at the sound of the horn. But if ever you do want to come back, we'll give you a pike to trail, and a play or two to botch up. Won't we, Master Henslowe."

"Oh, yes. And spread flowers before his feet," Henslowe said sourly. All this fuss about a hired man? Why, he might be a favourite bear, the way Ned was going on.

CHAPTER 4

ALAS! TO WIVE...

Scream after scream after scream rang out in the heavy silence of the night.

The young husband propped himself on an elbow, looking all prepared to leap out of bed and investigate, but hoping that his young wife would restrain him. She did. She clung to him, trembling. But Mistress Hathaway called out from her bed, "Anne! Stop your noise! What, are the devils of Hell at you already with their pincers, little whore?"

She spoke truer than she knew. Anne lay on her back, and devils with hooks and knives were tearing at her flesh, clawing at her womb to bring forth – what? She watched, horrified. They probed, and groped, and tugged. They clustered, gibbering, over what they had produced. Then, gleefully, one of them held it up for her to see.

A rat, dead and bloody! A rat, from the innermost core of her woman's body. She filled her lungs with air, and screamed in an ecstasy of defilement. She went on screaming...

Somewhere, outside the iron doors of Hell, her stepmother was calling. Anne woke; from nightmare to a nightmare world.

She lay, in utter darkness of her room, quivering. Had she, she wondered, been given a glimpse of the torments that awaited her after death, that awaited all unchaste women. She lay, eyes wide and staring. God, of Thy mercy let the night go on for ever. Cover my guilt forever in thy merciful darkness, O Lord. Christ, save me from the accusing eye of day.

Not that she felt very guilty, try as she would; a certain sign, surely, of her wantonness? But she had taken her love, in the fullness of her love. She had been kind, not cruel, generous, not mean, loving, not cold. Could that deserve the endless pains of Hell?

The Church said it could. Her stepmother said it could; all day she said it, and every day, her tongue stinging like the serpent's, whipping like a lash of scorpions.

The neighbours knew, and shunned her. Her young brother-in-law, who had managed to get his own bride to the altar intact and so felt justly proud of himself, treated her with contempt. Only her sister said little, and was kind and loving.

The cock crew. Anne braced herself for another day of scorn and contempt; worst, another day of waiting for a letter from Will.

It was a month now since she had written to him, and trudged into Stratford to give it to the Oxford carrier, with instructions to hand it to the London carrier at Oxford. And she had paid an extra penny to have it delivered specially in London.

If Will replied, he would have to use the same system in reverse. So it was perfectly possible that her letter, or his, had gone astray. It was also possible that her Will-o'-the-Wisp would *not* come dancing back to take up the burden of fatherhood. Many young men, receiving such a letter, would go down on their knees and thank God for the anonymity of London.

So might her Will. She didn't know. Her love for him was absolute. It was her life. Take away her love, and she became a husk, a dried husk. Not so with Will. Where Will was concerned, she knew instinctively, she had a great deal of competition; if not from other women, then from subtler, abstract things she feared but did not understand.

Suppose he *never* came! She would bear her bastard alone; in loneliness and poverty and scorn she would bear her child; in loneliness and poverty she would rear him; in loneliness and poverty she would live – until the griddles of Hell had been made white hot for her.

She sat up in bed, gnawing at her knuckles. She couldn't face it, yet she knew she *would* face it; she shared the patient, terrible courage of mankind.

Nevertheless, she sought to alleviate the iron hardness of life with daydreams. She lay back in bed. He *would* come. Already he would have made a little money in London. He would come, riding on a fine horse, and would snatch her up in his arms and bear her off to the Church. Then he would take her to a little house which, somehow, he had already bought, and there they would live forever in a garden of gilly flowers and sweet briar.

He sat beside the driver of the carrier's cart, and watched London slowly fall away, out of his very life.

They were rehearsing the last act of *A Sticke to Beat a Wife Withal* this morning. *His* last act. His first, and last, contribution to the professional theatre. He smelt the theatre smell – greasepaint and leather and canvas and sweat. He heard Alleyn's noble voice speaking *his* lines, he saw the stylised gestures, the hand sawing the air, the tossed-back head. Could he live without all this? Were the kings and queens, the princes and the prelates, who fought and strove and declaimed inside his head, to be locked in there for ever? Or, at best, trotted out to pass an hour for grinning yokels?

In the English way, last night's placid evening had been followed by a surly day. Clouds scudded low over trees that dripped rain and sodden leaves indiscriminately. Rain splashed miserably from the hood of the carrier's cart, and was thrown up from the ruts and puddles. A mean wind shook and savaged the canvas hood. Yesterday had been autumn, dying in majesty. Today was winter, snapping and snarling, sulkily determined to make everyone as miserable as possible.

Will, dozing, was awakened by galloping hooves. A horseman appeared, gesturing imperiously to them to pull into the side and stop.

He reigned in, until he was sure that the carrier's cart was almost in the ditch, and the way was clear. Then he rode on, leaving a cursing driver and a very scared poet. For on his breast Will had seen the arms of Leicester.

And now, a cavalcade was approaching, followed by a heavy baggage train. And at the front, proud, imperious, sitting his horse nobly, Robert Dudley, Earl of Leicester.

Will hid his face, and cowered. But my lord did not even seem to notice the carrier's cart. Slowly the procession passed by. The carrier whipped up his horse. And for Will, alarm gave place to intense relief. Judging by the length of the baggage train, my lord's stay in London was going to be a long one.

The last house was left behind. The trees closed over the quagmire of a road. The horse heaved and steamed in joyless toil. The driver sucked his teeth and thought of nothing. The cart creaked and squeaked and lurched and squelched. Fifty miles left to Oxford, at five miles an hour. Winter, in Merrie England.

The Oxford carrier left for London every Wednesday, and was always back by Saturday.

The carrier between Oxford and Stratford came to Stratford every Tuesday.

Every Tuesday Anne would walk into Stratford and join the crowd waiting for the carrier's cart.

And there she would wait.

Sometimes the carrier would be early. Sometimes there would be trouble with broken axles, footpads, Abraham Men, floods, horses frightened by dogs or hobgoblins, or other tribulations of the road. Then he would be late; sometimes very late.

But the crowd would wait, enjoying every garrulous gossipy minute. There was always so much to discuss, so much to learn about the fascinating world about them. It was said that an angel had visited Philip of Spain and shown him how men might be borne on clouds. And Philip had assembled an army of ten thousand men, ready to invade England from the air. It was said that one of the Queen's ladies-in-waiting had danced on the Sabbath, and the very next morning had made the alarming, though not in the circumstances surprising, discovery that where her feet had been were now cloven hooves. In Warwick a woman had borne a son with three heads and, nothing daunted, christened him Holy Trinity. John the Baptist had appeared to Matthew Wright in a vision and bidden him to walk to Coventry, but when Matthew got there he could find no purpose for his visit, and returned home a disillusioned man. John Shakespeare's son had got a Shottery wench with child, and fled to London. And who should blame him? said the men, guffawing. The women were inclined to agree. Only did it to trap him into marriage, I'll be bound. 'Tis said a bastard is always born deformed: a clubfoot, or a hare-shotten lip, or a birth mark like a gout of blood in the centre of the forehead.

Anne listened, pulling the hood of her old cloak about her face. She felt faint, and tired, and sick. Was it true, she wondered, about bastards? She'd heard it often enough, and her stepmother had crammed it down her throat almost daily. But was it really true?

The carrier was late today. The talk went on all round her, the soft Midlands burr of the men like a murmur of bees, the women clacking like goosefair. A light but steady rain began to fall; cold, with the sting of winter in it. After a time it seeped through the poor stuff of her cloak, it soaked her thin shoes, dripped miserably from her hood. "Clack clack," went the women, one of whom was announcing that, in her considered opinion, any unmarried girl found with child should be flogged. Her friends agreed with her wholeheartedly. Something had got to be done. They just didn't know what things were coming to.

Should she go home? The carrier might be hours yet. And there wouldn't be a letter anyway. Was it worth waiting, just to feel yet once again the sickness of hope deferred? To be soaked to the skin? To learn what charity she could expect from the virtuous when the time of her deliverance came?

To wait was sheer folly. But, for Will, she would gladly spend a lifetime of waiting, and not think it time wasted. She shrank more deeply into her cloak, pulled the hood about her ears, wriggled her toes for warmth in her sodden shoes, and waited.

It was dusk when the carrier's cart reached Stratford. A lantern glowed yellow by the horse's head.

Most of the crowd had disappeared by now. But Anne had waited. Though her hope was only a crumb, Anne would have waited till Doomsday.

The horse clip-clopped to a stop. The driver jumped down, flexing stiff knees, blowing on cold hands. "Sir, have you a letter? For Hathaway, of Shottery?"

She knew he was going to say no. He always said no. It would be nothing new. But the months of her pregnancy were passing; it was growing late. She was comfortless, and wet from the thin rain.

Desperately she searched his face. But he was looking at her as a man looks at a woman, considering her. Pretty, in a milk-and-water way. But not for him. He liked big girls, something you could get hold of.

Anne said, "A letter, sir? For Hathaway?"

"Damn you," he suddenly roared, snatching at the horse's bridle. "Get back." He dragged the horse cruelly back. The horse threw up its head in panic, eyes starting wildly. Like, thought William Shakespeare coming round the cart at that moment, like Ned Alleyn expressing royal anguish.

"A letter?" said the carrier. "No. No letters."

He'd never write now. If he hadn't written now, he never would. The time had passed. He'd washed his hands of her – and his child. But she could not help saying, piteously, "You are sure?"

"Yes." He glared at her balefully. "I am sure." He went back to tugging at the horse's bridle.

With an inborn courtesy she inclined her head. "Thank you, sir."

She moved away. She did not think she would meet the carrier's cart another week. It was too humiliating, and too painful. Besides, now that the days were drawing in, it meant returning home in the dark. Anne shivered. There were, according to reliable estimate, one hundred and twenty-seven hobgoblins dwelling between Stratford and Shottery. Anne thought of her long walk home – puddles at her feet, dripping trees overhead, darkness, and the powers of darkness, all about her. And no letter to comfort and console her.

Out of the corner of her eye she saw a bearded young man with a bundle of belongings. He must have arrived with the carrier. A scholar, maybe, from Oxford. Or a traveller from London!

People with letters to send sometimes gave them to a respectable traveller to carry. There was just a chance – Anne was a shy girl, and knew well the dangers of approaching a young man in the dusk. Young men were inclined hopefully to assume the worst about a girl in such circumstances, and act accordingly.

So. She dare not take the risk. She was wet, cold, wearily disappointed, and frightened – a fight for her honour was the last thing she wanted.

He turned away. She would let him go. *He* wouldn't have a letter. Will was lost to her. Will had disappeared into the smoky jaws of London, and been swallowed up. The sooner she started standing on her own two feet, and forgot about Will, the better.

He turned away. Since no one knew he was arriving, he could hardly complain that no one met him.

But it was a damned lonely, inhospitable homecoming. And would be more inhospitable yet, he feared. Good fellow Will, beloved by the Players, a fellow of infinite jest, had died in London with the summer days; and his pale silent ghost had arrived in its place of torment, winter Stratford.

And torment there would be: reproach, scorn, contempt, poverty, a dull trade, the life of a clod.

Coming through Oxford hadn't helped, of course. When he compared his circumstances with those of these supercilious students, strolling through their beautiful colleges with all learning, all beauty, theirs for the asking... But it was only now, back in Stratford, that he really began to see the very unpleasant situation he was in. Saddled with a wife and child before he was twenty, they'd never afford a home, it would be a case of living with whichever parents would take them in. *And* it would mean asking to be taken in. Will's nature was generous when it came to giving favours, not when it came to asking them.

Then he'd got to tell his parents. Endure the shame of knowing that every giggling maid, every yokel was laughing at him behind his back. William Shakespeare, poet, who entered the Earl's service, ran away to London, and was dragged back by a woman's apron strings.

Only one person would be pleased to see him: sweet, loving Anne. In the friendly world of London he had thought so little of her. Now, in the hostile world of Stratford, he yearned for the soft comfort of her arms. But not yet. No. He would see Anne Hathaway. He would marry Anne Hathaway. He would love and cherish Anne Hathaway till death did them part. But not yet. First he had to become young Will Shagsper, a despised nobody, of Stratford-upon-Avon once again.

Indecision tormented her. Suppose the bearded stranger *had* got a letter! But already it was too late. Almost, anyway. A few more steps, and he would be round a corner.

She began to run. "Sir," she called. "Oh, sir." What did honour or safety matter compared with the one-in-ten-thousand chance that this stranger might carry a letter from her William?

He paused, intrigued. The woman in the grey cloak, whom he had taken for the carrier's doxy, moving towards him. A decoy for cutthroats? A maid in distress? One thing, he thought wryly, if she has anything to sell it's not likely to be lavender at this time of night. But he wasn't interested. And if she was in danger, he was no gallant. He had his own problems. He made to move on. And then – something about her, even in the shrouding cloak, made him pause. His mouth was suddenly dry.

She stopped at a safe distance. "Sir, would you by any chance – ?"

Her voice – how well he remembered – was ever soft, gentle and low. "Anne!" he whispered. "Anne." He held out arms that suddenly longed and yearned.

She took a step back, fearful. The new law, that every householder must light the front of his house, was badly observed in Stratford. Will, under a lantern with a single guttering flame, had a black and horrifying cavity where his face should be. Anne heard of such creatures. They were said to be quite common, and usually presaged death.

If I take one step forward, he thought fondly, she won't stop running till she reaches Shottery. "Anne," he said again.

This time, despite the emotion that still tightened his throat, his voice came out clearly. He saw her stiffen. "Will?" There was disbelief and fear and longing and love and even hope in her voice. But mostly fear; fear of hope, with its lying promises, its tinsel, meretricious wares.

"Of course it's Will," he cried, laughing, stepping forward now.

She was very close to fainting. There hadn't been a letter, and she had followed a bearded stranger who wouldn't have a letter, but she had to make sure. And suddenly the bearded stranger had become Will, speaking, laughing like Will. It was the stuff of dreams. Next he would change into a bear, a dog, a cat. And then she would wake.

He stood before her, arms outstretched, patient with her fearfulness, waiting.

And then she knew. "Will!" it was a cry of such certainty, a paean of such joy that it deserved a velvet heaven of stars to fly to, it deserved to ring for ever down the corridors of time; it deserved more than this low-ceilinged winter's night, trapped between damp clouds and rain-pocked Avon.

"Oh, Will!" He was tight in her arms, now; it was a miracle so to hold a Will-o'-the-Wisp. But there were many miracles; a bearded stranger turning into her beloved; her Will back in Stratford, something she had never seriously hoped for; his arms about her and his kisses on her lips and eyes, wet beard against cold cheeks. Strangely, ridiculously in her mind the disappointment persisted that there was no letter. And a dread she had not yet defined.

She would have gone on kissing, fondling, embracing him all night. How else could she prove that he was real? But, significantly, it was he who tired first. Gently he held her away from him. "How did you know I would be with the carrier?"

"I didn't. I came for letters." She stared at him earnestly. She had defined the dread. "The Earl? Is it – ?"

"Safe? Yes." He smiled. "I saw him, approaching London, with a great train. He will be there some time, by the look of things."

She sighed with relief. But there was a question she must ask: "Will, is it – for good?"

"Yes," he said. "For good." It was well the darkness hid the bitterness in his face from her. But she heard it in his voice. She was silent. She had things to say, but few words with which to say them. She took his hand, as they began to stroll towards the Shottery Lane. She said, "I would not wish – an unwilling husband." He made to speak. "No, hear me," she said. "You – you're like a swallow, a wild goose. I could never hold you, my love."

She spoke with a matter-of-fact sadness that tore his heart. "I will – always stay, Anne." Oh, the spires and towers of London. Oh, the creak of the stage, the high, soaring rhetoric, the friendship and the laughter, forsworn, for ever, in five simple words!

She stood still, holding him close, pressing her cheek to his. "Oh, my Will," she murmured with such a world of sadness that he had to forswear himself still further. From its sheath he pulled out a small dagger he always carried. He held it up by the blade. "See, Anne, by this cross I will swear – "

Hastily she seized the dagger. "No, Will, no swearing. The time will come when – " She smiled, though he could not see the smile. "I have seen swallows gathering, remember, and the wild geese flying."

I am no wild goose, he thought wryly. My wings are clipped, the barnyard for me, from now on.

She said, "Besides, I am older than you. They will all say – they *are* all saying – that I trapped you, still a boy. Perhaps you, too, feel – "

"God damn their evil tongues," he shouted. He was a man, wasn't he, making his own destiny. And Anne – Anne had taken him in love and tenderness and compassion. How *dare* they besmirch and defile his manhood, her woman's honour?

He was not used to anger. It left him trembling and confused, as though a whirlwind had seized, and then dropped, him. He said, "I will take you home. Then I will go to my father's house. Anon, I will see the priest."

Anon! A vague word. But she wasn't afraid. Will might dance like a star, flit like a Jack o' Lantern. But when Will said a thing, he meant it. Will was as sound as a rock, and a very present help in time of trouble.

Mary Shakespeare sat by the fire, sewing.

Opposite her, John Shakespeare snored and wallowed, an empty mug of sack ledged on his heaving belly.

The children were abed.

Mary looked at her husband. Her thin, dark face showed – what? If there was contempt, it was softened by affection. And the outcurling lower lip showed amusement. Poor John! He was trying. With her help, with her unflagging help, he was slowly, painfully getting back to something like his old self.

But it was slow. A step forward. Then collapse, floundering drunkenly on the doorstep, groaning his way upstairs, his weight unbearable on her shoulder, gross oblivion. Then start again, start all over again.

Dear Mother of God, she was tired. Day after day, week after week, she gave him her strength, she *willed* her strength into him, she pleaded, cajoled, bullied, encouraged. She fought against sack and sugar as some wrestle with the devil. She looked at her husband. Gradually, she knew, he was sucking her dry. She had sold her precious Arden lands to pay his debts. But now he was robbing her of something more precious than money, more precious than lands even. He was robbing her of her youth.

Or, rather, she was giving it to him without stint, as she had given him everything else.

And he didn't even know he was taking it.

There was a tapping at the door.

John snuffled, stirred, was still again.

Mary stiffened. It was late for visitors. All too often people who opened at this hour wished they hadn't. Luke Grafton had opened, only to be carried off by the foul fiend. Rose Granthan had been so horrified to find Death, scythe and all, on the doorstep that she finished up in Bedlam. But Mary, sensible as always, took a crucifix in one hand and a candle in the other, and went and opened the door.

Despite the flickering of the candle, the stranger looked human, so Mary kept the crucifix hidden in her hand. Walsingham's spies were said to be everywhere. And in many minds Catholic was synonymous with traitor.

"Mother!" said the bearded stranger. And held out his arms.

She stared. Then urgently she grabbed his hand, scratching him with the crucifix. She pulled him inside, shut the door, bolted it, turned the great key. Then she straightened, holding up the candle, peering into his face. Slowly, as though scarce daring to look, her eyes moved down to his left hand. She caught her breath. Relief. It was bleeding a little, from a scratch. But it was there. Whole. That had been a horrible moment. "Will, is it safe? What about the Earl? And why –?"

"The Earl is at Court. I am safer here than in London."

She was steering him into the living-room. His father opened his eyes, peered, obviously decided he was dreaming, and went to sleep again. Mary said, "He's improving. Four nights a week you'd find him sober. But tonight's a bad night. Help me get him upstairs."

With a struggle, they did it. It was good, she thought, to have a sturdy son to take some of the weight from her shoulders. They came downstairs. "Now," she said. "Into the kitchen, and talk to me while I find some food."

There was cold rook pie, a mug of milk, home-made bread. He crammed the food into his mouth, bolted it down, washed it down with the milk. His belly received it with deep thankfulness, it was the most satisfying thing he had ever known. For the moment beauty, poetry, philosophy seemed shadowy things. Filling an empty belly was the summit of all human endeavour, the ultimate achievement and satisfaction.

His mother watched him across the table. London certainly hadn't improved his table manners, she thought wryly. Or his appearance. Could this bearded, ragged oaf, grunting, tearing at his food, really be her fastidious, fresh-faced William? "When did you last eat?" she asked.

He looked at her blankly, shrugged. "Yesterday – sometime."

That would account for much. "What brings you home?" she said.

He tore off a lump of bread, crammed it into his mouth. He seemed to cram half his fist in as well. He gulped the food down. Then he grinned. It was the first time she had glimpsed her William. So he could still smile. But something was wrong, badly wrong. Yet she must be patient. Men liked to do one thing at a time. A time for eating, a time for talking; a time for setting a mind at rest – or destroying its peace for ever. Not like women, eating, sewing, chattering all at the same time.

He finished the milk, grinned again. "I'm sorry, mother. I haven't really forgotten the manners you and father taught me."

"I'm relieved to hear it," she said drily. She rose, fetched a jug, filled up his beaker. "What brings you home?" she said again.

There was no smile now. "Nothing good, mother."

It was cold in the stone-flagged kitchen. She went and poked the fire. The ashes were grey, dead. She shivered.

Will said, "Honour? Dishonour? What you will, mother."

"A girl?"

He bowed his head. It could have been an affirmative, a gesture of shame, both. "Anne Hathaway, of Shottery."

"Oh, Will." It was the only reproach she uttered. But it nearly broke his heart. She had come back to her stool at the table. She sat silent. Then she said "Your father once did Richard Hathaway a great kindness. It seems she has repaid our family well – a woman of her age, snaring a mere boy."

He was on his feet, banging the table with that precious left hand. "*No*, mother. The fault was mine."

She gave him a long, cool look. "I'm sorry, Will. But any mother would have thought as I thought then." She said, with sudden passion, "We hold you at our breasts, boy. All innocence. Then, in a moment it seems, you are at another woman's breasts. And we can never believe – "

"The fault was mine," he said again, dully.

"So," she said, reaching out over the table, taking his hand in her cold one. "So, what is to be done?"

"Marriage. As soon as possible."

Well, the Hathaways had a certain standing. The sort of family an Arden could marry into without disgrace. Just. But that wasn't what really mattered. What mattered was Will's happiness. She said, "You can bring her here, Will. We can find room – "

"Father – ?"

"Your father's life is mortgaged. Any life he now has comes from me. He knows it. He would not try to cross me, Will."

"Poor father."

She looked at him keenly. Always she had tried to teach him compassion. It looked as though she had succeeded. "Yes," she said. "Poor father."

And poor mother, she thought, not with self-pity but with wry humour. Young children, a drunken husband, a disintegrating business, all dependent on her. A load of debts, an eldest son up to his ears in trouble, and now, to cap it all, a new daughter-in-law and a squalling grandchild to take under her wing. She thanked God for her proud Arden blood, for her sinewy Arden body. Somehow, *they* would help her carry the burden. And it was good to see Will again, her favourite, whatever the circumstances. She said, with a sudden grin that matched his own, "Are you tired?" He shook his head. "Then kindle the fire, and tell me about yourself."

They sat late, mother and son, their feet on the hearth, the fire dancing, the candle flickering on the table. They talked: gravely, of birth and life and death, of what was to be done, of the sweet, innocent past and the lowering future: two keen minds, sorting the tangled skein of disaster.

John Shakespeare slept late. Waking, he was troubled by a foul mouth, a desperate surging in his head, and aching limbs. And by a frightening, half-remembered, half-forgotten dream.

Nay, it was no dream, it was too real for a dream. It was a vision. His son Will had appeared to him in a vision, blood dripping from his left sleeve. There was only one possible interpretation. The Earl had had his revenge on William.

He stumbled out of bed, went to the top of the stairs. "Wife!" he called. "Wife!"

There was desperation in his voice, but she came up coolly. Like most people with the world on their shoulders she did not hurry to meet trouble. She braced herself, and went calmly to meet it.

By the time she reached the bedroom, John was sitting humped on the bed in his shirt, hands hanging down between his knees. He looked at her glumly. "Wife, I have ill news."

Well, a little more couldn't make much difference. But she felt a blow in the stomach, none the less. "What is it, John?"

He said portentously, "I have seen a vision." He shook his head mournfully. "A vision of ill omen."

Mary crossed herself. When it came to visions, you couldn't beat the old religion. The old religion had had a lot of experience of visions.

She waited. "Our son William appeared unto me, his left hand a bloody stump."

She caught her breath in a moment of horror. Then she understood. "Oh, John – "

But he was launched. "Clearly, Leicester has had his revenge. Oh, my poor son, why were you not content with the glover's trade?"

She said tartly, "It was not a vision, husband. It *was* Will, only you were too drunk to recognise him."

He stared at her dully. "Will is here?"

She nodded. "With a scratch on his hand. But the news *is* ill, husband."

"Will, here?" He scratched his knee irritably. "But what is he doing here?" It was all too difficult at this time of the morning.

She, too, hadn't wanted to tell him yet. Why, in fact, should she tell him at all? Why not let Will do his own confessing?

No. She was a practical, level-headed woman who looked after her husband and her children with brisk, unsentimental affection. But when it came to her nut-brown Will she couldn't always resist a little spoiling, a little show of love. It was, perhaps, the one luxury she allowed herself, apart from her warm pride in her Arden blood. "Will has got Richard Hathaway's daughter with child," she said.

He was silent so long she thought he had not heard. He had stopped scratching his knee and was rubbing his calf. "I stood surety for Richard for two debts," he said. "But they were both paid after harvest. A good man, Richard. And now – the worms are at him, Mary." His eyes filled with tears.

"And Will is at his daughter," she said drily.

"Yes," he said, the tears overflowing. "Do you remember – when I was Bailiff – how proud – a was a sweet lad."

"And still is," she said. "And will make a sweet husband. I only hope – she's worthy of him."

"Husband," he mused. "Young Will. But – " He looked startled. "Where will they live, wife?"

"Here, John."

"*Here*? But – we have no room – "

"We shall make room. And – " She was silent. Edmund, her own child, but two years old. Her last, she had vowed it. And now, it seemed, Edmund was like to be given a niece or nephew for a third birthday present. And another woman in the house, a stranger; milk and water by all accounts but she'd never met a woman yet who hadn't *some* vinegar in her blood.

"Young Will, a husband," John muttered again. "I must give him some precepts, Mary. Now what was it my father told me? About friendship. Binding friends with bands of steel. Something – ? Full of precepts, my old father was."

"Precepts?" she said scornfully. "He will not thank you for precepts. He will thank you for a bedroom to take his bride to, and – "

Something struck him. He looked at her in sudden astonishment. "Did you say – she was with child?"

"Of course I did."

"Will's child?"

"Will's child," she said with exasperation.

The tears came afresh. "And it seems but yesterday. Coming home from the petty school with his A per se A and his B per se B. And then his Master Hunt saith this and Master Hunt saith that. And now – "

She left him to his maunderings. Perhaps, she thought, it is hard for a man to discover that his begotten has now become a begetter. Perhaps with the discovery there comes a wind, blowing from the plains of death.

Perhaps. She didn't know. She was only a woman.

Fulk Sandells and John Richardson, those two old friends of Richard Hathaway, had brought their joyless faces to cheer his widow in her shame.

It was not a convivial evening. Anne was out, Anne's sister and her young husband had gone to bed out of the way. Fulk Sandells, John Richardson and Mistress Hathaway sat on three-legged stools round a cheerless fire and talked about sin.

It was a fruitful subject at any time. But now, and for months to come, they had a concrete example to discuss. "And she will not name the father?" Sandells was saying.

Mistress Hathaway shook her head.

"But the Lord knoweth his name," said Richardson with satisfaction. "And already for him the fires of Hell are being stoked, the pincers are being heated." John Richardson had a very high regard for Divine Justice.

"That doesn't help me," grumbled Mistress Hathaway. "A bastard to feed; and somewhere some good-for-nothing father living off the fat of the land."

Richardson was shocked. "Nay, sister. To realize that, though he may be living off the fat off the land *now*, his everlasting torments are already decreed and prepared – that should relieve some of the bitterness in your soul, surely?"

Mistress Hathaway seemed unimpressed. "*She* is the one should suffer."

"She will, sister, she will."

"Nay, but now. In *this* life."

It was into this unpromising atmosphere that Anne Hathaway stepped, leading by the hand a bashful William Shakespeare.

The room was dark, lit by a candle and the half-hearted flickering of the fire; and barely furnished. The stone-flagged floor was as cold and unwelcoming as a frozen pond.

But no more cold and unwelcoming than the three faces that swivelled round on dark shoulders to stare, to question, to examine.

Poor Anne! She disliked and feared both Sandells and Richardson. Bringing William to meet her stepmother for the first time had filled her with dread. But to be faced unexpectedly with these two as well –

Too late now, though. "Mother, this is William Shakespeare."

William swept a low bow. His mother had spent the day cleaning and mending his clothes. He had bathed, his hair had been cut, his beard trimmed. He was well fed. And he was behaving with impeccable honour, was he not? Frankly, he felt that anyone ought to be very grateful to have him for a son-in-law.

He was wrong. Three hostile pairs of eyes were boring into him. Or rather two hostile, one sorrowful. Fulk Sandells was always saddened by another's sin.

John Richardson rose, clapped his black hat more firmly on his head, pointed a denunciatory finger, and cried in a terrible voice, "Are you the father of this woman's child?"

"Yes."

Fulks Sandells groaned in spirit, and lifted his eyes to heaven. His lips moved in prayer.

But John Richardson, for once, was more concerned with a mortal than with the Almighty. He shouted at William, "Then you shall marry her, sir."

"I fully intend to – sir!"

"It's no use you trying to wriggle out of it."

"I have no intention of trying to wriggle out of it."

"Brother Sandells and I will see that justice is done. Won't we, brother?"

Sandells nodded. "Alas, yes." He turned his mournful basset-hound eyes on Will. "It's no good, lad. You'll have to pay for your transgression – in this world as well as the next."

Will said, "But I *want* to marry her."

John Richardson was working himself up. "Sinning before God, and then refusing to take the consequences of your evil doing."

"But – "

"Are you John Shakespeare's son?" Mistress Hathaway enquired.

"Yes," Will said eagerly. Anything to get away from the fruitless conversation with the two men.

"The man who led my husband into debt," Mistress Hathaway said sourly.

Will had heard the full story from his mother only that morning. He said hotly, "He didn't lead him into debt. He simply stood security for him when he needed money."

"What a family!" said Mistress Hathaway. "The father seducing my husband into debt. The son seducing my stepdaughter. What a family!"

"He'll marry her, though," said Richardson. "Sandells and I will see to that, never fear."

Sandells, tears in his eyes, said, "We always promised Richard. 'Look after my poor plain Anne,' he said as he lay dying. And promise him we did, on the Holy Book."

William had had enough. "*Listen* to me," he shouted, thrusting away Anne's restraining hand. "I have come all the way from London, simply to marry Anne. I am a man of honour. I would not think of evading my responsibilities."

"*And* we'll see you don't," said John Richardson.

"*And* quickly," added Fulk Sandells.

Then a surprising thing happened. Anne walked up to the fireplace. She turned and faced them all. She was trembling so violently that even the gloom failed to hide it. And her voice was so unsteady that twice when she tried to speak no sound came. But the third time it obeyed her. She said, "Sirs, I am poor Anne Hathaway. A woman, not beautiful, unmarried, and so of no account. But" – she swallowed – "I bear within my body a child. And I love, and am prepared to marry, a man of family and honour."

No one spoke, or moved. They were too astonished.

"So," said Anne, "I am no longer a person of no account. Henceforth, my life is my own. And I will ask you to remember it, sirs, stepmother." Her own voice lifted. "I am a woman with child. Not a bitch in litter."

Her head was high. But she had not finished. "As for you, Will," she said kindly but firmly, "I will not be spoken of as a responsibility. If you love me, you may marry me. But I would rather live my life with a bastard child, in despite and poverty, than be married for honour – or pity."

Will was silent. Once before, she had surprised him by a flash of spirit. But this – She was a woman to be reckoned with. For the first time it occurred to William that perhaps the bargain-getting wasn't entirely on Anne's side.

She was flushed. A tiny, tight smile was about her lips. But her eyes shone. She was elated. She – poor, plain, milk-and-water Anne – had asserted herself. And they'd listened. They hadn't shouted her down. For the first time in her twenty-six years she realised that, given strength and determination, one need not always be carried along by the current. One could kick out, lash out, against the flood, even if one was borne under in the process.

Her voice was steady. "Goodnight." She crossed the floor like the Queen of England, and went up to bed.

They watched her go. In silence; even Will, who was not usually lost for words.

At last John Richardson shrugged. "And now to business." He turned to his friend. "Tomorrow, brother, you and I and Shakespeare shall to my Lord Bishop of Worcester for a licence." He turned to Mistress Hathaway. "What day would suit you for the wedding, sister?"

"Monday is washing day. Tuesday?"

"Aye. The sooner the better when dealing with a slippery eel. And I will ask Vicar Barton to wed them. He hates a Papist more than the belly ache."

God's blood, he wouldn't stand for this. He'd get back to London, where he belonged, back to the Players, to whom he meant something. They didn't discuss him to his face, as though he were a child. A lascivious child. God's teeth, they could all stew in their own juice, Anne included. See how they liked that.

He flung himself out of the house. Anger! How he hated it. It was like a consuming fever, a raging madness. He could throw himself to the ground, froth, drum his heels on the earth like his brother Gilbert when the falling sickness was upon him. But he had no time for self-indulgence. He must to London, straight.

The night was dark. He lost the garden path, tripped over a strand of the dead husbandman's sweet briar. He swore, bringing in the Trinity, the Gods of Greece and Rome, half the Communion of Saints to witness his rage.

"Will," cried a piteous voice, "Oh Will. I didn't mean – "

Alone in her bedroom, Anne had soon come down to earth. What had she done? Swimming against the stream was all very well; but not if it lost her dear William. And at the moment it sounded as though her dear William wasn't likely to be very amenable.

But her anguish checked his wrath like holy water sprinkled on a charging bull. He looked up.

Her face showed in the darkness like the moon seen through veils of mist. "Anne," he whispered.

"I'm sorry, Will. They – mean kindly."

"Kindly? I'll not be ordered like a serf. We'll marry in our time, not theirs."

But now a segment of yellow light cut across the garden. Fulk Sandells and John Richardson, those indefatigable righters of wrongs, came bustling out with a lantern, found Will, and gave him orders: to be at Stratford High Cross at seven the next morning, prepared to ride with them to Worcester for permission from the Bishop to marry.

"I'll see you both damned first," said William, anger still choking him.

Fulks Sandells, the better to meditate on the stubbornness of sin, produced a small dagger and began to de-earth his nails. John Richardson, a less subtle character, whipped out a sword and held the point unpleasantly close to Will's right eye. "Now, Master Shakespeare. Do not underestimate me. Are you for Worcester?"

Fulk Sandells said pleadingly, "My friend is very zealous for the Lord, young sir, and is made impatient thereby. Do not provoke him, Master Shakespeare."

Will thought this very good advice. Far be it from him to provoke anybody. And after all he was going to marry Anne, so the visit to Worcester might save him some trouble. Advent was at hand, and he believed the Church made marrying in Advent both difficult and expensive. Yes, he supposed he ought to be grateful to those gentlemen. In fact, he said as much.

John Richardson sheathed his sword. Fulk Sandells seemed satisfied with his finger-nails, and put away his dagger. Anne, watching, saw the three of them go off amicably together through the garden gate. And Will – Will hadn't even turned, hadn't even waved. Desolate, she went to bed. Will had forgotten she was there!

He had, too. For Will was where he spent so much of his time – probing, examining, watching the workings of his own mind.

Had that rusty steel, almost caressing the apple of his eye, affected his decision?

Yes, he had to admit. It had.

He had come to Shottery happy in the knowledge that not many young men would have behaved as honourably as he. He returned to Stratford in a mood of bitter self-realisation. He was a coward. He'd always known he was unmanly. His secret pity for the bears, even while he screamed with the rest for their blood, had shown him that.

His revulsion, when a raven bolted some tit-bit of brain or eye from a traitor's head, showed he was more than half woman. But now! To be courteous at the prod of a knife, to dance at the prick of a sword! This was worse than unmanly. This was cowardice. This was for slaves and peasants, not for a poet, son of a Town Bailiff, grandson of a Gentleman of Worship, descendant, on his mother's side, God save the mark, of a Sheriff of the County. Oh, what a rogue and peasant slave am I, he murmured. And stopped amazed. The sentence had come into his mind ready-made. But from where? He didn't know. But it was a good line. If a man could write *more* lines like that he could write a play that would delight the groundlings.

His cowardice was forgotten in this new, absorbing subject. He walked on, feeling much better.

CHAPTER 5

A HOMELY SWAIN...

It was the dreariest of weddings.

The date was wrong, for a start. No one would choose 30 November who wasn't faced by the unfortunate combination of Advent, Lent, and a baby due in May.

Dawn painted a white frost under a porridge sky, but soon the frost turned to a foggy dew. Everything – trees, grass, flowers, berries and briars, the stone church, clothes, hair, boots, flesh, bones and marrow, mind and spirit – everything sweated with a chill, omnipresent dampness.

Vicar Barton and Fulks Sandells both had a rheum; and Will told himself glumly that the only thing more mournful and depressing than a Puritan with a rheum was two Puritans with a rheum.

Mary Shakespeare arrived with little Edmund in her arms, the other children in line astern behind her, and her husband by her side. She had supervised them all, husband included; and they shone like new pins. For herself, she had done her best with what finery remained to her. And, being still a slim and elegant woman, she knew she looked what she was: a gentleman of worship's daughter who had met poverty and was fighting it every inch of the way. Her nut-brown Will, isolated in the front pew like a prisoner in the dock, turned and smiled at her. It was, she thought sadly, a rather desperate smile. Poor Will! If it was true that the girl hadn't trapped him (and she'd take his word for that) then fate had. He shouldn't be standing there, at eighteen. He wasn't ready for marriage yet. In fact, she doubted whether he ever would be. Will, she suspected, had more important things to think about.

Here came Mistress Hathaway, on the arm of her son Bartholomew. Hard, cold and stupid, thought Mary dispassionately. Thank heaven she wasn't Anne's real mother.

The church was chill and damp, and some of the morning's fog had seeped inside and hung greyly about the grey pillars. No candle cheered the gloom, no coloured saints or altar frontal. It was a grey, puritan world on the last day of that puritan month, November.

Now the only sound in the church was the shuffling of cold feet, and John Shakespeare, maudlin today, weeping into his handkerchief. It was the sort of still morning when sounds are magnified. Through the open west door came the sounds of cattle cropping the wet grass, the neigh of a horse, the clatter of boots, a murmur of voices.

Mary Shakespeare turned. The bride, Anne Hathaway, spinster, of the Parish of Stratford-upon-Avon, entered the church on the arm of John Richardson, her father's friend.

So this was the girl fate had chosen to be her daughter-in-law! They'd been in such a hurry to get Will to the altar that Mary hadn't even met her yet.

She saw a head hung low, in shyness or in shame; country clothes that made the girl look as shapeless as a basket of laundry; a sad posy of November's dejected flowers. And, intelligent and perceptive as she was, Mary saw a fellow woman who walked in fear and doubt, and who needed, more than anything else in the world, love.

Anne came down the church. She reached the front pew, still gazing down at her feet, and stopped. John Richardson stepped back. Will Shakespeare came out of his pew to stand beside his bride. For the first time Anne looked up; and smiled at her Will.

It stopped Mary's heart. Never in her life had she seen a look of such love, of such sheer pleasure in the presence of another. Will's face she couldn't see. She could only hope that he was returning some of that tenderness.

So. Her Will was loved. And love made a penny go a little further, it stretched a mean room, softened a hard bed. It would straighten the path for them all. Mary Shakespeare settled herself more comfortably in her pew.

Vicar Barton wiped his nose on his cuff, and looked at the young couple with distaste. 'Hate the sin and love the sinner.' Vicar Barton found no difficulty whatever in hating the sin; he hated it so much that he found loving the sinner impossible; especially sinners who couldn't wait for the marriage service.

Almost the words of the Service stuck in his throat. But he got them out, and gave the couple his reluctant blessing. He had saved another whore, another bastard, from the calumny of men. But not from the wrath of God, he thought with satisfaction. Sometimes it was only the thought of Hell fire that made this sinful world supportable for Vicar Barton.

Eighteen-year-old William looked at his twenty-six-year-old wife with some astonishment. He had heard little of the Service. His mind, as very often happened with Will, had been elsewhere: in a cold room filled with the bustle and cheerfulness, the eager concentration of a rehearsal; with

Ned Alleyn and little Joan Woodward; with his friends the Players. And now, while he day-dreamed, this – this stranger had been bound to him by hoops of steel. What did he know of her, of her mind, of her likes and dislikes? Marriage, when you thought about it (and how many *did* think about it, till it was too late?), marriage was a frightening business: two comparative strangers, of opposite sexes, suddenly flung together in the closest intimacy of mind and body. And forever! But suppose the bodies grew to hate, the minds – suppose one mind tried to soar, the other, clinging to earth, held it down! The only surgeon whose knife could part those minds was death. He shivered. The body was nothing. The body would find its own rewards. But the mind – who could know the deeps and caverns of another's mind?

Then she smiled at him, so lovingly that he forgot the caverns and thought, poor fool, there could be only sunlit uplands in a mind of such sweet simplicity. And so he took her hand and led her out into the frore November day.

"Mother," said Will. "This is Anne."

Mary Shakespeare had done her best. A great fire leapt in the open hearth in Henley Street. The table was covered with an Arden carpet, laid with what was left of the Arden pewter. And if there was more pewter than food, well, she'd done her best. There were boiled capons, sausages, marrows on toast, turnips, quince pie, cheeses, apples and kickshaws; and John, cheerful now after his fit of weeps, was doing a job he understood thoroughly – mixing sack and sugar. The children stood around, wide-eyed, staring at their strangely transmogrified, married-man brother. (The Hathaways had returned to Shottery, Mistress Hathaway having said privily that the food of usurers and seducers would choke her, even if it was not actually poisoned.)

"Anne," said Will. "This is my mother."

The first two women to love William Shakespeare looked at each other.

Anne saw, or thought she saw, an erect, beautiful, amused aristocrat.

Mary saw a country woman who didn't know how to wear such clothes as she had; a woman startlingly old for her boyish Will; a shy, frightened creature suddenly, intolerably plunged into a household of strangers; to interweave her life with theirs, to accept their ways, their habits, their prejudices. And in this household of strangers she, Mary, would be the one to affect the girl's life most; more even, in some ways, than Will. Three things, she knew, could never work: two bitches in the same kennel; two she cats in the same basket; two women sharing a kitchen.

But the fact that it couldn't work was, for Mary, no reason for not trying. She reacted as she would to a trapped and frightened bird. "Oh, my dear," she said, holding out her arms. "Welcome to Henley Street. Welcome to our family." She enfolded Anne, feeling the stiff suspicious body slowly soften. "We shall, all of us, do everything we can to make you happy. Shan't we, John," she called to her husband who had just bustled in with the sack.

"Aye," said John, beaming. A man had to taste the wine. It would never do to make it too sweet. And John had tasted just enough to make him mellow. He kissed his new daughter-in-law with enthusiasm. Nowadays he was sometimes not altogether sure what was going on. But he knew what was what today. He'd got a new daughter: a pretty girl, in her way. And she looked kind. John often felt nowadays that he didn't get as much kindness as he would like. Mary would go to any lengths to stop him drinking. But Anne looked the friendly sort of girl who'd bring him a bottle quietly, when no one was around. He kissed her again. He and Anne, he knew, were going to be great friends.

But Anne was still afraid. She'd married Will, not a whole family. She wanted to be alone with Will. But that was the last thing she was going to be. In that gregarious world, it was the last thing anyone would expect her to want to be. Everybody jostled and elbowed merrily together. A married couple who desired privacy, except in bed, would be thought strange indeed.

Stiffly, because of her shyness, she said, "Thank you, Mistress Shakespeare. I shall endeavour – " she fell silent.

Mary laughed, patted her hand affectionately. "What have you done to my Will? Tongue-tied, for the first time in his life."

Will looked uneasy. He felt like an actor who has been o'er-parted, given a part beyond his range; and with an audience, not of strangers, but of those nearest to him.

It was a difficult, awkward meal. They ate it standing, saying little. Anne spoke when she was spoken to, responding eagerly; but then falling back into silence. Will was becoming sulky.

After the meal, John announced portentously that he wished to give his son a few precepts. Will listened courteously. He must not borrow, or lend, warned John Shakespeare, who had spent his life lending and losing. He must not always be seeking new friends. He must dress as well as he could afford, but not gaudily. "Yes, father," said Will dutifully. "No, father." Watching Anne, gazing as in a dream at this unknown girl, who, while he wasn't paying attention, had been made his wife.

Will and Anne went for a walk beside the Avon. Once outside the house Will took a deep breath and put an arm round Anne's waist. That was better. Suddenly, away from the family, she was no longer frightening "Wife". She was sweet, familiar Anne once more, whom he loved. And they were walking as they had walked in the acres of the rye, in summertime.

Only now – the golden rye was harvested, the fields were grey stubble, like an old man's cheek, the silver lantern of the moon was dowsed, spider webs hung with raindrops were now your only curtaining, the veils and tapestries of leaves were torn and down.

So was it, Will thought gloomily, with his life. The colour, the brightness of sun and moon, had departed. The future was as grey as this November landscape.

Anne laid her head on his shoulder. "Thank you, Will," she said simply.

He was startled. "For what?"

"For marrying me. Many men would not have done."

"You speak foolishly," he laughed. But he was glad she wasn't just taking it for granted. After all, he did deserve some credit for behaving so honourably. And he'd had precious little so far.

Anne said, "Your mother is a kind woman. Even so – she must be mistress. I will do her bidding. Otherwise, there will be quarreling."

"You and my mother would never quarrel," he said, manlike.

"We shall quarrel. Unless she is mistress."

"But – you're my wife. I can't – "

"At home, my stepmother was mistress. I was nobody, and treated accordingly. Here, I am young Mistress Shakespeare, and must be treated as such. But if that is borne in mind, then your mother must be my mistress."

Young Mistress Shakespeare! So. Anne would take her orders – but on her own terms. For the third time he realised that this was no country goose he was marrying. Tongue-tied she might be, awkward, even lumpish. But she knew her own worth; and he suspected gratefully, the worth of the man she was marrying.

The cheerless day had merged almost imperceptibly into night. The tapers had been lit, the children put to bed. Then, at last, it had been bedtime.

No horseplay, no bawdry; for a wedding night, with bride already three months gone, must in the nature of things be an anti-climax. Besides, Mary Shakespeare, unlike her Queen, was too ladylike for horseplay, and John was too drunk for bawdry. Will and Anne had crept away, alone.

Now, at last, she had him to herself, safe in her arms, doubly safe in a cocoon of bedclothes and darkness and crouching ceiling and night. And when at last he slept she cried a little, for she knew that holding to her breast a Will-o'-the-Wisp was a miracle that could not last.

Then she too slept; and, waking, saw through the uncurtained window that the stars were paling; and knew fearfully that another day, another month, another life was dawning; and, putting out a hand for the strong comfort of Will's found – nothing. Her Will-o'-the-Wisp had danced away even before the light.

Will had lain in his bride's loving, but somewhat over-soft embrace.

His bride had slept, breathing just a little too loudly.

So this, thought Will, was life. Of a man's life, tonight's pleasurable antics were the crown, the summum bonum.

To marry a wife, to beget children, to eat and sleep and toil, to be merry in season, to be plagued by the toothache, the belly ache, the itch and the scurvy, to suffer night terrors,

to die and stand before the awful gates of Heaven or Hell –
this was the life of man. And tonight was the crown.

God!

To hear music, to create beauty and laughter and poetry,
to people a stage with kings and queens and princes and
prelates, to taste of wit as it were a rare wine, to wanton with
women scented like the Indies, to sup with friends whose
lips were filled with laughter – this, too, was the life of a
man. Or could be. Or could have been. But for a bed of
moonbeams, and a man's honour.

Her embrace was stifling him. Carefully, for he wanted
this precious darkness for thought, he unwound her arms.
She stirred and moaned, but did not wake.

He couldn't bear it. *He could not bear it.* He loved Anne,
he pitied Anne, if he ever made Anne suffer he would
deserve all the pains of Hell. Life with Anne would be
pleasant, their love would grow and spread like a tree to give
them shelter and shade. But – poor Anne was no match for
kings and queens, the princes and prelates, the stringing of
words together like pretty beads, the twin intoxications of
creation and the theatre. Anne was no match for seething,
brutal, magnificent London. (She stood alone, in her country
clothes. Not very beautiful, not very clever, not very brave.
She fought alone, for her Will – not only against all these, but
also against the unborn generations, and the compulsion of
history. Poor Anne!)

He could not bear it. He must write, he must be of the
theatre. Oh, he'd earn a living somehow – father's business,
ploughing, schoolmastering – but he'd also write. And then,
one day, somehow, when the child was weaned, and he'd got
together a bit of money, then – somehow – he would once
again become William Shakespeare, poet.

There was not a moment to lose. It was in his nature not to squander money. Now he realised that to squander time was even worse. Quietly he slipped out of bed, groped his way out of the chamber, and downstairs.

What had Henslowe said? "A play about identical twins." Plautus had written a play about identical twins. Well, old Plautus was past caring if William stole his plot. Besides, what was wrong with using another's plot? It was the characters that mattered, he'd learnt that already. He was trembling, as much from excitement as from the December cold.

He lit a candle, found pen, ink and paper. He sat down at the kitchen table. He needed his school copy of Plautus and it was upstairs with his Ovid and his Seneca. Never mind. He could remember something of the plot. He could make a start, and check with the *Menaechmi* later.

He dipped his quill in the ink. "A Comedie of Errors," he wrote. "By Wm Shakespeare. Act 1, Scene 1."

He sat, biting his quill. The kitchen was bitter cold. Upstairs, Anne stirred, and sighed, and drifted into sleep once more. She was sorry, but not concerned, that Will was not at her side. Will would always have things to do – even, apparently, on his wedding night, she thought sadly.

William, scribbling away at Scene 1, asked himself whether he wasn't letting old Aegeon talk too much. Besides, Henslowe *had* asked for a comedy. Old Aegeon, all shipwrecks and death, wasn't likely to have the groundlings rolling about the floor.

He read through what he had written. And was appalled. It was dull, monotonous stuff. Old Aegeon could empty the theatre before the second scene.

He couldn't write! Fool, get you behind a plough, go stitch in your father's workshop, teach infants their A per se A. But don't imagine you can write. You need a university education to write. Will Shakespeare, up from the country, pitting his wits against graduates like Greene and Lyly and Nashe!

He knew it wasn't true. He *could* write. There was an itching, a yearning in his fingers. He could feel a power in his brain running down into his right shoulder, along his arm, into his hand. To hold a pen, to write, was a physical as well as an emotional compulsion. *He* could write. He just needed to find his subject.

He crossed to the window. His limbs were so stiff with cold that he could hardly move. He drew back the curtain. A clear cold light filled the eastern sky – and filled Will's mind with a torturing dichotomy that was to remain with him all his days: it was dawn, Anne would be waking, he must be by her side; yet if he went to Anne, there would be no more writing today. Never, by a moment's absence or neglect, must he hurt his sweet Anne. Yet Anne, he knew, was the unwitting enemy of his writing. And it was by his writing that he, a writer, would be judged at the bar of Heaven. (Would the man who buried his talent in the ground have been forgiven had he pleaded a contented wife, he wondered.)

He read again what he had written. No. This wasn't the way. He opened the curtains to the cold day, blew out the candle, and went upstairs.

Anne was up already, and dressed. She gave him her sweet smile, her fond embrace. "Will, where have you been? Oh, you're so cold. I was anxious for you."

Had he said, "Lighting the fires, cutting gloves, checking my father's accounts," she would have understood, and approved. But he liked to think of himself as at least indifferent honest, so he said, with a half-smile, "Writing a play."

She looked frightened. The last time he'd talked of plays, he'd had to flee for his life. She had hoped he had learnt his lesson. But no.

But now that he was her husband, it was her duty to try to understand what he was talking about. "What *is* a play?" she asked, wrinkling her brow.

He looked at her in alarm. This was worse than he had imagined. He knew by a sort of instinct what a play was, always had known. He couldn't believe that anyone didn't know what a play was. He sat down on the bed, pulled her down beside him. He tried to explain. She looked bewildered. At last she said, "But why do you want to write them? *I* don't."

"To make money." It was only part of an answer, but he didn't feel he could tackle the rest. Not now, in a cold December sunrise.

"But" – she played thoughtfully with his fingers – "couldn't you make more money in your father's business?"

"Much more," he said, and immediately regretted it. "I could write many plays, and might not earn a penny. Or I might earn enough to buy New Place."

"New Place?" She was suddenly angry; as, he was beginning to learn, his loving Anne could be angry. "Earn enough to buy me the humblest cottage, first, where we can live alone and in peace. Then you can start talking about New Place."

His heart sank. Even as a hired man, he had had his daydreams about living, a gentleman, at New Place. And they had burst, like bubbles. So perhaps it was as well Anne didn't fancy big houses, after all.

He said, "Listen, Anne. Edward Alleyn, he's a famous actor – "

"What is an actor?" Anne was determined to learn.

He explained. "Ned Alleyn thinks I could write good plays."

Anne was getting to grips with the subject, now. "How long would it take you to write a play, Will?"

He shrugged. "Perhaps a month."

"And how long to make a pair of gloves?"

"A day. Two days."

"And how much for the play? And for the gloves?"

For the moment *he* was angry. You could not weigh plays against merchandise. Then, feeling her cold hand tremble in his, he was suddenly all compassion. "Listen, Anne. I will work for you and the child. And in a year, two years, perhaps – we will find a cottage – "

He glanced at her. She was staring out of the window. The sun was up, now, and fell upon her face with a warm radiance. But it was nothing to the radiance that glowed from within. A home of her own, where she could live at peace with her Will; cooking his meals, washing his shirts, bearing his children! A snug, low-ceilinged cottage with a few flowers in summer, a pile of logs in winter. That was all she asked on earth, or yet in heaven.

Poor Anne!

Things went well at Henley Street.

Mary Shakespeare soon came to love her shy, helpful daughter-in-law; and she was a woman who, when she felt affection, knew how to bestow it gracefully.

Anne, robbed of a father she loved, brought up by a sour stepmother, responded slowly at first, unable to believe her good fortune. Then, when she learned that the affection was real, she opened to it like a flower in sunlight. The two women went marketing together, sewed and talked and laughed quietly together in the evening; and Mary soon realised that Anne, beneath her country ways, had character and intelligence, and she devoted herself tactfully to developing these qualities.

William, for all the pother of poetry in his brain, turned out to be a shrewd and uncompromising man of business. He hurt many not very worthy citizens deeply by calling in debts that his father had shrugged off long ago. He ensured that orders were ready on time. He was courteous and civil. He was handsome and sturdy. His colouring was as warm as that of an October woodland. Very soon his stall was the most popular in High Cross. Will Shakespeare, who had got a wench in trouble and slunk off to London, was forgotten. Young Master Shakespeare, with his friendly wit and pleasant ways, had become as much a part of Stratford as Clopton Bridge.

No one, not even Anne, knew how he loathed it.

He did it, because he had told Anne he would work to give her a cottage. He did it well, because if he did anything he always did it well. But he hated it. He wasn't born for this.

What was he born for? His *Comedie of Errors* was still in the first act, and getting nowhere. How could he learn his craft, when all his days were spent in marketing, and accounts? He felt desperate. But Anne must not know. To Anne, her Will was always kind, gentle, teasing. And he was beginning to enjoy, and even need, her company. Under Mary's guidance she was becoming less shy. She was learning that life could be more than a hard, grim struggle. She was learning that laughter *could* not be an offence to the Lord, as John Richardson claimed. In a family like the Shakespeares' it was a gentle and holy bond of love, a salve for life's harsh excoriations.

So with Anne he laughed, and played; keeping for his lonely walks his teeth-grinding rage of frustration.

In May, another shackle was hammered on to his leg. Little Susanna was born. Then, as though that were not enough, in February 1585, a pair of manacles. Fate's most vindictive joke. Twins! That ought to keep him in his place. "That young man," chortled Matthew Wright (he who had been so sorely inconvenienced by St John the Baptist), "that young man should go down in history. Three children, and not yet twenty-one!"

Twins! Will pretended to be delighted. But he was appalled. He had no taste for procreation, even though he appeared to have a bent for it. He had more important things than children to create.

But it was too late for that now. A father of three, living in the provinces? A successful glover? Such a man had as much chance of becoming a well-known poet as of becoming Archbishop of Canterbury.

So. He had a loving wife, a son to carry on the business, two daughters. He was popular, he had many friends in Stratford, he was on the way to becoming what he had always wanted to be, a man of substance. Keep on like this, and he could well finish up as a gentleman of worship.

If only – ? He could destroy his writings, burn his quill – but could he kill this fury in his brain? Did he *want* to kill it?

No. He went on writing: poetry, plays, more poetry. And destroying them all, hating what he had written, bad, bad, bad. And always before him was the unanswered question: *could* a man learn to write without a university education?

He began to notice his children. He wasn't much interested in the girls, but Hamnet, his little son, was beginning to toddle around now. As he watched the brave lurching steps, he began to feel a yearning love for the boy. Perhaps *he* would be the poet. If Will saw to it that the business prospered, he could afford to send Hamnet to Oxford. Then, who could say? *A Comedie of Errors*, by Hamnet Shakespeare?

No, by God. Will wanted no glory at second hand. Besides, that would not clear the turmoil from his brain, that would not stop this fever.

Susanna, gay eldest child, gathered flowers in the meadows; or played wonderingly with the snow, or scuffled joyfully in the autumn leaves. The twins cut their teeth, uttered their first words, smiled, wept, and began to stumble uncertainly about the house. Grandfather spoiled them with suckets, Grandmother soothed them when they fell, Mother saw them all as little Wills, and loved them accordingly, Father played with them when they laughed, and promptly handed them back when they cried.

As always, this pretty domestic scene was being played out against a bloody backdrop. Philip of Spain was getting together his Armada to crush England. In the Low Countries, the Spanish were killing and burning anything that moved; in the New World, they were enthusiastically ramming Christianity down native throats with a sword. Sir Philip Sidney died, nobly, an example to us all. Mary Queen of Scots died and, pitifully for so romantic a figure, was seen to lose her wig in the process. Elizabeth was at odds with everyone; and so beloved and feared was she that mighty men like Burghley and Leicester crept about like scolded children. The plague came and went as God's displeasure waxed and waned.

The world was full of weeping. But in the house in Henley Street, in the middle of peaceful Stratford, in the centre of still peaceful England, were peace, and love, and a growing security. Even Anne began to wonder whether life might not go on like this. Will seemed to be settling down. He seemed more contented. He was still writing and reading, giving her and the children a carefully rationed amount of attention each day. But he talked more of the business, discussing it at length with his father. And everyone knew that the Earl of Leicester was fighting in the Netherlands where, presumably, he had other things on his mind than William Shakespeare. Sometimes she really began to feel she could look forward to a home of their own, a long life with Will in Stratford.

But what first signalled the end of Anne's hopes was not war, or invasion, or the Earl of Leicester. It was the publication of the second edition of Holinshed's Chronicle History of England.

Will, in his newfound prosperity, bought a copy. And there it all was. The kings and queens, princes and prelates, conflict, battles, honour and dishonour, the slow building of order out of dissension and chaos. All he had to do was clothe these dusty names in flesh and blood. Harry the King, Bedford and Exeter! Names rang in his brain with the sound of trumpets.

He read, and wrote, turning Holinshed's prose into sword-rattling verse. Within a few months he had a great, sprawling mass of work. He was absorbed. He would hurry home from the market; a meal, trying desperately not to appear hurried, with Anne; a quick romp with the children. Then for the rest of the evening the scratching of a quill, urgent thought, while his father dozed in his chair and the women murmured no louder than the fire.

Then, one evening, as he came home from the stall, Anne came running to meet him, smiling, her eyes bright.

Anne and Will were always pleased to see each other. They still delighted in each other's company, even after five years of marriage. He held out his hands, smiling.

"Anne, this is sweet. You should meet me more often." And he was not the less fond of her because he thought he would then be able to spend a few minutes less with her in the evening, a few minutes more for his precious work.

She took his hands, panting, laughing. "Will, come for a walk by the river."

"Of course." They turned down Bridge Street towards the Avon. She took his arm, squeezed it. At one time she would never have shown this excitement. Mary had been good for her. "Will, old Eli Barford is dead."

He looked at her, amused. "I wonder whether Eli is as pleased."

"Oh! I had not thought." She looked ashamed. "But – Will, his cottage in Chapel Lane will be for sale."

He was silent. Another shackle. Wife, children, business; and now house. They'd got him trussed. And now they were going to drop the leaden weight of a house on his chest.

Yet it was what Anne wanted above all things. Which meant, for him, that there could be no question. Anne wanted it. He could afford it. There was nothing more to be said. He smiled at her. "If we were to walk that way – we might glance – "

It was a pretty cottage. The thatch came down over the upper windows like protecting brows. At the back, a wall of mellow brick surrounded a few apple trees. It was tiny, and made the house in Henley Street seem like a palace. The front windows looked out on New Place, that decaying hall built by Sir Hugh Clopton, Stratford's most famous son.

Small though it was, Anne would not have changed it for Kenilworth or Warwick Castles, or for Grandmother Arden's great house at Wilmcote. They walked past, pretending not to look, for Eli was still in occupation, stretched out with pennies on his eyes in the little front room. But Anne did not need to see it as it was. She saw it as it would be. Herself, busy in the hot kitchen, which would be fragrant with the smell of new-baked bread, and herbs, and roasting meat. The children, out in the garden, climbing the apple trees. Will, reading (always reading!) in the cosy parlour. And if Heaven, thought Anne, had anything more wonderful than that to offer, then it was quite beyond her to imagine it.

The cottage was behind them, now. She squeezed his arm again. "Can we? Can we, Will?"

He appeared grave. "It could be damp."

She shook him, in mock anger. "Do not tease me."

"It will need thatching before – "

"Before what?"

"Before I do," he grinned, tugging his crisp hair.

She clung to him. "Can we?"

"Yes," he said. "If you want it, Anne." Knowing that his tenderness for her would give her anything she asked. Anything.

Except, perhaps, himself.

For Anne, those were the sweetest of her days.

Cleaning, sweeping, polishing. Choosing the curtains and the linen. Getting together bits of furniture from Henley Street and the market; even her old bed from Shottery, despite her stepmother's grumblings. Cooking her first meal. Their first night under the overhanging eaves. Their first waking, with the sparrows fidgeting in the thatch, and a whole long day before her, mistress, queen of her own tiny kingdom.

Will, too, was as happy as a stifled poet could be. Coming home, at evening, to a smiling wife, a bright fire, supper on the table – wasn't that enough for any man?

And he had written what pleased himself. But would it please others? How could he find out, without journeying to London? But journeying to London took time. Besides, once there – dare he risk submitting himself to that temptation, to that torment of longing?

No.

One evening he surprised Anne by saying, "Would you like me to read you a play?"

She was afraid. She wouldn't understand. After that first difficult attempt to describe his work to her, he had kept it to himself. They had had plenty of other things to discuss – house, children, plague, relations, witchcraft, keeping the house free of mice and goblins – but not his work.

Nevertheless, she was flattered. And she would try, so hard, to understand this mystery. "*Please*, Will," she cried.

"It is about King Harry Six," he said shortly. And began to read.

Anne listened, entranced. To her delight, she found it wasn't the mystery she had feared. It was conversation, people talking, and much of it she could understand. But the wonderful, unbelievable thing was that all this had come out of Will's brain. She looked at him with awe. Will, knowing about kings and knights, and the way they spoke and behaved! For a fearful, disloyal moment she thought it smacked of witchcraft. But Will would have nothing to do with anything that was not of God, she comforted herself.

He read until bedtime. She listened, swept along by a river in spate, a river of words and poetry and ideas. She was a long time going to sleep that night. In one way, it had been the happiest evening she had ever spent, firelight and candlelight, her head on Will's knee, his hand on her shoulder, the two of them, alone, snug and safe as two hares in a form.

In another way, it had been frightening. For the first time she had peered dizzily into the gulf that separated her mind from Will's. A mind like that was not going to be content with Stratford for ever. Or with her? She held him close, in the darkness. She could encompass his body. But in her country wisdom she knew, more certainly than ever, that she would never encompass all the creature that was William Shakespeare.

"Read me some more," she would say now, when the children were abed, and supper was cleared away, and Will had put another log on the fire.

She never interrupted, far less criticised. She could as soon have thought of criticising Holy Writ. She listened, still filled with wonderment at her Will's cleverness, but engrossed now in the story, filled with sorrow for this sad, weak king. She hoped he would not die. No. Will was too kind a man; Will would not let him die.

The words flowed on. And then, suddenly and at last, Will was reading something that struck, not into her bemused mind, but into her very heart:

O God! methinks it were a happy life,
To be no better than a homely swain;
To sit upon a hill, as I do now,
To carve out dials quaintly, point by point,
Thereby to see the minutes how they run,
How many make the hour full complete;
How many hours bring about the day;

How may days will finish up the year;
How many years a mortal man may live.
When this is known, then to divide the times:
So many hours must I tend my flock;
So many hours must I take my rest;
So many hours must I contemplate;
So many hours must I sport myself;
So many days my ewes have been with young;
So many weeks ere the poor fools will ean;
So many years ere I shall shear the fleece;
So minutes, hours, days, months and years,
Pass'd over to the end they were created,
Would bring white hairs unto a quiet grave.
Ah! what a life were this; how sweet! how lovely!

For the first time she interrupted, turning her head and gazing up gravely into his face. "Read that again, Will. About – a happy life."

Pleased and flattered, he read it again. She sighed. "That is how I would live – always."

He looked, suddenly, careworn. He did not meet her eyes. He sat, playing with her yellow hair, silent. She said, anxiously, "But – not you, Will?"

"Yes," he said to her surprise. "I, too. If I were allowed."

"Allowed? But who would stop you?"

He touched his heart, his forehead. "There are demons, here, that give me no rest."

She gave a little cry, and crossed herself. Her stepmother would have been horrified, but sensible people like Anne believed in keeping in touch with both religions. It could do no harm, and might well do good. "Demons?"

He laughed, put his arms round her shoulders. "Not real demons, sweet." He had to explain what could not be explained, even to himself. He did his best, trying to define genius in human terms, and denigrating genius in the process. "Pride, ambition, lust for power."

She shook her head. These were not her Will. Oh, why couldn't he be content? *To be no better than a homely swain.* She said, "It is a good life, of which the King spoke."

On an impulse he said something he had wanted to say for a long time. He held her tight. "How would you like to live in London?"

"London?" He felt her body jerk convulsively. "London? Oh, no, Will. Not for me."

"'Tis a wonderful city."

"No." she shook her head violently. She looked terrified, but determined. "Not for me. Even Stratford, after Shottery – Besides, this pretty house – " She felt cold, and empty. Was her little corner of heaven-on-earth to be threatened already?

Normally, he would have had no thought but to soothe her distress. But this had to be discussed sometime. And now that he had made a start – "But I may *have* to go to London – if I am to sell my plays."

She was quickly out of her depth again. Why could gloves be sold in Stratford, but not plays? And since gloves could be sold in Stratford, why not stick to gloves? Will was being unreasonable. Night after night she'd sat, hearing nothing but the scratching of a quill. And had she complained? Never. But now that wasn't good enough. Now they'd got to live in London, if you please, to sell his plays. The whole thing was ridiculous. Especially when you'd got a thriving business here at home.

She said, "Then you go alone."

London, alone! The Players; his friends, Ned, Dick; the bustle, the excitement in the very air; the women, lovely as swans, scented like the Indies. O, brave London!

He put such disloyal thoughts away from him. He said, "Think, Anne, I could show you the Tower, the Queen's palaces; I could take you to the play. *My* play," he added quietly.

She said, "Once and for all, I will not live in London."

She was right, of course. She *would* be out of place. He could see quite a few smiles on people's faces if he took her there. Even though, thanks to Mary, her clothes were much less countrified than when he married her.

But she was being damned unreasonable. He began to feel that most dangerous of emotions, self-pity. Why! If he hadn't been such a man of honour, he'd still *be* in London. He'd only come back to save her from her shame. And now, having got him here, she was refusing to budge. Oh, it didn't matter that his whole success as a poet depended on his being in London. It didn't matter that he, William Shakespeare, poet, was living like a clod. So long as *she* was comfortable, and getting her own way. And what had *she* got to be angry about? He could be angry, too. And with much more cause.

His arms were no longer about her. He stood up. Anger welled in him like a spring. "Can't you see – ?" he shouted.

"I can see that you have a good business; that you have a duty to me and your children, *and* to your parents. I can see that you, a grown man, would throw it all away, duty and all, to go and live with shiftless harlotry players."

"God in heaven, woman, they're not the harlotry players. They're actors; fine actors. And I know now that *I* can give them the plays they want."

"And I suppose that's more important than giving your children the bread *they* want."

He hated anger. Always it left him drained and exhausted. And she – she was afraid. She had tried to bind Will to her with silken bands of love. And now, she was risking everything that she had worked for; because of the anger that filled her and Will, that filled the little, low-ceilinged room with knives and swords and lightning flashes. Will, fighting for his entire future, and against the person for whom he felt the tenderest love. Anne, fighting for herself and her children, against one who was more dear than life itself.

By bedtime, the storm had blown itself out. They were friends again, lovers again. Bruised and hurt, they now clung to each other for comfort.

But the question between them was shelved, not resolved. And for Anne something had been destroyed for ever. She had learnt that each could only have his life by spoiling the other's life. They would be like wild horses, pulling different ways. And the wretched victim torn between them would be their marriage. And this must never be. They went to bed, hand clinging desperately to hand, knowing that things would never again be the same. "O God! methinks it were a happy life, To be no better than a homely swain..."

Will would write many more things that Anne, with developing perception, would like. But, for her, he would never write anything more beautiful, more true, more deeply and terribly moving. For Anne, King Henry's meditation on Towton Field would always be Will's supreme achievement and the memorial of her abandoned hopes. She was defeated.

CHAPTER 6

THEN CAME EACH ACTOR ON HIS ASS...

In London Dock, History, in the form of a grey rat, left a by no means sinking ship.

It scurried down a hawser, tail snaking, button eyes coldly watchful. A darting pause; then it flickered into the kitchen of a dockside tavern.

The rat had bubonic plague.

Aboard the rat were a number of fleas, gorged with his blood.

The fleas, who by this time also carried bubonic plague, left the rat and began cheerfully exploring the tavern. They soon found sailors, whom they preferred to rats as offering more scope.

The sailors went to the brothels, where both they and the fleas had a high old time...

"Bring out your dead," cried the men with the death carts. "O wicked and perverse generation," thundered the preachers. "Once again is God's anger kindled against you." The people did what they could. They put rue in their windows, and tried to be a bit less sinful, but it didn't seem to have much effect on the plague. It just went on spreading. God, it appeared, was in a vengeful mood.

For the City Fathers, busy organising mass graves and days of prayers, half out of their minds with anxiety, the plague always brought one little ray of cheer. It gave them a perfect excuse for closing the hated theatres and sending the players packing into the country. This they did; and so serious was the outbreak that this time they even closed Henslowe's brothels; just at the very time, as that outraged gentleman pointed out, when people really needed something to take their minds off their troubles.

So, thanks to a grey rat, Edward Alleyn had ridden his nag morosely northward.

Behind him had toiled baggage carts, long, laden tumbrils that would help to set up the stage in inn yards (a weary business), lesser actors on nags, the boy actors squealing and giggling in a covered wagon, dogs, trollops. Is it not passing brave to be a player, and ride in triumph through Abingdon and Oxford, he had thought bitterly. He, Tamburlaine the Great, leading his rabble army on a nag!

By the time he reached Stratford, Edward Alleyn was feeling very sorry indeed for himself.

The play had gone well. They had put on Kyd's *Spanish Tragedy*. Alleyn had torn himself to pieces as old Hieronimo. He hadn't meant to. He was too important an actor to waste his energies on a lot of cowherds. But it was always the same. Once on the stage he got carried away every time. He felt drained. The things he did for his art!

The Stratford groundlings were drifting away now; staring back yokel-like, with shy grins or open mouths, at these gorgeous creatures from another world.

Alleyn, still in his grease-paint, was having to direct operations, of course. Without him, they'd never get the stage dismantled, the wagons packed, the boys to bed. It was very tedious. He shouldn't have to play an exhausting part like Hieronimo, *and* see to all this. The sooner Henslowe built that permanent theatre, the better, he thought morosely.

"Ned!" said a voice softly.

He spun round.

Will Shakespeare stood before him, holding his arms out. His eyes, in the light of the torches, were bright with tears. But his smile was one of ineffable joy. The Elizabethan male could watch with composure, and even relish, the disembowelling of a man. But he was very easily moved to tears. And Will had cried through the whole play. Not because the *Spanish Tragedy* moved him; it was poor, ranting stuff. But because he, an earth-bound mortal, was glimpsing through a rent in the clouds, as it were, the happy Immortals at their play.

He shouldn't have come. The torment had been too great. But once he had seen the play bills, nothing could have kept him away.

"Ned," he said again, as one might whisper the name of a saint. And Alleyn, larger than life in his vast cloak, his face fierce and tragic in its grease-paint, might well have been a Commander in the Heavenly Host.

Ned Alleyn peered. "Why, Will," he cried, remembering his old vision of Henslowe, himself, and Shakespeare, drawing all London to their permanent theatre.

"Ned, I came to ask you to supper. It is – humble, but – And I have written a play. Three plays, really, about King Harry Six. I – I thought the part might suit you well."

Three plays, with a continuing part for him! It was interesting. Supper sounded good, too. It would make a pleasant change from a shilling ordinary at the inn. He wondered whether he had sounded sufficiently welcoming. He held out his arms. "My dear Will, forgive me." He smote

his forehead. "So lost was I still in Hieronimo – exhausting."
He closed his eyes. "Exhausting!"

"You played it well, Ned."

Alleyn opened his eyes, stared at Will gratefully. "You
think so, Will? You *really* think so?"

Will's idol had changed; put on both weight and stature.
He had changed from an arrogant business-like young man
into a man who went on acting long after the play had
finished, and the stage had changed back into a couple of
tumbrils. A man, perhaps, who would never again speak one
sincere word, make one unaffected gesture, never think one
honest thought. But what did it all matter, thought not-so-
simple Will. It was more important for an actor to act on
stage than for him not to act off it. The man didn't matter.
Hieronimo, Tamburlaine, King Harry Six mattered.

The beamed ceiling was villainously low. Alleyn, who liked
to hold himself at his full height when making an entrance,
cursed silently, and bent his head.

"Anne, this is my friend Master Alleyn, London's greatest
actor."

Alleyn smiled graciously, putting the country creature at
her ease, and made as elaborate a bow as the small living-
room allowed.

To his surprise, the country creature did not seem to need
putting at her ease. She curtseyed gracefully and
composedly. (Mary had taught her well, and she was no
fool.) "Honoured, Master Alleyn. Pray be seated." She gave
him a three-legged stool.

"Thank you, Mistress." He sat down. Will and Anne sat
facing him on a wooden bench. He took in his surroundings.
Plaster walls, polished oak, firelight and candlelight, a fair
linen cloth on the table, pewter mugs and plates, a linen
napkin at each place. Master Shakespeare, it appeared,

wasn't doing badly for himself. He might need some wooing to get him away from Stratford.

Anne excused herself, and went into the kitchen. Despite her composure, she was frightened. Will had not gone to London. Now London had come to Will. Was this big, handsome stranger here to woo him away from her?

She began to carry in the food – fried rabbit, a hen boiled with leeks, bread, cheese, and a jug of beer. And as she set down the dishes she looked anxiously at her husband and the tall stranger.

They were poring over his precious plays. And she saw, with a sick heart, a new Will: not the gentle, courteous and loving creature she knew; but a man talking keenly and vivaciously on his own subject; a man filled, suddenly, with power and authority. And this great man from London was listening to him like a schoolboy at the feet of his master.

She called them to table. They came, reluctantly, still talking plays. They pulled out stools, sat down, still talking. They received their plates of food, their mugs of beer, still talking. They muttered "Amen" to Anne's grace, still talking. Anne, taking up her first forkful of food, said with a touch of frost, "You are heartily welcome, sir."

Alleyn was big enough to acknowledge that he had been put in his place by this country mouse; and was annoyed with himself. "Mistress Shakespeare, forgive me. I was most unkind to occupy your husband so. And how" – that untimely conception could no longer embarrass, surely – "how is the child?"

"Children," said Anne. "We have three."

God, they were fast workers in Stratford. He began to fear that Will had too many anchors in this backwater, and he wanted Will back in London.

These plays about Harry Six were not good. Yet, like that absurd Hamlet, they had hints of glory. As a resident playmaker, simple Will was a far better proposition than that firework Marlowe.

Then he knew what he must do. Anne Shakespeare suddenly found herself being treated to a smile which, since it normally had to reach the groundlings at the very edge of the crowd, had in that small room an almost overpowering intensity. "Mistress Shakespeare," cooed Alleyn in a voice overflowing with milk and honey, "I want you to do something for me."

Anne looked startled, and suspicious. "Me?" What could she do, for the greatest actor, whatever that meant, in London?

"I want you to bring your clever husband – oh yes, and your dear children, to London."

"Never!" said Anne. Will, Alleyn noted, looked unhappy.

"But Mistress Anne!" He spread his hands. "We need him. London needs him."

"So do his children, Master Alleyn."

"But they would *have* him. In London. There are good schools in London, Mistress Shakespeare." He wasn't risking *Mistress Anne*, again. Her *Master Alleyn* had put him in his place.

He pulled a shilling from his purse. "Here, Will, fetch a pint of claret from the tavern. We must drink to our meeting."

"No need for that," said Anne, rising. "We have our own." She went down into the cellar, brought up a bottle of Rhenish. She wasn't being left on her own with this smooth-tongued stranger. He wanted to break up her little corner of earthly paradise. Well, it wasn't going to last for ever, she knew that. Perhaps not for very long. But when she did have to give it up, it would be of her own doing. She wasn't going to have it taken from her by a passing stranger.

She came back. Will and the stranger had got those plays on the table now, Will was actually using his dagger to eat his cheese, he *must* be absorbed, he was usually very particular at table.

She poured the wine. "Ah," said Alleyn, his hand groping for the glass, his long fingers closing about it, his eyes still on the manuscript. Anne was incensed. With a sure country instinct she distrusted a man who treated you like a queen one minute and a serving wench the next. Will, she was pleased to see, spared a moment for them to share their own private smile. Then he too was back at the plays.

Alleyn remembered what he was about. He raised his glass, gazed almost amorously over the rim at Anne. "Will you not promise to think over what I have said, Mistress Shakespeare?"

She had had enough. "I should look well," she said angrily. "Taking my poor children into a city of plague, of cutthroats and harlots, of unbelievers and mockers of the Lord." Anne's Puritan family hadn't a high opinion of London.

Alleyn laughed. "Mistress, London is the home of the Queen, the Court. It is the centre of thought and knowledge. Men like Lyly, Greene, Marlowe – "

She hadn't heard of one of them. But she was being uncivil to a guest. "Forgive me, sir. But I will not adventure my children in London. Nor myself for that matter. If Will goes, he goes alone."

For a second, Will's face looked up eagerly. Then it became despondent again. He *couldn't* go alone. He was bound, hand and foot. And gagged. And blindfolded. He would never join the choir of sweet singers Alleyn had just mentioned. And if Henslowe's men did play Harry Six, he would never see it. Five pounds in his pocket, perhaps, and that an end of the matter.

"Now, if you will excuse me," said Anne. She carried the dishes into the kitchen. She washed up, cleared away. When she came back the men had drawn their stools up to the fire, the wine and the manuscripts between them. They did not seem to notice her.

She lit a candle, carried it to the door. "Goodnight, gentlemen."

They leapt to their feet, spilling the wine. Alleyn bowed low, but she wasn't interested in him. She was watching Will.

Will was flushed. Wine soon unsettled him. And he did not smile. He bowed, as to a stranger. Was there resentment, hostility even, in the look he gave her? Or was he, made unsteady by the wine, simply concentrating hard on keeping upright? Whichever it was, she sensed that if he thought of her at all tonight it was as a gaoler. Sick at heart, she went up the narrow, boxed-in staircase. Was it an omen that tonight she went up alone, no cheerful William creaking behind her?

In the bedroom, she stared at herself in the looking-glass. A woman in her thirties, across whose face the cold of bitter mornings, the sun of summer toil, unceasing work and care had drawn their harrows. And in London, it was said, were women soft as doves, smooth as the silks and velvets of their gowns.

The bedroom was tiny, cold, lit by a single candle. In London, it was said, the bedrooms were warmed by great fires, lit by a thousand candles.

In London, it was said, wickedness and lewdness were paraded openly in the streets. Whereas here was love, and gentleness, and peace; the laughter of children; a sweet and simple life.

Or had been, until that stranger came in at the door tempting her Will, behold the cities of the earth, all these things will I give thee, follow thou me.

And no "Get thee hence, Satan" from her husband. Will sitting mumchance, not a word; pitiful as a dog gazing patiently at a closed door, eager for the free world of the heath.

Edward Alleyn had destroyed her world. Oh, William would settle down again. He would never, knowingly, cause her pain. He would sacrifice his life to make her happy.

She let down her corn-coloured hair, began combing. She saw, dimly, that in some way she could not understand, he *was* sacrificing his life for her. And this should not be.

Her kingdom was her home; husband and children her subjects. Like most women, she would fight like a tigress to hold her home intact. But in her case the enemy was Will. She could not fight Will, she thought piteously. And anyway, Will would never fight her. She would never bring him to battle, even if she wished. He would lay down his arms, with never a word of complaint. But what would he be thinking?

William stood on one side, listened to himself speaking. The voice was a little slurred, the thoughts came and went like cloud-shadows on the distant Cotswolds. "Take them, Ned. I'll write more. Next time you come – Richard Three, perhaps, I have made a start. Now is the winter of our discontent Made – something or other. But that's good don't you think. Ned. Winter of discontent – Made glorious summer – "

Yes. Ned did think it was good. He'd always seen himself as Richard, with a monkey on his back. He would be so much the more impressive when he came back to being Tamburlaine the Great. "Come with me, Will," he pleaded. "I *need* you, man. London needs you."

Will shook his head. He smiled, wryly. "I am in the unhappy position of being too much loved, Ned."

"Won't she really come?"

"No. And she's right. She has a terrible country wisdom. It's something I could not, would not, argue with."

"Then come now. She's abed. We could be in Warwick before – "

Will rose, kicking over his stool. He might be a little tipsy. But he steered a steady course to the street door and wrenched it open. "Out," he said.

"But, Will – " Again the charming, enchanting smile. "I meant nothing. I – "

"Out," said Will.

Alleyn moved to the door. "My dear Will, I didn't mean – I'm sorry if – "

Will waited, silent. Alleyn came up to him, smiled again, put a hand on his shoulder, shrugged. "I'm sorry," he said most contritely, and made as good an exit as was possible in the circumstances.

Will shut the door, came back into the familiar room. He felt rather proud of himself, though he knew well the wine had had a part in it. William Shakespeare, sober, never had the courage for dramatic, decisive actions like that.

Yes. Decisive. Tonight, thanks to the wine, he had stood apart from himself, and watched himself choose between Anne and Alleyn. The choice was made. He had embraced domesticity, Stratford, gloves, the friendship of yokels and petty tradesmen. He had rejected the theatre, London, perhaps the friendship of people like Greene, Alleyn, the Queen herself. He picked up his upturned stool and sat, staring into the fire, leafing moodily through his plays. His pleasure in his own decisiveness drained quickly out of him. The fire was still bright. He took the plays – so many candle-lit hours, so much thought, so much weariness and doubt, so much elation when things went well

– and held them towards the fire. A clean break. Burn everything, smash your ink into the wall, stab your quill against your leather jerkin. Will Shakespeare's occupation's gone.

The fire was scorching his hands, curling up the edges of the paper. He drew back. No. He could no more cast those writings into the flames than he could have cast his flesh-and-blood creations.

He carried the bottle and the glasses into the kitchen, rinsed the glasses, locked the doors, made sure the fire was safe, blew out all the candles but one. Then William Shakespeare, of Stratford-upon-Avon, householder, husband and father, went up to bed.

He hoped so much that she would be asleep. But she was awake; and, he sensed, utterly wretched.

Tears were denied to Anne. But she could attain a state of dry misery that was worse than tears. As soon as he came into the room she said, "So? Are you for London?"

"No," he said. "Of course not."

"Why *of course* not?"

"I told you when I first came back, it was for good."

"I see." She was silent. "Not because – you don't want to?"

Now he was silent. "I would not leave you, Anne."

"But you would like to go to London."

"God, yes," he cried with sudden bitterness.

She was silent again, while he undressed and slipped in beside her. Her body was cold, and stiff, like that of a corpse. She said, and her voice was as comfortless as the winter rain, "Will, I want you to go to London. But only if you can earn enough to support the children and me. And you must visit Stratford often."

He propped himself on an elbow, stared at her. "You mean – alone?"

"I would never come. You know that."

He said, "I would never go without you."

She said, "One day you will go. I have always known it"

"I shan't, Anne."

"One day you will go. If you go now, you will go loving me. If you stay, you will come to hate and resent me for keeping you. And you will still go, in the end. And there will be nothing left between us, then."

He said stiffly, "You should know me better than to think I would ever hold it against you."

"Oh Will, you would always be loving and tender. But inside – there would be something in you that wanted to strike me dead."

"Anne." Laughing, he tried to take her in his arms. "You talk such nonsense."

"Nonsense? Oh, can't you see that I am breaking my own heart?"

It was a cry of despair. He tried to comfort her, but she held away from him, as though in her mind she had already made the break between them. She stared up at the ceiling. Then she said, sternly, "But you must promise to return often. And I am not giving this house up. I shall need money, Will."

Well, there'd be money, of course. He had put the business on a sound footing, and his father was sober five days out of seven, now. Will's share of the business would keep Anne going. Then six shillings a week as a hired man. And if he earned a few shillings botching up somebody's play and – exciting thought – a pound or two for a play of his own – really, when you began to look into it, it was a very sensible move.

He couldn't go, of course. He couldn't leave Anne. It would be a heartless thing to do. On the other hand, when you looked at it from the financial side alone, it had certain advantages. And if Anne *really* didn't mind too much; and she said she didn't...

Marry, that wine must have been strong. He was *so* sleepy. But he mustn't sleep yet. There was too much to talk about. He must argue Anne out of this London decision. It wasn't fair to her. His place was by her side. On the other hand, of course –

He was asleep, snoring cheerfully. Anne lay still, staring at the ceiling, until the sparrows began to chirp and bustle in the eaves, and morning, like a white blind, filled the window. *O God, methinks it were a happy life To be no better...* She slept at last. And tears, denied to her waking, flowed desperately in her dreams.

Sunday afternoon. Mary Shakespeare sat gazing into the fire. Her fingers itched for her sewing, her tapestry, her darning. But it was the Sabbath. A mended sheet wasn't worth eternal damnation. So she watched the flames leaping and writhing as she, a child, had watched them in the great hearth at Wilmcote, in the dusk of forgotten winter afternoons.

Across the hearth, John dozed in his big chair. Husband John! And sober. She stared at him fondly; she was winning. John was taking up the threads again. With him and Will both active in the business, life was starting to blossom once more. Her new yellow cambric ruff bore witness to that, as did John's silk doublet. Yes. There might be signs and portents dreadful to behold, Philip of Spain's Armada might be in the last stages of preparation, across Europe and the New World

there might be a bloody swathe of death and torment; but in
the Shakespeare family things were going well.

The door opened. Will came in, in his Sunday best. Beside
him trotted little Hamnet, in doublet of crimson satin, the
child's small fist trustingly in his father's big one.

Mary's eyes shone. She had never not been delighted to
see Will; and fond though she was of her daughter-in-law, it
would be pleasant to see him on his own for once. "Come
in," she cried. "Will, this *is* good. Hamnet, how you are
growing."

John Shakespeare woke, blinking. "Why, Will. What day
– ?" He shook himself. "I was deep in thought, boy." He
spotted Hamnet. "Ah, the pretty imp. Wouldst like a sucket,
little knave?"

The little knave, having been well brought up, was down
on his knees awaiting a grand-parental blessing. But a sucket
was a sucket; and blessings, so far as he could see, never
helped one very much. He jumped to his feet, danced up
and down for joy.

"There," said John munificently. Soon the crimson satin
was stiff and streaked with sugary mess. Anne was going to
be pleased! But Will had other things on his mind. "Mother!
Father! I have news you may think ill."

Ill news, crashing like a bolt into the peace and comfort of
a Sabbath Day! Ill news! It was always there, lurking behind
the laughter and the firelight and the quiet days; a Lord of
Misrule to turn happiness and an ordered life topsy-turvy.
"What news?" said Mary.

"Anne and I have decided. I must go back to London. My
work is there, with the Players. Not shearing gloves. I – I'm
sorry, father."

John, who had been in too great a haze to know much
about Will's previous London visit, was outraged. "What?
The players, those vagabonds? A respectable glover – ?" It

was all beyond him. Fond though he was of Will, he'd always thought he might be a bit of a fool. Now he knew it. "Here you are," he spluttered. "Three lovely children, a wife – no beauty I grant you, but capable and kind – " his voice began to quaver – "and two aged parents dependent – "

"Speak for yourself, John," Mary said, lower lip outcurling. "I am in no dotage yet. But, Will, how will you live?"

"Even as a hired man I can earn six shillings a week."

John snorted. "Six shillings? Why, it will barely pay your own lodgings. Now see here, Will. You cannot expect your mother and me to look after Anne and the children. Can he, Mary?"

"Indeed no," said Mary, who had already decided on this very course; but knew that, if she only waited, north-facing John would veer due south given time.

Will, who had decided last night that the business would support his wife, parents and children quite comfortably said, "I wouldn't think of such a thing, father. But there are my plays; and I intend to write poems. Oh, the plays are nothing; trifles to pass an afternoon for the groundlings. But a poem can open doors to a man: the Inns of Court, the great houses – the Court itself."

"Your children cannot eat open doors, Will," his mother said drily. But she was watching her husband, and waiting. The carp will not miss this bait, she thought comfortably.

John said, "Is this so, Will? In London, such a life might be open to you? Mingling with the gentry?" His eyes were big with amazement.

"Yes, father."

"You hear that, wife? Our Will, hobbing and nobbing with my Lord Burghley, my Lord – "

"While his wife begs in Stratford market place, is that it, husband?"

"I shall provide," Will said angrily.

"Nay, Will," said John. "Your mother and I will look after Anne and the children. The least we can do. And Will, if you *do* come to Court, and I" – he looked suddenly pathetic – "and I am still alive, as God knows I may well not be, I am nearing sixty, Will, nearing sixty – commend me to her Gracious Majesty."

"Yes, father."

"Oh, Will," said Mary, holding out her hands, taking his, her eyes too bright, her voice unsteady. "These last years, with you, and Anne; the happiest, perhaps, of my days."

He was so deeply moved that he knelt before her. "I shall be back, soon, mother."

"Aye, marry, and with a knighthood or I'm much mistaken," said John, getting carried away.

But Mary wasn't listening. She sat, gazing at her son's bowed head, her hands clasped in the warm strength of his. So, her Will was breaking out of the chrysalis. She wasn't surprised. Nothing Will did would ever surprise her. Will was for the heights, or the sunless valleys. Will would never stay on level ground.

CHAPTER 7

FOR WE WHICH NOW BEHOLD THESE
PRESENT DAYS...

There was so much to do, there was no time to be sorrowful.

Then, suddenly, he was gone. And there was all the time in the world.

At bedtime, Hamnet cried, wanting his father. Anne, who also wanted his father, grew angry with self-pity and scolded him; then hated herself.

The little girls, Susanna and Judith, were afraid. If father, that rock, could disappear, why not mother, house, sun, moon and stars, all the rest of their universe? It was a joyless, cheerless, dreary time. In the evening, Mary came round, bringing her sewing, and sat with Anne. Drunk or sober, John had always been at *her* side. She tried to imagine this fearful amputation. Anne gave no outward sign. She just looked like someone who has been struck across the face. But no tears, no complaints. Mary wondered whether *she* would be as brave. She said, kindly, "He may soon be back."

Anne shook her head. "No. Not Will. He is following a star." She went on, almost to herself: "None of us will ever know Will. Not even you, his mother."

Mary felt a small hurt. She, not know her friendly, open Will? But it was true. There *was* something – it was as though – as though Will knew the core of things. Nonsense! She laughed at herself. Honest, country Will, who had come close to making a complete wreck of his life before he was twenty, was now off to London, doubtless to finish the job?

Briskly she collected her sewing together. "I must be away, my dear. Your father-in-law will be for his bed." She kissed Anne fondly. For a moment they clung together. Then she went. Anne stood in the doorway and watched her go. Mary, looking back, thought she was the loneliest creature she had ever seen.

He sat his horse grave and melancholy, as befitted a man torn from his wife's arms (even if he had done the tearing). But inwardly he bubbled. He was like a dog let off the lead, a child out of school. His friends Philip, Ned and the Players would be there to welcome him. Oh, Ned might sulk a bit at first. But he would soon come round. Will was beginning to be humbly thankful for his ability to charm.

He exulted. Last time he came this way, he had been running away. Now he was running to London, with plays to sell. London little knew its good fortune.

He was right. London had other things to worry about, in the spring of 1588.

The year had begun with the most horrid portents and omens. From January onward the most alarming things happened. All over Europe, rivers ran blood; the blood of the martyrs flowed again from the painted wounds of plaster saints; in Stratford the Angel of the Lord appeared unto Matthew Wright, but did not give him any instructions (fortunately, since Matthew was now ninety-seven); in places as far apart as Nuremburg and Antwerp the clouds parted to show the night sky filled with marching battalions; a six-legged calf was born at Bury St Edmunds; but at Rheims the most disturbing thing of all happened: the earth opened while a man might count ten, and the alarmed inhabitants were able, not only to peer down into the flames and smoke of Hell, but also to smell the brimstone and hear the shrieks of the damned. An unnerving experience, all agreed.

As if all this were not enough, King Philip of Spain sat in the Escurial Palace, attending, in his fussy, pernickety way, to the final details for the invasion of England.

From dawn to midnight he worked, as always. Occasionally, when his eyes became too weary, or his pen hand too stiff, he would refresh himself by crossing to the window of his room; it looked out, not on to the sunlight and the scorched rocks of the Guadarrama, but on to the candlelit dusk that shrouded forever the high altar of the Escurial Church. For a few minutes he would watch the monks at their endless devotions. Then, fortified in body and spirit, he would return to the subjugation of England and her heretic Queen.

The Court danced. But, quietly, England prepared itself for invasion. No one had any doubts that the Spanish, victorious, would set up stakes in every English market place; that the sweet-smelling savour of a thousand roasting heretics would rise to the grateful nostrils of the God of Love.

It must not, could not, be. An army was formed at Tilbury to repel the invaders; another at St James's to protect the Queen's person. The Earl of Leicester was recalled from the Netherlands to command the armies and save England; on the frequently disproved, but yet pathetically held, principle that a noble was born, not only with nobility, but also with a sound working knowledge of tactics, strategy, and logistics.

At Whitehall, the Queen was in her closet, preparing a speech in case the worst happened, and the invasion became imminent.

She was enjoying herself. She was preparing to use this invasion, as she used everything else that came to hand, to increase her popularity with the people. "I have the body of a weak and feeble woman," she wrote. "But I have the heart and stomach of a King." She pondered, chewing her quill. Something to round it off? She got it. "Aye, and of a King of England, too."

God's wounds, that ought to rouse them. If she hadn't had to be Queen she could have had a good life, botching up plays for sweet Ned Alleyn and his boys.

She read over what she had so far written. She could hardly wait. She would address her army seated on a white horse, she thought; wearing a silver corslet; and with four attendants; no more. God, if Leicester let her make this speech (and she'd like to see him stop her) and the invasion was repulsed, she would be remembered as long as men told tales of England and England's glory.

If the invasion was *not* repulsed – she looked suddenly old – then, she supposed, she would be led in chains to Rome. Only the Vicar of Christ would claim the burning of so arch a heretic, so right royal a bastard.

And Philip of Spain would have earned the undying gratitude of the Holy Father, the Communion of Saints, and the Trinity, Individually and Collectively.

It was early days yet. But Elizabeth liked to have her speeches ready in good time. Then she could rehearse them over and over, polishing, pruning; perfecting them until they sounded like the spontaneous outpourings of a full and loving heart.

As, in some curious way, they probably were.

Embattled England.

Troops were everywhere. Pikes were being thrust into unwilling hands, rustics were being pressed into service, drilled, armed, assembled, marched away to foreign parts like Kent and Sussex. Plots were being uncovered, plotters hounded down, Catholics quietly rounded up, Jesuits executed. Nobles were having themselves fitted out in becoming armour. The regular soldiers, told that present battell would be given them, were as joyfull at such newes as if lustie giants were to run a race, dauncing and leaping wheresoever they came. On Cotswolds and Chilterns, on Malverns and Mendips, on Pennines and Cheviots, on the high, windy places, a chain of beacons was set up, ready to give the signal.

All England shivered with a high excitement. In the last few years, under this loved and incredible Queen, life had been transformed, miracles had been wrought in every sphere. Now, they had to perform the greatest miracle: to save their misty island from the determined assault of a great Empire. Failure meant, literally, death. But give us the victory, O Lord, and, united behind Her in peace as we now are in danger, we will make of this England such a place as never was before.

And the man who, above all others, was to speak for this brave new world was riding wearily into London on a jaded nag.

Great ships, towering like castles, might be stealing out of Spanish harbours, massing, turning northwards, their sails such as no man might number. But, in Stratford, winter gave way quietly to spring, and the cattle sauntered home for milking, the days lengthened. Susanna was bought a taffeta gown, Hamnet fell in the Avon and boasted of being near drowned, Judith cried with a toothache which even a boiled mouse, that most sovereign of remedies, failed to relieve. And Anne kept things together, the children neat and clean, the house tidy. Things must be right for Will – when he came home.

Will, too, had more important things than Spain to think about. He was going to see Philip Henslowe; not as a hired man, but as an author with a number of plays in his pocket, and, he hoped, the good wishes of Henslowe's chief actor.

Having dressed soberly, but with great care, he kept as far as possible from the central kennels where, thanks to the overhang of the buildings and the law of gravity, slops flung from upper storeys usually landed. He walked daintily, close to the buildings, where the cobbles were relatively clean.

So, of course, did everyone else; a fact that caused more brawling, thumb-biting, and knifing than all the Rhenish and claret, all the sack and sugar, all the ale and beer in Tudor England.

Three men were approaching.

Like Will, they were hugging the buildings, keeping out of the filth.

Someone had to give way.

Will did. He always gave way to superior numbers. There was enough trouble in life without seeking it.

"Will Shakespeare!" said the tallest man, stopping. "I heard you were in London."

Uncordial! But what could you expect? The last time Will had seen Alleyn, he had ordered him out of his house. He had regretted it, for he had never grown out of his desire to be liked. "Ned! I was just on my way to see Henslowe." He looked at Alleyn's companions. Villainous-looking creatures. But he did want to show Alleyn friendship. "Have you time – the tavern?" he said hesitantly.

Alleyn's two companions immediately began to hurry towards the Mermaid, on the corner. Alleyn gave an irritated shrug, and fell into step with Will. By the time they arrived, the two companions were already seated, ale mugs in front of them.

Will ordered more ale. He and Alleyn sat down. Alleyn made no attempt to introduce his friends. Will said, "Master Alleyn, I was unmannerly. You provoked me – sorely – but I was unmannerly. I am sorry."

Alleyn inclined his head, coldly. "It is forgotten. But you did promise – some plays. About Harry the Sixth."

"They are yours," Will said generously. "I will send them to you." He patted his doublet. "But first – a few alterations I have in mind."

Alleyn smiled. "Thanks, Will. And now meet my friends."

Will looked at the two men. One, a crouched, villainous creature, a cutthroat if ever Will saw one; the other a huge sack of a man with baleful, questing eyes and a red beard long and pointed like a weapon.

Alleyn said, "Robert, this is Will Shakespeare, who has written three plays about Henry the Sixth. Will, this is Robert Greene, the writer. And his, er, brother-in-law, Cutting Ball."

"Brother-in-law?" Greene laughed noisily. "Brother out of law, rather." He turned to Will. "His sister is my whore," he explained with sudden courtesy.

"I – see," said Will. So this was Robert Greene. A university wit! A famous writer of plays. And he looked like a hired murderer!

Greene heaved to settle his paunch more comfortably on his thighs. "So you would write plays, Master– ?"

"Shakespeare. Yes. I would, sir."

"Then you are as great a fool as I." He grinned mockingly at Alleyn. "The Players will make their fortunes at your expense. Hey? Won't they, Ned?"

Alleyn was silent. Greene turned to Will. Despite the coarseness, the gross figure, he had a courtesy and charm – when he felt like it. "Do you know Dick Burbage?"

"No?"

"A man of no parentage. His father was a carpenter, but he has a good company of players at Shoreditch. He will serve you better than that kite Henslowe."

Alleyn rose. He drew himself up to his full magnificent height. "I will not stay and hear a good man maligned."

"Suit yourself," Greene said contemptuously.

Alleyn hesitated. But he didn't think he need waste any courtesy on Greene. The man had produced some good work; but he was finished. His mind was dropsical as his body.

A man in Alleyn's position didn't waste time on a spent force. And he could whistle Shakespeare back any time. He nodded curtly to Will, and stalked out.

Will felt suddenly lonely.

Greene took another swig from the bottle, looked at Will with interest. "So. You write plays? Which university were you at?"

Will's heart sank. "Neither."

That red beard shot up in the air like a sword. "Yet you would write plays?" he put a hand on Will's arm. "Listen, boy. *I* was at both Oxford and Cambridge. Utriusque Academiae in Artibus Magister. And I cannot make a living from plays. So how do *you* expect – ?" He looked at Will with friendly irritation. "Have anything with you?"

"As it happens, I have," said Will. He pulled Harry the Sixth out of his doublet.

Greene pored over it, snuffling and grunting. Cutting Ball listlessly shaved the hairs of his wrists with a glinting dagger, an occupation that Will watched with a certain horror. Suddenly Greene slapped down the manuscript. He said, "Master Shakespeare, I seldom perform a kindness. But I will perform one for you. Why?" he looked at Will, one eyebrow cocked. "Perhaps it is your greenness. Come."

He strode off. Cutting Ball stuck his dagger in his belt and loped after him. Will followed. "But where to, Master Greene?"

"Burbage," said Greene.

All the way to Shoreditch, Greene talked. "Your Harry Six. It's good, man. Young, green, but good. You'll go somewhere. And by God I'll help you. I'm a fool. You'll use me as a ladder, then kick me from under you."

"I'll do no such thing," Will said hotly, vowing eternal gratitude.

Greene slapped a great fist down on his shoulder. "If you do, I'll crucify you. Or get Cutting Ball to." He glanced round at his shadow. "He pays my debts. With a slit throat." He laughed hugely at his pleasantry.

Will gave a strained smile. He could have wished for a more gentlemanly companion. But he wasn't complaining. He had found what every writer wanted, a disinterested helper; someone, moreover, who seemed to know what he was talking about. And, being a man who prized gratitude very highly, he warmed quickly to this alarming stranger.

For the first time Will found himself in a real theatre.

On the stage a man was nailing a loose board. Greene put a friendly arm about Will's shoulders, led him forward. He said, "You are going to meet the greatest actor of his day – a man not afraid to soil his hands – not like that jackanapes Alleyn."

The man looked up. Surely, thought Will, Greene must be drunk. There was nothing of the great actor about this man. He looked like a friendly hired man.

He rose stiffly, came forward, peering. Greene said, "Dick, fool that I am, I've brought you a new play writer." He turned to Will. "Richard Burbage, of the Theatre. Tell him your name, boy."

"Will Shakespeare, sir."

"An unlettered oaf," Greene said with the appalling rudeness that never seemed far from his tongue. "But he seems to have got the knack of writing plays with his mother's milk."

Burbage was smiling, holding out a friendly hand. "You must not mind Robert. Too many pickled herrings have soured his tongue. Now, can you act?"

"A little, sir."

"Good. We've been a man short since they hanged Job Carter. There'll be plenty for you to do."

Greene said, "If ever you feel grateful for my gift of the lily-white boy, Dick, you can repay me by performing my *Alphonsus*." He thrust his red beard at Shakespeare's face. "And if you find I have served you well, remember – a Master of Arts will not disdain a gift of wine from a clod."

With something between a sneer and a grin, he lumbered off, followed by his guard.

Dick Burbage and Will looked at each other, smiled, and liked what they saw. Will gazed around the great theatre, smelt the theatre smell, felt the latent excitement of the place. Then his eyes came back to the unassuming, friendly man before him. And he knew: thanks to Robert Greene, he had come home; come home as he had never done in Chapel Lane, Stratford; come home where he belonged. If ever he, humble creature that he was, could help a man of Robert Greene's eminence, then Robert would not have to ask twice.

Edward Alleyn felt well content. He'd put both Greene and Shakespeare in their places. *And* he'd have his Harry the Sixth. This Will might be a poltroon, a bit of a fool, but he'd keep his word. Revised, too; some of the rough edges knocked off, perchance.

And Marlowe was being unusually civil these days. So long as the mighty Marlowe was on their side, they didn't need to worry about fledglings like Shakespeare. For the time being, at least, Shakespeare could go hang. Let Master Shakespeare botch up a few plays for another company. It wasn't going to affect Edward Alleyn's fortunes. Once this Spanish scare was over, and Marlowe had written a few more plays like *Tamburlaine*, Philip Henslowe and Edward Alleyn were going to be in a very comfortable situation.

But the Spanish scare showed no signs of being over.

On the contrary. At Dunkirk, the cruel Prince of Parma gazed out across this grey, northern sea, awaiting one thing: the sight of the Armada, lumbering up from Spain to give him cover for his crossing to England. Under his hand were seventeen thousand soldiers, a fleet of flat-bottomed barges. Once let the mighty Armada appear, and the match would be lit. His barges, protected by the greatest fleet the world had ever known, would sail for England. His army would land on the Kent beaches. Then the struggle would begin. It would be long, bloody and remorseless. Parma knew these English. And he had rather less faith in the personal intervention of the Trinity than had his master Philip.

In Stratford, they were calling out the militia. The yokel-soldiers marched up Henley Street to High Cross, and back again. Three-year-old Hamnet trailed a pike with the best of them. "Little soldier," cried John Shakespeare, eyes filling with tears. "'Tis mercy he is not some years older. No battlefields for him, pretty nestling."

Not knowing that, of this hardbitten band, the pretty nestling would be first to go.

Flame, and a shower of sparks, leapt into the night sky.

Far away, on the dark horizon, another burst of brightness. And another. And another.

Men lifted up their eyes to the ancient hill places of England; and their throats constricted with fear, and pride, and love of country, and again fear.

This was it. The Spaniard was coming. Let him get a foothold, and the fires would rage again at Smithfield. Aye, and at more than Smithfield. At Exeter and Stratford and Daventry and Ashbourne; in every pleasant market-place of England. This must not be! By God, this must not be.

There was no time for poetry now. No time for love-making. Let the father leave his children, and the husbandman the ripening corn, and the bridegroom his bride. Let men prepare themselves for bloodshed, and women for weeping, and children for hunger. An end of kindliness and gentle peace. The Armada was in the Channel. Terrible as an army with banners.

Like the Queen herself, Will and his new friends, though deeply involved as were all Englishmen, were wondering how to turn the coming invasion to their own advantage. "What we want now," Richard Burbage was saying, "are stirring tales of war to match the spirit of the times."

"Aye," said Will Shakespeare fervently, and the kings and princes and mailed warriors clashed and roared defiance in his brain. He must to his Holinshed. There were enough warres and battells in Holinshed to fill out a dozen plays.

"Nay," said Will Kempe, the company's clown, scornfully. His pale, thin face gazed, unblinking, at the new man. He did not seem to like what he saw. He sneered. "What we want now is lusty comedy. Naught takes a man's mind off his troubles better than bawdry."

Henry Condell shook his head. "I am with Richard. The people want war; but preferably without wounds or bloodshed. That is what we can give them."

Richard turned to Will, smiling. "Now, Will. Your chance. Have you no tales of war? They say you are a poet."

Will was pleased and flattered. "I have written three such plays about Harry the Sixth," he boasted. "But" – he began to regret his boasting – "they are promised."

"Promised?" Burbage, who could flame with anger like dry kindling, flamed now. "Promised? To whom?"

"To Edward Alleyn."

Will was appalled. He had known these men but a few days, and already he and they were like brothers. They spoke the same language, were welded together by a love and a loyalty that were almost tangible. Condell, Heminge, Phillips, Burbage and himself – he felt he had known them all his life. Only in Kempe, the clown, did he not feel this love. Liking so much to be liked, he was distressed to feel Kempe's immediate antagonism.

And now, alas, he felt the antagonism of them all. *"Edward Alleyn?"* cried Burbage. "But – you're with us now. You owe *us* anything you write."

"The plays were promised before I became your hired man."

Burbage seemed to accept the point, but still looked put out. Will Kempe sneered. "Send him packing, Dick. We want no traitors in this camp."

Condell said morosely, "Even if the plays were not to our taste, we could have worked on them."

Phillips said, "Let us have them, Will. Believe me, Alleyn would not be so nice."

This, thought Will, was true. But – he remembered something Dick Field had once said, about being true to your own nature. What was right for Edward Alleyn was not necessarily right for William Shakespeare. He said, "I am sorry. But the plays are promised."

Will Kempe spat. The rest were silent. William Shakespeare, cheerfully gregarious as a starling, hated this cold disapprobation. He said, wretchedly, "I have another play, about a man whose murdered father's ghost appears to him and tells him to revenge him on his uncle, and – "

"Has it wars, and battles?"

"Not at the moment. I could give it some."

Burbage shook his head. They were still silent. Then Burbage said in a flat voice, "So. We will say no more. I would not stretch a man's conscience for him."

"Conscience?" sneered Will Kempe. "I think, rather, Master Alleyn is a good paymaster."

Will felt himself flush painfully. The remark called for a flourished dagger, or a pint of ale flung into that mean face. But Will did nothing, said nothing. The characters who peopled his mind might wave their swords and holla for revenge. But not Will. He took his wounds in silence, and nursed them in solitude like a hurt animal.

But the harsh facts remained. Of the two major companies in London, one had lost interest in him; and the other saw him as a kind of traitor.

It was not, for a play writer who at twenty-four had achieved absolutely nothing, a good beginning. And, had it not been for the Spanish Armada, that is where he might have stayed.

The Armada sailed up the Channel, the tiny English ships snapping like terriers at its heels.

So many galleons were sunk that the English sailors boasted the feathers of the Spaniard had been plucked one by one. The fact remained, however, that the plucked bird itself reached the Calais roads. It only needed now to make contact with the Prince of Parma, poised with his barges and his men, and the invasion and conquest of England could begin.

Eight fire ships, loosed to windward of the Spanish fleet by the dastardly English, put a stop to all that. Seeing these balls of furious fire bearing down on them, bewildered by the exploding of the charged guns, the Spanish sailors cut their cables and stood out to sea, where Drake was waiting for them.

All day the battle raged. The sun went down on a shambles of torn sails, splintered masts and blood. Poor Medina Sidonia who, being a court favourite, had seemed the obvious man to put in command of the Great

Enterprise, went quite to pieces. "We are lost, Señor Oquenda," he cried. "What are we to do?"

Captain Oquenda was made of sterner metal. "Your Excellency has only to order up fresh cartridge," he said soothingly.

But he was overruled. Such sail as was left was hoisted. The Armada was going home.

And since both the wind and El Draque lay south, they faced the singularly unattractive choice of returning to Spain round the Isles of Orkney; where those who were not drowned in the bitter sea were cheerfully plundered and butchered by the savage Highlanders and the wild Irish, to whom Philip's Great Enterprise must have seemed a veritable Godsend.

So the Prince of Parma was left with his flat-bottomed barges and no escort, impotent.

But no one in England yet knew this. The army at St James's, formed to protect the Queen's person, marched and drilled.

The army at Tilbury, formed to fling the Spaniard back into the sea, drilled and marched.

Elizabeth, having revised her speech to the last comma, and having had a satisfactory fitting of her silver corslet, announced her intention of addressing the troops at Tilbury.

The Council, the commanders, were appalled.

But if Elizabeth said she was going to Tilbury, Elizabeth was going to Tilbury. No use pointing out that an army was stationed at St James's solely to protect her. There was an army at Tilbury also, was there not, my lords. But if the Spaniards arrive when you are there, Majesty, the army will be too occupied to protect you. *Protect* me? Protect *me?* God's wounds, little man, I need no protection. I will hit the Spaniard as hard as any man living.

She went. And there to greet her was her sweet Robin of Leicester, who had been anything but her sweet Robin so many times since those ridiculous Revels at Kenilworth; and who now, as a sick and dying man, as Lieutenant and Captain General of the Queen's Armies and Companies, greeted her with the fond, sad kindness of one who knows that the race is run – and lost for ever.

That night they supped alone in his tent. They were both growing old. He, much married, but never to the woman he would have wished. She still the Virgin Queen, though now the tinsel was wearing a little thin. And both under a terrible danger that might, even tomorrow, end their bright world forever. No. There would be no scandal now. The time for dalliance was past. Reality had come.

The messenger spurred his horse on desperately. Pray God he might be the first to bring the news to the Queen. It would be worth a silver crown at least, at best a knighthood.

He came to Tilbury. He was taken straight to the Queen in Leicester's tent. Bowing humbly, he gave her Drake's despatch. And waited, smugly, for her cries of delighted gratitude.

Elizabeth surprised him, as she managed to surprise most men. She read the despatch. Then she turned to Leicester. "Have him kept under guard. See that he speaks to no one."

The messenger was outraged. After all, if you brought ill tidings you expected anything – cuffs, blows, even throttling. Good news meant silver, gold. It helped to even things up. If you were going to be arrested for bringing *good* news, there wasn't much point in being a messenger. "Your Majesty!" he protested.

"You will not be harmed," she told him. The guards led him off, not altogether reassured. The Queen turned to

Leicester. There was a tight exultant smile about her lips. "The Armada is scattered, and fleeing northward. But Drake warns they may refit in Danish ports. And Parma may still try a crossing."

"The Armada? Scattered? We must ring the bells. Put out the flags – "

"Fool. You will tell no one."

"But why?" he remembered something. "And the messenger? I thought his tidings had been ill."

She said, "I have prepared a speech for tomorrow." She drew herself up magnificently, lifted her royal chin. 'Therefore am I come amongst you, being resolved, in the midst and heat of the battle, to live or die amongst you all; to lay down for God, for my kingdom, and for my people, my honour and my blood, even in the dust.'" She sagged. "You can't expect me to waste all that, Robin."

"Waste it?"

"Listen. This is the best speech I've ever written. It's going to bind me to my people for ever. But only" – she seized his chin between finger and thumb, stared at him earnestly – "only if the troops think there are a hundred Spanish ships just coming up over the horizon. To bind me to my people, I need the putty of imminent danger, as well as oratory."

She came, erect on a white charger. She came, wearing a white velvet dress and a silver corslet, her silver helmet with its white plume borne before her. She came, attended by two boys in white velvet. She came, attended by four nobles: Leicester riding on her right, Essex on her left, Norreys walking behind; and in front, held aloft by my Lord Ormonde, the great Sword of State flashing in the August sunshine.

It was magnificent. In all that mighty throng, there was no sound. No eye but stared at Royal England.

She began to speak, her voice ringing out clear and strong.

They listened, in silence. Then as she went on, there were murmurs, a roaring as of a pride of lions.

There would be more yet, she thought, exulting. She lowered her voice. "I know I have but the body of a weak and feeble woman," she said pathetically, and saw male protectiveness glow in a thousand eyes. She paused, and took a deep breath. "But I have the heart and stomach of a King," she cried at the top of her voice.

Delighted, frenzied cheering. As soon as she could make herself heard she added in a growled aside, "Aye, and of a King of England too."

They loved her for this brilliant impromptu. And when she finished "...and by your valour in the field, we shall shortly have a famous victory over these enemies of my God, of my Kingdom, and of my People," they went mad. There was not a man in all that throng who would not have died for her that day. They would fight for her like devils out of Hell. And if, by God's Grace, they beat the Spaniard, they would work for her as they had never worked before. Aye, and tell their children of her glory.

She rode along their ranks; hoarse, exhausted, exultant. She had been right. It had been too good an opportunity to throw away.

So. The great ships, with their terrible cargoes of burnt and maimed and blinded men, ran the gauntlet to a home most of them would never find.

But there were few in England to spare them a pitying thought. The Queen's speech was quoted in every tavern, in every town, in every hamlet. England was like a banked fire that suddenly bursts into flame. With the defeat of the Armada she had cast off, like a cloak, a menace that had hung about her shoulders for years. Under her loved and brilliant Queen, she gazed into a future so bright with promise and hope that eyes were blinded to all else.

England! Her Court was the most brilliant in Europe, her Queen the cleverest, bravest, gayest, most beloved creature that ever sat upon a throne. The English were cock-a-hoop. This England, they felt vaguely. This royal throne of kings, this sceptr'd isle. Come the three corners of the world in arms, they wanted to cry, and we shall shock them. But they were inarticulate. And as the years of promise crept by, the people longed, they yearned, for someone to speak for them.

And, sure enough, someone did.

In March 1592, was put on, at Philip Henslowe's new theatre The Rose (yes, the cautious man had taken the plunge in 1587, and never regretted it), *Harry the VI*, by an unnamed author.

Harry the VI had all the warres and battells anyone could wish for, with the burning of a strumpet Joan of Arc thrown in for good measure.

Its success was phenomenal. House takings reached the astonishing sum of three pounds sixteen shillings and eightpence. Henslowe was beside himself for joy.

But William Shakespeare took it in his stride. After their first suspicions, Burbage and his men had taken him to their hearts. He had comfortable lodgings in Bishopsgate. He was writing a major work: a poem, *Venus and Adonis*, of which his friend Richard Field thought well. Richard was now a printer; for his master, Vautrollier, had died, and Richard, with a mixture of sentiment and business acumen typical of his age, had taken over the widow and therefore the business. Will thought *Venus and Adonis* was good. If Richard would only print it, Will might well make a reputation.

He was pleased, of course, that *Harry the VI* had so exactly caught the mood of the times; and, at the desperate urging of his company, was busy on a *Richard the III* with similar ingredients; and, to keep Will Kempe quiet, struggling on half-heartedly with his *Comedy of Errors*; and botching up some old thing about Titus and Vespacia. But, though he would gladly dash off the bloody histories that were taking London by storm, only two things really interested him. The poem that was going to bring him fame; and a deeper purpose he had discovered in his histories. Order. Degree. Oh, let the groundlings have their bombast, their clash of swords, their hymns of praise for England. All that he, too, loved. But beyond all that stood Order and Degree. God, the angels, man. Sun, planets, earth. Prince, Council, people. Each moving in precise and God-ordained relation to the other. But take away the sun, and you had planets wandering in disorder, plagues, portents, chaos. Take away the anointed Prince, and you had wars, dissension, misery. He must preach order. He had read too much about the Wars of the Roses. Chaos must not come again to peaceful England.

He was a peace-loving man. Often he had gazed at London Bridge, and shuddered at the rewards of treason. So now he shuddered at the old tales of civil war. Let Marlowe and Greene and Nashe fight and ruffle it in the stews and taverns. He, Shakespeare, would always have order in his own life. Neat of dress, sober, honourable, courteous to all.

Both in his thought and in his way of life, he would always be on the side of government.

Or so he thought.

Yet even now he was about to take the first step along a road that would bring him to the rim of a terrible vortex.

"Hey! You, sir!"

Will, lost in thoughts of *Venus and Adonis*, looked up at the arrogant cry; and saw two Adonises standing on the far, dry side of the street, across the filth of the kennel.

A courteous man himself, Will was angered by discourtesy in others. But it was unwise to show anger to two such young men as these; nobles, by their dress and bearing; born to expect instant obedience from every commoner. What could two such rarefied creatures want with him? Apprehensive, yet flattered and intrigued, he picked his way through the mud and filth, for one couldn't expect them to cross to him.

The younger looked him up and down arrogantly. "Are you not Shakespeare?"

Will bowed; more apprehensive, yet more intrigued.

"I saw your *Richard the Third*. I liked it well. Come to Southampton House, on Thursday, in the forenoon. I would speak with you." They moved on, leaving Will bowing. Southampton House! This must be the young Earl. And one of his friends. Perhaps the famous Essex himself!

They were, both of them, lithe as young deer, lovely as women, exquisite as peacocks. And yet, beneath the rich adornments, beneath the soft femininity, he sensed a hard masculine aggression. Creatures of earth and air, who would write a sonnet, tumble a wench, and run a man through, all in a summer's day.

He walked on in a daze. What could Southampton want with him? Did he want to commission a play or a poem, make the poor player dance a jig or recite some bawdry to pass an idle day? Was there (always the cautious Will's first question) was there danger? He remembered – oh those simple days – poor Anne's alarm at his summons to Kenilworth Castle. And how right she had been! Poor Anne! He *must* visit Stratford. He had found a way of sending money regularly, letters, little presents for the children, by an honest fellow, a friend of Richard Field, who often travelled on business between London and Stratford. Yes, he must get back to Stratford; but how could he find the time, what with *Richard*, and the *Comedy*, and *Venus*, and still working away, almost surreptitiously, on this Hamlet thing that no one would show any interest in; to say nothing of acting four or five days a week? And rehearsing. And now, my Lord of Southampton.

What could Southampton want? Will, with his gentlemanly aspirations, listened avidly to the unending gossip about the nobility. What did he know of this young Earl? Henry Wriothesley, they called him, third Earl of Southampton, baron of Titchfield. They said he was a Royal Ward, in care of Lord Burghley, the Lord High Treasurer. They said old Burghley wanted to marry him to his granddaughter, the Lady Elizabeth Vere, but the youth was digging in his elegant toes. They said he was learned in the classics, a patron of the arts. They said he was sulky, arrogant, charming, wayward, unpredictable, generous and wealthy.

Will, piecing all this together, felt his pulse beating faster and faster. Lady this, Lord that; it made even the Ardens look small beer.

Not to go would be an insult. Men had been run through for less. Besides, he thought with a return of spirit, why should he not go. He was not only a despised player. He was a poet, proud title. Poets had always walked with kings; and sometimes had their heads cut off by those same kings, he remembered glumly. No. It would be a frightening thing to go through the great doors of Southampton House, and hear them close behind him. But he would go. He could be brave enough when there was no choice.

He dressed with great care: nothing gaudy. He would be the poor but gentlemanly player who knew well how to comport himself.

He set off, trembling a little with nervousness and excitement, his mind concentrated entirely on the coming visit. And he had not gone ten yards when he met Robert Greene.

There was no escape. Robert almost filled the narrow lane. Not, of course, that Will would not want to meet his benefactor. But when you are on your way to visit an Earl, meeting a man who looks like a tousled bed calls for some adjustment.

"Why, the lily-white boy! Will – don't tell me – Shakespeare." He threw an arm like a bolster round Will. "Come and drink with me, boy."

"I cannot, Master Greene. I – "

The arm fell away. "Then I cannot drink either. My money is gone. My credit never was. Where are you going?"

"Holborn. Er – Southampton House."

The little pig eyes widened. "So? The country oaf has found comfort with one of my lord's serving women already?"

Gratitude flew out of the window. "No, sir. I am visiting my Lord of Southampton."

Greene whistled. "So high, so soon?" He looked waspish. "I served you better than I thought, Master Shakespeare."

Time was passing, and meeting this uncouth sot – who called *him* oaf – just when he was poised and prepared to be greeted by an earl, was curiously irritating. He said, "Sir, I am eternally grateful for your interest, and for introducing me to Dick Burbage, whose hired man I am at six shillings a week. But it is 'that kite Henslowe' who has so far brought me what success I have. And I knew him before I knew you. I hope we shall meet again, sir. But now – " He doffed his bonnet and ran.

Robert Greene watched him go. He looked very hurt. Like most men who pride themselves on their blunt speaking, he felt deeply resentful when anyone spoke bluntly to him. It was something his sensitive nature found almost unbearable.

My lord sprawled in a great chair. He greeted Will with a lack-lustre eye. "Is not the world a tedious place, Master Shakespeare?"

So deep was Will's bow, such a notable flourish did he give his bonnet, that he had time, before regaining the upright, to ponder the advisability of agreement or disagreement.

Well, at least it was *Master* Shakespeare, this time. He decided on disagreement. "I do not find it so, my lord."

The beautiful nineteen-year-old boy looked displeased. He sat forward in his chair. He pushed back the golden locks that draped his left shoulder. "Can you tell me why *I* should find it so; while you, a mere player, do not?"

"I am also a poet, my lord."

Southampton pouted. "And what difference does that make, pray?"

Will swallowed. Then he said, bravely, "To a poet, my lord, the whole of Creation is his plaything: clouds, music,

185

summer and winter, words, words, words. A poet could never find life tedious, my lord."

My lord looked unimpressed. "So. Recite me a poem."

Now by great good fortune Will happened to be carrying the unfinished manuscript of *Venus and Adonis*. This he read.

When he had finished, Southampton smiled.

It was the first time Will had seen Southampton smile. And it moved him deeply. The small petulance of the mouth was forgotten. The eyes lost their arrogant stare. Instead, there was warmth, friendship, even gaiety. "You have written this, Master Shakespeare? And *Richard the Third*, and, so it is whispered, *Harry the Sixth*? What else?"

But he did not wait for an answer. He went on rudely (or what would have been rudely in a commoner), "You should write more poems, Master Shakespeare. Any scribbler can please the groundlings. But your poem has a sensuous and pretty wit."

"Thank you, my lord." Will bowed and flourished again, dizzily.

There was a silence. "James," Southampton called. A servant appeared, bearing a beaker of wine and a single glass. "Pour Master Shakespeare a glass of wine," commanded the Earl. James did so, handed the glass to Will, withdrew.

Will stood before the silent Earl, holding the glass. The Earl sat watching him. Will, uncomfortable, felt like a beggar given a cup of water at the door. He was humiliated and angry. Was this how the nobility always behaved?

Humiliated and angry. Three courses were open to him.

To fling the wine in my lord's arrogant face? Instant death. No question.

To refuse the wine? An incalculable risk to his future.

To drink with as good a grace as possible, bow, flourish, say "Thank you, my lord," and go; and live to write another day.

There was never any question which line the amiable Will would take. He sipped, sipped again, smiling. And suddenly, to his astonishment, the young man was out of his chair, standing beside him, clapping an arm about his shoulders, laughing. "Oh, Master Shakespeare, Master Will, may I call you Will?" He looked boyishly alarmed at his forwardness. "You are so much older than I."

It was true. This dragonfly creature made Will, in his sober doublet, with his already receding hair, with his old married status, feel staid and elderly. But – to be called Will, by an earl! This would be something to tell his father. He stammered, "Sir – my lord. I should indeed be honoured."

That noble arm was still about his shoulders. But in his hand was still the empty glass. And not a single table in that silked and damasked room. Together they strolled towards the door. Southampton said, "You must read your *Venus* to some of my friends – Essex, Pembroke. I will send for you, Ancient Will." He slapped him on the back, pushing him towards the hovering James, who mercifully took the glass and showed him to the door. Will walked all the way from Holborn to his lodgings in Bishopsgate without seeing a thing. Southampton, Pembroke, even my Lord of Essex, the brightest star in England's firmament! He was to meet them, read them his *Venus*!

And when he had done that, he thought, it would be time to visit Stratford. He would, at last, have something to report.

He was almost home before he remembered his meeting with Robert Greene. But when he did he was appalled; and, as usual, set about analysing his motives for his churlishness; and – again as usual – putting the blame entirely on his own shoulders. Just because he was going to visit an earl, he had spurned a man who had shown him friendship and whom, in many ways, he liked. Just because Greene was the antithesis of all that he, Gentleman Will, held dear, he had run from him as though he had the plague.

He would visit Greene, apologise, take him to the tavern, fill him with wine, listen courteously while he boasted and ranted an evening away.

Yes, he would do just that, as soon as he returned from Stratford.

CHAPTER 8

HERE SHALL HE SEE NO ENEMY...

The children were growing up. Susanna was nine, now, would you believe it, a pretty, bright creature with much of her father's charm. And the twins, six; Hamnet a bit rude and boastful at times, needing a father's hand, riding his hobbyhorse, a present from someone called "father" whom the child confused with, but preferred to, God. Both were invisible and remote. But father sometimes sent toys and kickshaws which God, however much petitioned, never did.

And little Judith, a constant care. Always ailing, not long for this world perhaps; a quiet, withdrawn child who spoke thickly, as though her words were so much dough in her mouth. Sickly and pale. It was as though, at their double birth, her lusty brother had grabbed all he could of life, and left her the lees.

They were none of them getting any younger. John Shakespeare was sober again, but a sad wreck of the man who had once been Town Bailiff. Things washed over him, nowadays, passed him by. The business was doing well, but he still owed money here and there. It wasn't easy, he complained, to sort out what was what. He took little interest in his own children, except William, who, he explained to all who would listen, was in London rubbing shoulders with the great. His life now centred on his grandchildren. He would watch their pretty games for hours, frequently mopping his eyes, giving them suckets, reciting them old rhymes, riddling them merry riddles. They despised him utterly

Mary Shakespeare was grey, now, and walked a little stiffly. She was too intelligent, and too independent, to centre her life on her grandchildren. She still had her own life to lead, thank you very much. Her husband, her children, the business, the house on Henley Street, baking, cooking, preserving, curing, salting, praying – these were enough for any woman. The cottage in Chapel Lane must look after itself. Oh, there was always a welcome for Anne and the children at Henley Street, and many evenings Mary would take her sewing and sit with Anne by the lonely fire. But she would not interfere. If a son of hers had gone off to London, leaving wife and children, well, she wasn't going to look hangdog about it. Will was a good lad. If he and Anne had decided to go their separate ways, it couldn't all have been Will's fault. Fond though she was of her daughter-in-law, she felt Anne must have contributed her share to the breakdown. How, she could not imagine. But a marriage had more currents and crosscurrents and undertows and eddies, more deeps and shallows, than the most treacherous sea. When you really thought about it, a happy marriage seemed the unlikeliest thing in nature.

And Anne? Anne was in her middle thirties, middle-aged. The years had dealt kindly with her, not in the trite sense of leaving her unmarked. No. The years had added to her, giving a strength to her features, a strength and courage to her spirit.

Oh, she knew all the gossip: yes, he had to marry her, her family saw to that. But, by God, he was soon off. She won't see *him* again. They say he's living in a whorehouse by the Thames. They say he's wormed his way into Court, just suit him, always a bit big for his boots, that lad. They say, they say, they say; they say he never sends her a penny, John Shakespeare has to keep her, poor old devil, as if he hadn't enough on his plate, why they say he still owes seven pounds to William Burbage; and to others.

She knew the gossip. It flowed over her, and left her unmarked. She had her home, her children – and her faith in Will. She still knew, what she had realised from the very beginning: that she would never possess Will; but that for her a little of Will was better than the whole of any other man. She did not know Will. No one could. She did not understand him, never would in a thousand years. She just loved him.

And trusted him. He'd come back, when he'd done what he'd set out to do. In the meantime, she was the loneliest of women, yet happy in her quiet country way. Happy with her children, and the turning seasons, and the countryside. For Will had taught her to see it all with the eye of love: the flowers, the weeds, sun, moon and stars, the pretty darting birds, even the glistening worm, and the soft horns of cockled snails.

And now, at last, her faith was justified. Will was coming home!

They responded to the news in their several ways. John Shakespeare told all his customers: my son William is to pay us a visit. Now we shall hear all the Court news; and the latest fashions, I don't doubt. Very highly esteemed at Court, my son Will is.

Mary; pleased, but not showing it. "And about time, too. No, John, we are killing no fatted calves. Young Will can forget any fancy London ways he may have picked up, while he's with us. However big he's grown, I'll not forget I suckled him and gave him life." Knowing in her heart that she was being unfair; that her Will would always be the cheerful, loving son she remembered.

The children were scared. Susanna could just remember a deep-voiced, bristly creature who had filled the house whenever he was in it. A creature, moreover, who took too much of mother's attention. She didn't want him back.

Hamnet, confused as always between father and God, was secretly fearful. Father would descend from Heaven, bathed in unbearable light.

Little Judith, who could just about cope with life provided nothing strange or untoward happened, wept in anticipation.

The people of Stratford were, on the whole, unimpressed. While a visitor from faraway London must, in the nature of things, be as interesting as a dancing bear or a blackamoor, they were determined not to show it. He might be a London gallant now. But he was still young Will Shakespeare who had been no better than he ought to be. You could feel quite affectionate towards a sinner who stayed trodden in the dirt; but a sinner who prospered set himself beyond the forgiveness of both man and God.

And Anne? Anne scrubbed, and baked, and made new gowns for the little girls, and bought a blue silk doublet for her son; and, her country wisdom flung to the winds for once, bought herself a cone-shaped Spanish farthingale, a gored skirt to go over it, and a pointed bodice; not knowing that by now the London fashion was all for wheel farthingales, and that, in Will's eyes, she would have looked better in her homely gown.

She was anxious, yet composed. She too knew that, whatever had happened, Will would still be Will. We are what we are, was one of her dearest saws. And Will Shakespeare, above all men, would not change.

Will, being no fool, wore his soberest dress to visit Stratford. His doublet, breeches and stockings were brown. He wore a leather jerkin over the doublet, and a round, unadorned hat. He might have been some noble's man, visiting his master's properties.

But, if his dress was sober, his mind was aflame. Now, at last, he could stand away from himself, see his progress since he last travelled this road, *Richard*, *Harry*, playing to packed houses. Far more important, *Venus and Adonis* almost ready to show to Dick Field. The *Comedy of Errors* going well now. And for friends: the earls of Essex and Southampton, who jested, and danced, and diced with the Queen almost daily; and, on a lower but still important plane, a rising young publisher, and perhaps the most promisingly brilliant group of players the world had ever known. Good fellows, anyway, who appreciated their amiable Will; all except the mean-mouthed Kempe.

God, life was full: writing, reading everything that came to hand, botching up a play for tomorrow's performance, drinking with his fellow players (though you could have too much of that. Drink sat ill on his stomach, and he still could not with an easy conscience waste an hour), visiting Southampton House where the young Earl was beginning to accept him as, according to his changing mood, his own lost father, his father confessor, his jester, his whipping-boy; and, incredibly, his friend.

Friend! Friend to Henry Wriothesley, Third Earl! He, Will Shakespeare, who got his first child sprawled in the

Warwickshire clay. Bed of moonbeams and gossamer, forsooth! His thoughts turned sour. He should have come home sooner. Every year, he had intended to come. But the years had slipped by, as years do. Oh, he deserved an unkind welcome.

Marry, it was a long way to Stratford. He dozed, in the still noon day. His horse jogged on. When he woke he saw in the far distance, a church spire.

There was no other spire in England quite like that – self-assured, sturdy, yet unassuming, half hidden in the careless bounty of Stratford's trees, backed by the little hills where Wilmcote lay. He spurred on his horse, suddenly exuberant. He was coming home – in a sort of triumph. "Is it not passing brave to be a king, And ride in triumph through Persepolis?" he cried. Alleyn was not the only one who could quote Marlowe. "Holla, ye pampered jades of Asia," he yelled, as his horse thundered along the leafy road. He was coming home – Anne, the children, mother, father, family, sweet Avon, the house in Henley Street, the cottage in Chapel Lane; and, not a word to Anne, a quiet look at New Place, that commanding house built by Sir Hugh Clopton, whose achievements in London made Will's look poor indeed.

Holy Trinity Church, floating amid its water meadows, came slowly nearer. The horse had dropped back to ambling now. Will's cheeks were wet. "Is it not passing brave," he muttered, voice breaking. "To be a king, And ride – in triumph – "

He was among the houses, now. He pulled himself together.

He had come home.

Onomatopoeically, he clip-clopped and clattered over the cobbles of Clopton Bridge, followed the road along into

Bridge street, then turned left at High Cross into High Street.

Things hadn't changed. The Renaissance might be a flame in men's minds, an explosion in Europe's cities, but Stratford could comfortably ignore such things. Men needed food, and protection from the weather; they needed somewhere to huddle against the darkness; they needed company to help them forget foul fiends, hobgoblins, and Hell fire. And this they had in full measure: in a pretty, leafy, well-governed town. He was surprised to find how small and pleasant it was. No, things hadn't changed. There was Quiney's shop, with a new coat of paint, there his friend Henry Walker's with a new sign; there was New Place, he saw with rising excitement. As grand as he remembered it, but sadly falling into decay; it would need work, and money, spending on it. But it would be cheap. By the time he could afford it, it should be well down in double figures.

And here was Chapel Lane, running back to the river. And here was home. He looked in amazement. Was this tiny, humble dwelling really his? He realised, with a shock, that his ideas had changed in mighty London. The splendours of Southampton House; even Richard Field's tall, narrow, tottering house in St Paul's Churchyard, wedged upright, like a drunken man, by its neighbours; these made William Shakespeare's house look a hovel. He glanced back at New Place on the corner. That was where he would live, eventually, in still-distant summer days; Wm Shakespeare, Gent.; a morning stroll by the Avon, in the afternoon sleep, or a game of bowls; musical evenings with the family, or a glass with friends at the tavern. Dull, but pleasant, when words and rhymes and lines and kings and princes ceased at last their janglings in his restless brain.

But he was still young Will Shakespeare, about to meet a wife he had not seen for years, a wife he had neglected cruelly. He brought his mind back to the present. He hoped, humbly, that he would get a better welcome than he deserved.

She went to open the door.

A thousand times she had faced this moment; in her dreams, and day dreams, and longings, and nightmares.

A thousand times she had opened the door to a knock, suddenly trembling, thinking: it might be Will. Only to find a beggar, a neighbour, a peddler with laces and buttons. A thousand times she had opened the door in her dreams to find – Will; and had wakened to a joy that melted like snow before the searing truth of day. Often, when loneliness and longing became intolerable, and the children were abed, she had opened the door and gazed out into the empty lane, imagining what it would be like to hear his footsteps, to see his sturdy figure come swinging round the corner.

And now! He was here, and her hair was awry, and the kettle was coming to the boil, and Judith was crying because Hamnet had scratched his arm on a rusty nail and Anne could not find a spider's web to lay on the wound, so well had she cleaned the house against Will's coming.

She opened the door...

It was his smile she saw first. His smile hadn't changed; so full of laughter and love and understanding and compassion. He had gained: a little weight, a few years, a bearing and an authority. "Will," her lips said, but no words came. He took her in his arms; and for the first time for all these years she was safe from the world. They looked into each other's eyes, searching; and liked what they saw. A young, unsure man had parted from a simple country wife. Now, a man who had smelt success in the world's most exciting city, had come home to a woman deepened and strengthened by the unremitting trial of the every day.

She clung to his arm as they went towards the little parlour. She had had a curious fancy about time. Much as she had longed for him, she had known that the moment he arrived the clock would begin ticking his visit inexorably away. So, now, already the precious seconds were growing into minutes. And the minutes would grow into hours, the hours days, bringing her to the moment when they would walk the other way, from the parlour to the front door, and clinging would avail her nothing. Now she clung the harder. She didn't think she could face another amputation. Yet knew that frail human flesh and spirit could bear suffering that would appal the gods. "I bade the children wait in here," she said, opening the parlour door. "I wanted a moment – alone."

He kissed her again, smiling. Then faced his children's candid stare.

He might be making a name for himself in London. He might be made much of by a loving wife, by noble friends. But to these children he meant nothing. With them, he had got to start from the beginning. And work hard.

Susanna looked at him shyly, Judith fearfully. Hamnet scowled. Susanna curtseyed.

It was Hamnet who broke the silence. "How is the Holy Ghost?"

Will was not to know that, in his son's mind, he and God were hopelessly confused. Nevertheless, he smiled and said "Well, I thank you."

Hamnet said, "There is a dead cat down by the river, with worms in his belly." Since this fascinating piece of Stratford gossip seemed to amuse his unknown father, Hamnet went on, "And Master Smith of the tavern dropped a barrel on his foot so that his big toe burst."

Anne said, "Nay, Hamnet, let thy sisters speak."

But the little girls sat, tongue-tied. And Will, who was seldom lost for a word, was lost now. He could only smile, and nod, as though these his children were Danskers or Hollanders, without English.

However, children were not particularly interesting creatures, except as potential adults; especially girl children. Childhood, with its diseases and tears and tantrums, was something to be got over as soon as possible. The most desirable attribute in any child was precocity; and, Will hoped and suspected, Hamnet was precocious. So, perhaps, was Susanna. Poor Judith certainly wasn't. Judith was going to remain a child for an unconscionable time; perhaps, he thought, looking at her eyes which, in her pasty face, were blank as two currants in an uncooked bun, perhaps all her life.

Frankly, he wished the children had been abed. Trying to talk to Anne in front of them was like acting a part on the stage. And he hadn't come home for that.

Anne, to his relief, said, "Susanna, take the twins, to play in the meadow."

"But mother," cried Hamnet, "has father brought us no gifts?"

Will said, "Do as your mother says, boy. There will be gifts anon."

They went, closing the door behind them. The outside door slammed. The children swept past the window, like wind-driven leaves. Anne said, "They are good children. Susanna is already quite the lady." She smiled, a little mockingly. "I think the Arden blood – "

"Oh, Anne," he murmured. "Wife" – grabbing her to him. They stared at each other, gravely, almost blindly, their eyes too filled with love for seeing. They turned, together, and went up, trembling and silent, to the low-ceilinged bedroom, with the sparrows chirping in the eaves, and the light filtering through the thatch-hung window, and the warm, deep bed, and warmer, deeper, flesh, in the best welcome of all, the best coming-home; while the children shouted at play in the meadow, in the long, slow, drowsy afternoon.

Henley Street was much the same. William Wedgwood, the tailor, still seemed to be in business, Will noted, in spite of having two wives, and quarrelling with the neighbours, and his naughty goings-on generally. And Bradley, a rival glover. And Draper Whateley. Will remembered, nostalgically, the beehives in Alderman Whateley's garden, and the smell of the stored honey and wax and pears and apples – the smell, he had thought as a boy, of the slow centuries of rustic England – in the Alderman's apple chamber high up under the roof. And Hornby's smithy, whose dramatic contrasts of flame and shadow had so often fascinated the loitering Grammar schoolboy. They were all there. And had been. Will had lived in London, the Armada had come and gone, queens (one Queen anyway) had died young and fair, plague had emptied the cradle and the settle, and gone away, and come again, a whole world of monk-ridden superstition had passed away, a new world of thought and learning had exploded in men's minds; and Henley Street went on, untouched, unchanging. Henley Street would always go on. Men would want suits, women their gewgaws, horses need shoeing. With the new discoveries, the world, even the universe, was changing before men's eyes. But some things would always be needed: the midwife, the cooking-pot, the marriage-bed, the grave – and the Henley Streets of the little towns of England.

But if time passed Henley Street by, it did not pass its householders by. For here were his parents, hurrying joyfully to meet him. And the years had marked them. Father was slow, and paunchy. Mother was grey, she too a little slow.

He held out his arms. "Mother! Father!" He kissed them both fondly.

"Oh, Will," said his mother, smiling, laughing, folding his arm in hers. "And where is Anne?"

"She said you must see me first alone. She will bring the children later."

"Oh, she is such a sweet woman, your wife. I have grown very fond of her, Will."

"And she of you, mother. And of you, father. Except that you spoil the children."

"Someone has to. I sometimes think she is overstern with them, Will."

"Which comes of being mother and father both," Mary said tartly. But she would not spoil this joyful homecoming. Besides, it was none of her business. And Anne was content – and Will knew what he was about.

Will felt the slight stab. He was painfully vulnerable to criticism. But now they had come into the house. And here to greet him were his brothers, wary, suspicious, ill at ease: Gilbert, ungainly and shambling, loud of laugh and voice, who seemed to speak with his tongue rolled back in his throat; Richard, shy; Edmund, not much older than Susanna, a pretty, vain boy. Will embraced them all fondly and humbly. And now here was his sister Joan, jigging in in her best. "Why, brother Will, come to tell us of the London fashions." She hugged him gaily, and he hugged her back. He was fond of Joan. She was like sunlight on water. His father said, "Sit down, Will. Now, a cup of sack? I do not touch it myself nowadays" – he looked suddenly forlorn – "it is harmful to the spleen, I am told."

"One cup will not hurt you," said Mary. "We will all have a cup – now Will has come home."

John looked at her gratefully. And poured the wine. Mary said, "Tell us about your life in London."

Nothing he would like better. "I have joined a band of players, mother. We perform at the Theatre at Shoreditch."

"*Your* plays?" For once, Mary was prepared to allow her maternal pride full rein.

"We are rehearsing – "

"Tell us about the cock fighting, Will," called Gilbert in his thick voice.

"Nay, I want to hear about the Court," said John.

Will said stiffly, "I have been neither to the Court nor the cock fighting." Then remembered himself. No airs, no graces while he was in Stratford. He said, trying to make up, "But they say the cock fighting pleases the Queen greatly, Gilbert."

Gilbert slapped his thigh, roared. "Aye. I warrant it does." He could apparently see more in this remark than the rest, for he went on laughing hugely.

But John Shakespeare was looking disappointed. "So. You are not at Court, Will."

"No, father. But I have been much to Southampton House. Henry – he that is the Third Earl – and I have become friends. Also my Lord of Essex." God forgive him, he didn't want to boast, but he did want to please the old man.

He had pleased him too. "My Lord of Essex." John rolled the name round his tongue, and absent-mindedly filled himself another cup. "They say – " But Joan cut in, clapping her hands. "Oh, I have seen his picture. A proper man, indeed. Tell us about him, Will."

"Nay, tell us about London," grumbled Gilbert. "Is it true the honest burghers change wives every night, turn and turn about?"

"I have not found it so, brother," smiled Will.

Gilbert looked disappointed. Mary said, "Your plays, Will. Tell us about your plays."

"Gladly, mother," he said eagerly. "Oh, they are pleasant trifles. Though" – he looked suddenly far away – "there is one, written but roughly as yet, about a man whose father's ghost bids him revenge him on his uncle. I – "

"God's wounds," said Gilbert. "I had liefer watch a hanging. Why don't you write a play like *Gammer Gurton's Needle*, Will? As bawdy a thing as ever I see. 'But belly God send thee good ale enough,'" he suddenly sang in his tuneless voice.

"Gilbert!" his mother said sharply. There was nothing of the Ardens about Gilbert. Shakespeare through and through, she thought. She turned to Will, smiled. "Take no notice of him, Will. He's for a jig, or a tale of bawdry, or he sleeps."

Will made a mental note. Mary smiled, put a hand on his arm. "Your plays, Will?"

"Would that be the *young* Earl of Southampton, Will?" said John, who had been ruminating. "The one that is ward to my Lord Burghley?"

"Yes, father."

The old man ruminated further. "Aye. Fancy that, wife. Our Will, knowing two earls. I trust you are courteous and remember your position, Will."

"Of course, father. My plays, mother. I have done three about Henry the Sixth and – "

The door opened. Little Hamnet burst in, followed by Susanna; then by Anne, holding Judith by the hand. "Why, the pretty imp," cried John, as Hamnet knelt before him for his blessing. "The pretty, pretty imp." Mary rose, smiling, took her daughter-in-law's hands. "My dear, is it not good to have him home again?" The two women smiled fondly, and rather sadly, at each other: Anne hearing the clock ticking away the precious hours, Mary thinking, I shall never get him to myself, now. And there was so much I wanted to know, so much that he would tell only me; remembering that night, so long ago it seemed, when he had come home to marry Anne, and she had sat talking by the embers, closer than she had ever been to this sweet, yet somehow strange, son of hers.

It was a real family party, eleven people in the low hot room, with cakes and kickshaws, and the children chasing and weeping and laughing, and Gilbert, who, with his guffaws and his ungainliness, could single-handed make any room seem overcrowded, and Richard and Edmund flaring and flailing in sudden anger.

To most Elizabethans, the press and the crowding and the tumult would have been very heaven. But not to Will. The Stratford gossip – neighbour Wedgwood's naughty doings, the price of bread, the chance of plague this year – meant nothing. He fell silent; and was soon ignored, except for loving glances from his wife, and appraising glances from his mother.

He wanted to join in. He was the last man to want to sit and be superior. But he couldn't. He had lost the art of trivialities.

And he wasn't used to being ignored. Nowadays, in London, when William Shakespeare spoke, men listened. And when he didn't speak, they sought his opinion. He felt most uncomfortable, sitting mumchance. His mind turned to London. They'd be half-way through the performance now. The hired men would be going round with the bottled beer, the quinces, things would be livening up, a scuffle among the groundlings, a hand flying to a dagger among the gentry. And then: the next act, and everything suddenly stilled. The entire audience rapt, staring, lost in wonder, eager as children to find out what was to do; then joining in – an appreciative roar of laughter, heavenly sound to actor or play writer, thrice heavenly to one who was both; or a mounting exasperation with some dolt on the stage; half the audience eventually shouting to tell him that he is being duped; or the hush as the dagger comes through the arras, behind the unsuspecting victim's back. Then, when they could bear the suspense no longer, the cries: "Watch thy back, Master Burbage." "Turn thee around, man." God, this was life. Authors, actors, housemen, audience, all utterly absorbed and carried away by a tale of make-believe. Each, for an afternoon, making his contribution to something that had not happened with this intensity since the ancient Greeks. *That* was life, and away from it he would sicken and die. He must go back. A few more days, for Anne's sake. Then he would be off. He had no place here, anymore. And no one except Anne would really notice whether he went or stayed. And his mother, of course. He caught her glance across the room. She smiled, and waved her fingers. She had a clever face, he thought. One day he would write – He crossed the room, put an arm about her shoulders, rubbed his cheek against hers. "One day, mother, I will write a play about a woman like you – clever, witty, high-born."

She was delighted; especially by the high-born. "And what will you call her?"

He was silent. something was happening that she had known so many times. It was as though a shutter came down. One second, he was easy going, laughter-loving Will. The next he was aloof, almost arrogant, withdrawn into a world of his own, his eyes seeing nothing of the things before him. Then, suddenly he was back, with a smile flashing like lightning. "A *pretty* name, mother. What you will, so it be pretty: Rosalind, or Portia perhaps. Olivia."

She was entranced. "Speak the names again, Will."

Surprised, and pleased, he did so. The soft syllables hung on the air like the droplets of moisture in September mist. She put a hand on his. "When you were a little boy, and I touched your lips with honey to stop you weeping, I little thought – the honey would remain so long."

He smiled. And was away again. Olivia! A lovely, liquid name. Someone who loves an Olivia, and – halloos her name to the hills, no, to – the reverberate hills, that was good, halloo thy name to the reverberate hills, cry out, Olivia. Oh, that was good, he ought to be writing, not listening to this bibble-babble all around him.

His mother said, "Be careful, Will. The company of men like Essex and Southampton can singe a poor moth's wings."

"I know," he said. He too had thought of this. And so, of course, had Anne. "Will, do not fly too high," she had murmured in his sleeping ear. "Men like Essex make me afraid. As did Leicester, rightly as it happened."

He had stirred, and wakened to the river mist pressing white against the window, and soothed away her fears. But she was right. And his mother was right. When men like Essex fell, they brought down a great edifice with them; not of stones and mortar but of men. Yet what could he do? A poet befriended by a noble lord ceased to attend the lord at his peril. Besides, he needed patronage. And in many ways Southampton attracted him as no one else had ever done. Already, he was looking on the nineteen-year-old boy as a charming, wayward, petulant son; as, one day perhaps, he would look on Hamnet when the lad reached a more interesting age. Southampton, except for flashes of arrogance which only made his usual behavior seem the more attractive, treated Will like a revered father with whom, nonetheless, one could jest and play the fool. It was the most rewarding relationship of Will's life.

And yet? Friendship with Southampton meant friendship with Essex. And Essex was a different matter. Will was both attracted and repelled by him. Southampton, for all his petulance and arrogance, was not dangerous. Essex was. Essex combined great personal magnetism with a wild unruly temper. The question was, where would he lead them?

Suddenly, in a summer's dawn in Stratford, Will had seen, with dreadful clarity, the matted locks of men who had once been quick and gay as Essex and Southampton, before the word *treason* blistered their soft lips. And he had wanted to stay, here in the comfort of Anne's arms, here under the crouching ceiling of his Stratford home, forever.

But he knew it could not be. He could no more stay in Stratford than he could wear the breeches he had worn as a child. These were his people, and he loved them. But his soul was struggling desperately to take wing, while they would spend their lives happily earthbound. He had to go, even though a part of him longed to stay safely earthbound too.

Yet, for Anne's sake, he stayed on.

Sometimes, when they walked with the children by the river, or sat, alone together, after supper, she would forget the ticking of the clock, and feel a warm happiness, such as she had never known, fill her whole being; telling herself how foolish it was to spoil the present by forever bracing oneself against the bully-boy blows of the future. But then bedtime would come, and she would be sad, knowing another happy day had gone to join its fellows, and that her little store was dwindling.

And one day Will said, "Anne, I am but a poor father. Hamnet is my son and heir, and I scarcely know the lad. Dress him in his best, and let him accompany me on my walk."

They set off. And Will said, "See, there is a water rat. See his bright eye, his long whiskers. Is he not pretty?"

Hamnet said, "He is a rat. An I had a stone, I would dash his brains out – an he had any brains."

Will said, "I am glad I am no rat. Else would you dash my brains out."

The boy thought this very funny. Will said, "Why should you kill a rat, and not a man?"

"You are my father. If I killed my father, I should go to Hell fire."

"I think the rat would not approve your reasoning."

They walked on. Hamnet thought his father a strange man, all this about a rat. It must be living in London that softened people's minds. Nevertheless, he found he rather liked him. It was pleasant having a man about the place. As the only man in a feminine household, he himself had a great deal of responsibility, and, though he would never have admitted it, it was a relief to be able to share it. He slipped his hand comfortably into his father's. "Women are tedious creatures," he sighed.

"Are they?" said Will, who thought them anything but tedious. "You will not always find them so, Hamnet."

"Frightened of their own shadows. I do not think," said Hamnet thoughtfully, "that I am afraid of anything in the whole wide world."

"Not even of Grandmother Hathaway?"

"A *little*, perhaps, of Grandmother Hathaway. But of no one else."

"You are a brave imp," said Will. Suddenly, he knew one of those rare moods of happiness when past and future fall away, and the present is a crystal orb of perfection. The Warwickshire flowers were all about his feet. King cups and yellow irises stood up in the water meadows, the green reeds waved like swords, swans sailed, proud as Lucifer, on sweet Avon; and in his hand was the warm, living hand of his son, in his ears the boasting prattle of his sturdy son. God, it was good to stand foursquare on English soil. It was good to have a strong son. It was good to have a loving wife at home, cooking the dinner; good to have a home where you were Will, father, and had what you were given, and found it good. Not Master Shakespeare, the lodger, will you take a glass of wine with your supper, Master Shakespeare? London, the noble Essex, the noble Southampton, all seemed artificial. *This* was where he belonged, feet planted on this red earth, his son by his side. He moulded his hand round the fair head, pressed it to him. "Do you like having your father at home, imp?"

"Yes, father."

"Why?"

"The women are so fearful. It is good to have another man in the house, to soothe their fears."

"Oh, Hamnet," he said laughing. "They have no need of a coward like me, when they have you."

"You are no coward. You must be the bravest man that ever lived, father."

Will sighed. He would have liked it to be true. "Why, Hamnet?"

"Because you are my father."

They walked on in silence. The noontide stillness was all about them. The dragon-flies shimmered and darted over the Avon, the willows dreamed, there was the scent of growing green things. While in London – stench, filth, noise.

A respected glover, a respected father, a loved husband; friends: the Walkers, the Sadlers, the Quineys; good, solid tradesmen, with their careful wives, the cream of Stratford society. All this could still be his. O God, methinks it were a happy life – A big fish lording it in a little pond. Whereas in London – a minnow among carp: carp with savage teeth.

But of course there could be no question. And that night he spoke the words Anne had been dreading. "I must go back to London, Anne. There is much to do."

She paled. "When, Will?"

"Tomorrow."

So soon? You have ticked away to fell purpose, clock. Well, there was still this evening; and tonight, smothered together in bedclothes and darkness under the loving thatch. Nights were long, if you did not sleep, and tonight she must not sleep, waking would be too bitter to be borne. She must clasp her Will-o'-the-Wisp in her arms the long night through. For in the morning he would dance away.

She said, sternly, "Last time you went, I said you must return often. And it has taken you four years. This time it must not be so long, Will."

"I intend to come again soon."

"Soon?" Her heart leapt.

"Next summer. I have things planned. If all goes as I expect, I shall be in a position to – to take a holiday."

Next summer. It was sooner than she expected. Yet it was a lifetime. "And if all does *not* go as you expect – "

"I shall still get away. There will be plague, or riots. Something will give the magistrates a reason to close the theatres."

"So I must pray for plague, or riots?" she said tartly.

He looked forlorn. He came and knelt before her, buried his face in her lap. "Oh, Anne, Anne, I have been a poor husband to you. And you have never reproached me."

She clasped his head tight between her hands. "I have nothing to reproach you with. I knew how it would be. I knew I was marrying no ordinary man."

He looked up at her in astonishment. "But I *am* an ordinary man, wife."

"Are you?" she said. They stared at each other with a grave intensity. "I think you are," she said at last. "But you are also more besides. Much more. Something" – her shoulders sagged helplessly – "something a poor country woman like me could never understand. A sort of – splendour."

"Splendour? Me?" He laughed, putting on his thickest Warwickshire accent.

"I knew, always, that I should have to share you. There is too much of you for such as I. So – ?"

Will slept like a log. Anne watched the wheeling stars, and heard the cry of the night owl, and the hateful crowing of the cock. The day had come too soon. "O God! methinks it were a happy life, To be no better than a homely swain – "

Many hearts had a specially warm corner for sweet Will Shakespeare: his wife, his mother, Dick Field, his fellow players; even the wayward heart of Southampton. Yet now, suddenly, he had the most devoted admirer of them all: his son Hamnet.

After their walk together, the boy followed him round like a spaniel, gazed at him adoringly whenever he spoke. To Hamnet, brought up in a household of women, a man was someone like grandfather, old and foolish. To find a man who would run and play tag with one (when nobody was looking), *and* discuss women and rats with one as though one was grown up (as indeed one almost was), this was a revelation to the boy. And when he found that this *friend* – and whoever had imagined a father could be a friend? – when he found that this delightful companion was deserting him so soon, he was inconsolable. He didn't cry; that was for women. He just shut himself in an iron box of misery, and would speak to no one.

So, once again, Will took the London road: a more successful Will than last time; but less elated. Stratford was pulling at him. He had also an unaccountable sense of apprehension; like a climber, who looks back at the chasm beneath, and envies the crawlers in the valley who can never fall, even though they will never reach the summit.

He shrugged. It was due, of course, to the women's warnings about mixing with the mighty. But he could not shake it off. He looked back at peaceful Stratford, the smoke rising slow and untroubled in the morning air. Anne would be washing, his father setting out his stall, his mother deciding about dinner. Hamnet – ?

Aye. There was the rub. His love of the Warwickshire scene was woven into his very being – its flowers, and trees, the deer and the hares and the timid voles and mice, the singing birds – but now it had crystallised about the sturdy, vulnerable body of a small boy. Hamnet's pathetic devotion had won Will's heart. Fathers were to guide, reprove, chastise. Sons were to obey and show respect. This sudden love between them was something totally unexpected and delightful – yet it made returning to London all the harder.

And Anne? In the night Anne, usually so controlled, had clung to him and cried out, "Will, don't go! Don't leave me."

He had held her close, without a word, his heart breaking. He had to go. He knew it, she knew it.

CHAPTER 9

O! WHAT A ROGUE AND PEASANT SLAVE...

Robert Greene, MA Cantab., MA Oxon., died of a surfeit of that curiously fatal Tudor combination, Rhenish and pickled herrings.

He died as latterly he had lived – in unbelievable squalor.

As he lay dead, the rats flickered over his dead face, disturbing the flies. The fleas danced a jig on the rags that covered him.

When he died, his friend Cutting Ball spat. Since this was the only way of expressing emotion that Cutting Ball knew, it may be assumed that it expressed sorrow.

But the woman with whom he lodged went out into the lanes, and cut bay leaves; and made a garland; and set it about his head. So that, lying there in his filth, in a stinking room under the eaves, with the death carts rattling outside, and washed by his woman's tears, he might yet have been a poet of ancient Rome, crowned in the market place.

He died, hating the human race. It was unfortunate that his resentment fastened curiously on one of the most amiable of that race, a man in whom was no unkindness: William Shakespeare.

Yes. It was all "Sweet Will", "Gentle Master Shakespeare". Everybody loved him. And he revelled in it. *Richard III* was a great success. So was *Titus Andronicus*. But of course they were only plays, written in snatched hours at the theatre or while waiting for a meal at his lodgings. It was his poem, *Venus and Adonis*, that really occupied his mind and his talents. That was where reputation lay. Besides, he had a bold device for the poem that would kill three birds with one stone: repay a debt of gratitude, increase the sales of his book, and enhance his own prestige.

But in one quarter he was not "Sweet Will". One day, entering the tavern for a reading, he found the players already assembled; with Kempe, the clown, reading to them with sardonic enjoyment.

They were embarrassed when they saw him. Burbage leapt to his feet. "Why, Will." Condell looked up at him with evident pity. Heminge, ill at ease, drew up a stool. Only Kempe, crouched over the table, leered up gleefully. "So. Did you know you were mentioned in Robert Greene's will – Will?"

He was silent. Greene was on his conscience. He had come back from Stratford determined that the first thing he would do would be to visit Greene, apologise, have a night's drinking with him.

But there was always so much to do that must be done today. He would have to leave Greene to tomorrow. And tomorrow. Until, suddenly, he heard with a sick heart that Greene had run out of tomorrows. Greene was dead, and Will's churlishness must remain forever unshriven.

But a will? Greene, it was said, had died in extremes of poverty and squalor. No. Will knew by Kempe's pallid, gloating face that there were no benefactions in this document.

214

Kempe handed it to him with a mocking flourish.

It was a printed pamphlet, with a crisp title, *Greene's Groatsworth of Wit Bought with a Million of Repentance*. It viciously warned his fellow scholars against the players; and with all the venom of a dying and destitute man, robbed of the fruits of his wit and learning by an ignorant yokel, he attacked "an upstart crow that supposes he is as well able to bombast out a blank verse as the best of you; and being an absolute Johannes Factotum, is in his own conceit the only Shake-scene in a country."

It was cruel. It was monstrously unfair. Will remained silent. A blow on the face could not have left him more hurt and bewildered. Will Kempe squirmed round in his chair, ledged his arms across its back and his chin on his arms. "Well, Master Shake-scene?" he gloated.

"Quiet, Kempe," snapped Burbage. He was a good man, and hated unfairness and cruelty. And he liked and respected Shakespeare. Besides, he had a company to hold together. He couldn't afford to have either a popular clown or a very useful Johannes Factotum like Shakespeare killed in a brawl. And now that Greene had died untimely, London was short of men who could knock a passable play together. It looked as though this Shakespeare, whether he was capable or not, might have to fill a considerable gap.

Will looked at them all. He saw friendship, encouragement, pity in their eyes. In all except Kempe's. There he saw something like a glittering hatred as the clown, watching him closely, said, "And is our Shake-scene invited to the wedding of Master Alleyn and Mistress Joan Woodward next month? After all, the bridegroom should be grateful to him. Shake-scene's *Harry the Sixth* will have supplied the wedding breakfast – aye, *and* the bride's dowry."

It was a clever speech, reminding them that he had not always been their sweet Will.

But Kempe had not finished. Now he said, musingly, "But perchance our Ned will not be so grateful. Perchance he will find the pool has already been paddled in."

A rage, such as he had never known, surged though Will. Why, the last time he'd met Joan Woodward she had been an exquisite child of twelve, he a grown man. The foulness of the remark sickened him.

What sort of man, he wanted to demand of Kempe, do you think I am? But there were certain remarks to which etiquette allowed no spoken answer: only a snatched and upraised dagger. Will, determined to be a gentleman at all costs, fumbled his dagger out of his belt and raised it above that mocking face. And, in spite of his anger, was immensely relieved when Condell pinioned his arms behind his back and Burbage wrenched the weapon from his reluctant fingers.

Silence, as Condell released his arms. Silence, as Burbage sternly handed back the dagger. Silence, as he slowly backed away from them and out of the room. Their eyes, cold as stones, had all been upon him. He had been weighed in the balance, and found wanting. Sweet Will was a man of straw, a swaggering poltroon. Gentle Shakespeare was *too* woman-gentle. Not one of them but thought Will Kempe's visage would have been vastly improved by a dagger hole in the cheek. And Will, given a heaven-sent opportunity, had let them down. Besides, everyone enjoyed a good brawl. It was meat and drink to them. They were disappointed in him.

Will went back to his lodgings to hide himself from the world. His fellow actors had seen him for what he was, they had seen through the charm and the friendliness to the true

Will Shakespeare: a coward whose fingers grew palsied at the mere thought of shedding blood; who was too lily-livered even to defend his own honour; who, all unknowing, had been hated and despised by a man whose good opinion he could now never win back. He looked at himself in the mirror with loathing. He had always thought of himself as the sturdy yeoman with the poet's face. But those smooth, oval features, with the deep, sensitive eyes – take away the scrag of beard and what had you? A woman's face, weak as water. No wonder they all despised him! No wonder Greene had died with contempt in his heart. Oh, it was pitiful. A country grammar-school boy, imagining he could pit his brains against university men like Greene and Marlowe, could ruffle it with Sir This, my Lord of That. Well, his pride had been taught a sharp lesson. All London would be chuckling over Greene's "upstart crow". He would not dare to show his face. Nobody loved him who basked in being loved; except Anne, sweet Anne; and little Hamnet. He would enjoy some of Hamnet's adulation at this moment. The child, at least, loved him. Out of the mouths of babes –

Stratford! He was filled with a homesickness that was a physical ache. The trees would be turning already. Anne would be getting in the logs for winter, making everything secure. Safe, quiet, homely. God, he would give all he had, just to walk down Chapel Lane, just to stroll beside the quiet river, his son's hand trustingly in his. Why had he ever left such a haven of peace for this cruel, harsh London? He would have been a respected citizen there. Why, he might even have taken civic office, like his father. That would have been *solid* achievement. What, after all, were a few lines of poetry, an entertainment for the groundlings, an afternoon spent mouthing another man's lines? An actor, a rogue and vagabond still, detested by the City Fathers, driven and persecuted by them! What a profession on which to build one's life!

All that winter he stayed in the dumps. London was cold, snow hung about for weeks; not the clean, exquisite snows of Warwickshire, draping the trees in samite: but smutched and wet, stained by the filth of the streets. Rooms, more than a yard from the fire, were damp and dank as charnel vaults; day after day, dawn was a grudging lifting of the murk, sunset a sullen thickening of the gloom. Scurvy was rampant. The only creatures that seemed to thrive on the chill dampness were fleas and lice; and since scratching through four pairs of woollen stockings and two pairs of quilted breeches was largely ineffectual, an itch could drive a man to twitching exasperation. Tempers grew thin, and snapped. It was a winter of cold thaws and sleet, that most cheerless of all precipitations. It was a foul winter. Everybody said so. But for William Shakespeare it was fouler than for most. Despite the balm of a most generous apology from the publisher, the bitter wound Greene had given him refused to heal. There was only one comfort. If – as seemed unlikely – this surly, sodden earth ever managed to awake to the miracle of April, then *Venus and Adonis* would be published. And if that failed – and in his present mood he felt it was likely only to remind men of Greene's attack – if that failed there was only one way to restore his confidence: back to Stratford, and the glover's shears.

It was a bad winter in Stratford too. Avon sprawled apathetically across the countryside and seeped miserably into some of the low-lying cottages. The children sniffed and snuffled, passing round colds in a dreary game of catch-as-catch-can. Prices rose while spirits sank. Anne felt the cold and damp getting into her bones. For once, her solid acceptance of life forsook her. She began to look on the other housewives of Chapel Lane with something like envy. They had husbands to get the logs in, to clear the snow, to share the worry about the children's ailments. Their husbands didn't feel the need to go and lord it with the mighty in London. Besides, writing plays and poetry; it was a very peculiar way to earn a living. There were many in Stratford, she knew, who connected it vaguely with lying, loose-living, and even witchcraft. Why couldn't she have had a respectable husband, like the rest? Resentment was new to Anne. She hated it. It weighed on her like a physical malaise. It was one with the dark days and the damp rising through the kitchen floor and the unrelenting cold.

John Shakespeare, too, was being a bit of a burden to his nearest and dearest. Will's visit had left him vaguely disappointed. Will not at Court, still wearing homespun? Good stuff, it was true. But still homespun. Will without much to say for himself? John had expected a son, swaggering in the latest London fashions, who would have kept the table in a roar with his tales of Court life. "A should have stayed in Stratford," he muttered over and over again, crouched by the fire in his old gown, holding out his plump, mittened hands to the warmth. "A should have stayed a glover. A was a good glover."

Mary let him maunder on. Will had to go his own way, for success or disaster. But Will could have had his own farm by now, he could have been treading Arden land, deep-rooted in Warwickshire soil, a gentleman of worship like her father. She too felt depression gnawing at her with the cold.

But April came at last, as it comes to the most unlikely of winters. And with April came, for Anne, the realisation that Will's promised summer visit was not far off; and for Will there was Richard Field's beautifully produced *Venus and*

Adonis that was to bring him fame and fortune at last. Or so he hoped.

"I wondered, my lord. Would you graciously accept a small gift from your servant?" Will Shakespeare bowed deeply.

Southampton looked surprised, then a little weary. Tradesmen, hangers on, literary men seeking patronage, were always giving him little gifts. And it became so tedious. What could anyone, except perhaps the Queen, afford to give him he did not possess already? Yet he was too kind a person at heart not to feign pleasure.

Of course, he didn't mind the gifts being cheap. But they were always so tasteless. Frankly, he was a bit surprised at ancient Will joining the ranks of the present-givers. He'd thought Will would have more sense.

He opened the package. A book. *Venus and Adonis, by Wm Shakespeare.* So? Ancient Will was spreading his wings with a vengeance. He turned to the title page. "To the Right Honourable Henry Wriothesley, Earl of Southampton... I know not how I shall offend in dedicating my unpolished lines to your lordship... "

Will, watching with a fearful anxiety, saw the brows draw together, saw the impatient sweeping of the golden locks away from the face, sure sign of anger. Southampton went on reading the dedication. Then he looked at Will, furious. "This was ill done, sir."

"But, my lord, you liked the piece well."

"You should not have dedicated it to me without my permission. It was a liberty."

Will was trembling. Those who took liberties with earls made themselves a thorny bed indeed. His lips felt dry and cracked. "I do assure you, my lord, I had no thought but to give your lordship pleasure, to show my gratitude – "

"It must be withdrawn."

Will's whole mouth was dry. "Copies have already been sold, my lord. I should have shown your lordship sooner, only – your lordship was at Titchfield."

"Damnation." My lord slouched in his chair, scowling, biting his lip. Will had a picture of a man and his little son strolling together beside the unhurried Avon. That, he thought bitterly, could still have been his, but for over-reaching ambition, the sin that brought down Lucifer.

Oh, what a presumptuous fool he had been! Having nothing to say – there was nothing he *could* say – he hung his head. When he dared to look up at last, the anger was still in Southampton's eyes. But Will thought he saw another emotion – contempt.

Now an earl was an earl. God had set him above the common sort, as surely as He had set the sun to rule by day and the moon by night. An earl was a sure and certain part of that God-given universal order and degree that Will so much revered.

But, to Will, a poet also had a standing in the hierarchy. So, by God, had an Arden. Contempt, perhaps, for a fool whose presumption had led him by the nose. But when that fool also happens to be Master Arden Shakespeare, Poet and putative Gent., then contempt should be tempered, my lord. He said, "Sir, you do me much wrong. I thought merely to give your lordship pleasure."

"And sell more copies of your book?" the Earl said shrewdly. "*And* tie your – if I may say so – somewhat plebeian name to that of Southampton."

"*Plebeian!*" Will was really stung. "My father applied for a Grant of Arms, my lord."

"And had it refused, I do not doubt." But the contempt had gone from the eyes, though the anger remained. "Master

Shakespeare, like a strumpet you have pinned my name to a child that is not mine. You and I, sir, have nothing further to say to one another." He picked up his book, and began reading.

Will Shakespeare bowed low, and backed in silence to the door, where a servant came to his rescue and let him out of Southampton House. So this, he thought sadly, was the end of William Shakespeare, poet. A poet who had offended one of the nobility might as well burn his pens. No printer would dare to print anything of his again. The sensible thing was to go back to Stratford, while the family business was still there.

That was a terrible year for plague.

Eleven thousand people knew the despair of finding the bubo under the armpit, of knowing that nothing in this world awaited them now but a dreadful death and a perfunctory burial. For those, and they were many, who also feared that some peccadillo or some error of doctrine had condemned them to everlasting fire, the outlook was unpleasant indeed.

The theatres were shut. Will, unable to act; unable, for once, to take any interest in his writing; Will hung wretchedly about his lodgings. And finally, almost without volition, set off for Stratford.

He was still sore from his wounds. Anne soothed them with her love. The countryside enfolded him to its quiet breast. It was a wet summer; but he and Hamnet sat for hours under the dripping eaves, poring over a Book of Wonders, both father and son learning a great deal about the natural world around them: about a dolphin's love of music, and how the amiable creature rejoices to be addressed as "Simon"; about the gentlemanliness of lions, who have to be very hungry indeed before they will attack a woman; about the delicate feeling shown by panthers, and the innate courtesy of dragons; all these things attested by the most sober and reputable travellers. They also learned of less happy creatures, sent as signs of God's displeasure: the monstrous pig of Hampstead, a pig born with hands at Charing Cross, the terrible Black Dog of Bungay, the Headless Bear of Ditchet (though there was some reason to believe that this last was the Devil in disguise; several of the witnesses had caught a distinct whiff of sulphur).

It was heady stuff. Hamnet vowed that when he grew up he too would be a traveller, and find even stranger dragons, even more dreadful pigs. And Will? It confirmed Will's view of a fascinating, ordered universe, infinitely enriched yet infinitely bedevilled by that creature, man: noble, excellent, execrable, villainous man; pitiful, suffering, sorrowful man; man wallowing like a pig in the muck, or soaring to the stars; laughing, rejoicing, weeping, bleeding, dying man. Thank God, thought the writer of plays, for his infinite complexity.

Man's life: that was what he must write about. The pity of it, the tragedy of it, the nobility, the striving; man brought to destruction, not by blind fate but by some flaw in himself. Man against Man, Man against men, on the long, rearguard action to the grave. Death? Oh, the groundlings would want their deaths; but it was life that mattered. And, in all this, not to forget the other part: the sparkle of wit, the laughter of the taverns. Must a man still laugh, then, though the death carts creak through the infected night, and the husband gazes despairing at his fevered wife, and the mother clasps her tormented child? Yes; because mankind, beset by pestilence and darkness and devils and damnation, by hunger and the itch, by terror and pain; by, worst of all, the cruelty of his fellows; mankind *could* still laugh. It was the unfailing miracle, greater even than the miracle of spring.

This time he went back to London eager, his fingers twitching for his pen. In Stratford he had been able to stand outside himself, take a long look at himself and his life. And he had learnt: that, for a writer, it is what is inside himself that matters; not the accidents of everyday, or even the wrath of princes. That his mind is an everturning mill; and that all experience, pleasant and painful alike, is grist to it.

He was proud, too, of his relationship with his children. Despite all his efforts, poor Judith still gazed at him as fearfully as though he were old Harry the Bear. But Susanna was a thin, long-legged ten-year-old now; at one moment a singing child, the next a young woman teasing and provocative towards this flattered male creature, so that Anne noted with shame within herself some needle pricks of jealousy.

But he was most happy about his son. Hamnet was his devoted slave. Father and son were inseparable companions. Will was surprised and pleased by the warmth of his love for this ridiculous, strutting manikin. "Goodbye, Hamnet," he had said, laying both hands in blessing on the fair head. "Take care of the womenfolk while I am gone."

"Aye. That I will, father." Adoration in the brown eyes. Will said, "It is a grave responsibility I lay on you. Not too heavy for your young shoulders?"

"No, father." He had raised himself on to his toes, sunk back on to his heels, flexed his muscles. He would take on the world. Oh, to be young, and unafraid, thought Will. Not to be aware of one's own helplessness, one's awful vulnerability.

The boy ran beside his horse all the way across Clopton Bridge; then fell back, panting, grinning, waving. Will waved, with a sad heart. But five minutes later his mind was completely absorbed in his profession: Burbage wanting a history, the groundlings blood, Kempe a jig (well, Master Kempe could write his own jigs; he never kept to the script, anyway) and himself itching to rewrite the thing for which there was never time, the thing that no one wanted: the Hamlet; which, like his saddle bag, would hold everything he cared to put into it. Murder, incest, love, a notable ghost, pirates, warres and battells, his own views on acting; a garrulous old fool (no, *not* his father; he would never have that), and the flawed marble of a noble spirit; the flaw so little, yet so tragic. One day. One day, when people stopped pestering him. One day, he would take paper and write: Hamlet, Prince of Denmark. Act I. Scene I. Elsinore. A Platform before the Castle…

It was like a roll of drums in his head. His scalp prickled. Shivers ran down his spine. His writing-fingers itched. One day. Whether anybody wanted it or not, one day he *had* to write Hamlet.

Chapter 10

And bitter shame hath spoil'd the sweet world's taste...

The pestilence raged on. The theatres stayed shut. The players scattered to the provinces. The rain fell remorselessly. Performances in inn yards often had fewer in the audience than on the stage. Money was tight, valuable costumes became soaked. So did the players. Will very sensibly sat snug in his London lodgings, protected (obviously effectively) from the plague by a gift from his mother, a decayed object said to be one of St Luke's molars, worn round his neck in a silk bag.

And he wrote, and wrote and wrote.

Then, to his delight and alarm, he received a letter from Southampton, curtly summoning him to Titchfield, the Earl's house in Hampshire.

He went.

The Earl received him very formally. And said, stiffly, "In view of the success of your poem, Master Shakespeare, I have decided to overlook your presumption."

Will bowed deeply. "I thank my lord."

Southampton lolled in his chair, staring at Will arrogantly. Then, with the suddenness that characterised him, he grinned. "I was too hard on you, ancient Will. Why, half the Inns of Court men sleep with your poem under their pillows. I am the most envied of men."

"Your lordship is too kind."

"Oh, Will, why so stiff? Come. Stay with us at Titchfield. We will hunt together, and you shall write me more pretty poems, to fill my friends with envy."

Impetuously Will stepped forward and kissed the young man's hand, as he might have kissed the hand of a prince or a saint. "I will write you such a poem as shall set all England talking," he said devoutly.

Nor was it an idle boast. Most of the poem was written already.

The great house dreamed in the late summer days. The Earl was a capricious, but usually charming, host. Other guests came and went; witty, wealthy, powerful, they treated this quiet friendly Master Shakespeare with careful respect. Obviously, he was not one of them. Equally, he was obviously not a servant or even a secretary, for he was placed high at the table, and was a constant companion of Southampton.

There were rumours, of course. It was said he was a player, aping the gentleman. (Really, Henry picked up such strange friends!) It was said: his father was a provincial tradesman, and he himself had a wife and ten children tucked away in a Midlands hovel. It was said: he had been the laughing stock of London, something that that lewd wag Greene wrote. But to some, of course, he was sweet Master Shakespeare, the witty author of *Venus and Adonis*, and they treated him with reverence and warm affection. These were the London men. The Hampshire landowners had never heard of either Venus, Adonis, or William Shakespeare, and were at a loss accordingly.

As for William, he fitted in curiously well. He might have been born to great houses. His natural courtesy, added to his acute observation of the ways of others, helped him not to offend. Good manners came natural to him. Nevertheless, he watched his neighbour intently, so that when it came to something he had not experienced, like the use of forks at table, or the latest flourish to a bow, he was always prepared. No one was going to find William Shakespeare, grandson to Robert Arden, Gent., countrified.

Will revelled in it all: the beauty and splendour of his surroundings, the wit, the fashion, the deference shown him by the Inns of Court men, his wary acceptance by the nobility, the guests' unflagging, unrelenting zest for living. The appalling summer had given way to a golden autumn, day piled on slumbrous day. So, while London sweated out the plague, Will and his new friends played bowls under a sky of blue gauze, and shot their arrows at gay targets in a ride of the forest, and rode, thundering across the dreaming parklands, and danced, and diced the night away. But when they hunted the hare, or the pretty deer, Will pleaded work. He was coming, gropingly, to the conclusion that there was enough pain in the world without his adding to it.

It was a far cry from the Players. It was an even farther cry from Stratford, and Anne, and the cottage in Chapel Lane. He was sensible enough to realise that it was no more than a pleasant interlude. His place was in the theatre, botching up a play, trailing a pike, selling bottled beer, even nailing a loose board. Not for nothing, he thought wryly, had Robert Greene called him Johannes Factotum.

It was time to go; but each autumn day was like a cornucopia, overflowing with golds and ochres and russets, with a fading, dying blue. Besides, Southampton had become such a delightful companion; and now, just when Will had decided to tell him he must leave, something else happened.

It wasn't much. The flick of a skirt at the bend of a corridor. A white hand, resting on a balustrade. Candlelight, on the sheen of a dark head. A woman's laugh, tinkling like glass behind an open door. Looking up in the dance, and finding two black eyes watching him thoughtfully, boldly meeting his glance.

It was disturbing. It was time to go. High time.

But he didn't go.

"Are you not Master Shakespeare? The author of *Venus and Adonis?*"

He bowed with a flourish. But his heart was pounding. She had suddenly appeared before him at the foot of an oaken staircase, in the dusk of the day. She stared at him unsmiling, never taking her eyes from his face; she made him feel that her interest in him, in every part of him, was absolute.

Yet she was no beauty. Her eyes and hair too black against the pallor of her face; her mouth wide and stretched, full-lipped, challenging. And no girl, either. An ageless woman. She might be his own age, older even.

And he was trembling.

She said, "Your Venus was a ninny, Master Shakespeare. Too much talk. *I* would have had the young man."

He bowed again. "I am sure, madam, he could not have resisted you."

Somehow, without apparent movement, she had come nearer. Her breast, under its carapace of jewelled brocade, touched his. He watched, fascinated, as her hand fondled the oak baluster. Her look was long, and level. "I have not Venus' charms, sir."

"That I find hard to believe." His lips were dry. "Without proof, madam."

"Proof?" The black brows arched. But not in anger. "You could – " She smiled mockingly.

"Yes?" It was a croak; the best he could manage.

She was silent. She seemed to be making up her mind. "Ask my Lord of Southampton," she finished coolly.

For a moment he stared at her. Then he grabbed her jewelled shoulders, dragged her to him, forced his mouth against hers. God, it was dangerous to play with a lord's toys, but for once caution had taken second place. By the time he had finished with her, love, honour, loyalty strewed the stage as in the last act of a tragedy. Only revulsion, self-hatred and fear remained. And memories: a terrible, unspeakable joy; the stars bursting in their courses; a whitely wanton, under the wanton moon.

He had been bewitched. That was his first thought.

Often enough he had been attracted by women. Lovely creatures, with laughing mouths and flesh like a ripe peach. But something had always come between him and them: loyalty, his sense of that universal order that must rule, not only the stars, but also his own life; and, most of all he strongly suspected, caution: the fear that giving himself to another woman, however secretly, might prove, too late, to have been the slow poison that would rot his marriage, his love for his children, his own warm regard for that model of gentlemanly behaviour, William Shakespeare, Gent.

And now? He had resisted a hundred swans, only to fall for a brown goose; a brown goose, moreover, belonging to a man he called friend. Will Shakespeare, who so admired loyalty, had been disloyal to his wife, his children, his friend and patron; above all, to himself. What had Dick Field said, all those years ago? If you were true to yourself, you could not betray anyone else. Something like that. He was filled with self-loathing. He must go, leave Titchfield at once.

But he didn't go.

She came and went mysteriously, like the mist in the autumn meadows, like the cloud on the hills.

It was always the same. He would hate, detest, fear her. But as time passed his longing would, not cancel, but overcome them all. His eyes would be hunting desperately for her everywhere; in the gardens, in the rooms and galleries, on the stairs. Longing would drive him nearly to madness. If he did not find her he would be consumed by it, like a paper twisting and writhing on the fire.

He would rake hungrily round the great house, yearning to find her, yearning *not* to find and be once again betrayed. And then, suddenly, when he was at breaking-point, she would be there, in front of him, standing close, silent, staring.

And she would empty him of honour. She would make of Will Shakespeare, Gent., an alley cat; sans love, sans thought, sans poetry, sans past and future; all drowned in an ineffable, despairing, desperate joy.

He never found out who she was, did not trouble even to learn her name. She was woman, Eve, Venus; dark-haired, black-eyed. And when at last the fever died, he knew that she had taught him much that he would have given a world not to know, about William Shakespeare, Gent. That he was *not* compounded all of courtesy and poetry and compassion. That he was *not* one of the best-ordered creatures in an ordered universe. That he was capable of disloyalty to a friend, unfaithfulness to a wife; not once, but every time a pair of not-very-beautiful eyes beckoned. He had assumed it

231

was probable that he would be seduced one day; you couldn't expect a poet to be able always to resist the loveliness of the creatures. But he had always assumed it would be by a woman whose beauty he found irresistible; that love and admiration would light the fuse – not loathing and fear.

Had the fire really died? It had been quenched, anyway. They had been standing, silent, in a way they had, not touching, just staring at each other, in a quiet corridor. Southampton had come along the corridor; and, not even glancing at Will, had put out a hand, and linked a finger in hers, and led her away.

She had followed, instantly obedient. Not a word was spoken, not a look exchanged. There was no backward glance. Will had been left standing foolishly in the corridor; and suddenly he was the poor player, befriended by an earl; the provincial tradesman's son, with thinning hair and a bit paunchy. Southampton's gesture of ownership was magnificent, unmistakable, and, to someone of Will's percipience, ominous. The dying fires were quenched. Will left Titchfield the following day.

The next time he visited Stratford he was laden with presents. Anne looked at him shrewdly. She never asked whether there were other women. Knowing Will better than he knew himself, she thought there probably were. But, in her country wisdom, she preferred not to know. All she said, laughing, was, "Is something on your conscience, husband?"

He looked, she thought, unhappy. Poor Will! He was an uneasy dissembler. Then he pulled himself together and grinned. "No, wife. But things are prospering. Dick Field has published my new poem, and my Lord of Southampton is vastly pleased with the dedication."

"What is it called?"

"*The Rape of Lucrece.*"

"Will!" She was horrified. As a country girl, she had a matter-of-fact view of these things. But rape was not a thing to write pretty, make-believe poetry about. It was nasty, brutish. There had been a Shottery girl – pretty and singing one day, broken and drooping the next. She wished he would more things like his *Harry the Sixth*. Even *Venus and Adonis* hadn't appealed to her. There were pretty things in it, like the poor hare, pretty country things, she told Will. But Venus should have been thoroughly ashamed of herself, talking like that to a young boy; and she was tedious withal.

"Tedious?" cried Will, who could accept most of life's ills with reasonable fortitude, but not adverse criticism. "Tedious? The Earl of Southampton did not think her so. Nor my Lord of Essex. Nor Dick Field."

"They are men; flattered no doubt by her yearnings. But ask any woman."

He asked his mother. "My dear Will, a fat goddess begging a young man to roll her in the hay? Of course she's tedious. Flesh-and-blood women have other ways, haven't you discovered that yet, my handsome son?"

He actually began to sulk. Mary's lower lip was outcurled with an amusement he knew so well. God, why had he come to this backwater? They appreciated him in London. He sought comfort from his own sex. "Father, have *you* read *Venus and Adonis*?"

"Read what, son?"

"*Venus and Adonis.* My poem."

He waited. The tumblers in John's mind fell into place slowly, these days. But they got there in the end. "The one dedicated to my Lord of Southampton? Yes. A fine dedication that, Will, respectful without being too obsequious. There is a balance in these things. I always found, when dealing with the nobility – "

"But the *poem*, father? Did you read the *poem*?"

John's mind began to drift away like an unmoored boat. "No, son. No. I have not read any poems."

"A fine, bawdy piece, that Venus," guffawed his brother Gilbert. "She would not have found *me* so backward, I warrant."

Only little Hamnet was on his father's side. "I vow father's book is the best poem ever writ," he said stoutly. Will loved his son more than ever, not even the fact that the child had read neither this nor any other poem could destroy his pleasure.

At long last, the plague began to recede. God's anger, it seemed, was abating.

But it had left its mark. Citizens who should still have been caught up in the cheerful bustle of the everyday sprawled in the death pits. The mother's breast, the father's hand, the child's smile had all been snatched away. Families had been sliced down the middle: this side to the grave, that side may go on living, but take care not to kindle God's anger a second time.

But the players weren't worrying about God's anger. Reluctantly, the magistrates had opened the theatres again, and there were costumes to be replaced, bellies, cheeks and coffers to be filled. It had been a lean time. A few provincial tours couldn't make up for the daily revenue of a London theatre. Some companies had gone out of business, others had merged.

Besides, a new threat was looming on their horizon. Burbage said, "Do you realise, men, the lease of the Theatre expires before long?"

"Giles Allen will renew," Kempe said comfortably.

"Yes. At his price, though. We're going to need money. Not only to cover our recent losses, but to prepare for the future."

And now, a time of the most intense activity. Burbage's company were thin-cheeked but happy. "We *must* have a play, Will. Something to pack in the groundlings."

"I've been doing some work on this revenge tragedy. The one about the man whose father's ghost – "

"God's death," cried Will Kempe. "Most of these people will have lost a wife, a son, a whole family. They've enough troubles of their own without taking on your man's. They want something to start them laughing again."

The others murmured in agreement. One day, thought Will morosely, they'll let me write something to please myself. He'd done *Lucrece* for the Earl, comedy for Kempe, sword-rattling for the groundlings. When were they going to let him write the things he wanted, those tragedies still vaguely stirring, vaguely heard in the far recesses of his mind, like distant thunder, like the tide roaring through unfathomed caves, like the beat of surf on an undiscovered shore? Now more than ever he needed to write them, now that his soul was in a torment of revulsion and self-loathing and, God forgive him, renewed longing. An absent and faithless husband, a neglectful father, a false friend, an unshriven sinner. He needed absolution – not from the Church but by a veritable bonfire of creation.

Instead, amiable and helpful as ever, he worked away at *The Taming of the Shrew, The Two Gentlemen of Verona, Love's Labour's Lost, Midsummer Night's Dream*. And was Master

Kempe grateful for all these comedies? Not a bit of it. It was all too literary for him. You didn't want all these damned *words* in a play. He sighed for the old, happy pre-Will days, when with a pig's bladder, a few bawdy gestures, a leer and a wink, you could keep the audience happy for a whole afternoon. Damn his quiddities and quibbles and conceits, his tortured puns. It had been, thought Will Kempe, a bad day for them all when "sweet" (he screwed up his face as at a sour apple) when "sweet" Will Shakespeare had charmed them all (all except him!) with his winning ways.

The others would not have agreed. Especially not John Heminge, the business manager, who realised more than the others how a performance of *Richard III* or *Titus Andronicus* swelled the takings; especially not Dick Burbage who, sensing his own growing strength as an actor, felt that Shakespeare was the man to provide the kindling for his fire. This new thing he was writing, for instance, *Richard II*. It had a part such as he had never even dreamed of: a part of infinite subtlety; a man being brought to the dirt by the flaws in his own personality. The part was not one man, but many. Here was arrogance, irresponsibility, profligacy, self-pity; a pathetic weakness leading in the end to a sort of despairing dignity. Here was something the world had never seen before. Your magnificent Tamburlaines, your Jews of Malta, became lay figures beside this poor, sad king.

A time of flux, a time of intense activity. The loose-knit band of players coalesced into the Chamberlain's Men. There had been Chamberlain's Men before, companies of players saved from the brand of vagabondage by the patronage of the Lord Chamberlain. Such patronage was common. The only way for a band of players to survive was to seek the patronage of a noble; and Leicester's, Strange's, the Admiral's Men were all respected actors' companies. But *this* company, they all felt with a high excitement, was something different. With an actor like Burbage, a business manager like Heminge, a protector as powerful as the Lord Chamberlain, with Kempe, who could bring the house down with a flicker of his eyebrow, with cheerful Shake-scene, the most useful man any theatre ever had, willing to knock up a play or blow the opening trumpet, or take a part at a moment's notice, or act as Guider for one of his own plays, or sell apples; with a growing and devoted audience; and with their own theatre in Shoreditch; the Chamberlain's Men breathed deep of the enthusiasm, the soaring optimism that was in the very air of England. A joyful gusto was in their daily work, their relations with their audience, their friendships, their quarrels, their acceptance of new plays, their pleasure in old ones. Days were too short, the mind too slow, the emotions too sluggish for life to be lived as it should be lived. But they did their best. It was a brave, swaggering, hurrying world.

Only at night, in the quietness of one's lodgings, did the mind's predators creep out from their holes: remorse, self-loathing, yearnings, longings, night-fears, night-terrors. By day: sweet Will, gentle Shakespeare. By night: a crawling, lusting worm.

Despite his lack of interest in religion, he expected chastisement for his sins. The fact that he now began to flourish like a green bay tree increased his doubts about divine justice. If anyone ought to have been carried off by the plague, he ought. Yet here he was, not only alive but with his plays being performed almost daily in London, his poems selling like hot cakes, men like Southampton and Essex and their circle pressing their friendship upon him. And now here to buttress his literary reputation was a fine pecuniary increase. He was invited, despite Kempe's querulous objections, to become a sharer in the Company. This meant that at each performance he received a share of the entrance money, a share of half the gallery money, but was required to help pay for the hired men, candles, musicians, boys. This just suited Will. Poet he might be. But he was a poet who knew the exact value of money; who loved the stuff, not for itself but for what it could buy in the way of gracious surroundings, honour and respect. And to be a sharer in a brilliant company; not only to know that his own income would keep pace with the company's, but also to have a considerable share in shaping policy, this was heady wine indeed. His thoughts returned to New Place, that most imposing of Stratford's houses. He even began negotiations to purchase. And, crowning symbol of his growing strength, he persuaded his father to do what, long ago and unsuccessfully, the old man had done before: apply for a Grant of Arms. The poor player would be a gentleman yet.

Will Shakespeare was on the crest of the wave. Or thought he was. But there was more to come. The greatest honour of all. The Chamberlain's Men were summoned to play at Court. At Christmas. They had reached the dizzy summit of their profession.

That was a bad Christmas in Stratford. Little Hamnet was seized with an unaccountable fever.

It was only a childish complaint, Anne told herself. Had it been poor little Judith she would not have thought twice about it. But the sturdy Hamnet, who never ailed! And, being a man, and unused to illness, he made the most of it. He railed, he wept, he prayed, he gave himself up for lost.

By Twelfth Night he was quite himself again, poring over his beloved *Book of Wonders*, clamouring to go out and run in the snow. But it had given Anne a fright, and brought home to her her loneliness. Will should have been here. Look at it how you would, a man should be at home at Christmas, a man should be home when his son was sick. And life was short, and slipping by. Whatever came after death (and a woman who had given herself before the marriage service couldn't, in the nature of things, expect much happiness in the next world), this life should surely hold some pleasure. Yet here she was, nearing forty; a woman who asked little of life; a woman, in fact, who asked only one thing to make life perfect, very heaven, and that one thing denied her: her husband.

But Will thought little of Anne, or Hamnet, or provincial Stratford that Christmas. Even the midnight searchings of his muddied soul were forgotten. Will was at Court.

True, he was not strutting it in the Presence Chamber. He and his fellow players were being looked after by Lord Hunsdon, the Lord Chamberlain, a fussy, anxious man who imagined that players, even *his* Players, had little regard for, and less knowledge of, Court behaviour. Little did he know this man Shakespeare, who could bow and flourish and turn a pretty speech with the best of them. They were all, he felt, servants, without the discipline and training of servants. He kept them in their place, and on a tight rein.

But now, here to confound my Lord Chamberlain was my Lord of Southampton, holding out his arms to one of the players, embracing him fondly. "My dear Will, why have you been so long from Southampton House? We have been hurt, Will."

Because I am a false friend. Because I could not look you in the eye. Because I feared, hoped, yearned that I might meet again *her*, that she would drag me down once more into the mire, the mire for which my squalid soul so yearns.

He did not say these things. They did not even trouble him greatly. He was too busy enjoying this exquisite moment. To be embraced by an earl before his humble friends, and particularly before that pompous ass with the staff – this would have been a rare moment even for someone far less class conscious than Will.

Still, he was never one to allow himself to be set up above his friends. He said, "My lord, may I present Master Burbage, Master Kempe, Master Condell?"

Southampton doffed his bonnet most civilly. "Your servant, gentlemen." He turned to the Lord Chamberlain. "Sir, are the players comfortably housed?" He caught a leer on Kempe's expressive features. "Well bestowed?"

"According to their desert, my lord." Hunsdon too had caught the leer. Well, he didn't mind that. He'd see the fool didn't leer twice. He could still have a player whipped, if necessary, high and mighty though they seemed to have grown. But this young upstart, trying to tell *him*, the chief officer in Her Majesty's household, how to treat a rabble of players!

Southampton said coldly, "*Their* desert? Nay, my lord, treat them according to your own honour and dignity." Then, turning his back on Lord Hunsdon, he threw an arm round Will's shoulders. "Ancient Will, you must sup with me tonight."

With innate courtesy, the other three players were effacing themselves. Will said quietly, "I thank my lord. But my place is with my fellows."

A flash of irritation? But then, the slightest non-compliance irritated a noble. And immediately the sun shone again, its warmth embracing them all. "Gentlemen, you must *all* sup with me tonight." He swept them a bow, and was away.

"Come, sirs," said Hunsdon, thoroughly disgruntled. God's body, the very scullions would be invited to dinner next.

Even Will's far from inadequate imagination had never pictured such splendour.

A vast chamber, all gold and silver, dazzling the eyes with its jewels. A thousand candles.

A chamber adorned, not only with honest English craftsmanship, but with tapestries and precious objects brought from the world's farthest corners.

A chamber adorned, not only with objects, but with men and women strutting and preening like peacocks, the highest, cleverest, ablest men and women in this new and thrusting land; the men and women whose success was England's success. Silks and velvets, brocades and jewels, adorning the most brilliant Court in Europe.

Suddenly the chattering was hushed. Double doors were thrown open. The Great Servants of the Household entered, led by my Lord Chamberlain with his staff. They turned and faced the doorway.

The Ladies-in-Waiting entered; creatures lovely as angels. They turned and faced the doorway. Breath-holding silence. Every eye strained on that open double doorway.

Quite alone, as she had all her life been alone, especially since sweet Robin of Leicester's death: alone, unattended, Elizabeth of England entered. The Court bowed like a field of corn rippling before a summer breeze.

She was in a superb gown of white satin, embroidered with gold. Perched over her forehead was a bird of paradise for a head-dress. Jewels flashed and glowed through floating filmy draperies. Straight and imperious, she glided into the room like a swan. She was breath-taking. She was magnificent. Courtiers who had seen this entrance a hundred times still felt a constriction of the throat. But Will Shakespeare, seeing it for the first time, was completely bowled over. If only they had a boy actor who could make an entrance like that! God, he'd write him such parts: Cleopatra, Helen of Troy, Antigone?

The spell was broken. The Ladies-in-Waiting ranged themselves behind the Queen. Lord Hunsdon, leaning heavily on his staff, stood beside her. Essex and Southampton rushed forward like lovers, hand on heart, and, kneeling, kissed her fingers. The Queen looked arch, and delighted, and tapped them on the shoulders with her fan. "Arise, Sir Devotion. Arise, Sir Lovelorn." The daily make-believe had begun – that every courtier, whatever his age, was desperately in love with this tired, ageing, jewel-encrusted woman; who, in her sixties, could outdance them all, out-think them all, outwit them all, outdare them all. A shrewd, brilliant creature who had given her life to working, thinking, scheming, calculating for one thing, and one thing only: the greatness of England.

A friendly hand gripped Will's elbow. "Her Majesty wishes to meet the author of *The Comedy of Errors*. Come with me. And answer her boldly. It is only the tongue-tied fool who irritates her."

Will followed the Earl of Essex in a daze. The Queen! This would be something to tell his father, with a vengeance. This would please the old man.

His heart was pounding away. But he was not afraid. He was of good stock. And a poet. It had always seemed to him quite fitting that one day he should stand before his Sovereign.

He knelt before her. She tapped him with her fan gesturing to him to rise.

He rose; and allowed himself a quick glance before dutifully lowering his gaze. Thin lips, eyes hooded with fatigue, a beak like a bird of prey. And for a moment he was afraid. The eagle, tearing at his victim, knew as much of mercy as this creature.

Then she smiled.

There was nothing gentle about Elizabeth's public smile. It was brittle, mocking. But it was welcome. The Court, who always watched her face as earnestly as a mariner his weather-glass, relaxed, murmured, smiled too.

The Queen said, "I liked your *Comedy* well, Master Shakespeare."

He bowed very low; giving her, he realised, a close view of his thinning hair. But it couldn't be helped. "Your Majesty is very kind."

"It was a pleasant trifle. Well suited to this present season."

Pleasant trifle, indeed! He was stung. But when you are stung by Majesty, you hide your hurt. He bowed again.

"And what are you writing now, Master Shakespeare? More pleasant trifles?"

He would let her see he was no mere trifler. "An historical piece, your Majesty. About the deposition of King Richard the Second by Henry Bolingbroke."

The royal eyebrows shot up. "About the putting down of an anointed Prince? This is dangerous ground. Have a care, Master Shakespeare."

The Court shifted uneasily. They hoped this fool of an actor wasn't putting her in a bad mood.

Will swallowed. "If your Majesty would prefer – ?"

"Indeed not, sir. I shall wish to see your play. See what kind of a rogue you have made of our cousin Bolingbroke."

"No rogue, your Majesty, I assure you."

"No rogue? A man who deposes his anointed King, no rogue? Come, sir."

Will was sweating. He stammered. "No cousin of your Majesty's, ma'am, however distant, could be a rogue."

"Fiddlesticks, man. We've *all* been rogues, who sat upon this Throne of England. But – mark me well, Master Shakespeare – *anointed* rogues."

There was only one answer, when the wind blew easterly: to bow in silence. Elizabeth looked down at the thin thatching. Poor little man! After all, he had given them good entertainment. She need not be so hard on him. He didn't look the kind to set the kingdom alight.

But who had introduced him? Essex. Strange. She knew very well Southampton was his patron. (She knew everything.) But Southampton, she noted, was too busy making sheep's eyes at Mistress Vernon, a fact that did not improve her temper. So he had left it to his friend Essex to present his William. Essex, her new "Sweet Robin", the man of less than thirty, who was so madly in love with his sixty-year-old Queen. The man she loved but did not trust. The man so spoilt, so vain, so ambitious – and so beloved of the people, and so foolhardily brave – that, in the end, frustration or over-reaching ambition might teach him treason.

Treason! There was no need to be anxious yet. But her mind, that stored *everything* pertaining to England's past, present and future, had already drawn a triangle – Essex, the leader, Southampton, the led; Shakespeare, pen in hand, inciting the rabble. And the least ineffectual of the three, she thought – Master Shakespeare.

But not yet. Let the young nobles go on delighting her with their courtship. Let them all laugh over Shakespeare's pretty quibbles. Let her old limbs go on dancing a few more nights, a few more years. Let her people not be seduced from their love of her, for then she would die. She lived only in her people's love.

Meanwhile: "Come, Master Shakespeare. You are but poor company." Tonight, she would be kind. "You are not, I think by your speech, a Londoner?"

"No, your Majesty. My mother was a Warwickshire Arden. My father was Bailiff of Stratford-upon-Avon which, as your Majesty doubtless knows, is also in Warwickshire."

"My Majesty does know." But she was smiling.

He hung his head. *It is only the tongue-tied fool who irritates her,* Essex had told him. He said, "I saw your Majesty once. At Kenilworth."

Kenilworth! Sweet Robin of Leicester! God, would they never let her forget past happiness? Past happiness, whose memory squeezed the last tears from a withered heart!

The Court realised the clouds were down again. Damn this actor fellow! What was he saying to her?

"Indeed? And what passed between us at Kenilworth, Master Shakespeare?"

"I cried, 'God save your Majesty'."

"A notable remark. And what said I?"

"You said, 'Ah!' ma'am."

"'Ah?'"

"'Ah', your Majesty."

Kenilworth! The great redstone Castle brooding among its English meadows. Kenilworth, still, remote, under a soft sky, where she walked and talked with her Robin so long ago. Kenilworth, lost among its woodlands and the mists of time. Neglected now, no doubt, the rooks beating their black wings in the Great Chamber. She sighed. The Lord Chamberlain, seeing she had fallen into an old woman's reverie, led away the deeply bowing poet. It hadn't sounded as though the upstart had had much success, he thought.

Serve him right! It had been his, the Lord Chamberlain's place to introduce him to her Majesty. But these young gallants like Essex cared nothing for Court behaviour. He really didn't know what the world was coming to. The Queen, receiving a strolling player! And not at the Lord Chamberlain's hands. At some sprig of a lord's, God save the mark!

Will said anxiously, "I am not at all happy about *Richard the Second*. To the Queen, the deposition of a king is abhorrent. I think she feels that such a play might – give the people thoughts."

"Of treason? Then make the usurper a villainous creature," said Burbage impatiently. "Show where your sympathies lie."

"But the usurper – Bolingbroke – was a kinsman of the Queen's," groaned Will, with the wretchedness of one caught in a regal cleft stick.

Burbage's quick temper flared. In Richard, Will had written him the best part a man ever had. And now here he was, shilly-shallying over something the Queen had said. Will could be ridiculously fearful at times. Besides, they needed all the money they could get. Giles Allen, ground landlord of their theatre, was certain to put the screw on when it came to renewing the lease. Burbage knew Giles. He was determined to be able to meet his terms. He said, "Will, we are doing *Richard the Second* as soon as it's finished. I'll see the other sharers vote against you if you try to stop it."

Will groaned again. There would have been much to be said for being a glover, back in peaceful Stratford. Life in London wasn't all it was said to be. Southampton was too taken up with Elizabeth Vernon to have much time for his

old friend. Essex was being very friendly; but Essex was too
unpredictable, too confident, too swaggering, too affected,
too much the Queen's favourite for an ordinary man like
Will to feel anything but clumsy and loutish in his presence.
And the Queen? Quite frankly, Elizabeth had frightened the
life out of him.

He soon forgot his dumps. The New Year was a river in
spate, he was swept along from day to day in whirls and
eddies of work. As a sharer in a popular theatre he had to
read plays, attend sharers' meetings, decide policy, rehearse,
act, attend to the business side, teach the boy apprentices
and keep an eye on the little devils, see to the repair and
upkeep of the costumes, their most valuable asset, intervene
in brawls, and wage a running war with the Puritans to keep
the theatres open at all. There was little time for brooding.
He was writing *Romeo and Juliet* and *A Midsummer Night's
Dream*, and loyally finishing off *Richard the Second*.

Only at night, still: the shames, the hateful longings, the
peering and poking into the heaving corruption that was his
soul, the wonder at God's apparent prospering of the sinner
(or was God crouched, like a tiger in the undergrowth,
waiting to pounce?), the purging of his conscience in black
and tortured sonnets.

In the summer, he made his now annual journey to
Stratford. New Place was a little more dilapidated; a few
more pounds off the asking price, but a few more on to the
cost of repair. Anne, mother, father, brothers and sisters, all a
little older but otherwise unchanged, like the dial of a clock
that has crept on an hour since one's last looking. Only the
children had changed: Susanna now suddenly shy, Judith
occasionally smiling out of her shell; Hamnet?

Hamnet had shot up. But he was thinner, paler. "Father, I was ill at Christmas, and like to die," he announced proudly. "Was I not, mother?"

For a moment it was as though a hammer had struck Will above the heart. He looked anxiously at Anne. But she was laughing, thank God. "Oh, Hamnet, you had a little fever. It was nothing."

Hamnet looked affronted. "I *felt* like to die," he grumbled.

But afterwards, when they were alone, Anne said sadly, "I could have wished you at home at Christmas, husband. Hamnet – I *was* afraid, Will. Besides, there are not *so* many Christmases in a marriage that one can waste even one."

He had been so looking forward to telling her about his Christmas at Court, where he had even met the Queen. But it looked as though he might not be able to tell that story, after all. Will never liked to exacerbate a situation, and he sensed that Anne, with all a woman's illogicality, resented the fact that Will, though he could not possibly have known his son was ill, had not come posting home. To tell her, remembering her miserable Christmas, that he had been lording it at Court, might just be the match to spark off one of Anne's rare, but impressive, explosions of anger. Many men would have vowed to come next Christmas. But Will, though craven, was reasonably honest. All he said was, "This year, if there be not snow, and if we be not wanted at Court – "

"Aye. And if the roads be not too mired, and if the world do not end – " She stared, miserably, away from him. He looked at her profile. Sad, weary? Anne, he sensed, was beginning to find his absences more than she could bear. He was filled with a desperate compassion. Next Christmas, he vowed to himself, he would come to Stratford whatever happened.

But he did *not* go to Stratford the following Christmas. The Chamberlain's Men were summoned to Court again.

Fortunately, on Christmas Eve, a great sheet of powdery snow blew a whole day across southern England. It filled every hollow, piled itself against every obstacle, levelled hills and valleys. From London, Stratford was as inaccessible as the moon.

Will was relieved. In some devious way it satisfied his conscience to know that he *couldn't* have reached Stratford even if he'd wanted to. And when he saw Anne in the summer it would be so much easier to say, "The snow at Christmas, Anne! Not a road out of London but was impassable." It would save any awkward references to the Court.

The Queen did not ask to see him this time. This poet, with Warwickshire loam in his speech and on his boots, brought back too much of the happy past for comfort.

But the woman he had known at Titchfield was there; flitting, ghost-like, in the winter's dusk of a long gallery. Dark, pale, she might almost have been a shadow, her laughter might have been a late bird calling. She might have been a succubus of waking, a hundred demons in one woman's urgent body.

In her arms, he knew that away from her he had been nothing, a homeless wanderer, an outcast naked to wind and rain, an amputated limb; yet he hated her for holding up a mirror to his soul, for fanning the flames of guilt and shame and self-loathing that he had thought were dying, for giving him a squalid heaven at the cost of hell; for playing both Mephistophilis and Helen to his pitiful Faustus.

Then, once again, she was a memory, no more; a searing excoriating memory; she was revulsion, hatred, intolerable longing, she was the Destroyer. She had destroyed peace of mind, gentleness, self-respect, a man' innocent love of wife and children; and bitter shame had spoiled the sweet world's taste.

And surely, he thought, trembling, God would not allow Himself to be mocked a second time.

Nor, as it turned out, would He. Nevertheless, He waited with His usual patience until high summer.

Life was like a spinning bobbin, ever gathering more and more strands. The Chamberlain's Men were called to perform at Whitehall, at Nonsuch, at the Inns of Court, at the great houses of the nobility. Such popularity did not come for the asking. It came because the company worked with a dedicated friendliness, chose the right plays, were brilliant actors, and had a resident author who worked himself to the bone writing unconscionably long plays that they could then tailor to suit an afternoon.

He was up at dawn, seldom abed before midnight. Work! He revelled in it, which was just as well since it was all-demanding. There would, he thought ruefully, be no Stratford this year. He wanted to go, he *ought* to go. Sometimes he thought wistfully of the country peace, the slow country days; and of Anne, poor Anne, who wasn't having much of a life. Anne, who accepted her loneliness with such gentle resignation; even though for her the sun shone only when Will was there.

Poor Anne! But if *she* wanted him, so did the Court, the nobility, the prentices, the small tradesmen, the street sweepers and the labourers of London, many of whom were beginning to think a Shakespeare play beat even the bear-baiting.

So. Anne could only wait and take her turn. She wouldn't complain, that was one good thing. Hamnet, too, and the girls. Just let him get them all settled in New Place. Then he *would* go to Stratford more often. Sit in the window of his stately house and watch, with pride, his son coming home across the road from the Grammar School. Teach the boy to shoot a straight arrow, to fence (though his wind wouldn't allow much of that nowadays), to learn the run of the biased bowls, wayward as women. It would be a good life, when he was a little older. But now – the laughter and friendship of the Players, the dazzle of Nonsuch; or sitting in his room, like God in his Heaven, dealing out to his creatures life and joy and suffering and death. Now, the crammed, boisterous, responsible noontide of life; tomorrow, the quiet afternoon, the lengthening shadows of the Stratford poplars.

It was early August when Richard Field brought the news.

They were at rehearsal. Will was acting as guider. The play was one of his own, a comedy called *A Midsummer Night's Dream*. There was a scene (some country folk putting on a play) that made gentle fun of Kyd's *Spanish Tragedy*, and of Edward Alleyn's heavy style of acting, and of the celebrations attending the baptism of Prince Henry of Scotland.

The players loved it, especially Burbage. He had a lighter, more natural style of acting than Alleyn, and found this parody of his old rival very flattering. Will, too, was enjoying himself hugely. Laughter was on all their lips. Then he looked up and saw Richard Field's face.

Field was always a little on Will's conscience. Will liked and respected him, no man better. Yet he never sought out his company. It was not only, he thought, that Richard was a bit of a dull dog. He was also a sort of embodied conscience; or rather, since he never reproached Will for his absence from wife and family, he was a sounding-board from which Will's conscience reflected back into his face.

Will came flying across the room, hands outstretched. "My dear good friend. What brings you here?" He laughed, mocking himself. "Not *another* printing of *Venus*?"

"No, Will. I am from Stratford."

Will looked at Richard's face. And knew. Tragedy. Father? Oh, the old man should have lived till the Grant of Arms came through. It would have pleasured him so much. But for a long time now he had been – what? – anchored not very firmly to this present world. Poor old man! And mother? She would bow to the storm, but she would not break. But – the old man, who gave me this harsh, turbulent thing called life. God rest his soul.

Richard said: "Hamnet is dead."

The old man must have a funeral befitting a Town Bailiff. He must – Will looked at Richard. "*What* did you say?"

"Hamnet – your son – is dead. I'm sorry, Will."

It was a mistake. It must be. His father, frail, never quite sure whether it was today or a week last Thursday; the boy, robust, feet planted firmly on the earth, knowing exactly who he was and where he was going; the boy, who was to go bowling with him, and live at New Place in gentlemanly style, Hamnet Shakespeare, Gent. A mistake had been made somewhere. By Richard? Or – he felt himself trembling – by God?

"Hamnet?" he said.

Richard looked down at the floor, nodded.

The rehearsal had fallen silent. Here was drama of another kind. Will was weeping.

"Grief fills the room up of my absent child,

Lies in his bed, walks up and down with me…" Already in his sorrow, because of his sorrow, new characters were stealing out of the shadows to stand upon a tragic stage.

It was Anne who opened the door to him.

If anywhere in the world held any comfort for him now, it was in her arms. But she shrank from him. Her features were stiff, like the face of a corpse. "You should have been here," she said. Her voice was like the rattling of bones.

"I didn't know," he said helplessly.

"You should still have been here. It isn't natural, living away, year after year. God is not mocked."

He shuddered violently. So she too thought it was God's anger, though for different reasons. He said, "How did it happen?"

"Another fever. It burned him like – a scrap of paper." She would not meet his eye. "And Judith: she will not eat or speak or sleep. It is as though a half of her had died."

Life, he thought, had always been a little too much for Judith. The death of her twin might well push her over into madness. God, to what had his loveless lust brought them all? Not only had it spoiled the sweet world's taste for him. It had brought God's anger, like a lightning flash, into this pretty innocent cottage. Helplessly, beseechingly, he held out his arms. "Anne, if ever we needed each other, it's now."

She shrank away.

Had he come to her covered with buboes, stinking with the plague vomit, she would have taken him tenderly to her breast. But not now. She was like a hurt animal, seeking a solitary cave ion which to lick her wounds. Deliberately she was cutting herself off, comfortless, from God and man. She was cocooned in her own misery.

She said, "Your father has received his Grant of Arms. What is the loss of a son, compared with that honour?"

He said, very gently, "Anne, it is not my fault that Hamnet died."

She said, "You sought honour, rather than love. Well, you have found honour."

"And lost love?" he said humbly.

She was silent, still staring away from him. Then she said, "Back to London with you now, Will." Her voice was flat, and dead, and grating, as it might be a voice coming from the parched lips of a skull.

"I – not yet," he said uncomfortably.

She flared at last. "God's mercy, man. I've managed alone all these years. I can manage now."

"But Judith? She needs – "

"Nothing you can give her. A strange man, of whom she has always been afeared? You are best away."

He said, with terrible humility, "I had planned so much for Hamnet. I've lost a son. I need you, Anne."

"I've often needed you, husband. When there was plague in Stratford. When I was sick. When a madman lurked o' nights in Chapel Lane. *I* needed *you*. But I managed. And so will you."

"But why must I go?"

For the first time she looked at him. He was appalled to see how she had aged. "Would you stay always, Will?"

"I couldn't. You don't understand. There are plays, rehearsals, a thousand reasons. But I could manage a few days, a week – "

She rose. "All or nothing, Will. Away you go. I have a daughter to pull back from the brink."

Susanna was staying at Shottery. He did not see her.

Judith, reluctantly, gave him a death-cold cheek to kiss.

He did not visit Henley Street. Father would be full of the Grant of Arms, his mother *might* be a comfort, but her tongue could have a cutting edge, and he could bear no more reproaches.

He went into the churchyard. Strange to think that this little grave could hold the boastful, strutting Hamnet. God, I have sinned, he cried. And so a pretty child must lie in the dirt, and a gentle wife be frozen with misery. And, for me, a bitter shame spoiling the sweet world's taste.

A little boy, playing in a summer garden. A mother, contented, watching. Both blasted, by my own defiance of the Universal Order.

He dragged himself up on to his horse, and rode off towards London.

CHAPTER 11

WITHIN THIS WOODEN O...

Anne Shakespeare tended the grave of her dead child, and worked ceaselessly to bring his half-dead twin back to life.

With heartbreaking slowness, her tenderness bore fruit. Judith took a little food, spoke a few words, smiled. The smile was like a gleam of yellow sunlight after a week of rain and wind.

Nevertheless, that August, when the frosts of winter were far away, a bitterer frost had visited the house in Chapel Lane. It withered Hamnet. It had touched Judith. It had frozen Anne's heart within her breast.

Anne did not know what had happened to her. It was almost a physical sensation, as though her warm, beating heart had changed to a cold lump.

Love had died. She knew only three emotions: grief; guilt (it was not right for man and wife to live apart, and God had shown his displeasure); pity: for little Judith, for Susanna, most of all for herself. Love was dead. Will? She had no time for Will, a foolish, clumsy creature, a broken reed. She felt resentment against him growing in her like a cancer, and she could no more stop it than she could have stopped a cancer.

Nor did she want to. She fed it – titbits of remembered irritations, morsels of neglect – as assiduously as she fed little Judith. And it waxed, and grew fibrous and strong, a malignant growth in her once-gentle mind.

She shut herself away with her little girls. Guilt and self-pity, those predators of the soul, gnawed at her self-respect. She began to look unkempt, to neglect the house. What did it matter anymore? Hamnet was not there to see. And Will? If Will came and found a scarecrow of a wife in a pigsty of a home, what did *she* care? The sooner he went back to London the better.

Winter dragged itself by, all mud and misery. And the spring brought William.

William Shakespeare, Gent., spoilt by success; a brilliant new character, Sir John Falstaff, filling his mind with inner laughter; a Grant of Arms; the praise of London ringing in his ears; and the deeds of New Place, Stratford-upon-Avon, in his pocket!

He did not notice the shabbiness of the cottage. A poet is above noticing dust and disorder. He did not notice the bleakness of his wife's expression. A keen businessman who has just bought the second-finest house in Stratford for sixty pounds will soon bring a smile to his wife's lips. He did not notice, God forgive him, the absence of his son. He had written that unhappiness out of his system with his new play about King John, weeping with a bereaved mother for her lost son. For Anne, since Hamnet's death, winter had come and gone; no more. For Will, the child was already buried under a great mound of activity. Life had hurtled on at an ever faster rate. No time for mourning, now. The sweet world's taste was on his lips once more.

She let him kiss her cold cheek. "You are early this year," she said, with a cruel bitterness. "Perchance you thought I would be lonely."

He gave her a quick look. It occurred to him that she was not as welcoming as usual. Well, he'd soon put that right. "Wife," he said, "we must sell this house."

She looked at him in sudden fear. And saw he was smiling – grinning even. But it did not quench her fear. "Sell this house?" Her precious, loved home? "Sell this house? What do you mean, Will?"

He was still grinning down at her, as excited as a schoolboy. Nevertheless, a little wary. This wife of his could be very down to earth. She had sometimes hurt him deeply by laughing at his gentlemanly aspirations. However: "I have bought New Place, wife."

While it was sinking in, she thought: he's getting like his father. I've never seen it before, but he is. The foolish grin, the complacent air of success, even the hint of stoutness. In that moment she hated him. "You've – *what*?" she said.

"Bought New Place. And guess for how much. Oh, it will need some repair, but – "

She said, "You've bought New Place? But – for what?"

"To live in, of course." He was growing irritated.

She looked incredulous. "You expect *me* to take my two little girls and live in style in that great tumbledown barn? Why, I should be the laughing-stock of Stratford."

"It will be repaired, set in good order. And I shall spend more time at home when we are settled in New Place."

"I see. We shall be honoured. You will find wife and children more attractive when they are housed like the gentry?"

"Of course I don't mean that. But I am becoming a rich man, wife. I can soon afford to leave some of the work to the others."

She looked at him with contempt. She spoke slowly. "Sweet Will! Gentle Will! Charming to everyone, courteous, considerate. Everybody's favourite. Yet underneath steel. All your life you've been a steel bolt, flying straight towards the target."

"And I have hit the bull." His chin came up, this time like his mother's.

"You have hit the bull. A Grant of Arms, visits to Court, friends, women no doubt, and now a grand house. What do *my* years of loneliness matter, or my grief?"

He said, dully, "It was not my fault the boy died."

"Nothing was your fault, husband. It was just that you could have done better."

New Place. It had been the bull. And he had hit it. A moment of humble – yes, *humble* – pride. How he had looked forward to the rebuilding, the furnishing, the installation of his family and, eventually, his own apotheosis into William Shakespeare, Gent., of New Place, Stratford-upon-Avon, late of London! And now this – this *peasant* – had ruined everything for him. The infection of resentment spread from her mind to his. They sat in the little parlour, silent, not looking at each other, smouldering. At last he said, "Since that is how you feel about me, I shall return to London as soon as I have put the repairs in hand and found a buyer for this – hovel. In the meantime, I shall lodge at the inn."

She was silent. He looked at her. Her frock was old, and shabby, her hair dull and unkempt. Her cheeks were grey, and drawn, her face weary. But the compassion that was so large a part of his nature lay unmoved. He said coldly,

"When you are mistress of New Place, you will need to look to your appearance, wife."

They were both silent. He rose, and went out of the house without a backward glance.

She went on sitting there. She had lost a son. Now, it seemed, she had also lost a husband.

Burbage said, "Fill your cup, Will." He leaned over the inn table, resting comfortably on his folded arms. He had reached the stage of mild intoxication when a man so loves his fellows that he speaks freely and sensibly what is in his heart. "Will, this acting. I am discovering things, depths, I had never dreamed of. Subtleties, suggestions, quirks – you yourself have taught me much, with your *Richard the Second*. Taught me that a man, even a character in a play, can have many sides."

Will sipped his ale carefully. The damned stuff always made him queasy. But he felt a strange excitement. "I think, Dick, there are in the drama far, mysterious lands yet to be discovered. I think you and I, speaking between ourselves, that is – I think we could go on voyages of discovery as strange as Drake's or Raleigh's." He was undoubtedly a little drunk. But he had had these feelings for a long time. Now, at last, drink had unlocked his tongue.

"God, yes." Richard Burbage put a hand on Will's forearm, squeezed it friendly. "Write me a many-sided man, Will. A part I can really get my teeth into."

"Perhaps," said Will, "you would care to glance at my *Hamlet*. I have done much polishing of it lately."

Burbage looked unimpressed. "That damned ghost?"

"There's more than the ghost," said Will, really drunk now. "*Hamlet* is my brains and my bowels, *Hamlet* is every tiniest vein in my body, *Hamlet* is my joy, and my sorrows, my loves and lusts and fears. *Hamlet* is me, you – Everyman."

"I'll have a look at it sometime," said Burbage, "if you'll remind me."

"As a matter of fact," said Will, "I happen to have it here." He pulled a bulky manuscript out of his doublet.

"Why in God's name," cried Burbage an hour later, "did you not show me this before?"

"I did *try*," Will said meekly.

"But this is what I've been looking for. *What* a part!" He went on reading. Something struck him. He looked suddenly dismayed. "Oh, Lord. Is there anything in it for Kempe?"

"There's a comic gravedigger in Act V."

"Only in Act V? That won't suit him. Can't you write in a Fool?"

Will said, "I am not having Kempe romping and jigging round the Castle of Elsinore. He can be First Gravedigger or nothing."

But Richard Burbage was back at his reading. "To be, or not to be. That is the question." This was the stuff to give the groundlings. At the moment he didn't care who played what part; so long as – and this was a foregone conclusion – so long as *he* played Hamlet.

But Will's troubles were falling about his ears thicker and faster. One day Burbage came into the tavern looking almost as wan as he did in the last act of *Richard the Second*. They stared at him in alarm. "Dick, what is it?"

He dropped on to a stool. "I've seen Giles Allen's terms for renewal of the lease. They're impossible. We're ruined."

Will the poet, Will the actor, stepped down. Will the keen businessman took their place. "We must beat him down, Dick. He'll have his price."

"He won't. He says he wants the Theatre pulled down. Because of what he calls great and grievous abuses. But it's my belief he wants it for himself."

This was serious. A blow in the teeth, just when everything was going so well. It was more than serious. It was disastrous. Without a theatre they'd be back to playing in inn yards; inn yards, when other companies – and their audiences – were snug in their own theatres! That wouldn't last long. And yet – this band of brothers threatened with extinction? It was unthinkable. Will said, "Could I see the original lease?"

"Of course." Dick drew it from his doublet.

Will pushed his cup of ale over to Burbage. He looked as though he needed it, and Will was glad to get rid of the stuff. He read the lease.

He handed it back without a word. Dick, searching his face for hope or comfort, saw none. Or was there a glitter in those troubled eyes? He didn't think so.

But there was. Two days later, Will was back, bubbling with suppressed excitement. "Friends, I shall need money. On your behalf I have taken a lease of a garden plot on the south bank, near Henslowe's Rose Theatre. We'll draw some of his groundlings, or I'm a Hollander."

"You've done what?" said Kempe. "A garden plot? Are we to dance among the roses, then?"

Condell said, "Will, you fool. What use is land without a theatre?"

Heminge said, "You haven't *signed* anything? For a garden of weeds?"

Augustine Phillips said glumly, "We could never afford to build another theatre."

Will let them talk. He was enjoying himself. Then he said, "You forget that I read Giles Allen's original lease. There is a valuable clause. The Theatre is ours, provided it be moved before the lease expires."

They were silent. Then: "Move the Theatre?" cried Kempe scornfully.

"Across the Thames? In winter?" said Phillips.

"Winter or summer makes no difference," Condell muttered. "I had as lief move Nonsuch across the Channel."

They thought Will mad. "Carry a theatre across London Bridge?" sneered Kempe. He shivered, blew on his nails. "'Tis bitter cold; and a fool for a companion! No comfort anywhere."

Will said, "I have already thought of that. Now listen."

By the time he had finished talking they were looking at him in wonder; then slapping their thighs; then roaring. Will, who had given them so much laughter, had now given them the finest jest of all – something that would keep London laughing for years. Sweet Will! He'd been in the dumps lately. They were glad to find he was himself again.

At dawn on Christmas Day the work began. The Chamberlain's Men, respected actors, crept through the silent streets. They converged on the Theatre. Then, at a signal – oh, what a heathen hullabaloo shattering the Christmas peace! Sober citizens leapt from their beds as though stung, ran and peered through their lattices. Giles Allen, pausing only to pull on a gown, ran through the icy dawn. "What is this? What are you about?"

"Just removing our property," said Will sweetly, who was wielding a pair of pincers with the best.

"But it's *my* property, now."

Patiently, Will showed him the clause in the contract. Giles Allen cursed and swore. No man heard him. Dismantling a wooden theatre is a noisy business – especially when it is being done against time.

Carts were waiting. Soon they were trundling off with their loads of beams and timbers. And there was no need to go the long way round by London Bridge. The Thames was obligingly frozen. The Chamberlain's Men crossed London's river as safely as the Israelites crossed the Red Sea.

And Giles Allen, the ground landlord, stood like Pharaoh, helpless, and watched them go.

By evening, the garden plot on Bankside was a litter of planks and beams, baskets of costumes, bundles of swords and staves and pikes, a clutter of armour; which, before winter had dragged by, would grow into a new theatre.

That night they sat long in the tavern. They were weary, but content. And bubbling with laughter. Men, good friends, used to working together with humour and forbearance, had today worked with such a will, such comradeship, as never before. They had moved a mountain. They sat silent, hands on weary thighs, smiles on their faces, staring at their ale mugs or at the table. And suddenly one would give a hiccup of laughter, and the smiles would broaden. Then another. Then Will began to sing in his pleasant tenor. But quietly. They strained their ears. At last they got it. "I saw three ships come sailing by, Come sailing by, Come sailing by. I saw three ships come sailing by – " And suddenly there was a great roar from every throat. They had seen the joke. "On Christmas Day in the morning," they sang. They sang it, laughing helplessly, until half of them were under the table. Never was such a flowering of friendship among a group of men, passing the love of women. And the cornerstone of all this love and friendship was William.

By spring, all that remained was to name the new playhouse. "The Theatre," said Richard Burbage, nostalgic.

"The Elizabeth," suggested Heminge. But the Queen was sixty-five. They didn't want to have to re-christen it in a few years.

"The Thistle," said Will, "for will it not prick Henslowe's Rose?"

"It is round, like the great globe itself. And, like the great globe, it shall contain all of life and living. Let us call it the Globe," said Condell.

And that, since it was growing late, and since no one could think of anything better, was what they called it.

CHAPTER 12

AS MAN'S INGRATITUDE...

That summer, and the following, he paid several visits to Stratford, and supervised the repairs to New Place.

He stayed at the inn. He visited neither his wife nor his parents.

He was in too black and angry a mood. He hated everyone; and, like most men who hate everyone, he hated most of all himself.

With the help of a little talent and a tremendous amount of hard work, and with no help from anybody else, he had risen to heights one would have thought impossible for a local grammar schoolboy.

He had wanted to share the fruits of his success; and had been laughed at. So. He would enjoy them alone. He would hug them to his breast in a private, gloating joy. Surely Will Shakespeare, Gent., of London, could visit Stratford without always having friends and relations hanging round his neck!

Now the house was ready for furnishing.

It was, indeed, a gentleman's house: red brick and timber, with five gables, two gardens and two orchards; a fine dignified house, a fitting crown to any man's ambition.

And already he hated the place. Already he was finding that fruits, unshared, can have a bitter taste.

He had seen it for so long in his mind's eye: three children, playing happily in the orchards, while he and Anne set out the new furniture, chose linen and carpets and glass, engaged servants. And now he knew it could never be like that. To begin with, there were only two children.

He had not seen Anne during all the alterations. Now he went to the cottage and knocked.

She came to the door. He said, "New Place is built. I want you to help me choose the furnishings, the servants."

"Very well, husband," she said. She stepped outside, took his arm.

She had been baking. She was sweating. Her face was mottled, grey and red. Her hair was awry, her dress soiled. He said dismally, without anger: "Would you make me a laughing-stock, wife?"

She looked at him with wide-eyed innocence. "Why, husband? Because I am not as elegant as the ladies of the Court?"

He was still gentle, coaxing even. "Put on your best, Anne. We are going to our new house, remember."

She let go of his arm. "I come like this, or not at all. If you are ashamed of me – "

He said, "You would never have gone out in the streets, thus, at one time."

"I was proud, then," she said. "My husband loved me; and my child had not died."

Tenderly, he led her back into the cottage. "Is this really where you want to be?"

"Yes. Oh, yes, Will."

"I'll have to think," he said. "Consider." A dream had ended. Anne did not speak. He came away. That night, after

267

supper, he walked around the little town that held all his boyhood: the river, the willows, Henley Street, High Cross, Chapel Street. Did he really want to come back? To a wife who no longer wanted him, to friends whose talk was all of trade and prices, to a little grave? There were other fine houses for the buying, and the world was wide.

Chapel Street, Chapel Lane. On the corner, New Place towered up against the night sky. Its windows were dark and shuttered.

Riding back to London disappointment, irritation, and a curious feeling of helplessness and frustration weighed him down like a heavy cloak. A life's ambition had been snatched from him at the very moment of achievement, and he had nothing to put in its place. There was no other path he wanted to follow.

God, he'd worked. Admittedly, he had a little talent; but that wouldn't have got him far without all his strivings. It hadn't all been pleasant, whatever Anne might think, living in London. Gloomy lodgings, a stranger in a strange town, the summer's stench, the winter's cold, never able to draw up to your own fireside. Celibate – well, mostly. Yes, he's made many sacrifices. And how had he been rewarded? By sheer ingratitude. Worse! By having the gift he had saved and toiled for flung back in his face.

And Anne had grown into a slut. Well, that wasn't his fault. He'd always sent money when he had it. Aye, and had often gone short himself to send it. How he hated ingratitude!

Slowly, the rust of self-pity went on eroding his cheerful nature. His wife preferred his absence to his company. His son was dead. He was Sweet Will to no one anymore. For someone who was always so hungry for men's high regard, it was a bitter and a lonely time.

And now, it seemed, even Stratford was out of the question. A fine fool he would look if he went back to Anne and the cottage, while his grand new house was left to rot. A fine fool – and knave – he would look if he lived alone in the big house, like a bean in a quart pot they would say, while his family stayed in the cottage. Anne, he thought glumly, had made his native town impossible for him.

Mary Shakespeare said, "John, Will has been staying in Stratford. Not with his wife, God save the mark. Not with his parents. But at the inn. He must be out of his senses."

"Will who?"

"Your son, man." Oh, life was difficult these days. "But that's the least of it. He's bought New Place."

"Who has?" Sudden interest.

"Will. Our son."

At last she had made an impression. "Will? Bought New Place?"

"I heard it was being repaired. But – I go out so seldom now. The news passes me by."

"Will? Bought New Place? Why, that is a fine house, befitting a gentleman. Perhaps the finest house in Stratford."

"I would have liked it better had he told us."

"Our son, wife, living in the house Sir Hugh Clopton built for himself." His eyes filled with their accustomed tears. "The name of Shakespeare may mean something yet in Stratford, lass."

"Yes," she said absently. She had other things on her mind. She set off for Chapel Lane.

It was a long time since she had been thus far. A long time since Anne had visited her. She was shocked by her daughter-in-law's appearance. The Hathaways, she thought, had always shown a certain lack of breeding. An Arden would never have let herself become so unkempt.

She came straight to the point. "What is this I hear about Will?"

"Gentleman Will? He has bought New Place. He can live there with the rats and mice for all I care."

Mary looked at her. Then she went and threw her arms about her. "Oh, my dear. What has he done to you?"

It was a long time since anyone had embraced Anne. She clung.

And she wept for almost the first time since her girlhood. "Nothing," she murmured. "He has done nothing. I always knew I could never hold him. I just thought – I might keep a little part."

Mary held her, silent. Then she said, "When do you go to New Place?"

"Never!" said Anne.

Mary said, gently, "The world will say he neglected you."

Anne shook her head dismally.

Mary said, "The world will say he destroyed your virginity. And yet – you were a grown woman, he a boy."

"I had compassion, God forgive me. Foolish compassion, I know now."

"Yet it is he the world blames. And soon the world will be saying he lords it in New Place, and abandons you in a tumbledown cottage. You have given the world an ill picture of him, Mistress Anne."

The two women looked at each other. "Dress yourself up," Mary wanted to cry. "Go and stand proudly in the place your clever husband has won for you." But she said, pleadingly, "Look, Anne, all men are fools. They're only little boys, playing at being men. They'll do foolish things. We just have to go with them and see they don't come to too much harm."

Anne was still silent. Mary said, "I would have gone with my husband to the ends of the earth. But then we are, of course, all different."

Anne said, "Do they really speak so unkindly of Will?"

"Of course they do."

"Poor Will," said Anne. "I would not wish that. But I could not take the girls and live in London."

"But you could live in New Place. Oh, Anne, I would help you buy clothes and linen, and engage servants. You and I could prepare such a place for foolish Will, if only you would."

She came away; knowing, womanlike, that Anne's tears had thawed a little of the ice that still enwrapped her heart; perhaps, she thought, she had done a good day's work for Will. But she would certainly have a few words to say to that young man, when next he condescended to call.

CHAPTER 13

THE WIND AND THE RAIN…

"Hey, ho, the wind and the rain," sang Robert Armin.

"But that's all one, our play is done, And we'll strive to please you every day."

The pleasant voice ended, on a dying fall. The sound floated away among the great hammer beams of the ceiling, the high tapestries of the hall. There was silence – one of those rare moments at the end of a play when the audience sits unmoving, unwilling to destroy the magic, unwilling to quit the make-believe for the wind and the rain of every day.

The moment passed. They put their hands together, waiting only for the Queen to clap first.

She did not clap. She rose, and swept from the room, followed by her ladies. And if the Queen did not clap, nobody clapped. There was hurried rising, bowing, curtseying. No one was troubling his head about a poor playwriter's feelings when there was every sign of a royal storm.

It was Twelfth Night, in more ways than one. The Twelfth Night of Christmas, at the Palace of Whitehall; with Master Shakespeare's new comedy to grace the revels.

But Master Shakespeare's new comedy had proved not to the Queen's taste. Despite the drolls, despite the excellent wit, i'faith, despite the well-proved plot about identical twins – despite all this the piece had an inescapable melancholy. And an ageing, weary Queen, gazing forward into the dark of a New Year, has enough melancholy of her own.

Armin's sad little ditty of the wind and the rain was still in her heart later when she said, "Master Shakespeare, we asked you for a comedy. And you have made us weep."

A royal reproach! He trembled. But he was learning to speak up for himself. "Your Majesty, the comedy was there." He sighed. "Perhaps the sadness was in our own hearts."

She looked at him searchingly. "Nay. It was engendered, sir. What was the last line of that other song: something about youth?"

"Youth's a stuff will not endure, Your Majesty."

"Aye." She was silent. "You do well to remind us, Master Shakespeare," she said bitterly.

She was silent again. Then she said, "You are too cunning with words, sir. Other men bludgeon us about the ears. You slip a bodkin into our very heart."

She swept on. Will bowed very low. The Queen, he thought, had paid him a reluctant compliment. But she didn't like him. She admired his work, but she didn't like it. And if the Queen didn't like it, the Court didn't. He was finished. He had had his times of glory: sweet Will, loved by the fellowship of Players, adored by the groundlings, made much of by the Southampton circle. And now – what had he? Riches. A fine house in Stratford. And the love of no one. The end of the road.

And the sixty-seven-year-old Queen? What had she?

No one knew, in that January of 1601. But the old, wise woman had her inklings. This year would see her out, as like as not. Youth, life itself, was a stuff would not endure. She did not need a Warwickshire poet to tell her that. But there was more to it than the slow erosion of the years. She had reigned too long. She had taken a divided, bitter country from the hands of her dying sister; and she had made it great. She had inspired every citizen to work for his Queen, his country, and himself. She had kept the peace, and filled her coffers, while Europe bled almost to death. She had made England.

And now they were forgetting her, an untidy old woman muttering, clasping a rusty sword, about the great cold rooms of Whitehall and Nonsuch. She should have died before. A prince did well to die before his fickle people forgot what he had done for them.

Yet there was more to it than that. Those beaked nostrils had picked up a smell they remembered and dreaded. The smell of blood. The smell of guts, sliced from a living body. The foul smell of treason.

Essex was plotting something. Essex and his friend Southampton. And their friend Shakespeare? Had they embroiled him? Somehow she didn't think so. Master Shakespeare, she thought, would run a mile if you did say "boo" to him. But one never knew. You could not assess a poet as you assessed other men.

Things had never been the same since old Burghley died. His cautious wisdom, her brilliant opportunism, had been a formidable combination. She needed him to help her deal with temperamental creatures like Southampton and Essex.

Both were disaffected. It was a far cry from Sir Lovelorn and Sir Devotion. Well, let them be. Southampton had committed the most heinous crime, short of High Treason, in Elizabeth's calender. While claiming to be madly in love with the sexagenarian Queen, he had consoled himself with one of her young gentlewomen, got her with child, and married her at seven months. Elizabeth had clapped them both in the Tower to cool their ardour. Southampton had been bitterly resentful. Proud, rash, spoilt, he was prepared now to follow any leader except his Queen.

Essex was another matter. She had sent him to quell the Irish; and, once in Ireland, he had shown quite incredible incompetence and irresponsibility. As a result he had committed the second most heinous crime in Elizabeth's calendar. He had put her in a position where she had to send him money, more money. When at last he came home, nothing achieved, she dealt him the most bitter blow she could have devised. She revoked his monopoly of imported sweet wines, and with it most of his income. It was his turn to be beside himself with fury. She fanned the flames by having him harangued for eleven hours by a disciplinary tribunal, threatening him with the Tower, and finally placing him under house arrest.

Essex, in his middle thirties, still had the emotional make-up of a charming, but spoilt and pampered small boy. He expected people to love and admire him. And when they unaccountably failed to do so, and even admonished and punished him, then he behaved like any other spoilt child. He stamped and screamed; and was filled with a deep desire to hurt.

Elizabeth let him stamp and scream. But she watched. She watched his friends. She watched his servants. No one called at Essex House these days unknown to the Queen.

A far less astute Government than hers would have realised something was afoot. Essex House was alive with visitors: visitors, furtive in the winter's dusk. Visitors swathed in cloaks, their hats about their ears. Scotsmen, Frenchmen, Spaniards, Jesuits, hardbitten mercenaries in battered steel, courtiers sly and insinuating as worms. And, of course, spies, counter-spies, counter-counter spies baked the bread, brought away the laundry, took my lord's dictation, served my lord's wine. Under Elizabeth, spying was a highly regarded part-time occupation.

Rumours were everywhere. Essex heard them all. His followers seethed like a pan of hot beans. They thought up plan after crack-brained plan. Attack the Palace, seize the Queen. Rouse London, rouse the country, proclaim James of Scotland, kill Secretary Cecil. Essex seized upon each new one with avidity, pondered it, said yes, pondered again, said nay, pondered again, said maybe. Everyone was getting exasperated. If somebody didn't do something sensible soon, somebody was going to do something unbelievably rash.

And that is just what happened.

But first, in the sound belief that the pen is mightier than the sword, they brought Master Shakespeare in. Had not Will written a play in which the deposition of King Richard II by Bolingbroke was shown to be a good thing? If people could only see that play they would be the more inclined to agree that the deposition of Elizabeth by Essex was also a good thing.

It was perhaps the first recorded attempt at brainwashing in history.

Go to Essex House? Will shrank back from the cloaked messenger. He had heard the rumours. And they filled him with enough dread already. He could not deny his connection with Southampton. That was in print for all to see. "To the Right Honourable Henry Wriothesley, etc." God.

That youthful dedication of *Venus and Adonis* could still bring him to the rack. His only hope was that for a long time now he had seen nothing of either Southampton or Essex. He hoped, knowing the hope to be false, that the Queen's memory was short.

And now, here was a letter from Southampton begging him (Southampton, begging!) to go to Essex House. And a messenger awaiting his reply.

Will was not a brave man. Yet he said, through parched lips, "Tell my lord I will attend upon him."

Why? Loyalty, old friendship? More discreditably, his old longing to be liked, not to be thought ill of?

He went, muffled, flitting through the February morning like a brown ghost. He went early, because this afternoon he was needed for the long-awaited performance of his *Hamlet*.

Essex House was like a fortress, shuttered, not a light showing, armed sentries at every door.

Will gave his name, and was admitted. A clanking soldier marched him along corridors to a small ante-room, showed him in, left him.

This military atmosphere frightened Will more than ever. So it *was* going to be rebellion! God, why had he come? He must have been mad, quite mad. Even now, perhaps, it was not too late. He crept over to the door, opened it. A soldier with a drawn sword eyed him sourly. He went back into the ante-room, shut the door. What did they want of him? To carry a pike and cry, "Death to Elizabeth!"?

He knew they would not think twice about killing him if he refused. It seemed he was lost either way. A quick death now; or the long, dreadful road to death that awaited the servants of traitors. Unless, of course, the rebellion succeeded. But he had no illusions about that. Essex was a fool. And so, Will was afraid, was his friend Southampton.

"My dear Will!"

"Why, ancient Will. How goes it with you, man?"

Suddenly they were in the room, holding out their arms, smiling, laughing, embracing him.

They had both changed. Essex had the pale, fine-drawn look of a man tense to breaking-point. Southampton looked as though either marriage or a spell in the Tower had quietened him. But at the moment they were both ebullient at the sight of their dear old friend.

Southampton came straight to the point. "Will, we would ask a boon."

There was a time, Will would have said, "With all my heart, my lord." Now he said, dully, "What boon, my lord?"

The two men noted the difference. But Southampton, with undaunted friendliness, said, "Your most excellent play, *King Richard the Second*. Robin and I would dearly like to see it again."

A private performance at Essex House, to help pass the time until – ? No. He and the Players weren't putting their heads in *that* noose. He said, "In the circumstances, my lords – " He shrugged. But he might as well speak plainly. "I could not ask the Players to come to Essex House."

Much water might have flowed under London Bridge. But the two noblemen had not learnt to brook disobedience from commoners. Southampton said coldly, "We were not suggesting a private performance. We want a public performance, at the Globe."

A *public* performance! But why? Gentlemen like these summoned the players to their houses. It was one of those signs of power and affluence that the Elizabethans loved. Besides, *Richard the Second*? He had never been easy when the play had been produced. The Queen had personally warned him against it. He had always tried to have his name kept off the playbills. Or had used one of his less likely spellings – Shaxberd, for instance. But to perform it now, with all London in a ferment! He said, "It is an old play, my lords." He laughed uneasily. "My prentice hand."

"Nonsense. It's one of the best things you've done."

They looked disappointed in him. Southampton said, reproachfully, "It is a small thing to ask, Will."

Essex said, "It seems, Henry, that a poet, once successful, soon forgets those on whose shoulders he climbed."

Southampton almost spat out the words. "We would pay you fellows. We know how much money means to you. Would forty shillings be a suitable indemnity against loss of takings?"

Will said with sudden heat, "Do not offer me money, my lord." He went on calmly, "I would persuade my company to put on any other play for you, my lords. But not *Richard the Second*."

"Why?" The word came like a blow across his cheek.

"The Queen would take it ill, my lords."

"The Queen," sneered Southampton.

"That old carcase," whispered Essex savagely.

Will was deeply shocked. He didn't like Elizabeth much himself. But she was the anointed Queen of England. And here, in this armed camp, he became acutely aware of what it was these two foolish young men were trying to do. He said, "My lords, if you once loved me, as I think you did, let me speak plainly."

Petulantly, Essex flung himself into a chair. Southampton looked – what? Wistful, regretful, sorrowful? Will said, "I do not know what you purpose, my lords. But – let it not be against the State, or against the Queen's majesty, or against the ordinances of God."

"Preaching, by the Mass," murmured Essex. But his friend was listening intently.

"God is not mocked," said Will, speaking from experience. "And – the State is merciless – and all powerful. It crushes everything in its path like an iron wheel." He shuddered.

Essex said contemptuously, "These are days for men, Master Shakespeare. Not for poltroons." But Southampton said, sadly, "So you will not help us, Will?"

There was a long silence. Then Will shook his head. "I cannot, my lord."

Southampton went and opened the door. "Escort Master Shakespeare to the main gate," he said to the soldier. Will bowed deeply to the two noblemen. Both of them looked away.

Nobody loved Will Shakespeare nowadays.

He followed the soldier down the dark corridor. Then, suddenly, the man was no longer there.

But *she* was. No more beautiful than she had ever been. Yet as soon as his eyes saw, his whole body sprang towards her. Eyes, body. The brain had been by-passed, it seemed.

She waited for him, unsmiling. Just that long, intense, unblinking stare.

The sight of her overwhelmed him. The world had been harsh lately. In her embrace was shame, revulsion; but also comfort and homecoming; a fleshly heaven where mind and fear and memory, those cruel tormentors, could not exist.

They stood close, staring. "Come," she said at last. She led him through a door, along passages busy with men-at-arms, up small, twisting staircases, through silent corridors to a room perched under the great roof. All day she kept him there; everything, even *Hamlet*, forgotten. And when finally he left Essex House (and no one barred his way) he walked like one who has been near-drowned in a turbulent sea. This time there was no revulsion; only a deathlike emptiness of spirit, in a disintegrating world.

It was dark. *Hamlet* would have finished hours ago.

The noble Dane, who was so much a part of himself, would have gone to his long home. And in the Inns of Court gentlemen would be telling their friends about the latest Shakespeare. The only way to learn how it had gone was to find his companions at the tavern.

Will never felt that the tavern was quite the place for a gentleman. Tonight, particularly, he needed to be alone, to relive this extraordinary day. So many questions he had still to ask himself. Was it by chance that she had appeared so strangely? He thought not. It was almost as though he had been tricked, prisoned at Essex House not with drawn swords, but by the shackles of his own lusts. Why? A dreadful reason presented itself. But no. Southampton would not be so base. The Players would not be such fools.

Would they?

He hurried on to the tavern, marched in. Burbage and Heminge were there, sitting with their backs to him. He went and stood behind them. "Well," he asked, in a taut clipped voice quite unlike his own. "And how went *Hamlet*?"

They turned suddenly, startled. Burbage half rose. "Will, you surprised us. Sit down, man."

This time he almost shouted: "How went *Hamlet*?"

They waited for him to sit down. And now it was as though he were playing a part. He knew exactly what was going to be said before anyone spoke.

Burbage: We did not play *Hamlet*.

Shakespeare: Why not?

Heminge: We were offered forty shillings to put on another play.

Shakespeare: What other play?

Burbage: Your *King Richard the Second*.

The dull predestined question and answer were over. Will sprang to his feet. "You – you didn't *really* play *Richard* this afternoon?"

Burbage said reasonably, "After all, Will, you were missing. Phillips would have had to play the Ghost at short notice. So – when these gentlemen arrived with their offer, we naturally accepted. Forty shillings, Will. We couldn't lose."

Will's anger was the darting, quivering anger of fear. "Who were these – gentlemen?"

Burbage did not like being cross-questioned. He said sulkily, "Heminge dealt with them."

Heminge said, "One of them was a Welshman. Never thought I could do business with a Welshman, but this one had forty shillings in his hand."

"And his name?" Will asked. Heminge's stage Welsh had left him unamused.

"Oh, I don't know." Now Heminge was becoming irritated. They all liked old Will, but once he got a bee in his bonnet...

Will said coldly, "*I* will tell *you*. It would be Sir Gilly Meyricke."

They looked at him in surprise. Burbage said, "And who is this Sir Gilly what's-his-name?"

Will spoke the words like a man dropping coins to pay a resented debt. "Steward to Robert Devereux Earl of Essex."

They were silent. They knew the rumours. But they couldn't see. You couldn't refuse a man because his foolish master happened to be making warlike noises. Heminge broke the silence with exasperation. "But forty shillings, Will! We couldn't lose."

"Only our hearts and entrails. Only our limbs. Only our precious lives."

Heminge and Burbage paled. They had never heard such blistering bitterness on Shakespeare's lips. And there was no doubt what he was talking about. The hangman's trade had no secrets for any of them.

Will said, "You fools! What have you done to us all? I told you, from the beginning I told you the Queen sees treason in this play. And treason is in the very air of London. I tell you: in a month's time, the head of Essex – Sir Gilly Meyricke's master – will deck London Bridge. And he will be the lucky one. For us, the underlings, it will still be the question, the irons and the rack."

Burbage and Heminge sat, dumped on their stools, staring before them. They sagged like men who have already known the torture. Will sat across the table from them. And the old, generous Will, who had been buried deep these days, sprang to the surface at sight of another's fear. He seized their hands. He even managed an anxious smile. "Don't look so glum." He added, with a trace of his late bitterness, "*You* did not write the play."

Heminge looked at him beseechingly. "Where *were* you, Will?" Had you been here, it would not have happened, was implicit.

Where, indeed? So this was where his lusts had brought him. God, who is not mocked, had taken his son, so estranging him from his wife; and now had brought him into the shadow of the Tower. While he had spent the day in wicked pleasures, his innocent, foolish friends had been preparing, not only *his* death, but also their own.

He could have stopped them. If only, if only he had been there. The blame was not theirs. It was his, his alone.

They sat late in the tavern, frightened, desperately needing each other's company. "Perhaps – ?" one would say. "Essex may not move," would say another. They were like three famished men, desperately scraping a bowl, the bowl of hope.

And the bowl was almost empty.

Will did not sleep that night. He was composing another play. But this was no make-believe. This was a play they were all going to act in, whether they liked it or not. Essex and Southampton, leading their crazy rabble against the Court. The rising put down, brutally, swiftly, ruthlessly. The witch hunt. The interrogations, the dispositions, the manic search for a needle of truth in the lies of terrified men. "Your name is William Shakespeare? You visited Essex House on Saturday, 7 February? You were there all day? In your absence you caused to be produced your own play, *King Richard the Second*? To what end? I will tell you. To prepare the people's minds for the deposition of an anointed Queen. Your name is William Shakespeare? You dedicated a lewd poem to the man Southampton? Evidently you thought highly of this man. Do you still think highly of him, Shakespeare? Your name is William Shakespeare – ?"

He lay, biting his knuckles. Something, in his fearful heart, he had always wondered: what happened when you were made to bear the unbearable?

In the slow weeks ahead, it seemed to him, he was going to find out.

The play began just as Will had imagined.

He lay late abed, listening to that most peaceful of all sounds – church bells on an English Sunday morning.

He would have stayed in bed for the whole day – or forever. Not that he was safe, even in bed. Those who smelt out treason would soon drag him from his feathered nest.

But he had to know what was happening. He dressed, with trembling fingers, thinking of days when putting on good clothes had been a pleasant thing. Breakfast? It would choke him. How little, in the old days, had he appreciated a good breakfast of beef and ale, eaten with a contented man's appetite!

It was a raw February day; a good reason for wearing his heavy cloak, and for pulling his hat down well over his eyes.

He made for the Strand, attracted like a moth to the scorching flame; and stood, in a doorway, watching Essex House from afar off.

Men were pouring in, armed with pikes and swords and guns, pitchforks and pruning-hooks. Shouting, jostling, angry men.

He watched, fearful. And at eleven o'clock the ludicrous tragedy began. Out they came, brandishing their swords, hollaing for vengeance, rolling their eyes in the most alarming manner. And there, borne along protestingly in the middle, like a cork on a rushing tide, was my Lord of Essex. Clearly, lacking decision and a lead, the whole boiling of malcontents had erupted into sudden, purposeless action.

For one who loved order and degree, it was a terrifying sight: the moment when stifled resentment explodes into violence, the moment when the dam breaks, and the sweet world is swept away by a flood of madness; when irresponsible men have but one thought: to hurt, to wound, to kill.

Once in the Strand, they milled about in frenzied irresolution, like ants whose nest has been disturbed. Some waved their swords westward, crying "To the Court! Seize the Court!" Others pointed to the east. "First rouse the City. Thousands will flock to us. *Then* march on the Court."

Essex stood, chewing his lip. Then he drew his sword and pointed dramatically eastward. A frantic, gesticulating argument broke out; but slowly the noisy rabble moved off towards Ludgate Hill.

Will watched them go with a sick heart. Hundreds of foolish, doomed men, proclaiming their folly and their treason for all to see.

He waited, shivering. It was dangerous even to be in the neighbourhood of Essex House this brooding day. Most people were sensibly in their houses, the doors bolted, the curtains drawn. Other men's treason could bring death to the passer-by as surely as the plague. But he could not tear himself away. Would Essex rouse the City? Would a river of armed citizens flow back along the Strand, to engulf Whitehall? Or would the people stay silent in their houses, like rabbits in their holes when the fox is abroad?

The only hope for Will was that Essex and Southampton should be victorious, should depose a Queen who had shown little friendship to Will. Yet he could not wish this. He could not wish chaos to come again to his country, even to save his own skin.

The cold was bitter. There was no break, no movement, in the grey blanket of sky. The streets were empty, silent. He heard a few shots, far in the distance.

The government seemed to be making no move. But in the Palace of Whitehall, he knew, there would be intense activity. The old Queen would know every step. She would be waiting, watching, like a spider at the centre of her web. Clever, cunning Cecil, and the Council, would be doing the same. Waiting, watching; always leaving the other fellow to make the moves – and the mistakes.

It had been the same, all through the long and glorious reign. Elizabeth had been the stillness at the centre of the whirlwind, the rock unshaken by the demented sea.

There was a commotion at the far end of the Strand.

They were coming back.

Essex led them, now; not a great army of vengeful citizens; but a pitiful rabble that had lost half its members since leaving Essex House, and lost all direction.

Will could see Southampton in the depleted throng: a man who looked as though already he gazed on the headsman's axe. But even he did not look as dreadful as Essex. Essex staggered, using his sword to support him. He had lost his hat. His hair was wild. His eyes gazed about him like those of a man entering Hell. He led his ragged army into Essex House. The great doors slammed behind them.

And now, at last, Elizabeth acted. Troops came pouring down the Strand, thousands of them it seemed. They surrounded Essex House. They brought up artillery, pointed the guns squarely at the great mansion. Clearly they were prepared, with Tudor whole-heartedness, to blast it off the face of the earth.

The doors opened. Essex and Southampton came out, and were promptly marched towards the Tower, surrounded by a veritable ring fence of pikes. A troop of soldiers doubled into Essex House. Guards were set at the doors. Someone leaped from a high window. Will heard the dull crack of bone as he landed on the paving.

It was tragedy; a pitiful tragedy of a spoilt, foolish but by no means worthless, man acting as a catalyst for the resentment of others.

Will had seen more than he could stand. He retched, violently; it was as though his body struggled vainly to rid his mind of horrors. And still he could not tear himself away. Some of the rebels were being brought out, now: shoved, kicked, cuffed, prodded with swords and pikes; marched off to the Brideswell or the Marshalsea prisons.

A frore winter's dusk was already closing in. Will, emptied of body, numbed of mind, turned for home.

The soldiers had done a good day's work. Now it was the turn of the gaolers, the questioners, the tormentors.

That night he groped his way through the dark, subterranean caverns of his own mind.

He would be adjudged a friend of traitors, and the writer of a traitorous play. Thanks to him, his good friends the Players would be condemned. Even his wife, his children, his parents would not be safe.

If, as he believed, a man's character largely dictated his life, what flaws had brought sweet Will, everybody's favourite, to this state, he asked himself.

Ambition. Cowardice. Lust!

Cowardice had run like a yellow thread through his life. Oh, call it caution if you would. But fear of saying "no" to a lord had brought him to Essex House that fateful Saturday. Lust had kept him there, while others made a decision that should have been his. A decision that would destroy them all.

And ambition, that had suggested the dedication to Southampton. Ambition, that brought him to London, to Southampton House, to friendship of the rebels. Ambition, that had robbed poor Anne of the one thing in life that mattered to her: his company.

All night, he knew, in the Tower, in the Brideswell, in the Marshalsea, the work of questioning would go remorselessly on. Every now and then a name would be wrung from some wretch. The name would be handed to an officer, the officer would spring to duty, collect a few men, and clatter off through the midnight streets to bring in another suspect. The hammering on the door, the white, terrified faces at the window, weapons winking malevolently in the torchlight.

How long, he wondered, before they decided to see what the man Shakespeare could be induced to tell them.

The blow fell during the last act of *Twelfth Night*.

It had been a charmed performance. The players, under the shadow of death, acted with a desperate gaiety. The audience, escaping from the brooding tension of London into the make-believe of Illyria, were quite carried away. They roared, they wept, they cheered, they hissed.

And now, the February dusk had fallen about the rapt playhouse. The torches had been lit. Armin had been left alone on the stage to sing his little nonsense song about the wind and the rain. The torchlight played on his lute, on his pale, sad features, on the absorbed, muffin faces of the groundlings on the front row. The spells of music and poetry, laughter and sorrow, hung like a blessing over this lighted O.

It was broken by the clank of armour, the tramp of men. An officer and three men were pushing their way forward through the crowd.

The rain it raineth every day. Armin went on singing. The soldiers went round into the tiring-room. The more cautious members of the audience began to slip away. When the soldiery were out, one was best at home these days. The spell was broken. The cloth of make-believe was rent. The chill wind of everyday was blowing through.

" 'Tis a good play, Will," Malvolio Burbage was just saying to Orsino Shakespeare, as they waited to take their calls. Will's plays never failed to surprise him. However often you acted in them, you always found something new. However many layers you peeled away, there was always another.

Will looked delighted. He was always childishly pleased when someone enjoyed his "pleasant trifles". "It was – " he began.

"Master Shakespeare?" asked a coldly polite voice.

Will spun round. A military man in a broad brimmed hat, steel breastplate, and leather breeches. And with his hand on his sword.

Will didn't trust his voice. He nodded.

"Did you write a play called *King Richard the Second?*"

Again Will nodded. "And did you cause it to be shown at this playhouse on Saturday, February the Seventh, in this present year of our Lord?"

Will was about to nod miserably when Augustine Phillips, a quiet unassuming member of the company, said stoutly, "No, he didn't. We did."

"We, sir?"

Phillips swept an arm round the tiring-house. "We, sir. All of us. Except Shakespeare. He had nothing to do with it."

"Then you will be required to justify your choice of play to the Council, sir," said the soldier.

Phillips swallowed, but lifted his head boldly. "Tell your masters the drama will remain stunted so long as there is this state interference with writers and players."

"Tell them yourself," said the soldier. "You will," he added nastily, "have plenty of opportunity."

It was, perhaps, as well that Augustine Phillips and not the honey-tongued Shakespeare spoke for the Company before the Council, for, incredibly, the charge against them was dropped. Men were being ritualistically disembowelled for even being a friend or a servant to one of the rebels. Yet somehow the stolid honesty of Augustine Phillips won the day.

"I told them," he said as the Players crowded anxiously round him on his return. "I didn't wait for them to attack us. I attacked them."

There were murmurs of wonder, and approval. "How, Augustine?"

"I told them that unless a writer had freedom of speech he would never produce anything worthwhile. I told them that the Lord Chamberlain and the Master of the Revels were no better than the old Roman *Censors*."

"And they listened to you?" There were smiles now, even laughter, hands slapping down on thighs.

"They listened to me. I said, 'Take Will here'" – Will looked as though he would have preferred his name to be left out of it – " 'Take Will Shakespeare,' I said. 'He's a promising writer. But he'll never produce anything of value while he's writing under the dead hand of a *Censor*.' "

Will tried not to look glum. He'd rather hoped that people thought he had produced something of value already. He also felt rather ashamed of himself. Frankly, it had never occurred to him that he was being stunted as an artist by not being allowed to write anything he wanted. He was not, he decided, a very percipient person.

Augustine Phillips laughed. "No, friends, it wasn't my oratory won the day. It was the fact that we're too good a company to lose. If we were not available when the Queen desired a play, someone would have some explaining to do."

And sure enough, a few days later they were commanded to perform before the Queen on the eve of the execution of the Earl of Essex. The play? *King Richard the Second*. Ageing Majesty, it seemed, had not lost her gift for unpredictability.

Everyone at Court – except, it seemed, the Queen – was on tenterhooks that Shrove Tuesday Night. Essex was in all their thoughts. Essex, spending his last night upon earth. Essex, watching from the Tower as his sun went down for the last time. Essex, seeing the tapers lit, the gentleness of night, the preparations to bedward – all for the last time. He was on everybody's mind, in everybody's heart; he and death. Scarcely one person present, in that glittering Court, but knew that one night he too might lie where Essex lay, think Essex's thoughts, face Essex's fears. A thoughtless word, a moment of folly, were enough to start the journey on the long road to where Essex lay.

The players were nervous, fearing a trap, fearing a royal outburst as the treasonable play proceeded. The courtiers were tense. Tomorrow, one of their number was setting out on the greatest voyage of discovery of all – a voyage, moreover, that each one of them must make, sooner or later, and alone. All eyes were on the Queen.

She sat there, old, mumbling, majestic. At times she appeared to doze; but everyone knew that those hooded eyes were not missing a thing, either on stage or off it.

It was a stilted performance. Everyone was very thankful when it came to an end.

The players bowed, knowing that this was the moment for anything to happen: a few gracious words of approbation, a royal outburst, a charge of treason.

None of these. Elizabeth went on sitting. Her once-beautiful hands lay folded in her lap. The eyes remained hooded.

Then she rose, and the Court stirred. And she showed that *her* mind, too, was with him who was about to take a journey. Her lips moved. "*He* is no Bolingbroke," she murmured scornfully. And suddenly the royal chin was up, it seemed that lightning flashed about the room from the royal eyes. "And by God, *I* am no Richard Plantagenet," she cried. She swept from the chamber. She had given her warning. She was Elizabeth Tudor. And if the only usurper strong enough to challenge her was death, then let death take heed. He would not find her easy to depose.

They cut his head off the following morning; privately, at his own request.

Southampton they reprieved. But kept him in the Tower.

Will Shakespeare heard the tolling of the bells, and shivered. He remembered the two friends as he had first seen them: arrogant, wealthy, powerful; yet lithe and beautiful as young stallions. And now? A bloody head, lifted between calloused hands, and jabbed down firmly on an iron spike on London Bridge; the rusty metal, forcing through bone and muscle and brain; the squirt of blackening blood on hands and aprons.

He felt sick, faint with revulsion. And that other friend: alive, but shut away from the sunlight and the pleasant air, from the wind and the rain. Shut away from love, and all hoping.

Like many Londoners, that grey Ash Wednesday, he strolled towards the Tower.

There it stood, the ancient citadel, the Thames licking its walls. Somewhere, behind those grim stones, lay his friend

Southampton; hearing, no doubt, the marching, the prayers, the psalm-singing, the oratory, without which no execution of any standing was judged complete.

Also behind the walls of the fortress – and this was even more to the point – was almost certainly a paper on which it was recorded that the friends of the traitors Essex and Southampton had included one William Shakespeare against whom, *so far*, no action had been taken; but who would doubtless repay watching.

It was a terrible and frightening thing to believe that one's name was recorded in that prison with a black mark against it. He was finished. No one, not even Dick Field, would dare to publish any more poems by a friend of traitors. His plays would be suspect. He hated London, with its ailing queen, dangerous now as a cold-drowsy wasp, dragging herself about the rooms of Whitehall or Greenwich; with this dank prison-fortress by the river; with its overhanging houses and stinking ways. He feared it, now, this cruel, vengeful city. He had stayed with his fellows when they were in danger, and perhaps he was even more proud of this fact than of his Grant of Arms. He had satisfied honour and, perhaps even more important, kept the love of his friends.

But now, he couldn't leave London fast enough. The quiet ways of Warwickshire were tearing at his very heart. He would find some corner, sheltered by kindly trees, carpeted with grass and the pretty buttercups, and there live out his days; the slow pageantry of the seasons would be his theatre; the gentle countryside, his first love, would be his wife; and peace of heart would be the rich reward of all his labours.

So he thought, in the uncaring tumult of London.

CHAPTER 14

OUR PLAY IS DONE…

But, as he rode homewards, soothed already by the country quiet, he began to think differently. God, he had aged since Hamnet died. He had known little happiness, and much perturbation, since then. Well, he could make up for it now; but only if Anne would move into New Place with him. He was, he thought, beginning to need Anne. He had married before he was ready for marriage. Now, at last, he *was* ready. No more lodgings. No more loveless loving in high, forgotten rooms of empty palaces. No more roving. If – it depended on Anne. And Anne had a will of her own. He would be very humble, very gentle. Brash, swaggering Will was buried deep.

He stopped his horse outside the cottage in Chapel Lane.

The litter of autumn still lay strewn about the garden, sodden with winter snows.

He went and hammered on the door. He peered through the windows, knowing the only occupants would be the mice and the spiders.

He was suddenly afraid. Plague could easily carry off a whole family, only the house being left as a witness, like the shell of a dead snail.

Henley Street! That was the quickest way to find out what had happened. He leapt on to his horse, cantered off. For perhaps the first time in his life he really needed Anne. And she wasn't there!

His way took him past New Place – *his* New Place. He scarcely noticed it, perhaps would not have done had there not been a lamp burning in a window that cloud-racked February day.

A light, in New Place?

Trembling, he dismounted, went and knocked on the door.

He waited, knocked again.

Slow, shuffling footsteps were approaching the door. Not, surely, Anne's? But then, whose?

There was much drawing of bolts, turning of keys. The door was opened at last. By Will's father.

The old man stared, with sagging eyes.

Will said, "Father, what are *you* doing here? And where is Anne?"

John Shakespeare went on staring. "Who is it?"

"It's Will, your son."

"Who?"

"Your son, Will." Suddenly moved, he stepped inside, seized the old shoulders, kissed the white forehead. "But where is Anne?"

"Will?" The old man stared at him fearfully. "Nay, that is not possible."

Will smothered his irritation. "Not only possible, but true, father."

"Will!" A voice spoke behind him.

He turned. Anne, in cloak and bonnet, with a shopping-basket on her arm. Anne, staring as at a ghost. Anne, deathly pale, looking about to faint.

"Anne!" he said tenderly, taking her in his arms. "Anne!"

She peered at him earnestly. "Is it really you? Oh, Will, we heard you were dead. It was said Essex had rebelled – with ten thousand men – and there had been a great battle in the London streets – and you had been slain."

"I am no fighting man," he said, kissing her hair, her eyes, her nose. "Oh, Anne, I have come home."

She looked at him with an incredible, dawning hope. "Not – not for good?"

He nodded, grinning like a schoolboy. She clung to him. He hugged her like a bear. John stared at them both, solemnly shaking his head. "It cannot be Will," he said gravely. "Will was slain, fighting for the rebels. It was a foolish thing to do, though of course my Lord of Essex was of good stock. A Devereux, a good family."

"Will! I was resting. I heard the commotion." His mother came down the hall, walking briskly but with obvious pain. "So they didn't kill you, my pretty boy. I'm not surprised. I said Will would never be where the fighting was."

"Thank you, mother." But they kissed fondly.

There was so much to say that no one said anything. But there was something Will had to know. "You said you would never live here, Anne," he said gently.

"Your mother persuaded me. She showed me I was ungrateful, Will."

"And we came with her," said Mary. "It would have been too ridiculous, three women in a house of *this* size. Besides, your father loves the *grandness* of it so. He has attained his heaven without the inconvenience of dying."

Now they were all talking and laughing. Suddenly a girl stood before him – poised between girlhood and womanhood, with the bloom still on her.

He stared. She smiled, enchantingly, and kissed his cheek. "Father," she said.

"Susanna!" Susanna! Had he really helped to form this exquisite feminine creature, for some other man's delight? God, the man had better be worthy. Not, he thought wryly, some foot-loose harlotry player.

And here was Judith, a very different Judith, her curranty eyes friendly, her plain, homely face exuding pleasure.

He loved them all. Oh, it was good to be home.

Home! For perhaps the first time in his life the word stirred him. Home had been somewhere to write, and snatch a little food. Even, in the old days in the cottage, sometimes a prison. Now it was a place to love, to tend; a place in which to entertain friends, watch over one's daughters, aye, by the Mass, a place in which to give one's wife some of the happiness of which he had robbed her. He took Anne's arm. "Show me the house, wife."

Almost beside herself with happiness, she led him off. It was a fine house; and she, with Mary's help, had furnished it fit for a gentleman of worship. Yet, without Will, it had been nothing but a shell. Without Will, one place was as good as another.

And now, here was Will, back from the dead. Had she really believed the rumours? She did not know. All she knew was that the burden of sorrow had been lifted from her limbs. She straightened, filling her lungs with air, and walked with a brisker step.

The wind had been savaging the sky all day. Towards evening it succeeded in tearing great rents in the clouds. Through the rents could be seen the clear brightness of the lengthening days, the far wastes of eternity, the first pinpoint brilliance of the evening star. It was as though the drab curtain of winter had been dragged aside, to glimpse a hope-filled universe.

Will and Anne, in their tour of New Place, had reached a high, unfurnished room near the top of the house. Together they leaned on the window ledge, her right arm comfortably pressed against his left, and gazed out at the shredded clouds, the yellow shafts of sunset, the swollen river, the indignant wind-tossed rooks, the shouting elms.

A glimpse of turbulent spring. In another hour, darkness. Tomorrow, perhaps, winter would be in the saddle once more – greyness, sleet, the sun swamped in a plethora of cloud.

So this moment was rare. They gazed out, saying nothing. Then they turned, and regarded each other gravely.

He had filled out. Responsibility, success, having to fight a little, had given him authority, a presence. The chestnut, the neatly trimmed beard, were touched with grey. His face anxious, grave; but now he smiled, carefully, as though smiling were something he had not done for a long time. He said, wistfully, "I have been a poor husband, Anne. But now" – he gave a modest shrug she remembered so well – "I will do my best to make up." – he gave a shamefaced smile – "I think perhaps I have grown up, wife."

She squeezed his arm, turned back to stare out at the passing day. The sunset flared like a dying fire, lighting her face.

She, too, had changed. The slow country girl, the dowdy bride, the woman beaten to the ground by sorrow – all these gone. In their place was the mistress of New Place, the wife of William Shakespeare, Gent., a person like her husband, of authority. Yet, unlike her husband, with both feet still firmly planted on the soil of Warwickshire; a woman who had taught herself to live up to her station because it was her duty, once her mother-in-law had pointed out what was her duty; but a woman who would still be happier in a cottage, a woman who would live, and die, as simple, unaffected and natural as her native flowers. A woman who asked nothing of life except the love of one man.

Her face was a little wizened, now, like an apple. But sweet. Staring out at the sunset she said, "I thought I had driven you away for ever, Will, after Hamnet died. So – when your mother showed me how foolish I had been – I set myself to turn New Place into a home for you. But" – she rubbed her cheek against his sleeve – "I feared I was too late."

The sun was getting very low, now. The clouds were driving up again. She gave a little laugh. "I think – standing here, in this little room, with our elbows on the window ledge, watching clouds – "

She fell silent. "Yes?" he prompted.

"I think it is the happiest thing I have ever done in my life," she said slowly. Then, suddenly, she was in his arms, weeping a lifetime's tears.

Will's trunks arrived with the carrier: clothes, books, candlesticks, quills, inkhorns. Anne and Susanna were interested in the clothes, Mary in the books: Holinshed, Plutarch, Ovid, Seneca; even Cinzio, in Italian. They looked as though they had been read, too. She was impressed. She was always finding new depths in Will.

So. He had sent for his trunks. Anne said, "Have you really come to stay, Will?"

The whole world rested on his answer.

Had he? Life at New Place was delightful. A loving wife, a beautiful daughter obviously enchanted by this distinguished, courteous father, another daughter his devoted slave; friends – he had already done a little entertaining; Stratford society paying its respects. A path that wandered all day beside a brook. And, even more important, ninety miles between himself and that dreadful old Queen, ninety miles between himself and the Council, ninety miles between himself and the Tower.

And yet – things were already stirring in his brain: a story in Cinzio, for instance, about a black man who thinks his wife unfaithful. That was the stuff of plays. And a bloody tale of Makbeth, a Scotsman, in Holinshed. His fingers began to itch for a pen.

Well, he could write in Stratford as well as in London. And then, when things were forgotten… Perhaps a breath of London air would not hurt him?

No. Things would never be forgotten. Not while the old Queen lived.

He took his wife's hand. He smiled. "I have come to live and die in Stratford."

She gazed at him fearfully. If only he would leave it there, with that definite statement. But no. He was going to qualify it, she knew with a sinking heart.

He said, "It is possible that, when the old Queen dies, I may have to visit London occasionally. But certainly not while she lives."

Anne smiled, hiding her bitter disappointment. "Then I shall pray that the Queen be granted long life, husband," she said lightly. "For I would have you with me always."

It was good to be loved. Not with simple adoration. Anne knew his faults, and checked them tartly. But she loved him in spite of them, and that was good. His self-regard, that had lately taken so much buffeting, began to shoot again like the sturdy daffodils in Stratford meadows.

When the old Queen dies… Then he would be off, Anne thought. She had no illusions.

Not for long at a time, perhaps. He wasn't as young as he had been. He was beginning to like his comforts. And it pleased him, living at New Place. She could tell; the grandeur, the spaciousness, the beauty of these surroundings appealed to him. He was at home here, like a peacock on a lordly terrace.

Dear Will! He'd always wanted to be the gentleman. Now that he had achieved it he wouldn't lightly give it up. Herself, she felt much more at home in the old cottage. In fact she would often stand at the window of the big house, staring at he cottage with a desperate nostalgia. Foolish, she knew. One only had the present, and the future. The past was buried deep; deeper than Hamnet in his little grave.

The future? With her Will-o'-the-Wisp dancing away once more? That left only the present. And the present was so sweet. Oh, let not the future tarnish the shining present. It did her good to see Will so happy. Off to his bowls of an afternoon, or strolling with Susanna; an evening cup of sack with his father, who thought he was Gilbert but no matter; then, after supper, out with music books, and Susanna fetching her lute, and it was part songs till bedtime. A loving wife and daughters, a fine house, comfort, the pleasantest of routines. What man could ask for more?

In September, the old man died.

He found great satisfaction in dying in the solid middle-class grandeur of New Place; his wife and children about him.

Joan was the only one weeping. She was a good girl. But his sons had been a disappointment. Gilbert was a fool. Richard and Edmund would never make much.

Will, handsome with his trim chestnut beard, his troubled eyes, his face heavy with compassion? Will? No one would call a son who could afford New Place a *total* disappointment. And yet? Had Will stayed in Stratford and built up the business he might still have afforded New Place. *And* been a respectable citizen, instead of a foot-loose actor who did a bit of scribbling in his spare time. A strange way to earn a living; nothing *solid* about it, thought John, who loved solidity. A play was a play, something for an afternoon, forgotten as soon as seen. But a pair of gloves was a pair of gloves…

Judith, button-eyed and solemn, brought the old man a bunch of wild flowers. Too late. The child wept a little, with the April grief of childhood. Then she went off to play in the sunshine. What was one old man more or less, in a world where lads could wither like burnt grass?

It was often rumoured that the Queen was dead. But she was not. And there were many wise and learned men who declared, after giving much thought to the matter, that she would probably live for ever.

If one could call it living. She ate little but succory potage, slept little. She would sit for hours, silent and vacant, touching a golden cup to her lips. She would sit for hours, in a darkened room, weeping for Essex, sweet Robin, whose head she had, very properly, cut off. Sweet Robin, her last love, who had loved her and then risen against her. Who killed Cock Robin? I, said the sparrow, with my… And she would fall again to weeping. It was as though Essex's treachery, and his death, had killed her spirit while her body lived on. The music was stilled. The dancing days were done.

And yet? And yet? Lord Sempill glanced in through a window in a winter's dusk and saw, by the light of a single candle, the gaunt Queen and her faithful old servant, Lady Warwick, dancing solemnly, stumblingly, to the thin music of a pipe. An eerie, ghostly picture. Lord Sempill had seen what no man should have seen. It was more shameful than seeing the old women naked. He hurried to his chamber, and prayed that God would erase this pitiful sight from his memory.

The summer came, and died; and few thought she would see another summer, yet she did. *And* another winter; mumbling, huddled in shawls, skeleton claws clutching vainly at the fire's heat.

And Anne Shakespeare, too, began to think the old Queen would never die. And that she would have her Will with her always.

For years now, that sound of surf beating on undiscovered shores had been growing louder in his brain. That distant thunder, those tides roaring through ocean's deepest caves, were nearer now. He was busy with his Cinzio, his Holinshed. Even as he watched the bowls run, or brought his pleasant tenor to bear in a round or a madrigal, or smiled across the fireplace at his Anne – even then mighty and terrible figures were moving, mist-shrouded, across the stage of his creative mind: Othello, Makbeth, Lear. Sometimes, when he was alone, the mists would clear for a moment, and he would tremble. Could a mere mortal man take these tremendous figures, and dare to let them grow in his brain?

They were waiting, crying out for life and form. And here he was, idling his life away. Where now were those voyages of discovery he had spoken of, with such enthusiasm, to Dick Burbage? Life went on. Other play writers would be only too eager to fill the hole left by Master Shakespeare – Dekker, young Jonson, Fletcher, Webster.

Yet life was sweet; ordered and gracious, and reasonably safe. Whereas, in London, so many dangers lurked.

Southampton, he heard, still lay in the Tower. So, still, must many of the rebels. It needed only a word – the name Shakespeare, perhaps, murmured by a sleeping prisoner, or screamed out during some night of mindless agony – and he would be brought in. Perhaps even from Stratford, he knew. But at least he was not advertising his existence daily from the London stage.

Besides, he had promised Anne. So long as the Queen lived – He could not disappoint her again. Her happiness in his presence was too great. Sometimes he would watch her waking to a new day; see her, eyes still closed, frown. Then, opening her eyes, look at him, discover him by her side, and smile like one entering paradise. Sometimes, at table, he would find her watching him, telling herself it was true, her Will *was* home, it was no gossamer dream to tear at waking.

No. He could not leave her. Not while the old Queen lived.

Would they be waiting for her? Old, grave Burghley? Whether in Heaven or Hell, *he* would have learnt the ropes. He would know his way about. "If I might suggest your Grace, it will be advisable – I have managed to keep a throne for your Grace. Not quite what we were used to at Whitehall. But as a Protestant – "

And Philip of Spain, who had wooed her so coldly and so long? No. She would not meet Philip. He would be in a more select Heaven than hers, reserved solely for Apostles and Popes and Catholic Majesties.

Her witty, boisterous mother whom she had always felt she would have liked so well had father not cut her head off? And Robin, Robin of Leicester, slim, erect, laughing, as he had once been? Oh, if he and she could hunt the heavenly deer as they had hunted once, so long ago, at Kenilworth! If he and she could spend the nights in dancing and laughter, as in the old days! Watched, she thought glumly, by those damned wives of his.

With the turn of the year she fell into a deeper and more terrible melancholy. But it was not until 23 March that she finally announced, with true Tudor arrogance, that she had decided to die. "I wish not to live any longer," she said, "but desire to die."

And die she did. At three o'clock of the following morning.

For her, who had known so little of tenderness (a mother's love cut off by the headsman's axe when she was two; the rare, exuberant dandlings on the knee of her terrifying father; her gaoler, her own sister; the barren courtship of men to whom she could never give herself, for the Queen could give herself to no man; the hard comfortlessness of a throne) for her it was an end of melancholy, and weariness, and struggle. An end of treachery and loneliness.

An end of laughter. An end of summer days.

Everyone was really rather relieved. She had gone on just a little too long. Much as they loved her, they were ready for a change now. She had finished her work, and it was only proper that she should move on. They would show their appreciation, of course. She should have a notable funeral. Then: see what Scotch Jamie could do.

The Queen was dead. Long live the King!

After the dead days of winter, the early spring day had held a high excitement. Sunlight, bird chatter, the protesting bleat of newborn lambs, the broad sweep of river bearing away the last of the winter snows; the bright sky, piled and littered with clouds of every colour, the wind frisking with the lambs, the lambs frisking in the wind. Will and Anne had walked the lanes about Shottery, thinking (though not saying. There was always a certain shyness between them) thinking, here did we kiss, here did we lie when the corn was ripe to harvest, and the moon was lantern to our loving. They walked with their arms about each other's waist, tender, each utterly content with the other's company; two country lovers; he a middle-aged man, well dressed and prosperous; she approaching fifty. Two ageing lovers, trying to make up for the years that ambition had eaten, the sweet world's taste again unspoilt upon their lips. Even the fears that still lay heavy on his soul served only to intensify and sharpen his happiness.

And now, the evening was a fitting close to that perfect day. The fire leapt in the great hearth of New Place. There were friends: the Sadlers, the Quineys; there was music, and laughter; of all the things Will loved, two that he loved the best. Warmth, the living brightness of fire and candles, love, friendship.

They sang. "*Johnny, Come Kiss Me Now*", "*The Twelfth Day of December*", "*Greensleeves*" (inevitably) and, with much laughter and stumbling of words, a catch: "*Hold Thy Peace, Thou Knave*".

They finished the catch; laughing, breathless, gasping noisily. Will went round with the jug, smiling, courteous, filling up glasses. Slowly, the noise and chattering subsided.

And then they heard it: the low, slow tolling of a bell.

And, in the street outside, a murmur, like the wind in dry reeds: "The Queen, the Queen, the Queen, the Queen, the Queen." As it had been among the mists of Kenilworth, on that day of his youth.

And then, from the direction of High Cross, a distant cry: "The Queen is dead. Long live the King!"

A surge of excitement – and fear – lifted him like a great wave; and would carry him, aye, and fling him down –

where? Where he would not go, yet would go: London, with the prison doors thrown open; the theatre, the Players! Voyages of discovery? Yes, by God. Suddenly his mind was like a coiled spring. It was as though some giant power had seized his writing-arm, and was pouring into it a terrible strength, a ranging knowledge of good and evil and the souls of men.

A terrible strength; a terrible love; a terrible compassion such as, surely, only a God could feel; and, knowing himself mortal, a terrible humility. Who was he, to create giants?

The Queen is dead. Long live the King!

Anne looked across at her husband. He was standing with the jug of wine and a glass in his hands – staring into eternity.

She knew that look. His other world was claiming him. His world of make-believe. It would not be long, she knew, before he was off, now. Yet again, her Will-o'-the-Wisp would flit away. Oh, he'd come back. New Place would draw him, even if she didn't. Besides, she knew now, he was rooted in Warwickshire soil as deep as she.

What had she had? Marriage to a man she loved but would never know. Many women, she suspected, would have liked to be wife to Master Shakespeare. Women who would have understood what he was trying to do, who would have helped him in so many ways. They would have been beautiful. They would have known how to spend his money in order to make themselves more beautiful. He would have been proud to introduce them to his noble friends. They would have been able to talk wittily and gaily, to dance a measure, to play upon the virginals. And Will would have taken them to his heart, opened his mind to them as he had never opened it to her. How wonderful it would have been, she thought sadly, to be able to *talk* to Will; not only about household and family affairs, but about books, about a whole world that was closed to her. A husband who could read in

Latin and Greek and Italian; a wife to whom reading even English was a labour.

She had, she supposed, failed him. She supposed she had never even tried to keep up with him. All she had ever done was to love him. It never occured to her that such devotion, such selfless love, was the rarest thing in life, and its richest jewel. Sweet William! Sweet Will-o'-the-Wisp! Without you there is no comfort, no sunlight. Come back, before I am old. Bring back the summer days.

Yes. He would come back. She knew it. There was hope, beyond the summer's heat, the winter snows. There would be happiness again, together, happiness at evening; before the long night, and the drawing of the curtains.

ACKNOWLEDGMENTS

Ivor Brown's *Shakespeare* was *my* Chapman's Homer. When I read it, a new planet swam into my ken: that delightful man Shakespeare.

Since then I have read, with profit and great pleasure,   A C Bradley, Anthony Burgess, M St Clare Byrne, F E Halliday, Elizabeth Jenkins, Peter Quennell, A L Rowse, George Bernard Shaw, Edith Sitwell, Lacey Baldwin Smith, Lytton Strachey, J Dover Wilson, and many others; all of whom have increased my knowledge of, and love for, either the man or his times.

I am most grateful to these authors for their splendid books.

ERIC MALPASS

BEEFY JONES

Beefy Jones is a lovable rogue. Not very bright, but strong and kind-hearted, he lives with a gang of petty criminals and Jack-the-Lads in the disused loft of the church hall in Dandy. The Vicar, meanwhile, is blissfully unaware of this motley gang of uninvited occupants. Returning home early one evening, Beefy overhears a meeting of the Church Council where under discussion is the demolition of the church hall – their home. The gang then embarks on a series of adventures with one aim in mind – to sabotage the vicar's plans by any means they can in order to save their home. In this hugely funny and intriguing story, they find themselves plunged into a series of wild, madcap escapades with the willing, naïve Beefy always at the centre of the action.

Eric Malpass

The Lamplight and the Stars

Nathan Cranswick's third child comes into the world on the day of Queen Victoria's Diamond Jubilee. Whilst the Empire celebrates, Nathan's concerns are about his family's future. A gentle and wise preacher, he gratefully accepts the chance to move from the dingy, cramped house in Ingerby to the village of Moreland when he is offered a job on the splendid Heron estate. Anticipating peace and tranquillity for his wife and young family, his hopes are cruelly dashed when their new life is beset by problems from the beginning. A family scandal and the Boer War menace their whole future, but finally it is the agonising choice facing his gentle daughter which threatens to tear the family apart…

Morning's at Seven

Three generations of the Pentecost family live in a state of permanent disarray in a huge, sprawling farmhouse. Seven-year-old Gaylord Pentecost is the innocent hero who observes the lives of the adults – Grandpa, Momma and Poppa and two aunties – with amusement and incredulity.

Through Gaylord's eyes, we witness the heartache suffered by Auntie Rose as the exquisite Auntie Becky makes a play for her gentleman friend, while Gaylord unwittingly makes the situation far worse.

Mayhem and madness reign in this zestful account of the lives and loves of the outrageous Pentecosts.

Eric Malpass

Of Human Frailty
A biographical novel of Thomas Cranmer

Thomas Cranmer is a gentle, unassuming scholar when a chance meeting sweeps him away from the security and tranquillity of Cambridge to the harsh magnificence of Henry VIII's court. As a supporter of Henry he soon rises to prominence as Archbishop of Canterbury.

Eric Malpass paints a fascinating picture of Reformation England and its prominent figures: the brilliant, charismatic but utterly ruthless Henry VIII, the exquisite but scheming Anne Boleyn and the fanatical Mary Tudor.

But it is the paradoxical Thomas Cranmer who dominates the story. A tormented man, he is torn between valour and cowardice; a man with a loving heart who finds himself hated by many; and a man of God who makes the terrifying discovery that he must suffer and die for his beliefs. Thomas Cranmer is a man of simple virtue, whose only fault is his all too human frailty.

ERIC MALPASS

THE RAISING OF LAZARUS PIKE

Lazarus Pike (1820–1899), author of *Lady Emily's Decision*, lies buried in the churchyard of Ill Boding. And there he would have remained, in obscurity and undisturbed, had it not been for a series of remarkable coincidences. A discovery sets in motion a campaign to republish his works and to reinstate Lazarus Pike as a giant of Victorian literature. This is a cause of bitter wrangling between the two factions that emerge. For some, Lazarus is a simple schoolmaster, devoted to his beautiful wife, Corinda. For others, who think his reputation needs a sexy, contemporary twist, he is a wife murderer with a deeply flawed character. What follows is a knowing and wry look at the world of literary makeovers and the heritage industry in a hilarious story that brings fame and tragedy to an unsuspecting moorland village.

ERIC MALPASS

THE WIND BRINGS UP THE RAIN

It is a perfect summer's day in August 1914. Yet even as Nell and her friends enjoy a blissful picnic by the river, the storm clouds of war are gathering over Europe. Very soon this idyll is to be swept away by the conflict that will take millions of men to their deaths.

After the war, the widowed Nell leads a wretched existence, caring for her husband's elderly, ungrateful parents, with only her son, Benbow, for companionship and support. But Nell is a passionate woman and wants to share her life with a man who will return her love. Meanwhile, Benbow falls in love with a German girl, Ulrike – until she is enticed home by the resurgent Germany.

This moving story of a Midlands family in the inter-war years is a compelling tale of personal triumph and disappointment, set against the background of the hideous destruction of war.

TITLES BY ERIC MALPASS AVAILABLE DIRECT
FROM HOUSE OF STRATUS

Quantity		£	$(US)	$(CAN)	€
	AT THE HEIGHT OF THE MOON	6.99	11.50	15.99	11.50
	BEEFY JONES	6.99	11.50	15.99	11.50
	THE CLEOPATRA BOY	6.99	11.50	15.99	11.50
	FORTINBRAS HAS ESCAPED	6.99	11.50	15.99	11.50
	A HOUSE OF WOMEN	6.99	11.50	15.99	11.50
	THE LAMPLIGHT AND THE STARS	6.99	11.50	15.99	11.50
	THE LONG LONG DANCES	6.99	11.50	15.99	11.50
	MORNING'S AT SEVEN	6.99	11.50	15.99	11.50
	OF HUMAN FRAILTY	6.99	11.50	15.99	11.50
	OH, MY DARLING DAUGHTER	6.99	11.50	15.99	11.50
	PIG-IN-THE-MIDDLE	6.99	11.50	15.99	11.50
	THE RAISING OF LAZARUS PIKE	6.99	11.50	15.99	11.50
	SUMMER AWAKENING	6.99	11.50	15.99	11.50
	THE WIND BRINGS UP THE RAIN	6.99	11.50	15.99	11.50

ALL HOUSE OF STRATUS BOOKS ARE AVAILABLE FROM GOOD BOOKSHOPS
OR DIRECT FROM THE PUBLISHER:

Internet: www.houseofstratus.com including author interviews, reviews, features.

Email: sales@houseofstratus.com please quote author, title and credit card details.

Order Line: UK: 0800 169 1780,
             USA: 1 800 509 9942
             INTERNATIONAL: +44 (0) 20 7494 6400 (UK)
                       or +01 212 218 7649
             (please quote author, title, and credit card details.)

Send to: House of Stratus Sales Department   House of Stratus Inc.
           24c Old Burlington Street   Suite 210
           London   1270 Avenue of the Americas
           W1X 1RL   New York • NY 10020
           UK   USA

PAYMENT

Please tick currency you wish to use:

☐ £ (Sterling)　　☐ $ (US)　　☐ $ (CAN)　　☐ € (Euros)

Allow for shipping costs charged per order plus an amount per book as set out in the tables below:

CURRENCY/DESTINATION

	£(Sterling)	$(US)	$(CAN)	€(Euros)
Cost per order				
UK	1.50	2.25	3.50	2.50
Europe	3.00	4.50	6.75	5.00
North America	3.00	3.50	5.25	5.00
Rest of World	3.00	4.50	6.75	5.00
Additional cost per book				
UK	0.50	0.75	1.15	0.85
Europe	1.00	1.50	2.25	1.70
North America	1.00	1.00	1.50	1.70
Rest of World	1.50	2.25	3.50	3.00

PLEASE SEND CHEQUE OR INTERNATIONAL MONEY ORDER.
payable to: STRATUS HOLDINGS plc or HOUSE OF STRATUS INC. or card payment as indicated

STERLING EXAMPLE

Cost of book(s):..................... Example: 3 x books at £6.99 each: £20.97
Cost of order: .... Example: £1.50 (Delivery to UK address)
Additional cost per book:.............. Example: 3 x £0.50: £1.50
Order total including shipping:........... Example: £23.97

VISA, MASTERCARD, SWITCH, AMEX:

☐ ☐ ☐ ☐ ☐ ☐ ☐ ☐ ☐ ☐ ☐ ☐ ☐ ☐ ☐ ☐ ☐ ☐

Issue number (Switch only):

☐ ☐ ☐

Start Date:　　　　　　　　Expiry Date:

☐☐/ ☐☐　　　　　　　　☐☐/ ☐☐

Signature: _____

NAME: _____

ADDRESS: _____

COUNTRY: _____

ZIP/POSTCODE: _____

Please allow 28 days for delivery. Despatch normally within 48 hours.

Prices subject to change without notice.
Please tick box if you do not wish to receive any additional information. ☐

House of Stratus publishes many other titles in this genre; please check our website (**www.houseofstratus.com**) for more details.